Alexandr
Welco

Goddam...

[handwritten inscription and signature]

MW01290836

The Nightly
Disease

a hotel novel

Max Booth III

PMMP

Perpetual Motion Machine Publishing
Cibolo, Texas

The Nightly Disease
Copyright © Max Booth III 2016

SECOND EDITION
Perpetual Motion Machine Publishing 2017

All Rights Reserved

ISBN: 978-1-943720-24-8

www.PerpetualPublishing.com

Cover Art by Matthew Revert
www.matthewrevert.com

Praise for
The Nightly Disease

"*The Nightly Disease* is a trip through a nightmarish service industry purgatory that heralds Max Booth III as a voice to be reckoned with. My favorite hotel book since *A Swell Looking Babe* and my favorite work novel since *Post Office*. Fuck yeah."
—Jedidiah Ayres, author of *Peckerwood*

"The book begins as a workplace novel and almost imperceptibly drifts into surrealism. Think *The Grand Budapest Hotel* meets *Lost Highway* if written by a prime Haruki Murakami. It might seem to be an unlikely mix, but it works. If it was a drink, they would be two-thirds David Lynch, one-sixth Wes Anderson and one-sixth Murakami."
—*Dead End Follies*

"*The Nightly Disease* is snarky and surreal, bitter and biting, and above all relatable. Booth writes with a sly bark that lets you know he's maybe kidding, a little but probably not, that he really means the horrible things he says, probably. maybe."
—John Boden, *Ginger Nuts of Horror*

Also by Max Booth III

Toxicity
The Mind is a Razorblade
How to Successfully Kidnap Strangers
Escape from Dinosauria (w/Vincenzo Bilof)

Anthologies Edited:

Zombies Need Love, Too
Zombie Jesus and Other True Stories
So it Goes: a Tribute to Kurt Vonnegut
Long Distance Drunks: a Tribute to Charles Bukowski
Truth or Dare
Lost Signals
Lost Films

This book is dedicated to:

Lori Michelle, John Corona, Javier Flores, Jose Hernandez, Matt Mattila, Diana Marin, Jason Haugh, Ed Kurtz, Garrett Hicks, Ed Strapkovic, Karli Trevino, Jesse Luan, Norma Ramon, Tianna Bebley, Taylor Spragling, Sabrina Smitley, Ashley Conway, Ron Schoonover, Diana Coleman, Ronnalyn Davis, Kali Sadiku, Loli Marin, Juan Sandoval, Kevin Bell, Yasemin Wray, Ernest Palomo, Joshua Olaes, Justin Kattar, Scott Nicolay, Erika Instead, Jennifer Wilson, Tracie McBride, Dominic Gonzalez, Laura Sebera, Franco Guarino, Lane Hamilton, Michael Kazepis, Jolene Casko, Glenn Rolfe, Mike Monson, Shane Douglas Keene, Christopher L. Beck, Eleanor Stitt, Laura Hickman, Brandon Vaughan, Jannett LaQue, Blake Burkhead, Emilie Schneider, Ryan Young, Amanda May, Goldie Schemanski, Bob Bates, Dawn Cano, Heavenly Wilson, Isreal Casias, Sam Cadle, Alexander Valhart, Doug Heller, Sonja Bratz, Alyson Hames, Mike Cruz, Cameron Crielaard, Sean M. Cogan, Julie Zanon, Stephanie Tohalino, Autumn Rae Craigo, Anna G. Kavanaugh, Aye Graves, Maggie Taylor, Lisa Johnson, Bobby Krstulovich Sr, Ken Gordhamer, Jeremy Baltimore, Paul Dagnan, Palanakie Franks, Jenny Sirocky, Tsunami Sprinkle, Joel Schram, Devlin Volungus, Kimberly Acabeo, Diego Orellana, Scott Watson, Sarah Read, Devin Anderson, John McColley, Belle Summers, Ted, Chet, my father and mother, and any other poor soul unfortunate enough to have worked in the hotel industry. May sweet, beautiful death find us all as soon as possible.

A History of Hotels

An Introduction from the Author

1983

The steelworker purchases a hotel with two of his coworkers. According to one of the men, there's no way in hell this won't make all three of them very wealthy. He frequently approaches the other two with get-rich-quick schemes, and they always, without doubt, fail. The aftermath of a disastrous greyhound sponsorship remains lingering in their memories like the ashes from an arson. Abandoned Amway products litter each of their residences. What makes this hotel idea any different, no one can quite say, but the steelworker goes along with the plan nonetheless. Later, when asked why he agreed, he will say: "I don't know. That's a good question."

This choice will trigger a chain of events that will result in the steelworker, almost a decade later, penetrating a woman with his penis and impregnating her with what will eventually evolve into the author of the novel you currently hold in your hands.

The hotel is located on the corner of 119th Street

and Atchison Avenue in Whiting, Indiana. It's called The Illiana, a term often used to describe the general area bordering Illinois and Indiana. The location leaves much to be desired. Bikers and drug addicts quickly start favoring the hotel bar as a preferred hangout spot. Every guest is a potential meth freak capable of murdering the front desk clerk and running off with whatever's in the register. Space exists in the building for a nice restaurant, but none of the three owners ever take advantage of the opportunity and the room remains empty for the entire six years the building lasts in their possession.

The steelworker and his two coworkers continue working at the mill while sharing shifts running The Illiana. Will the hotel eventually start feeling like a smart business decision? No. It will never feel like that.

1984

The woman who will go on to become this author's mother walks into The Illiana's bar with her fiancé. The steelworker who will go on to become this author's father serves them their drinks, and tells the woman he just returned from a trip to Jamaica, and he's curious if she'd like to join him next time he goes. The woman doesn't respond at first, since she's positive he's fucking with her, but the steelworker is sincere. He wants this woman he's only just met to leave the country with him.

"Well? What do you say?" says the steelworker.

"What the fuck? I don't even know you," says the steelworker's future wife, and her and her fiancé leave the bar. Later that night, her fiancé will tell the woman she is forbidden from ever returning to The Illiana, and a few months later, the woman will break up with her fiancé and apply for a job at the hotel. In the afternoons she will work at a hot dog stand, and in the evenings she will work the front desk. At home are her two sons, being watched by their grandparents. These dumb little babies have no idea their mother is in the process of getting to know their future stepfather.

1985

The steelworker and the new front desk girl decide to get married.

1989

The three owners of The Illiana declare bankruptcy and give up on their dreams of running a hotel.

1993

I am born inside of a hotel. A storm outside prohibits my parents from driving to a hospital. The night auditor on duty is burdened with the responsibility of delivering me into this cold, unforgiving world. He has my mom lay down on the floor in the lobby and he tells her to push, goddammit, push. A line grows at the front desk. People wanting to check-in. Guests demanding pillows, blankets, you name it. Everybody in the hotel is suddenly inconvenienced by my life. After I am free, the night auditor wraps me in a blanket and kisses my forehead and whispers into my ear: "I pass the curse onto you. I pass the curse onto you."

I'm just kidding. I was born in a hospital somewhere in Hobart, Indiana. But imagine if that really happened. Holy shit.

2003

I am ten years old and going on my first real vacation. Orlando, Florida. Disneyworld. Universal Studios. Islands of Adventure. Daytona Beach. My father stays home. My grandmother on my mother's side is treating us to this trip: me, my mother, my nephew, my niece, and my half-brother's half-brother. Only my grandmother has a driver's license. It takes us two days to reach our destination. Along the way, we stop at a Days Inn and I sleep in a bed with my mother and my nephew. The next day we make it to Orlando and check in to our new hotel. I don't remember the name. We are all excited to start the vacation. After we check-in to our room, my grandmother informs us today everybody must attend a meeting with her. "We're going to a timeshare presentation," she says, "since they were kind enough to help discount our room." Somehow, she forgot to mention this until right now. It is at this time that I decide I hate my grandmother. I hate her for sneaking this on all of us. I hate her for being a liar. I haven't yet learned that everybody on this planet is a liar. I haven't learned that lying is the only way people survive. Later, when I am an adult with my own family, I'll think back to this trip and realize I would have done exactly the same thing if placed in her position.

2006

I am a few months shy of thirteen. The mold in our ceiling has started spreading like an infection. A hole in our living room remains open like the eye of a conspiracy theorist. I rent *Kiss Kiss Bang Bang* and Chuck Palahniuk's *Survivor* from the library. I watch the movie and fall asleep. The next morning, I wake to a house without power. This is not a surprise. Bills are frequently overdue. Sometimes the power is shut off. It usually comes back on after a day or so. There is never a need to worry. I go to school, and when I return home in the afternoon, the power is still off. My mother tells me we are going to stay the night at a hotel, and then tomorrow the electricity issue will be resolved.

She has a little over a week of free rooms saved up for the Majestic Star Casino & Hotel in Gary. Casinos don't mind gifting their best customers room comps. It encourages them to never leave. And, once a week passes and we still haven't returned home, I begin to wonder if we ever *will* leave. My father drops me off at school in the mornings then I take the bus home and sit in our house without power and read books and pet my dog and apologize for leaving her alone every night, that I wish she could be with us at the hotel. I read Chuck Palahniuk's *Survivor* and Richard Price's *Clockers* and I stare at my X-Box 360 and wonder how to eject *Kiss Kiss Bang Bang* from the disc tray without power. My father picks me up each day after he finishes his shift at the mill and we return to the hotel and eat McDonald's. We are always eating fucking McDonald's. The dollar menu is our religion.

Another week passes and my parents decide to pull me out of school. It's too much of a hassle for my father to drive from the hotel to my school to his work then back to our house then to the hotel again every day. My mother tells me they will just homeschool me for the last couple weeks of the school year, then enroll me in high school come August. When we run out of free room comps at the casino hotel and my father's paycheck has dried up, we stay at my grandparents' house in Hammond until payday comes around again. Every day after work my father drives to our house and feeds my dog and takes her out for a walk. One evening he pulls up in my grandparents' driveway and gets out and tells me my bedroom window has been smashed in and the dog is gone. It is my thirteenth birthday.

Eventually a fight breaks out between my mother and grandmother and our presence is no longer welcome. We find a Super 8 in Portage that'll give us a generous weekly rate. Just another week or two, I'm promised, then we will return home. I ask why we can't just go back home now. I ask why this is happening. I ask why she won't explain anything to me. She tells me to stop being a smartass. She tells me she means it. Over time I give up asking for answers. It's clear I will never have them. I can make an educated guess and assume my mother's gambling addiction has played a significant factor in our current lifestyle. Still, eventually this mess will work itself out and we will return to our house. I tell myself this over and over for months, until I finally realize I'm living in a fantasy world, that we will never go back there again.

We continue to live in the Super 8 for three more years.

2009

When I am sixteen, my parents rent a house with my brother and his girlfriend. I enroll in an adult high school and earn my diploma within two years. Sometimes we drive past the Super 8 on our way to Walmart and I place an open palm against the backseat window and stare at the building while my thoughts whirl up a tornado of depression.

2011

At age eighteen I buy a bus ticket to Texas with the funds earned from writing Wikipedia articles for indie authors. The articles last barely six months before an admin deletes them all. I take my copy of Chuck Palahniuk's *Survivor* with me. The Lake Station Public Library will never see it again. I don't know what happened to my X-Box 360 or the *Kiss Kiss Bang Bang* disc inserted into it. Probably pawned for extra double cheeseburgers from McDonald's.

I vow to never step foot in another hotel for the rest of my life.

2012

I get a job as an overnight stocker at Walmart and last almost eight months before quitting for a new job with a retail warehouse called Garden Ridge. A month into the new job, I start applying elsewhere. The managers at Garden Ridge are monsters and treat their employees like garbage. The Atrium Inn interviews me for the night audit position. It goes well and I get the job. I sign the paperwork and shake the manager's hand and I start walking across town to tell the managers at Garden Ridge to go fuck themselves. The Atrium Inn manager calls my cell phone halfway through Garden Ridge's parking lot. He tells me somebody called in sick tonight and they need me to start immediately. I will be expected to work the shift by myself, with zero training provided. I suggest this might be an irrational plan, and the manager promptly fires me. My first hotel job lasts barely a half hour. A month later, Garden Ridge fires me for developing pneumonia. I spend the next three weeks applying to every business in town. Eventually I decide fuck it and try my luck with another hotel. Let's call it The Goddamn Hotel, because that's its name. I walk into the lobby and ask for an application and the lady behind the front desk tells me their full-time night auditor just put in her two weeks, so I apply for her position. I'm interviewed the next day and a month passes before they offer me the job.

2013

The city of Whiting, Indiana officially takes possession of the former Illiana Hotel via the county property tax sale process.

I create a Facebook group called Confessions of a Hotel Night Auditor to post about the weird shit constantly occurring at The Goddamn Hotel. It doesn't take long for me to realize a novel needs to exist with similar content, and I begin writing one while working the night shift.

2015

I finish the final draft of the hotel novel. I title it *No Sleep 'Til Dying*. It's the weirdest thing I've ever written, and probably the best. I lose track of what's autobiographical and what's fiction. It doesn't matter. It's all the same. Nothing is true. Everything is a lie.

I submit the manuscript to a handful of publishers and wait.

2016

DarkFuse, a small press of dark fiction, accepts the novel eight months after I send it to them. Their first editorial note is to change the title. I send them a list of possibilities and we eventually settle on *The Nightly Disease*. DarkFuse releases the novel as a serial on their website throughout the month of October. One chapter a night. They also open pre-orders for a limited edition hardback. It's the first time one of my books has been published in hardback. We sell our fifty copies at $60 each by the end of the month. I sign the signature sheets with immense pride. We settle on a publication date for the trade paperback and ebook: April 2017. Then, in December 2016, I randomly notice the book is already on Amazon. I email DarkFuse and ask why it's out early, why nobody told me. They explain they were going to tell me, they just haven't gotten around to it yet. I think about why a family might move into a hotel and never return home. I think about my mom telling me not to be a smartass.

2017

Six months after *The Nightly Disease* is released, DarkFuse emails their authors and announces they will be discontinuing their paperback and eBook distribution. All titles published before 2017 will be released back to their authors. The authors are given a chance to sign a new contract to keep the books in print, but no author in their right mind would sign such a terrible document. Six months after my hotel novel came out, it died. Six months after I finally felt free from the hotel's grasp, it had its hold on me all over again. I think about houses without electricity. I think about the Super 8 in Portage, Indiana. I think about how the owner of DarkFuse lives in Indiana, and how the state follows me wherever I go. Eventually DarkFuse will file bankruptcy and I will never see a dime of royalties from January—June 2017. All of my promotional efforts for the book have been wasted. I get real fucking depressed.

I have to email several websites who had agreed to review the hotel novel and let them know not to bother wasting their time. If a new audience can't purchase the book, then hustling for reviews becomes meaningless.

A question I start asking myself: "What's the fucking point?"

Now that the book has been removed from distribution, the way I see it, I'm left with three options going forward.

I self-publish it.

I convince another press to reprint it.

I let it die and move on to the next project.

A History of Hotels

Going the self-publishing route doesn't seem too far-fetched, considering I've operated my own small press, Perpetual Motion Machine, for the last five years. I've yet to publish my own writing, not because I view self-publishing negatively but more because I prefer to keep my own writing and my publishing business separate. I feel like if I start publishing my own work through PMMP, then I risk criticism of playing "favorites" over the press's catalog. It's less complicated to just let another publishing company handle my writing.

The problem with approaching another press, of course, is that it's going to be difficult to convince someone else to reprint a book that came out six months ago.

Which brings me to option #3: forgetting I ever wrote the damn thing and focusing on new books.

The process of writing a book is a lengthy endeavor. Even when you think you are finished, its completion will continue to stretch on and on until you've successfully pulled every strand of hair from your scalp, and even then it probably won't quite be done. All writers must face the cold reality that no book is ever actually finished—they're abandoned. Either you give up and send it out into the wild or you never stop fidgeting with it.

Solace is only gained once the book has been published, because the time to edit has passed. It's too late to make any additional changes. Once it's out, it's out, and if you decide you want to change a couple things, well tough shit, it's too late. It's difficult to describe the relief that hit me once *The Nightly Disease* was released. I had been working on this book for a couple years, writing a scene here and there between interactions with guests at my job. After a while, like with any book, you start getting sick of it. You just want to be finished so you can move on to the next thing. I haven't thought about writing the hotel book in a long time. I thought I was done with it. I thought I could wipe it from my memory. This is how I imagine most writers feel once they release a new title. They delete it from their brains to clear room for the next project consuming their every waking thought.

It makes sense, but it's also foolish, because what happens when that book unexpectedly goes out of print and you're forced to revisit it all over again?

Maybe it's selfish to assume a novel will live forever. Maybe a novel should only last as long as its initial interest. Maybe six months is the perfect lifespan for a book. Any longer, and it's just outstaying its welcome. There are so many books on this planet being published every single day, and it's rude to take up any further space than we rightfully deserve. I think about my novel and I wonder if there would be any point in bringing it back to print. It had a good run, even if I didn't receive any money from the piece of shit publisher who originally released it. The readers who would find it entertaining have probably purchased it by now and if it had stayed in print it would have just slowly faded into oblivion. Or maybe it was just about to hit a point where hundreds of new readers discovered it. There's no way to tell with these things, especially now that it's gone.

But will it stay gone?

No. Of course not. I consider letting it die every day, but the thought makes me sick. I can't decide why I need it to be published again. I can't force myself to forget it exists. It's the most personal thing I've ever written, and to dump it in the trash feels like a sin.

So I go through the goddamn book again. I add a couple scenes here and there, but don't change anything too drastically. I write a new introduction for it. I decide to call the introduction "A History of Hotels" because my life has been nothing but one hotel after another. Sometimes when I'm lonely at The Goddamn Hotel I call the Super 8 in Portage, Indiana and hang up after the front desk clerk asks how they can help me. I hang up and I cry and I don't know why.

I will self-publish the book through my own press. Fuck it.

Five years after starting my employment at The Goddamn Hotel, I'm still here, writing this introduction behind the front desk while guests get drunk in the lobby. I will never leave. I will die here and management will simply bury my remains in the flowerbed in front of the building and a new night auditor will emerge from the earth. The cycle will never end.

Hotel is god. Hotel is god. Hotel is god.

Max Booth III

The Goddamn Hotel
August 25, 2017

"For the rest of the earth's organisms, existence is relatively uncomplicated. Their lives are about three things: survival, reproduction, death—and nothing else. But we know too much to content ourselves with surviving, reproducing, dying—and nothing else. We know we are alive and know we will die. We also know we will suffer during our lives before suffering—slowly or quickly—as we draw near to death. This is the knowledge we 'enjoy' as the most intelligent organisms to gush from the womb of nature. And being so, we feel shortchanged if there is nothing else for us than to survive, reproduce, and die. We want there to be more to it than that, or to think there is. This is the tragedy: Consciousness has forced us into the paradoxical position of striving to be unself-conscious of what we are—hunks of spoiling flesh on disintegrating bones."

—Thomas Ligotti,
The Conspiracy Against the Human Race

———

"This job would be great if it wasn't for the fucking customers."

—Randal Graves,
Clerks

Seeking Friendly & Outgoing Night Auditor

Do not apply if still in possession of hopes or dreams.

The hotel is currently searching for a manager during the overnight hours, while providing a smooth transition between the evening and morning shifts. This position requires knowledge of accounting skills, computer skills, and a natural ability to handle obnoxious drunks without committing murder. Should an instance arise where a potential candidate goes over the line and ends a guest's life, the hotel will not supply you with bail money, nor will the hotel contribute to lawyer fees. The hotel's use for your existence will be immediately terminated, and once again, you will be forever, blissfully alone.

Potential night auditors will be responsible for: maintaining and promoting hospitality at all times, even when depression is at its highest (which will be every shift) and happiness is at its lowest (which never existed, anyway); welcoming and serving guests in a courteous, efficient and friendly manner, both face-to-face and on the phone, perpetually maintaining the widest smile physically possible despite how gory and disgusting a situation will probably become. As part of the job, this individual is required to: perform and manage standard accounting tasks; handle guest concerns and answer questions, such as "what is the meaning of life?" and "why won't my toilet flush?"; perform necessary audit tasks, which will range from backing up the previous day's work to assisting pregnant guests give birth or, if they aren't quite ready to be a parent, abort (remember: this is their choice, NOT yours; we don't need a repeat of New Years Day 2010); greet guests and assist them with check-ins and check-outs; demonstrate good computer skills, but not great computer skills (intelligence is not something to boast); accurately handle cash and charges; stand for long periods of time, perhaps forever, even when your body has been lowered deep into the hotel's garden with the previous night auditors; present a friendly, outgoing, energetic and guest-service-oriented demeanor. The night auditor will be left alone for the majority of their shift, although there will always be somebody or something, somewhere, watching, but you will never personally see or hear this person or thing. The night auditor will be expected to maintain order in the hotel at all costs, even if the night auditor must sacrifice his or her own life for the benefit of the hotel. The hotel is god. The hotel is god. The hotel is god.

Other duties include but are not limited to: Perform the balancing, reconciliation, and closing of various daily accounts and prepare the daily statements to provide accurate, timely information to management while ensuring proper controls are maintained, unless a guest passes away while staying at the hotel, in which case you will be required to dispose of the corpse in secret and hide all evidence the guest checked-in to their reservation. Do not tell management. Do not tell anyone. Serve the hotel.

Further shit expected of you:

Stocking the front desk with daily supplies. Ability to operate multi-line phones. Providing guests with information on local attractions (for instance, if a guest asks you to recommend the best bridge to leap off of, you don't want to be unprepared and direct them to a bridge without enough drop to properly end a life). Resolving or referring to management all guest concerns, complaints, or suggestions in a continuous effort to provide heartfelt, but insincere care to our guests. Remaining current on in-house groups and property events. Responding to customer issues/complaints/problems in a quick, efficient manner to maintain a high level of customer satisfaction and quality service, which involves never, absolutely never denying a guest's request, no matter how illegal, no matter how immoral. Maintaining preparedness and implement emergency procedures when appropriate to protect the hotel guests, staff, and assets.

Must be prepared to die for the hotel. Must be willing to prove it.

An ideal employee will have no social life. An ideal employee will not be close to family or have any friends who might ask questions should the employee suddenly disappear. An ideal employee will also be flexible with schedules and be willing to work holidays.

An ideal employee is you.

Compensation: Commensurate with experience.

Part One

Where Are The Owls

#100

"**T**hank you for calling the Goddamn Hotel. This is Isaac. How may I help you?"

This is how I'm supposed to introduce myself.

"What brings you to the area? Business or pleasure?"

Sometimes they're here to cheat on their lovers. Sometimes they're in town to attend a funeral. Other times, they just need to get away from their shitty, miserable lives for a few hours. To forget about the mistakes they've made, to ignore the pool of consequence perpetually drowning them. If only for a moment.

"What are you escaping from, sir?"

"Why are you hiding?"

This is the script management makes us practice during training. The diarrhea they shovel up our assholes and out of our mouths. Lava trickling down greasy chins.

"Will this just be for one night, ma'am? Or forever?"

"Will that be cash or credit card? Blood sacrifice or semen deposit?"

These are the words I've recited for hours, days, months, years. Two years? Three? Clocks don't work when the sun's down. Calendars lie. Seconds are days and days are seconds.

"I'm so sorry to hear that, sir. I understand how frustrating it must be to walk around in life with a gargantuan penis dangling from your forehead."

These are the apologies imbedded into my brain. My promises for resolution. My vows for vengeance.

"I can assure you, ma'am, that the Goddamn Hotel will do everything in its power to track down and punish the heartless bastard who coughed while passing your room. If not, we would be honored to purchase you some Goddamn Hotel rewards points.

Always say "purchase". Never "give" or "compensate". "Purchase" implies I'm personally reaching into my own wallet to resolve the conflict, even if it's a lie. Never tell a guest the truth. Night auditors are the FBI of sleep, the *X-Files* of dreams.

"Once again, ma'am, I deeply apologize for not warning you in advance that you'd have an upsetting nightmare tonight. Obviously you did not read the fine print on our website: every stay here is a nightmare. Life is a nightmare. You will never wake up. The Goddamn Hotel has failed you. How can we make this right?"

These are the questions I have to memorize. The same formula repeated on myriad blank faces. Everybody becomes nobody. Nobody becomes everybody. Adult infant doppelgängers stumbling in the lobby demanding a tit to suck and a customer service representative to stomp on.

The Nightly Disease

"Hello, sir? This is Isaac, from the front desk. I was just calling to ask if the kick to my balls earlier was satisfying enough, or if you needed to go for a second round. Also, did you ever figure out how to turn the TV on?"

In hotel bootcamp, the drill sergeant will scream the following into your face approximately one thousand times a day: "LEARN. LEARN. LEARN. LEARN, YOU MAGGOT. LEARN."

L.E.A.R.N.

Listen.

Empathize.

Apologize.

React.

Notify.

Listen to the way they cry. Empathize with their phantom, agonizing pain. Apologize for everything. React to the nausea. Notify the deceased.

Learn learn learn learn learn learn learn learn learn.

Repeat the word until it's the only word in the English language. Every hotel associate is required by contract to carve the word into their flesh. Become the word. Give the hotel your blood and become one.

Learn.

I am a prisoner in a kingdom of tiny shampoo bottles.

When the hotel doors slide open, reality blinks back into focus. I've lost count of how many times I've listened to these doors open and close, open and close. Sometimes I wonder how it would feel to lie down perfectly still on the floor and allow the doors to slide shut against my skull. How strong are they? Strong enough to shatter my cranium, squeeze my eyeballs out of their sockets?

Strong enough to fill out my resignation papers?

I straighten my tie at the front desk and clear my throat, because it's action, it's go-time, it's red alert. *Here we fucking go.*

"Good evening, sir." I smile at the guy approaching the front desk. He's wearing a business suit, but the top buttons are undone and his tie hangs halfway down his gut like a suffocated snake.

"Hey boss," he says. "How's it going?"

He reeks of whiskey and I gag when I open my mouth. "All right, and yourself?"

"Well, I'll be a whole lot better if you have any rooms."

"Then you're in luck. What are you after? One king bed, two queens, or a suite?"

"All depends, don't it? How much we talkin' for a suite?"

"Single king suite is gonna cost you one-seventy-nine, and a double queen suite will be one-eighty-nine."

The guy steps back, offended. "Jesus Christ. You talk to your mother with that mouth?"

"I don't make the rates. I'm sorry."

"You just give them out."

"Correct."

"Ain't that some shit. Okay, what about the standard one? The, uh, single bed."

"One-nineteen."

"Holy shit. Just stab me in the fucking face, why don't you."

"That still wouldn't make the price go down any, I'm afraid."

"One hundred and nineteen dollars? At this hour? It's two in the morning for Christ's sake."

The Nightly Disease

"Yeah, that's the rate. I think the Other Goddamn Hotel down the street is ninety-nine, if you'd rather do that." I motion at the door. Just fucking leave, I want to tell him. Fuck off and die.

"What if I was just going to be here a few hours? Can't you knock it down, like, fifty bucks?"

"This isn't the Days Inn. We don't rent by the hour. It doesn't matter what time you check-in or how long you stay. Housekeeping still has to clean your room the same way."

"All right, fine. I'll take it. Christ."

"Fantastic. I'll need a license and credit card."

The guy pauses, scratching his cheek. "Actually, I was hoping to just pay in cash. I don't need anyone tracking my expenses. Fuckin' divorces are brutal, kid."

"That's fine, we accept cash. The only thing is, you have to put down an extra one hundred dollar deposit that you'll get back once you check-out."

"What? Why the hell would I do that?"

"For incidentals."

"*Incidentals?* The hell's that?"

"You know, like, in case anything in the room is damaged during your stay, we'd have collateral."

"Do you honestly think I'm going to break something?"

"Honesty has nothing to do with it, sir. It's just policy."

"What if I promised I wasn't going to break something?"

"You'd still have to put down the deposit."

"Okay. Fine. What do I owe you?"

I bust out the calculator and do my magic, then tell him the total.

"Jesus. This is turning into the most expensive screw of my life." He opens his wallet and I manage to sneak a peek inside. There must be at least a couple thousand stuffed in there. He tosses two hundreds and a fifty on the counter.

"Are you a Goddamn Hotel rewards member by any chance?"

"What do you think?"

"Probably not."

"That's some wise thinking."

"All right, here's your change and license. Did you have a floor preference?"

"I don't really give a shit."

"Okay. I'm going to put you on the fifth floor, away from the elevator, so you don't bother anyone and nobody bothers you as you do . . . uh, whatever it is you're doing."

"Peachy."

"Internet is free, there's no code for the wifi. Just follow the directions prompted on the screen. Breakfast begins at six and ends at nine-thirty. Check-out is at noon. Are you going to be needing a wake-up call?"

"Why would I need a wake-up call? I got a cell phone, don't I?"

"I have no idea. Do you?"

"Are you being a smartass?"

"I don't know. Probably."

"What's your boss's name?"

I pause, then shrug. "I call him 'Boss'."

"Give me my damn license back, boy." He pats his pockets.

"I already gave it to you . . . man."

"Then where is it, smartass?"

"I assume your wallet."

He glares at me. "Give me your boss's information. I want to call him."

"Okay, sure. But I assume he's asleep at this hour."

"I don't give a shit. Give me his card."

"Fine." I toss the business card on the desk, hoping he gets a paper cut picking it up. A paper cut so deep he bleeds to death here in the lobby. I could display his corpse in front of the entrance as a rug for other guests to wipe their muddy shoes on. Impale a sign down his throat that reads: "ABANDON ALL HOPE, YE WHO ENTER HERE".

"You're in for it now, dickhead," the guy says.

The guy dials the number on the business card into his cell phone and brings it to his ear. The phone at the hotel begins ringing a few seconds later. I hold my finger up at the guest and tell him to hang on just a moment, then pick up the work phone.

"Thank you for calling the Goddamn Hotel. This is Dickhead. How may I help you?"

The guest across the front desk stares at me with death in his eyes, then lowers his cell phone. I keep the hotel phone to my ear. "Hello? Hello?" I hang up and shrug. "I guess they had the wrong number."

"Fuck this," the guest says, "and fuck you." He grabs his room keys from my hand, turns around, and storms out of the hotel. Then he immediately walks back into the lobby and asks for directions to his room.

I return to my seat and unpause Netflix. Five hours remain of my shift. In another hour, I will sneak up to the roof, take off my pants, climb up on the ledge, and masturbate onto the cars in the parking lot. Afterward, I'll wipe my penis off with a guest receipt and climb back down to the lobby and watch another episode of *Gilmore Girls*. Then I will go home, sleep, shower, eat, and do it all over again. The cycle will only end when I either quit or burn the fucking building to the ground.

#101

A **girl** I don't recognize is standing behind the front desk when I enter the lobby. She's dripping of sweat and her hair's a mess. Classic "I'm new here and I'm freaking out because I don't know what I'm doing" look. The same kind of look I have every night when anything happens that results with me having to do any sort of work. I empathize, which is the second step of the L.E.A.R.N. program.

"Are you Mandy 2?" I ask, pressing in the passcode and walking around the front desk.

"What?"

"You know, like the sequel to our other Mandy?" I'm referring to the Mandy who works night audit on my two nights off of the week. Part-time Mandy.

She pauses, then nods. "I guess."

"I'm Isaac, the night guy. It's good to meet you."

She smiles at me, her braces glistening off the ultra bright lights above the front desk, which I'll turn off once she leaves. Light is the enemy. Keep your guard down long enough and it'll wreck you.

"So, hey," she says, "let me ask you a question."

"All right."

"Where could someone pet an owl in this town?"

The laughter escapes before I can even understand why I'm laughing. "What the hell?"

She looks at me, insulted, confused at why anyone could possibly laugh over such an important question. "No, I'm serious. I really want to pet an owl. I've been trying to find out all day, but I just don't know. Any ideas?"

"I . . . I don't know? Maybe the zoo."

"Do they have owls at the zoo, you think?"

"It's possible."

"Would they let me pet them?"

I shrug. "If not, you could always break into the owl cage. Or whatever they're kept in."

She thinks about it a moment, seriously considering it.

"Why do you want to pet an owl so badly?" Might as well play along with this lunatic, and that's exactly what she is, for only a lunatic would bring up owl-petting inquiries two seconds after introducing themselves to somebody.

"Well, okay." She pauses and clears her throat. "I know this is going to sound a little crazy, but just hear me out."

"Okay."

"So, like, all right, for the last year or so, there's this owl that comes to my house every time I'm sad."

"It . . . comes to your house?"

She nods, glad I'm finally understanding. "Yeah, like, it hangs out on my roof, I guess? And it hoots, you know, like an owl hoots? All night. Every time I'm sad."

The Nightly Disease

"That sounds a lot like a Disney cartoon."

"Aw, thank you," she says, genuinely appreciative. "But the thing is, every time I go outside and try to find the owl, I can only see its shadow. Once I even climbed onto my roof, but it was gone by the time I made it up."

"Owls are sneaky."

"Ideally," she says, "I'd love to pet *that* owl specifically, but I'm trying to be realistic here, you know? So I guess *any* owl would do at this point."

The phone rings. Mandy answers it and redirects the caller to a guest's room. She turns back to me and asks what I think.

"I don't know. Sorry. Maybe you could try leaving mice around your house. Owls love mice, right? So if you plant them around your property as bait, maybe the owl will fly in through your window."

She doesn't answer at first, just stares at me, and I'm waiting for her to tell me to go fuck myself for not taking her question seriously. But then she smiles, showing me her braces again.

"You know, I would have never even thought about that. Wow. That's a really good idea, Isaac."

"Uh, thank you."

I've never met anybody so sincere about petting an owl before. Although, come to think about it, I've never met *anybody* who's ever shown even the tiniest interest in any kind of bird, so hell, what do I know?

"You really think that would work?" she asks.

I shrug and tell her I don't see why not. It sounds logical enough. She thanks me again, finishing the last of her cashier paperwork as I count the register to make sure it balances out. It doesn't. It's short two dollars. I don't bring it up. I doubt she would know the reason for the shortage. Plus she's kind of cute, and I want her to believe she's doing a good job. This probably makes me a sexist asshole. Would I be as lenient with a male coworker? Shit. Probably not. Yeah. Sexist pig. That's me.

"So," I say, "how are you liking the hotel so far?"

"Oh, it's not too bad. It's more complicated than I imagined."

"How so?"

She pauses, thinking. "I guess I didn't realize how much work goes into checking somebody in."

I want to laugh, but this time I'm able to restrain myself. "You'll get the hang of it."

Her braces respond with another shine, and I'm half in love with this strange owl girl. I feel like I'm betraying my other pretend-girlfriend: the homeless girl who sneaks into the hotel once in a while to steal breakfast food and puke it up in the bathroom down the hallway. I've been in love with the bulimic girl a lot longer, yet I've never said a word to her. With Owl Girl, at least we've shared a conversation.

She thanks me again for my advice. As I watch her walk out, slightly hypnotized by the way her butt bounces, a man clears his nicotine-rotten throat to the side of me and I turn to find a platinum member named Mr. Yates who frequently stays here. He's wearing long johns and a plain white T-shirt so clean I'm convinced he buys them in bulk and disposes of each one after their initial use.

I nod at the guy. "Yo."

"Don't you 'yo' me, young man."

"Okay."

"My toilet is clogged."

"I see."

The Nightly Disease

"What are you going to do about it?"

"Well, I can give you a plunger."

Mr. Yates bursts out laughing. "I don't think so. I—" he points to his face with both thumbs "—do not *plunge.*"

"No shame in plunging once in a while."

He chuckles again. I'm the funniest night auditor in the world over here. "You see," he says, "I am the vice president of a very, very important company. You, on the other hand, are paid to clean up the shit of vice presidents of very, very important companies. Therefore, you will go fetch the plunger, and *you* will operate its wooden, archaic handle. Are we understood?"

A thousand responses plead to escape my thoughts. I could tell him to go fuck himself. I could tell him I'd be happy to plunge the toilet with his face. I could just shove the plunger up his ass. I could leap over the front desk and tackle him and beat him senseless. Hell, I could even throw him off the roof. But all of these reactions would most likely end with my termination from the hotel. And maybe that's not such a bad thing, but where else would I go? Every other possible job I could get will end the same way: with a noose wrapped firmly around my neck while I flip the universe the bird.

Upstairs, plunger-in-hand, I stare at the brown, turd-infested water one soft breeze away from spilling over the bowl. The smell is death. I debate kneeling down and sticking my face in and gently floating away in its mystic depths. What awaits me below? Heaven or Hell? Freedom or imprisonment? Another hotel? An infinite layer of hotels, one after the other, each one more foul than the last.

Yates sighs. His breath hits the back of my neck and suddenly the toilet's stench is preferable. "Well, what are you waiting on? I'd like to go to sleep sometime tonight."

I bite my tongue until it bleeds then slide the plunger into the water, holding my breath and praying it doesn't overflow. It doesn't matter how deep I push it in, the rubber cup seems incapable of reaching the bottom. The water's now halfway up the plunger's stick and there's more room to go. I crouch, slowly lowering it, convinced it's sucking me in, eating me. The toilet's a bottomless pit and I'm its main course. Devour me. Fuck me. Use me.

The cup smacks against the bottom of the bowl. For a moment, I'm relieved, but as soon as I get some suction and jerk it up, a wave of shit-water splatters against my pants and I want to die, I want to deteriorate from view and never return.

Yates hovers over me as I plunge and shouts, "I want to know what kind of compensation's coming my way."

I stop moving and cock my head to him. "What?"

"What, you got shit in your ears, too? What kind of compensation am I getting?"

I look down at the shit-water leaking down the toilet, then back at him, at a loss for words. "Nothing. You're not getting anything."

"That's unacceptable."

"I . . . I don't—look, you made this mess, man."

"Your poorly designed toilets made this mess, young man!"

"No, your disgusting asshole did."

Yates gasps. "I will not have you talk to me that way."

The Nightly Disease

I open my mouth, fully intending on telling him where he can stick this plunger, when the toilet empties into the bowl and regurgitates clean water. Without another word, I walk around Yates and exit his room, leaving the plunger in the toilet in case he ruins it again. He knows damn well not to bother me again. Downstairs, there's a line of guests in the lobby waiting to talk to me about Jesus Christ or their toilets or loud noises or whatever the fuck, I don't care. I am not their god. I am not their father. I am not their savior. Let them figure out their issues by themselves. Just please leave me alone—now, forever, always.

I brush past them and go into the laundry room and take off my pants and throw them in the washing machine, then clean my arms and face and hands for a solid five minutes with scathing hot water. The line in the lobby undoubtedly grows, so to continue killing time I bust out a disposable toothbrush and give my mouth a thorough scrubbing.

When I return to the front desk, sans pants, the lobby is empty. Perhaps the guests had been a hallucination. Or maybe they'd gotten the hint and leapt off the roof together in a beautiful mass suicide. Outside, the parking lot might be littered with corpses. Just as it should be.

I approach the front desk computer and discover, like the majority of my other coworkers, Owl Girl also does not understand the concept of closing out of Internet browsers after she is finished searching for something. The screen is littered with dozens of Internet Explorer windows. The browser is outdated, since my manager forgot the admin password and we can no longer perform simple system updates.

All the opened windows contain various searches inquiring about how to pet an owl.

"where can i go to pet an owl"

"i want to pet an owl how can i do this"

"please where can i pet the owls"

I click through them until my finger's aching, then finally come across the last window. I stare at the words in the search bar, mesmerized.

It says, simply:

"where are the owls"

#102

The bulimic homeless girl I'm in love with but have never spoken to eats four waffles, two plates of scrambled eggs, and a cup of fruit. Then she throws her trash away and hides in the bathroom to regurgitate. She's been coming in for a few weeks now, performing the same routine every other morning or so. When we had chorizo and eggs, she skipped the chorizo altogether and opted for ten waffles. I didn't know it was possible for a human being to eat ten waffles in one sitting. But that was before I met my pretend-girlfriend-hopefully-one-day-real-girlfriend. No, I do not know her name.

I watch from behind the front desk, pretending to file paperwork. She is an eating machine, yet she remains the size of a twig. The sound of her vomiting is audible if I stand close enough to the restroom door. Revolting enough to make my own stomach churn, and I have to step back before I begin gagging. Once I've safely returned behind the front desk, I stare across the lobby at the restroom, wondering why she's putting herself through such hell. Is it a mental disorder? She can't possibly be enjoying herself. Or maybe she is. Hell. I don't know. A person doesn't know anything until he tries it, but this isn't something I intend on trying. Sticking my fingers down my throat and emptying my stomach sounds about as appetizing as tying my testicles to a tree branch and leaping off. Of course, maybe I could benefit from it. One look at my stomach and it's a miracle I haven't died from a heart attack already. Or, at the very least, tripped over my sagging gut.

The bulimic girl isn't the first non-guest to steal breakfast in the mornings. We usually get one or two every couple months. Homeless people stumbling through the lobby, dragging in the stench of shit like a reaper herding souls. They tend not to last long. They get too greedy and start making mistakes, like coming in on more than two consecutive days in a row. They wear the same dirty clothes that reek of paranoia and guilt. I never have to say anything. Either one of the breakfast ladies catches on or Kevin, the maintenance man, notices. If it were up to me, I'd just let them eat. The hotel isn't going bankrupt over bagels. I try telling this to Kevin, who has shared with me his suspicions toward the bulimic girl, but he either doesn't understand or doesn't care.

"She's stealing from the hotel. She must be dealt with."

"Is she taking *your* money, though? Your own personal money?" I wish he never noticed her.

"It's our jobs to protect the hotel."

"What? Your job is to fix shit when it breaks. If this place was so concerned about security, they'd hire a security guard. Or, hell, at least install cameras."

I fight off the urge to continue criticizing his

clearly bullshit motives. All this coming from a man who routinely smokes joints out by the dumpster when he's supposed to be taking out the trash. I may not be around when the sun's present, but if the day shift loves anything, it's to gossip. News travels. Besides, protecting the hotel has absolutely nothing to do with his desire to confront the bulimic girl. Kevin is an asshole by nature. Kicking this girl out of the hotel is his idea of a fun time. Ruining people's lives and watching them break down are the kinds of things that get him hard. Back in school, he was probably the kind of kid who shoved dirt clumps into the faces of those weaker than him. I wouldn't be surprised to discover a dozen nerds had, at one point in their lives, placed Kevin's name at the top of their to-kill lists.

"Someone needs to stop her," he says, gumming his chewing tobacco. "Yesterday I followed her after she left. She got on this bike and rode over to the Other Goddamn Hotel and did the exact same thing she's been doing here."

"All the more reason not to send her running for the hills. She's clearly unwell. Maybe this is the only thing keeping her from robbing a grocery store or committing suicide. Who knows? We kick her out, she ends up in prison stealing from someplace less reasonable."

Kevin laughs and spits tobacco in his empty coffee cup. "I don't give a shit what happens to that disgusting bitch. I know you're desperate for pussy, Isaac, but come on. Her snatch is practically dripping STDs."

I rub my eyes, exhausted and sick of the words leaving his mouth. Maybe the bulimic girl has already left, and me keeping him in the back office was enough of a distraction. It's almost seven, anyway. My time here is coming to an end.

"Oh, hey," I say, "I just remembered something. A guest turned in a comment card earlier."

"Okay. And?"

"It was about you."

His eyes brighten, full of promise. "Yeah? What'd it say?"

"That you're an asshole."

She rolls up on her bike just as I'm unlocking my car, and I don't understand, just an hour ago she had been inside the kitchen. Had she already left and returned for another round?

My body tenses, thumb frozen on the "unlock" button attached to my keys. She doesn't seem to notice me staring at her as she props her rusted bike against the front of the building. She's wearing a stained jacket on top of a black Social Distortion T-shirt and dirty jeans with wide, wet holes cut out at both kneecaps. I don't doubt that she's homeless, and an idea forms to tell her about the rumors I've heard of the abandoned shack behind the hotel. Facing the front of the hotel, there is a highway, but on the backend of the building, there is nothing but woods. I've never explored them myself, because a forest is scary as fuck in the middle of the night, and if someone ever tries saying differently they're obviously the slasher in a horror film, but I've heard from various employees from both my hotel and the hotel next door that there's this old shack a mile or so into those woods, mostly disintegrated from rain and age. Maybe the girl might like to live there until she's back up on her feet. Maybe she might like me to accompany her on the search for it. Or, if not the shack, maybe she might consider staying a few nights in my studio apartment. Sometimes it gets awfully cold in my apartment at night, and she might be tempted to snuggle up against my bear-like body for warmth. I've watched enough low-budget pornos to know what would happen then.

She focuses on the front doors, determined. But when I shout, "Hey, excuse me!" all confidence drains like the shit-water from Yates's toilet and she spins around toward her bike. She mumbles out a series of apologies and hops on the seat. I leap in front of her before she can take off and realize far too late I'm doing more to frighten her than comfort her. "No, no, it's okay," I say, "please, I want to help you."

She responds by smashing her fist into my nose.

I stumble back and trip over a bush. By the time I've sat up, she's already halfway across the parking lot.

Well, shit.

#103

The next time I relieve Mandy 2, I tell myself over and over on the drive to work not to mention our previous encounter. Don't say owls. Don't say owls.

Don't. Say. Owls.

The first thing I say upon entering the lobby is, "Owls."

Mandy 2 stops typing at the front desk. "What?"

I choke and spit out gibberish. "How are? Uh. How are . . . you?"

"I'm . . . fine. Thanks. And you?"

I come around the front desk and tell her that I'm all right, *all things considering,* and I immediately regret my words because I have no idea what they mean, and I pray she doesn't ask me to clarify, but of course she does, so I shrug and tell her I don't know, and she smiles.

"So who punched you in the face?" She nods at my bruised nose.

"Oh, just some guest."

"Did you deserve it?"

24

The Nightly Disease

"Undoubtedly."

"Well, I hope he broke his hand."

"She."

"What?"

I clear my throat and begin counting the drawer. "So, how was tonight?"

"You're going to have fun tonight."

"What now?" Based off our last conversation, I can't quite predict her definition of fun. Perhaps her stalker owl has discovered where she works, and is now outside the hotel, waiting to hoot all the guests to sleep.

I've already looked it up, and yes, in Amsterdam there's an establishment called The Owl Hotel, and here's a two-star review on TripAdvisor written by someone named BiznessGangBang:

"At first this 'never in a good mood' chinese dude gave us a room so tiny that we couldn't properly undress or even copulate. My wife complained and he gave us a room in a higher floor that despite being bigger still obligated us to move in strategic movements around the room. We'd already prepaid so could not stay elsewhere. Plus I was already erect. The room as I said is too little. The bathroom is for kids and dwarves but I did not see a single dwarf during our stay which was to say the least misleading. There was this tiny tub, good for bathing a pet, but we did not have a pet, although sometimes my wife tries to make me defecate in our front yard, but I don't think that's relevant. No fridge, no water, no coffee, no complimentary prophylactics. During the second night there was this drunk guy making noises at his door and we could hear everything. I think he was trying to devour the wood. It was 1 a.m. and I had to open the door of my room and yell at him and he spat in my face. And during the second night we had to bang on the walls so the drunk man would stop talking to god knows who, perhaps god, perhaps our lord lucifer. Not good at all. In summary, if you don't have quality standards and you just need a place to sleep then you're good. If, however, you need minimum comfort, run like hell before hell runs after you. Oh, they have decent coffee."

Seems like a nice place.

"You remember that lady in five-oh-four?" Mandy 2 asks.

I sigh and stare at her, closing the cash register. Fuck counting. Half the time my mind drifts off as I count and I forget what I'm even doing. "The hot chocolate lady?"

Mandy 2 nods, rolling her eyes.

This woman and her kids have been staying in room 504 for over a week now, and every morning she goes a little crazy over the fact that we're out of hot chocolate. I had brought this up with my manager one morning, and his only response was, "Fuck that bitch." He is not the best manager in the world, but he is probably not the worst.

"Bitch has been at me all night about this and that," Mandy 2 says. "She just screamed at me maybe ten minutes ago. I want to chop her head off and roll it down the street for cars to run over."

The Nightly Disease

"That's . . . that's kind of graphic." I picture an owl swooping down and picking up the decapitated head, but decide against sharing the imagery with her.

"She comes down, screams at me because she saw some guest has a trash bag outside his door. She told me I should be up there, taking everyone's trash out. Lady's nuts."

"Once you work here long enough, you'll begin to realize anyone who chooses to stay at a hotel is a lunatic."

"No kidding."

"So," I say, trying to stop the words from coming out of my mouth and predictably failing, "you find any owls to pet yet?"

She blushes and laughs. "No. Not yet."

If I was a pervert, I might claim to have something similar to an owl in my pants that she could potentially stroke. Correction: if I was a pervert without fear of consequence, without fear of rejection.

She rests her hand on my arm and the tiny television set in my heart switches to a channel broadcasting loud, disorienting static, and I'm worried the bulimic girl might witness this scene and crush all chances of us ever marrying.

"Listen," she says, "I just wanted to apologize if I came off as a little weird the other day. I've been going through . . . a lot of stuff lately . . . and I guess it's all made me a little . . . loony."

"Everybody's loony. It's all good."

"Thanks. But seriously, though . . . I wasn't kidding about the owl outside my house. I want you to know that. Just in case."

"The one that hoots when you're sad?" I smile, but I'm the only one.

"I think it's stalking me." She flinches and covers her arms over her head, as if expecting a strong blow from above.

"Are you okay?" I try to help her but she backs away, shaking. Lines of blood trickle out of both nostrils.

"I'M FINE! Sorry. Just a bad headache. Been having them a lot lately. You think about owls long enough and you start to become one."

"Sure. That makes sense."

Blood continues to drip down her face, but she doesn't seem to give a shit. "Anyway, the drawer's at three hundred. The only thing to pass on is that Yates guy has a clogged toilet. He's expecting you."

"Awesome."

"I gotta go now, okay? I gotta go."

"The owl awaits?"

Mandy 2 closes her eyes, blood dropping from her face to the carpet. "The owls always await."

#104

Hotel guests are not human beings. At best, they are dogs too dumb to ever be properly house-broken. If not for night auditors, hotel guests wouldn't survive the night. They might freeze to death after failing to comprehend the thermostat, or they might starve on the toilet while trying to figure out the flusher. If the hotel caught on fire, the guests would just sit in their rooms watching the flames spread onto the beds, waiting to receive directions to stand up and exit the building. Most guests would request the front desk staff to wipe their asses if they thought they could get away with it. Hold them on our laps and burp them at the climax of their meals.

It's bad enough we have to smile and ask how they're doing. But the truth is, nobody gives a shit about how anybody is doing at any point in time, and we all know it's bullshit yet we all continue playing along lest we disappoint a make-believe business executive jacking-off behind an invisible desk in an office that doesn't exist. We tell the guests good morning even though the morning is nothing close to

Max Booth III

good and we ask how they're doing and sometimes they nod and tell us they're doing all right and sometimes they spit in our faces and they shit in our mouths, they shit right in our goddamn mouths and we don't break our smiles even as their massive turds trickle down our throats and stain our teeth brown and even as we choke to death we still smile, we still ask if there's anything else we can do to accommodate their stay, and of course there's something, there's always something.

Night auditors do not see hotel guests as human beings and guests sure as hell do not see night auditors as human beings. Perfect example: cell phones. Guests *love* to check-in while on their cell phones. They'll typically enter the hotel, already on the phone, and toss their license on the front desk. Direct eye contact is unfathomable. Any sort of recognition that I'm a real person and not another automatic robot designed to satisfy their every need is a laughable dream. The frustration builds up to volumes so immense I have to bite my knuckles. There are many questions I need to ask this guest before I can complete the check-in process. Even if they already have a credit card on file, I still need to swipe the credit card again. I need to inquire about the purpose of their stay. I need to inform them of breakfast hours and the Internet passcode and various other amenities. I need to inquire which hole of mine they'd wish to penetrate. However, even when I try to gain their attention, they shun me, like a small child trying to impress their overworked parents with crayon drawings.

Being ignored is a direct cause of anger and depression. We all believe we are the center of the universe, and when this delusion is shattered by something as irritating and harmful as neglect, it beats the shit out of us. Few things are more dehumanizing than someone refusing to acknowledge our existence. We all share this rock together. We all burn under the same stupid, bastard sun.

The truth none of us are willing to admit is that, while we all view ourselves as the protagonist of our life stories, there are an infinite amount of other stories being written at the exact same moment, and the significance of each one is incomparable. What doesn't matter to one person matters a great deal to someone else, and vice versa. It is extremely difficult for myself to recognize that, because I tend to view others as side-characters in my life, others will thus view me as a side-character in their own. Maybe this is common knowledge to others, but for people like myself who spend the majority of their time isolated with only their thoughts to keep them company, this can be a difficult truth to accept.

Nobody's duty on this planet is to serve some other person. We are all serving ourselves, in one way or another. We all have our own desires. Our own plots.

The rude guest on his cell phone does not see me the same way I see myself. He doesn't see the hero to an uneventful, anticlimactic story about owls and masturbation. He sees a blurry face whose sole purpose on this Earth is to further delay the time it takes for him to walk into the hotel and to enter his reserved room. To him, I am a film extra unrecognizable in the background. The guy on the subway reading a newspaper with one leg crossed over the other. Instantly forgettable.

But now there's an issue with the reservation. Maybe the credit card he gives me is declined, or the type of room he reserved had been sold to another guest sometime earlier in the day. Shit happens. Now I've delayed his plot. This was supposed to be a simple process. Maybe he's on the phone with somebody important, maybe he's just shooting the shit with some girl he hopes to one day fuck, I don't know—the phone call is important to him, and that's all that matters. Now not only does he have to delay entrance to his room, but he also has to interrupt his phone conversation to further deal with what he expected to be a brief and forgetful moment in an otherwise significant story. Imagine Atticus Finch attempting to check into a hotel, only to be delayed thanks to the desk clerk having trouble locating his room key. Nobody wants to read about him standing at the front desk, sighing with impatience. No, we want to skip this scene and fast-forward to the cool bird-killing chapters.

So, understandably, the guest is pissed. He is pissed the same way he might get pissed if his WiFi was slow or his car battery died. He paid a certain amount of money for these things and he expects them to do their jobs without any issues. Now I've become yet another problem in an ocean of problems that should not exist.

I've reluctantly evolved from side-character to antagonist.

Thinking of the guest with the cell phone in this manner does not comfort his inevitable temper tantrum any more than showering the wilderness in gasoline extinguishes a forest fire. But it does help me understand why the guest reacts this way. Many times a guest will shout and slap the front desk and I will be left baffled. I think, what kind of human being treats another human being this way? And the answer to this is: all human beings. Because when Person A is expecting some type of service from Person B, Person A no longer views Person B as a human being, but as another machine with specific coding installed to exclusively serve Person A without failure.

And the truly terrible and funny thing about all of this is that, meanwhile, I'm viewing the guest as somebody who has interrupted my own story. I don't want to be stuck dealing with this asshole any longer than I need to. There are other tasks I'd like to accomplish and cross off my never-ending list of shit. Because he or someone else screwed up somewhere down the line and I have to deal with the problem, I am bitter and my hate for this guest increases. I hate the guest for no other reason than he is standing in front of me and is not already in his room. And the guest hates me for the same reason.

We are two main characters clashing against two supporting characters.

We are fighting ourselves, pissed at the reflection in the mirror.

If I can keep this in mind, maybe the next time a guest screams at me about something beyond my control I won't completely break down and spend the rest of my shift wishing I had some whiskey. The ability to not only understand empathy but to utilize it as much as possible is essential in not losing what little of our sanity we have left to lose.

But this is all easier to think about than it is to actually initiate.

Guests don't give a good goddamn if I empathize

with them. All they want is free shit, and they think if they scream and bitch long and loud enough, they'll get it.

And they are one hundred percent correct.

#105

The clock reads 1:30 A.M. and I'm fucking exhausted. This shift is murder. The number one cause of mind-decay, ask any reasonable doctor around. The night shift destroys not only your body, but also your mind. It's a whackjob psycho killer with a taste for blood. I need a better job, one with day-time hours and more pay. One that someone would be proud to claim. Like a hot dog vendor or a televangelist.

Later, if the hotel quiets down, I'll go up on the roof and masturbate. It's the only way to relieve stress these days.

The elevator dings open down the hallway. I sigh and wait. The scariest sound in the world is the elevator descending to the first floor.

A few minutes pass and nobody bothers me. False alarm?

"Hey!" a man shouts from the elevator doors. "Hey, is anyone here?"

"Uh, yeah."

A series of heavy footsteps follow as a man runs

down the hallway, into the lobby, wearing underwear and a tank top and nothing else. Beer drips down his face, soaking his hair, soaking everything. Waving an empty can of Cools Light, he says, "I couldn't find you. I was scared."

"Well, I'm here now."

"Thank the gods. Can you tell me where the Wendy's is? I'm so fuckin' lost, dude."

I tell him where it is, but remind him of the time and that they won't be open right now.

"Okay, yeah, okay, but where is the Wendy's?"

I repeat myself.

"Look, I just want some goddamn breakfast."

I tell the drunk guest that the restaurant is going to be closed, although I don't know why I'm even bothering. Just let him go and figure it out. Screw it.

Then the guest says, "Okay, yeah, sure, but what about the other place? Wendy's?"

I open my mouth to respond, but the guest interrupts with a scream: "NO, WAIT, I MEAN DENNY'S! FUCKIN' DENNY'S! YEAH!"

He spins around, runs out of the lobby, and punts the empty beer can across the parking lot, yelling, "GOOAAAALLL!" as he sprints away from the hotel.

After ten minutes of silence, I sit back down behind the front desk and try to relax. I grab my copy of Michael Cisco's massive novel, *Animal Money,* and flip through a couple pages, then set it back down. Too tired to read. Too tired to live. My eyeballs are dying planets under an exploding sun.

The doors open. Shit. The guy's returning already. He's going to bug me all night, I just know it.

I peek over the front desk. No, not the crazy guy. Just some woman. Probably also crazy. Her hair stands straight up like she's recently been electrocuted. Her grey sweater is clearly covered in animal hair. Most likely a cat's.

"Hi, ma'am, can I help you?"

She brushes her hands through her hair and starts rambling. "I'm so, so sorry, young man, this was a bad idea, just ignore me."

She flees from the hotel.

Well, that was remarkably painless.

Two seconds pass and she storms back into the lobby, rambling psychotically. She tells me that she's terribly sorry but she's afraid there are people after her. "I don't know how but they're . . . well, they're following me, okay? They're all around. They're in my GPS."

"They're in your GPS?"

"I am so, so scared, and they are closer than ever. They are in my GPS and they are screaming and I can't, I can't take it anymore, I just can't." She pauses to catch her breath. "Come with me. Please, just come outside. Please. You can hear it screaming, too."

"The GPS is screaming?"

"Nothing has ever screamed louder."

I have never heard a GPS screaming before, so of course I can't pass up on this opportunity. I lock the register and follow the lady outside. As we walk through the parking lot, it occurs to me that this could be a set-up. She'll get me to the other side of the hotel and bam, I'm face-to-face with some guy holding a knife. But after considering my wallet and the laughable amount of money in my bank account, I manage to relax a little.

We arrive at her car and she grabs my shoulder, trying to shush me despite the fact that I'm not making any noise. "Quiet! Do you hear that?"

"Uh, no."

"Shhh!"

We lean forward off the curb, straining to listen to nothing.

She shrugs. "This always happens."

She takes out her cell phone and squeezes it until her knuckles turn white, then pulls her arm back like she's going to throw it, then thinks better of it and returns the device to her pocket. She tells me "they" are using her cell phone and GPS to stalk her and she is so fucking sick of it.

"Those fuckers are out there. Just listen."

"Ma'am, do you want me to call the police?"

She shakes her head. "Fuckin' pigs are useless. Already talked to 'em and they said to consider a restraining order. CAN'T GET A RESTRAINING ORDER AGAINST THE GOVERNMENT, NOW CAN I, DUMBASS PIGS?"

Her screams unravel into incomprehensibleness. I slowly back away and return to the lobby. I'm fumbling for the front desk phone to call the police when her car screeches out of the parking lot. I stand like an idiot with the phone in my hand and watch the car disappear into the darkness.

Sure. Why not.

I return to *Animal Money* and continue consuming dead trees.

The phone rings. I slam the book down.

Room #504.

I stare at the ringing phone and gulp, seriously debating not answering. Shit.

But of course I answer it. It is my job. My duty. My only purpose in life is to answer this phone. My father and mother fucked and pried me from her vagina just so one day I could answer a telephone in South-Central Texas. This is my moment. This is my destiny. So I do. I answer it and ask how I can help her.

And she responds, "It's about fucking time!"

"Sorry, ma'am, I was helping another guest."

"Yeah, right, and I was born with a dick."

I almost choke. "Uh . . . were you?"

"I gave birth to these children, didn't I?"

The only thing stopping me from hanging up is knowing that she'd just come down to the lobby to scream in person. "Ma'am, how can I help you?"

"I need some wake-up calls. Seven-fifteen and seven-forty-five. Think you can manage that?"

"Yes, ma'am, of course."

"Good." She hangs up. Thank Christ.

I start to enter the wake-up calls she requested, then stop. I'll be out of this place by seven in the morning. If she happens to not receive a wake-up call for some reason, I won't have to listen to her bitching. Maybe by missing a single alarm, her entire day will be ruined.

I erase what I had already entered into the system and smile. The night is just beginning but it's already looking up. It's amazing what spite can do for the soul. I leave the front desk to store my lunch in the break room refrigerator. When I return, the phone's going insane.

504. Again. Somehow she knows I didn't enter the wake-up calls. Oh crap, oh crap.

"What do they even pay you people for?" she says after I answer.

"Sorry, ma'am, you caught me when I was helping another guest."

"Whatever. My son is sick. I need some extra towels. Now."

"Sure. How many do you need?"

"A lot! Jesus, do I have to hold your hand every step of the way? Just bring up some fucking towels already."

I hang up without another word and rush into the backroom for a stack of towels. A part of me wants to just forget she ever called and make her come down and pick up the towels her own damn self. The thought makes me smile deep down inside. But she would just end up bitching at me even more. It's not worth it. This lobby is my home, my nest. She is not welcomed here.

I knock on 504 with about ten towels stacked against my chest. On the other side of the door I can hear the woman saying, "Jesus Christ, it's about fucking time. I'm so sick of these lazy hotel assholes."

The door swings open and the woman stands in the opening wearing only a bathrobe, practically snarling at him. The bathrobe is not tied properly, revealing one enormous, sagging breast poking out. Purple veins have rotted it like the dead roots of a tree. She grabs the towels from me and holds up a plastic grocery bag. The top is tied in a knot.

"Throw this away." She shoves it at me until I accept it.

The door closes and I'm left alone in the hallway, holding a mysterious soggy grocery bag. The smell hits me hard. Vomit. The bitch has given me a bag of vomit.

"Fuck this."

I drop the bag on the carpet and it explodes like a grenade in front of 504. I confirm the cash register is locked, turn off all the lights, and exit the hotel. The humidity should not be so strong at this time of night.

The Nightly Disease

But hey, at this point, I'm used to Texas being an asshole. The anger fuels me across to the Other Goddamn Hotel directly in front of my own hotel.

George is sitting behind the front desk, watching *Pulp Fiction* on his laptop. The volume's cranked to full blast and the sound of Ving Rhames being raped by skinhead perverts can be heard throughout the lobby.

"My God, man, have you no shame?"

George looks over his shoulder, surprised to see someone standing there. "What? This is a good movie."

"I think you give less of a shit about your job than I do."

"That's highly possible." George mutes his laptop. "Speaking of which, I see you've already given up."

"This lady is going to kill me, man." I tell George about the hot chocolate lady. He proceeds to laugh like I've just finished telling him the greatest joke in history.

"She handed you a bag of *vomit?*"

"Yeah."

"How did you not strangle her?"

"My hands were too busy . . . you know, holding the bag."

"Of vomit."

"Yeah."

George keeps laughing. I sigh. Enough already. "You gonna bust out the flask, or what?"

He tries to calm himself. "This friendship is a sham. You just want my booze."

"Pretty much, yeah." I grab the flask and pour a healthy dose in a plastic cup on the front desk. "After tonight I am going to need all the whiskey you got."

41

"Well, drink up." George gestures to the empty lobby. "It's not like we have cameras or anything. Fucking idiots."

I gulp the whiskey down and refill the cup. "Do you think we're the only two hotels in existence without actual cameras?"

"Probably."

"One day someone will walk up to the front desk, shoot me in the face, take all the cash from the register, and walk out. And no one will ever know who did it."

George seems to contemplate the idea, then nods. "Yeah, I can see that."

The whiskey flows down my throat, warm and cathartic. "It would be a fitting end to a perfectly shitty life."

George raises his own cup and we bonk them together. "Amen."

We drink and discuss owls.

"She definitely sounds crazy," George says. "But is she good looking?"

"I don't know, man. I guess."

He laughs. "You're still in love with that fuckin' bulimic chick, aren't you?"

Shoving the whiskey down my throat seems to work as a decent excuse for not responding.

George shakes his head. "Have you even talked to her yet?"

"I told her 'good morning' the other day."

"And what did she say?"

" . . . Nothing."

"She just went into the kitchen and stole food, right?"

"I guess."

"Then she puked it out in the bathroom?"

The Nightly Disease

"I don't know."

"Did you hear her throwing up, yes or no?"

" . . . Maybe."

Before finishing off the flask, George says, "Just don't forget to make me best man at your guys' wedding."

"Deal." I pause, debating telling him about the way she'd assaulted me the other day, but decide to drop it. He's already laughed enough tonight at my own expense.

Back at the Goddamn Hotel, breakfast has been served and I'm just counting down the clock. Mostly sober at this point, but still in desperate need for a bed to crash upon. A group of men loiter around the lobby, fiddling with their cell phones. They belong to this oil company that often stays at the hotel. They're waiting for Kevin to arrive and drive them all to work in the hotel shuttle.

One of them, this big son of a bitch wielding a lovecraftian mustache on his upper lip, turns to the smallest of the bunch and says, "So, you gonna be my dance partner today, baby?"

The skinny one lowers his cell phone and looks at the big 'un. "I don't know. I'm kind of sore from working with Mike yesterday."

The big one sighs. "Oh, come on, don't be a wuss."

The smaller one pauses, seeming to consider his options. "I don't even have the right shoes."

"You'll do fine. Come on. I need you to dance with me. You're small, you can fit right up in there."

"All right! Fine. Jesus."

The big one grins, although it is almost completely hidden by his mustache. He holds out his hand and high fives his new dance partner.

I try to return to *Animal Money* but am once again interrupted when a man dressed in a business suit strolls inside. Despite being dried and sober, there is no mistaking him as the nearly naked man who had previously punted a beer can outside the hotel at the beginning of my shift. He nods and says, "Hi, how's it going, sir?"

I stare at him, amazed with the universe. "Did . . . did you find Denny's?"

He smiles and rubs his stomach. "Boy, I really love their omelets."

Just as he disappears, the woman from 504 takes his place.

"Hey, you can cancel my wake-up calls," she says, seemingly materializing from nothing. At least her terrifying breasts are thoroughly concealed. "I need to extend my stay another two nights."

I nearly start crying. "Sure thing, ma'am. You got it."

Before she leaves, she says, "Make sure to have your little illegals replace my dirty towels with new ones. I'd like some actual goddamn service for once."

And the tears finally arrive.

#106

The alarm clock screams. Somewhere inside this contraption resides a tiny man being tortured to death, and I am stuck listening to his suffering. My body remains still, lifeless as a corpse. If I don't move, maybe the laws of time will dissolve into the unknown. But the shitty song playing on the radio won't end until I get up and turn it off. I piss and get dressed in jean shorts and a Bad Religion T-shirt, then head out the door.

On the way to the hotel I stop at a gas station and buy a Red Bull. The drink's empty by the time I make it back to my car. I swerve into the hotel parking lot as sloppy as a drunk driver, punk music blaring through my speakers, guests outside for a smoke glaring at me like I'm the Anti-Christ arriving to claim all the hotel sinners. My windows are down, which makes Jello Biafra's lovely vocals all the clearer. The AC has never worked on this car, and it's typically never much of a problem considering I do the majority of my driving late at night or early in the morning. But in the afternoon, with this Texas heat?

Max Booth III

I might as well be swimming in a pool of lava, in the thick spunk of Satan himself.

Karen's at the front desk stapling paperwork. She tells me good afternoon and I grunt without further response. Simply put, Karen is an asshole. The kind of person who wastes your time ten, twenty minutes after your shift ends by complaining about every wrong thing that's ever happened in her life. "My little Rufus woke me up an hour before my alarm went off because he just loves me so much," she's told me on many occasions, "but you know how my legs are, they need their rest, if I don't let them sit long enough I'll get them stress hives again and my doctor specifically told me them stress hives are bad news, so I told Rufus he had to wait a little bit longer, and he ended up peeing on my carpet, can you believe it, Isaac, can you believe what I am telling you, can you, can you believe I am a waste of cells, can you please please bash my face in and end this faulty design as quickly as possible, thank you, Isaac, you are a hero, Isaac, Isaac, I said you're a hero, kill me, ruin me, end me, please, Isaac, Isaac," and so on. Like anybody gives a shit about her dumb dogs. But of course I can't say that, because my boss inexplicably loves her. I doubt it's her looks, and it sure as fuck ain't her personality.

There's a taco bar set up in the dining area. Most of my coworkers have already begun eating. I pour a cup of coffee and sit down, leaning my head back, closing my eyes. Next to me, Yas says, "What's the matter, Isaac? Aren't you going to eat?"

I don't respond. I'm too tired to open my mouth. She asks the same question every meeting. And I always tell her the same answer—that, for me, it's really midnight right now. It's the middle of my sleep

The Nightly Disease

schedule. How would you like it if you had to wake up in the middle of the night, drive to work, and eat a full meal while your boss said a bunch of pointless shit everybody already knew?

She usually gets quiet around this point.

To be honest, though, there's a more complex reason for my refusal to eat. It isn't like my stomach isn't growling right now. The smell of those tacos are like heroin. At home, the contents of my fridge consists of expired milk and tuna. But if I don't eat at this meeting, then management gets pissed off, and that, to me, is worth starvation. They go out of their way to buy a shit-ton of food every monthly meeting as a "thank you" to the employees for showing up, and I never touch a bite. They can't grasp how selfish these mandatory meetings are for some reason, no matter how many times I explain it to them. Anything that's said this afternoon can easily be texted or emailed. They could pass on the information the next morning. They could just leave a note. But no. Instead they force my ass out of bed with only an hour or so of sleep and put my own life and everybody else's in danger as I drive across town to the hotel. Then when I get home, my body refuses to go back to sleep, and I'm awake until the next day.

One of these days, my eyes will burst from their sockets. Sleep deprivation will consume me. It will become me.

One of these days, the world will be on fire, and I'll be holding the empty gas tank.

My boss asks me if I'm going to eat and I start laughing.

"Just thought I'd ask," he says.

I sip my coffee, close my eyes again. Fuck this

place. It means nothing. It means everything. In the day, it's foreign territory. Come night, it'll transform back into familiar land, and I can loathe it properly.

I don't belong here, out in the sun, like some kind of scumbag.

Fifteen minutes pass. Nobody says anything. They all just eat. I drift off for a few, wake back up and my boss is in the middle of a speech, saying something about a funeral being scheduled next Friday afternoon.

Sweaty and delirious from my brief nap, I bolt up and shout, "What funeral?"

Everybody in the dining area looks at me, shocked. Some of them have been crying.

"I'm sorry." I sink back into my seat, wishing I was invisible.

Javier stares at me for a moment longer, then returns to his speech, ignoring my question. "As I was saying, for those who wish to pay their respects to Mandy, the funeral will be held tomorrow at the Fisher-Diaz Funeral Home in Universal City."

"Wait, Mandy's dead?" I stand up, frantic. "Which one?" I quickly scan the crowd of employees and spot Mandy 1. The sequel's missing. "Holy shit! I just saw her. We . . . shared a moment. Wait—she's dead? What the fuck?"

Javier groans and motions for me to take a seat. I refuse. "Isaac, please try to control yourself."

"How did she die?"

"Now, we aren't quite sure yet, but . . . "

"It's all over the news," Kevin says. "Stop trying to act like you don't know, man."

I turn to Kevin, shaking. "What happened to her?"

Kevin laughs, and I want to beat his face in until

his smile erases. "Fuckin' owl killed her. Ate her face off."

A guest passing through the lobby laughs.

"Kevin, that's enough," Javier says.

"Wh . . . what?" I'm choking on vomit. "An . . . an owl? What? I . . . how, what. *An owl?*"

He nods. "Yeah, man. An owl."

My legs betray me and I collapse back in my seat. One of the housekeepers sitting next to me gasps and motions to her nose, then points at me.

"Te sangra la nariz," she says.

And I don't need to understand Spanish to know my nose is bleeding.

#107

There is nothing to eat in my apartment and I regret my stubbornness against participating in the free lunch back at the meeting. I find some crackers on the floor and drown them in ketchup and eat and stare at the wall thinking about Mandy 2, thinking about owls, thinking about the cosmic horror of the universe swooping down on us all with its hideous goddamn talons and tearing us apart. Clawing at us until we're nothing, until we're everything, which means the same thing so who really cares, who can really care, hoo, hoo. Our previous scheduled continuation of sleep has hereby been cancelled. The day's activities will now be replaced with the following: terror, insanity, nail-biting, and more terror. If time permits, perhaps we can fit in another delightful round of insanity.

There's only about fifty dollars in my checking account, which I was saving for filling up my tank throughout the rest of the month, but gas only remains important when you aren't worrying about inserting food into your stomach. I order a pizza and pace around my studio apartment as I wait for it to arrive.

I have no food in my stomach, and I must vomit.

I am a Troma adaptation of a Harlan Ellison story.

The urge to eat and be sick overwhelm each other, and I can't help but wonder if this is how the bulimic girl feels. Does her stomach also send her mixed signals? I curl into a ball on the floor and rock myself like an infant. Blood drips down my nose and soaks into the carpet. I lost any chance of regaining my apartment deposit a long time ago, so a little blood won't hurt anything.

How can Mandy 2 be dead? We had just spoken. What the fuck kind of crazy shit was she into? Had she actually tried to pet an owl? Had my mice idea worked? This could be my fault. She could be dead because of what I'd said. But still, sure, owls are cranky bastards, but I don't remember ever hearing anything about them fucking *murdering* human beings. How did this happen? Maybe everybody at the meeting had just been screwing with me. They noticed I was taking a nap and decided to pull a practical joke.

Ha, ha, ha.

I search "girl killed by owl" online and the article about Mandy 2 is the first result. Well, the first result after the surprisingly massive amount of owl-related porn.

The headline: "Woman attacked and killed by feral owl".

I already know what the words say before I read them.

Her window was open. It flew in. She was in bed. Maybe she was awake and aware. Maybe she even smiled as the owl landed on her chest. What transpired between the time the owl flew into the room and flew out will never be exactly known. Nothing about that night will be one hundred percent concrete. But somewhere in that time period, the owl scratched and pecked Mandy 2's face off. The article perhaps goes into too much detail. The journalist will probably be demoted, or depending on the page views, maybe a bonus will be given out instead. According to the article, Mandy 2's head was mostly hair and skull when she was discovered in the morning. The owl was nowhere to be found. Police say if you see an owl in the sky, you should find cover immediately. Close your windows. Lock your doors. Do not walk outside at night without some form of protective headwear. Do not trust the owls. The owls are not your friends.

Do.

Not.

Trust.

The.

Owls.

The comment section is mostly full of people making fun of Mandy. People calling her a dumb bitch, saying something like this would have never happened to a man. Other people arguing with those people about being sexist. Someone else selling discounted sunglasses. Another person claiming to have committed the murder. "I am the owl," the comment reads. "Hoot, hoot, hoot."

Another comment includes a link promising to be a photo of the crime scene.

Against my instincts, I click it.

What I see will haunt me both in sleep and

consciousness, which are really the same thing, when I think about it.

Mandy's on the bed, on her back.

No more smile. No more braces.

Like she was chewing gum and tried to make a bubble only to have it explode across her face. Except in this photo, there's no gum.

What happened to you, Mandy? What did you do?

What kind of owl were you fucking with?

The doorbell rings and I scream.

My pizza has arrived.

#108

There are one hundred eighteen rooms in this
hotel. One hundred eighteen corpses available
for one hundred eighteen lost souls to step into
and try on every night. Thirty-four standard kings.
Thirty-nine standard double queens. Twenty-four
king suites. Thirty-two double queen suites. Five
floors. One hundred eighteen potential rooms to fuck
a stranger or blow your brains out in.

"Do you think blood has spilled in every hotel
room throughout the world?" I ask George., who's at
my hotel for a change. Since hearing the news about
Mandy 2, I haven't found the courage to abandon the
premises at night. Maybe depression is to blame.
Maybe I'm simply afraid of the same shit happening
to me. Lots of owls outside this place. Who's the next
victim? The next meal?

George nods. "That seems like a pretty safe bet. If
I was a smarter man, I could probably come up with
some kinda fancy graph charting the statistics of
menstruating women who stay at hotels. But, alas."

I grab the flask from his mouth and shake my

head like a disappointed parent. "Nah, man. I mean, like, blood spilling from a violent means. Like stabbings or gunshots or whatever."

"I don't know, blood pouring from a vagina seems pretty hardcore to me. Imagine if you one day started bleeding from your dick. Not only that, but it bled every month. Like, holy shit, man."

"You're terrifying when you're drunk."

"And you're ten times sexier when I'm drunk."

I hand him back the flask. Somewhere down the hall, a guest is screaming about something too difficult to decipher. Fuck him. "I'm serious," I tell George, "I bet you, throughout history, blood has fallen in at least eighty percent of hotel rooms."

"I think you may be curious about the wrong kind of bodily fluid, my friend." He belches, loud and disturbing.

"What?"

George wraps his fingers around a ghost dong and jerks it off for a moment. "One hundred percent of every goddamn hotel room that's ever existed. Semen! Semen everywhere!"

"HELLO?" someone shouts from the lobby, and I jump up from my seat in the back office and rush to the front desk.

A guest slams a laptop down on the counter, most likely cracking the bottom in the process. "I CAN'T GET ON THE INTERNET!"

"Oh. Well . . . have you connected to the WiFi?"

"Of course I have!"

I wipe sweat out of my eyes, trying to convince myself that I'm not drunk. "Have you agreed to the terms and conditions?"

"No. What does that mean?"

"Well, with our WiFi, once you've connected to it, your browser will ask you to read and agree to our terms and conditions. Basically, you are agreeing that you won't download anything illegal, stuff like that. It should pop up when you try to get online."

"But that's the thing, your goddamn Internet isn't letting my browser come up!"

"Just let me see it."

He stares at me, sighs, and pushes the shitty laptop across the counter. The first thing I notice is that the wallpaper is littered with shortcut buttons to various pornographic websites. Not only that, but his mouse cursor is a tiny pistol.

I restart the computer, have the guest log on to his account, then try to connect to the Internet. It spends a few minutes "connecting" then dies a tragic death. It's difficult to come up with a solution when a giant baby man pounds his fist in front me and screams.

"All you fuckin' hotels are out to get me, I swear. Last night, at the Days Inn, same goddamn problem. Then again at Starbucks. Why won't you give me your WiFi? I just want to watch a movie!"

"Sir, if you haven't been able to connect to WiFi at *all* of those places, then I am afraid you have a virus."

"What the hell is that?"

I return the laptop to him. "It's like when your computer gets sick, it can't function properly. Since you can't get online to download any type of system mechanic, I would advise you either do a system recovery, or consider sending it in to Geek Squad or something."

The guest stands there for a moment, quiet, staring at me, then says, "So, how do I get to the Internet?"

The Nightly Disease

I point down the hallway. "Try looking that way."

The guest grunts at me and turns around. Before he can say anything else, I've returned to the back office and pried the flask from George's hands.

"Did he find . . . the Internet?" George asks, and I flip him off.

I set the flask down and close my eyes as the liquid burns through my chest. A minute passes and I've reprogrammed myself. I belch and tell George to consider Elisa Lam.

"Who?"

"You know. The lady who drowned in that hotel water tank."

"What? Here?" George looks around for extra effect, but I'm not buying it.

"No, man. Don't play stupid. Like three, four years ago, that hotel in Los Angeles?"

"Why are you talking to me about hotels in Los Angeles, Isaac? That doesn't concern us. Haven't you heard? Texas is gonna be its own country practically any day now."

"Oh fuck off. Remember the video that went viral of the girl who was being chased by something in a hotel hallway? She was in the elevator, freaking out, hitting all the buttons. Then she went missing. Two weeks later, an employee found her in one of the water tanks up on the roof."

"That never happened."

"Sure it did. For two weeks, the guests at the hotel drank the decomposed remains of the girl floating in the water tank."

"I bet they sued like a motherfucker."

"Wouldn't be surprised. Anyway, but that's the kind of bloodshed I'm talking about. Not bloody noses or paper cuts. Not menstruation blood. But gruesome, unexplained insanity. Do you think there's a similar story in every hotel?"

"I don't know. When was the last time you checked your water tanks?"

"That's not what I'm—"

"Wait, how did the girl get on the roof?"

"What?"

"Surely only an employee could unlock the door leading to the roof."

"True."

"Bam." George fist-bumps the air. "The night auditor did it. Mystery fuckin' solved."

"It's always the night auditor."

"We're a bunch of homicidal motherfuckers." George finishes off the flask and falls into a coughing fit. "Oh man, I may have overdone it tonight. Fuck, my chest."

"C'mon, I'll walk you next door."

My arm around his, we look like two lovers taking a midnight stroll. George sings a unintelligible song about making love to peanut butter. A man waits in the lobby of the Other Goddamn Hotel, and when George sees him he can't stop laughing.

"Look at this fucking guy," George says. "Actually expects some kind of service."

The guy checks his watch. "As a matter of fact, I—"

George makes a fart noise and flips him off. "No vacancies, dickwad."

"But . . . I already have a room."

"Not anymore. I sold it to your mom."

I sneak out of the hotel before they have a chance to drag me into their argument.

The bulimic girl is waiting for me when I return to

my own hotel. I stumble up the walkway, drunk, focusing all my energy on putting one foot in front of the other. She's standing in the foyer, arms crossed, staring at me. She's wearing the same clothes as the morning she punched me. Her odor is both erotic and repulsive.

"Wow, man," she says "Your nose is really fucked-up."

"I wonder who I have to thank for that."

She smiles. "You're welcome."

I step around her and unlock the entrance. She follows me into the lobby.

"So, where were you?" she asks.

"The Other Goddamn Hotel." I refuse to turn around and look at her. What if I try to kiss her? What if she punches me again? What if I punch *her?* Shit, the possibilities are endless.

"You work here *and* the Other Goddamn Hotel?"

"Nah, I just . . . go there sometimes." I sense her nearing me, so I flee behind the front desk, where the fairy tale of safety is much easier to swallow. I gather some random sheets of paper and pretend to organize them. She leans over the counter and I try to avoid eye contact, but her gaze is magnetic.

"Are you afraid of me?" she asks, giggling.

"No, of course not."

"Oh my God, you totally are."

I hold a stack of receipts closer to my face before answering. "Well, you did almost break my nose. Maybe you *did* break it."

"You don't expect me to defend myself when some random dude tries to grope me?"

I forget about being shy and drop the papers to look at her directly. "I did not try to grope you."

She shrugs and backs away, then sits on the lobby sofa. "Well, you at least thought about it."

"I was trying to warn you."

"Warn me about *what*?"

"Our maintenance guy, he has it out for you. He wanted to confront you this morning. Embarrass you in front of everybody."

"Embarrass me for what?" This time she's the one avoiding eye contact.

"We can hear you, when you're in the bathroom. Plus the maintenance guy followed you to the Other Goddamn Hotel once."

She stands up and tightens her hands into fists. "He *followed* me?"

"Yeah. He's, uh, pretty creepy."

"Ya think?" She shivers. "Jesus Christ, why would he *follow* me?"

"How many hotels do you go to every day?"

"It's not *every* day."

"You've been here every morning this week."

She opens her mouth, then closes it. She paces around the lobby furniture, mumbling profanities.

"Are you okay?" I consider going over there and consoling her, but fear another facial injury.

"What do you mean, you can hear me in the bathroom? You don't hear anything."

"I mean, aren't you, like . . . bulimic?"

She stops, staring at her feet, breathing heavier. "You can just go fuck yourself," she says after a while, and runs out of the hotel.

#109

"We accept the love we think we deserve."

A **quote from** *The Perks of Being a Wallflower* by Stephen Chbosky. The movie might be better than the book, which is rare, but in this case true. The quote originates after Charlie asks his English teacher, "Why do I and everyone I love pick people who treat us like we're nothing?" The character is referring to this girl he likes, but she's already dating a known scumbag.

The teacher answers, "We accept the love we think we deserve."

This quote won't leave my brain tonight. It is such a simple sentence, yet it is so heavy in truth it could sink a warship. I see fucked up relationships every day, and I'm constantly wondering why anybody would stay with someone else who constantly makes them so miserable.

Then I think about the hotel, and the way it treats me, and my refusal to end the relationship, and I don't know what to think.

Max Booth III

My older brother is married to someone who is going to kill him in the end. They had five kids together before they even got hitched, because apparently that's the next step you take after you conceive almost half a dozen children. They used to break up every other week, and they still do, too, if my mom's updates from Indiana are at all accurate. Physical beatings from both sides of the party is a regular thing for them. I had a hard time imagining two grown adults spitting in each other's faces until the day I had dinner with my brother and sister-in-law.

They fucking hate each other. They say this on a daily basis. It's as common as a normal marriage's "I love you" before heading off to work. At least until they finally break up and a few days pass, then my brother's crawling back to her, declaring his undying love with a knife to his own flesh. One day he will kill himself. This is a truth that I've long accepted. Everybody else in the family is still in denial, but not me, but of course, that doesn't do any good, seeing as I live in Texas now and the rest of my toxic, shitty family is back in the Midwest.

There will come a time when no one will be there to stop my brother from committing suicide, and he will finally be dead. In my brother's mind, it will be romantic, but in reality, it will be irrational and stupid. He will do this not for love, but for the idea of love. For the misplaced notion of what he *wants,* not what he actually *has.*

Deep down, my brother knows he is not a good person. He is right. But he could change. He won't, though. This kind of relationship is what he subconsciously believes he deserves. This lack of happiness is his own self-punishment.

The Nightly Disease

I have witnessed the same kind of shit over and over at the hotel. The bars in town close during the middle of my shift, so the lobby is every drunk's salvation. This is when their true feelings come out. They are ugly, and they do not care.

There's this one couple who stay at the Goddamn Hotel quite frequently. John Hobbs and Brenda LastNameUnknown. Usually for about three to four days, then a couple weeks will pass and they'll stay again. I don't know why they stay so much. Maybe they're homeless, maybe they have a tiny shampoo fetish. I don't care. What I do know is, at least one of those nights on each reservation, the woman will stumble up to the front desk at about two-thirty in the morning, reeking of alcohol. Voice slurring, she'll tell me that she's going upstairs, and no matter what, I am not to give her boyfriend a key to their room. Since the room is technically in her name, she gets to call the shots. Then, sure enough, an hour or so later the boyfriend will come waltzing into the lobby. I will watch with dread as he nods at me and heads up the elevator, only to return to the front desk a few minutes later complaining that his old keycard no longer works on the door. This is when I have to explain to a very drunk and obnoxious man that his girlfriend requested for the locks to be reset and I can't give him a new key. The boyfriend will ask what the hell he's supposed to do, where the hell's he supposed to go.

I hate the girlfriend for the situation she constantly puts me in. I hate the boyfriend even more for the things he says.

When people are drunk, sometimes they say things they would never in a million years say while sober. This does not make what they say any less the truth. If anything, the alcohol takes off their protective shields, allowing their inner thoughts to finally come out into the cold.

The boyfriend is a horrible human being. Imagine a ball of dried dog shit you one day discover on the bottom of your shoe. That is John Hobbs. When I talk to him, I visualize breaking his jaw. Sure, it wouldn't do any good, but it still helps me cope with our interactions. The first night I had to lock him out of the room, the boyfriend spent almost two hours hanging around the front desk, trying to shoot the shit. Of course, he was drunk off his ass, so "shooting the shit" basically broke down to him telling me how his girlfriend's father was currently on trial for molesting her and her sister's children. The boyfriend said he despised his girlfriend, yet he had to be with her anyway, because what else was there? All woman were pretty much shit, he said, but you aren't left with much choice. What else are you going to do—fuck a *man?* Hobbs then went on a rant about how homosexuals are not a part of God's plan, and proceeded to yell in the lobby that "God created Adam and Eve, not Adam and Steve," because if bigots are one thing, it's original.

This has happened about seven times now. Two nights ago, the girlfriend came in again, but with a new guy, the other boyfriend nowhere in sight. She told me she'd finally dumped that no good son of a bitch of hers, and she was never taking him back. This is a line I have heard from many other people about other boyfriends, other girlfriends.

Never, never, never.

As they walked toward the elevator, her new guy

started howling like a dog and shouted, "I'm a cheap little slut who needs to be punished! I'm a little whore, Mommy, a smelly little whore!"

I doubt I will see this new guy again. By now, the woman has probably already gotten back together with her bigot boyfriend. Of course they have. It's a story that's been played out a thousand times before, and it'll happen a thousand times again.

People's self-esteems are a dying fire under a black cloud. The rain will kill everybody soon enough, so why should they bother trying to breathe the oxygen required to survive?

"We accept the love we think we deserve."

This does not have to be a bad thing. But first, people have to stop being so goddamn cynical. Happiness is not something reserved for characters in movies. It is something people *can* have, dammit. At least that's what I try to convince myself. People will not achieve contentment with a partner by acting out some shitty cliché movie montage. It is something people have to work at, something they have to actually try for.

People need to have the strength to push, the strength to search for not what they *think* they deserve, but what they *do* deserve. They must purify the waters in their toxic relationships. They have to know when to hold on, and they have to know when to let go. They must have the willpower to say *no*, even if it means completely reprogramming their lives. Inconveniences are worth it if they are putting an end to a future of misery. They can either put out the fire with their hands, or let it consume them whole. I think these thoughts without ever having had my own partner. I don't know why I believe it to be true.

Maybe this is all a delusion on my part. Maybe I only feed the fire.

I wonder what the bulimic girl would say if she knew I thought like this. Would she fall in love with me? Would she think I'm a fucking weirdo and tell me to piss off?

One day, I'm going to find out.

But not today.

#110

I smell him before I see him. It's a familiar scent, one I've come to recognize with John Hobbs. Him and his girlfriend probably stay here more often than anyone else I know. Brenda supposedly works at the call center of one of the Goddamn Hotels, some building located into the heart of San Antonio, so she's always getting a $35 or $17.50 rate, depending on the time of year. Out of everybody who stays at my hotel, I despise this couple the most, especially the boyfriend. Like me, Hobbs is an owl, which means most of the time he's here, he's roaming around the lobby trying to talk to me. Most of the time he's drunk. Other times, he just smells like he is. And he's always bitching about his hands and showing me the latest scars his job has inflicted on them, crying that one day he's going to get a real job where nobody treats him like shit, which might be the funniest thing anybody has ever said.

I'm in the back office when the lobby doors open. The smell drifts from the entrance, over the front desk, and to my chair within seconds. The scent of booze and unwashed genitals. I'm caught off guard by the smell, because last I checked, I had no more reservations for the night, and Hobbs isn't currently staying with us. So what the fuck is he doing here?

My body is frozen. I pretend that if I sit here for a while, not moving, maybe he'll go away. But he starts slapping the front desk and yodeling, and I surrender to his redneck charm.

"Hey, boy!" he shouts at the sight of me. "How the fuck ya doin'?"

"I'm all right, thanks."

He nods, smiling, revealing teeth stained black from a lifetime of chewing tobacco. "I just need to check-in to my room. It's been a hell of a day. Gotta clock in to the good ol' shoe farm, if ya know what I mean."

I, of course, do not have the slightest clue what he means. I check the system to make sure a new reservation hasn't been made since the last time I checked. There's nothing there. When I look back up at him, it's a struggle to force my smile into a frown.

"Sorry, but you don't seem to have a reservation tonight."

"Well, that simply isn't true."

"I'm afraid it is. Are you sure Brenda made the reservation?"

"Of course I'm fuckin' sure."

"Maybe she made some type of mistake."

He's shaking his head, staring at me like I just killed his mother. "*You* made the mistake, boy. *You.*"

"I've done no such thing."

Every time he talks, my face is assaulted with another blast of his breath. A few more sentences from him and I'm likely to pass out.

The Nightly Disease

Hobbs pulls out his cell phone and dials a number, then holds it to his ear. It rings for a while and finally someone must answer, because he says, "Brenda! Goddammit, woman, wake the fuck up. What? It's *John*. Wake up. No, I don't give a shit about any goddamn owls. Now, will you listen? I'm at the hotel. Yeah, the Goddamn Hotel. They're saying they don't have the reservation you made. What? No, I don't fuckin' know. Look, Billy's on my ass about the latest orders, I gotta get this shit done *tonight*. No, Brenda, they don't got it. That's what I'm sayin'. Wait, what? What the fuck? Goddammit, Brenda. I ask you to do one fuckin' thing and you can't even do that. No. Ugh. Just go back to sleep, you worthless cow."

He returns the cell to his pocket and looks at me, pissed off and not trying to hide it.

"Did you say something about owls?" I ask.

He raises his eyebrow, confused. "I guess the stupid bitch forgot to make the reservation. Can I just get a room?"

I nod, only half-there, the other half of me focusing on conspiracy theories. I'm sure he mentioned owls. But why?

I tell him the rate for tonight and he flips out again.

"That ain't the usual rate."

"Well, your usual rate is the associate discount."

"So give me that, then."

"Well, I can't, considering you're not an associate."

"But Brenda is."

"But she's not here."

"Come on, man. You know me."

I shrug. "Sorry, but I would need her here

personally, plus I can't just give out the associate rate. That kind of reservation has to be made online. Hotel policy."

"Well, ain't that some shit."

"It is indeed."

He pauses, contemplating. He eventually throws his hands up in surrender. "All right, fine. Fuck it. I don't have time for this shit."

He throws two hundred dollar bills on the front desk, along with his license. I get him checked-in for the night, hand him his keys, and he's on his way, dragging a bulky duffel bag behind him. Of course, he makes sure he gets one last word in before hopping on the elevator:

"Fuck your faggot hotel policies!"

Then he's on the elevator, and momentarily out of my life. I wonder if tonight will be a night he falls asleep in his room or a night insomnia guides him around the lobby, looking for conversation. When he isn't talking about Brenda's most personal secrets, he's talking about shoes. It gets him hard, I think, talking about the different brands and styles. Lately, whenever he starts talking to me, I just pretend I get a phone call and walk into the back office. Then I don't return for at least an hour. Usually he's gone by then.

Twenty minutes pass. He doesn't come back down. Maybe I'm safe. Regardless, I need to refill my coffee cup. I walk around the front desk, heading toward the kitchen, but stop in the middle of the lobby at the sight of a wallet on the marble floor. On the front of the wallet, an owl has been stitched into the leather.

Because of course.

The Nightly Disease

After scanning the area and ascertaining nobody is watching me, I retrieve it and stuff it into my pocket. I wait until I've refilled my coffee and have returned to the back office before I take the wallet out of my pocket and flip it open.

John Hobbs's ugly mug stares back at me. The wallet is thicker than I expect, coming from him. Inside, there's a stack of cash. All one hundred dollar bills. I count it, heart racing, pounding against my chest, paranoid that someone's going to walk in on me.

After I finish counting, I put the money back in the wallet, then stick it in my pocket. I sit down, staring at the wall. The hotel is silent. I can't stop breathing like an asshole.

$4,500.

What the fuck is John Hobbs doing with that kind of cash?

I'm not even sure what he does for a living. He's told me before, but his words tend to drift until they dissipate. Something about shoes, maybe. Nothing to do with shoes is bringing in this kind of money.

The thought of giving the money back to him enters my mind only briefly. He's not getting any of this shit back. After all the nights he's spent annoying me, talking and talking and talking, nigger this, faggot that, yeah, fuck him, he doesn't deserve a good Samaritan.

I lock up the register, dim down the lobby lights, and head for the Other Goddamn Hotel next door. I need to tell somebody about this. Fucking $4,500. Goddamn, son.

George is sleeping at the front desk. The paperwork underneath his face is soaked in drool.

I nudge him. "Wake up."

He grunts, but doesn't wake. I slap the front desk and shout, "FIRE!"

Nothing.

I try again. "DO YOU HAVE ANY ROOMS AVAILABLE?"

He screams and sits up, eyes wide, jerking his head around for the source of the disturbance. At the sight of me standing in front of him, he sighs and says, "What the hell, Isaac? Never wake an auditor from his nap. That's hotel law."

"Fuck hotel law. You gotta check this out."

"Did you just say 'fuck hotel law'?"

"Shut up." I shove the wallet into his hands.

"Why is there an owl on your wallet?"

"It's not mine. Open it up."

He stares at the money for a long time. So long, I begin to think he's broken down. Just the sight alone of so much cash has fried his brain.

Then he asks how much it is.

"Forty-five hundred."

"Where'd you get this?"

"You know that asshole guest I'm always telling you about?"

"You're gonna have to be a bit more specific."

"The one who told me his girlfriend was molested by her father."

"Oh, yeah. That asshole."

"Anyway, that's his wallet. Dude dropped it in the lobby."

"Shit."

"Yeah."

He tosses it on the front desk, unable to take his eyes off it. "What are you gonna do?"

"I don't know. I guess I'm going to keep it."

"You thief."

"Some people deserve to be stolen from. Hobbs is one of such people."

"True."

"What do you suppose he's doing with that kind of money?"

"I don't know," George says, reaching out and caressing the torn leather of the wallet. "He's probably mixed up in drugs or something."

I lean on the front desk, considering the idea. "He does look the type."

George laughs. "And how do you know what 'the type' looks like?"

"I don't know." I shrug. "I've seen movies."

"So have I. And usually, whenever someone takes a drug dealer's money, they get shot."

"I'm not gonna get shot."

"We'll see."

"I doubt he's even a drug dealer, anyway," I say. "Maybe he's a drug *addict*, but I doubt he deals. Maybe he earned this money the legit way."

"So what, now you're gonna give it back?"

"Fuck no."

"Good." George opens the wallet again, fingering the bills. "The way I'm seeing it is, if you're stupid enough to lose this type of cash, you don't deserve to get it back. This is the price you pay for being an idiot."

"And an asshole," I add.

He nods. "And an asshole."

He runs into the back office and returns with his flask, which is the real reason I came over, anyway. Maybe that makes me a shitty friend. Maybe that isn't even true. If I had to pick anyone to be my best friend, it'd be George. Hell, he's my only friend, when I stop and think about it. Night workers don't exactly have the strongest social life. They're always working when everyone else is partying, or mini-golfing, or doing whatever it is that people do together for fun.

As we drink whiskey and recount the money, he asks me what I'm gonna do with it. I can tell he's a little jealous, and a part of me thinks I should give him a small percentage, but I don't, and I won't.

"I don't know," I say. "I guess the smart thing to do would be to save it. But then again, how much do you suppose a down payment on a brand new Mustang costs?"

George laughs. "Assuming you get approved? Plus, ya know, the monthly payments, which I doubt you could afford."

"I'll worry about the monthly payments once the creditors are at my doorstep."

George gulps down the last of the flash, which hadn't contained much to begin with, and says, "You should rent every room at the hotel for a night, and spend the entire shift guest-free."

"I think I'd be better off just quitting the hotel and living off the forty-five hundred for a couple months."

"And when it runs out?"

"Kill myself, I guess."

George nods, not smiling, but seriously considering the option. "Yeah. Yeah, that ain't half bad."

"Sometimes I have decent ideas."

George snaps his fingers, leaning forward. "Or, you know what? You could totally fuckin' buy an owl."

"Shut up."

The Nightly Disease

"No, seriously. You tellin' me a man can't buy an owl for forty-five hundred dollars? Of course he can."

"That isn't funny."

"I'm not being funny, man. You could buy one, keep it as a pet. It would be the ultimate tribute to Owl Girl, one of our own fallen heroes."

"Fuck you." I stare at the stitching on the wallet and fight the urge to faint. "Don't you find it a little weird he has that kind of wallet? After everything that's happened."

"I find a lot of things weird. It's a weird world."

I check my cell. It's nearly four-thirty. I should've already slid receipts under doors by now. Hell, I should be starting breakfast any minute.

"I gotta get going."

"All right, man. Congrats on the stealing. You're an expert thief."

"Thanks."

"Think about it, though. Hoot, hoot."

"You're an asshole."

As I walk back to my hotel, my mind is racing with possibilities. There's many ways I can spend this money. Maybe a Mustang isn't the wisest idea, but then again, maybe stealing somebody's wallet also wasn't very smart. I never claimed to anybody that I was intelligent. But fuck it. Thanks to my lack of morales, I'm now forty-five hundred dollars richer than I was a few hours ago.

Hobbs's bound to notice the wallet's missing, eventually. The question is when. Has he passed out 'til morning? Or is he awake right now, already searching for it?

My body's feeling pretty heavy from the whiskey, and I know if I go inside and sit down, I'm liable to fall asleep. But breakfast needs to be done, so I can't afford to pass out until I get home. I linger outside for a few, hoping the cold will wake me up. By the dumpster, a deer cautiously eats something in the grass. There's no sign of its herd anywhere, but that doesn't mean anything. There's never just one deer. There's probably others, in the woods behind the dumpster, watching me. Staking me out. Forming a plan to murder me. Maybe this deer is just a distraction, and there's a dozen others sneaking up behind me, preparing to feast on some juicy night auditor flesh. Are deer even carnivorous? Does it matter?

Someone in the parking lot screams, and the dumpster deer freaks out and sprints into the woods. The scream isn't short-lived, but long and impossible to ignore. I follow the sound through the parking lot, to the back of the hotel. Someone's on the cement, between two parked cars, shaking. I step closer and the screaming ceases. The body goes limp. Oh shit. I rush to the person, asking if they're okay, asking what happened. I'm taking my cell phone out and attempting to dial 9-1-1 as I kneel down to inspect the body. Then the person sits up, ski mask over his face, and presses the tip of a blade against my abdomen.

"Put the phone down, cocksucker." No, not a man. A woman.

I drop my cell. The blade digs deeper into my stomach and I've returned to reality. The blade hasn't entered my flesh yet, but it's cold against my skin, so it must have cut through my work shirt, at least.

I try to scream, but my voice is MIA.

The girl climbs to her feet, not moving the knife from my gut. "Empty your pockets."

The Nightly Disease

I don't react. I'm too cold, too scared. This can't be happening.

She slightly pushes her arm inward, and I feel something warm and wet drip down my stomach. The fucking bitch stabbed me. Shit, shit, shit.

I empty my pockets and throw the contents on the ground. Two wallets, a ring of keys belonging to the hotel, and my own car keys. She scoops up both wallets, ignoring the keys, and tells me to lie down, tells me to kiss the cement. And I do. I plant my lips against it. The parking lot is cold and wet and fucking dirty as hell but I kiss it like it's my goddamn prom date. Of course, I've never been to prom and I sure as hell have never kissed somebody, but I imagine this is all very similar.

"Count down from fifty," the girl says. "Don't look up 'til you reach zero, or I'll cut a lot worse next time."

Next time?

"Fifty, forty-nine, forty-eight . . . "

Her feet slap against the wet parking lot as she flees the scene. I stand up once I reach forty. Fuck her. Fucking thief.

I collect my phone and head inside the hotel. I'm so pissed, I can barely contain myself. I can't call the police in case they test my system for alcohol. I can't do shit. Not only did I just lose my own wallet, which contained my license and debit card, but I also just lost forty-five hundred fucking dollars that didn't even realistically belong to me. Motherfucker. My shirt is ripped, as I suspected, and slightly stained with my blood. The cut isn't very deep. It won't require stitches. I rub a washcloth over it and slap a bandage down. I wash my face, brush my teeth, and give myself a long stare in the mirror. What I see is pathetic. I'm looking at a man who should have died at birth. Fuck everything. Fuck this whole goddamn world.

In the kitchen, the cook has already arrived, and she's cursing me out in Spanish for not having the coffee or cold foods prepared. I curse her back in English, and neither of us know what the hell we're saying to each other, but we get the gist of it.

Nearly an hour later, I'm scrambling back at the front desk, printing out my auditing reports, which should have been printed out before four, and it's already six. Fortunately there's only thirteen scheduled check-outs this morning, so I get the receipts slid under the designated doors in less than ten minutes.

I breeze through the audit pack, not really paying attention to the numbers, but reading enough to catch anything out of the ordinary. I've been doing this job long enough, I don't need to read every line, every statistic. I know where to look and I know when a mistake has been made. A half hour later, I have all my paperwork documented and filed away. I pick up the hotel phone and call the Other Goddamn Hotel. George answers on the seventh ring.

"Thank you for—"

"We gotta talk."

"Uh, right now?" he asks, hesitation in his voice, then he whispers, "My fucking boss came in early."

"After work. Meet me at IHOP?"

"Yeah, all right."

I hang up without saying anything else. A guest at the front desk waits for me to finish my phone call, tapping his fingers against the marble tabletop, rolling his eyes and whistling. I want to murder him before he even speaks.

"You're out of paper towels in the men's restrooms."

"Okay."

He holds up his hands, flinging water at me. "How am I supposed to dry my hands?"

"Use your pants."

His jaw drops and I turn away, not giving a shit about his reaction. I close my shift just as my relief strolls into the lobby. I'm outside before she finishes telling me good morning.

In my car, I'm punching the steering wheel and shouting every profanity in my vocabulary, fantasizing revenge plots and knowing I'm too chickenshit to actually do anything about it.

Fuck.

Part Two

The Art of
Throwing Up

#200

George walks into IHOP around a quarter 'til eight. The restaurant's only down the street, and we both get out at seven, so I've been sitting here a good half hour at this point. I've already gone through a pot of coffee. I'm too stressed to eat. I'm only chugging coffee because I don't know how to do anything else.

I wave him over from across the restaurant and he sits down in my booth, on the opposite side of the table.

"You look like shit," he says. "More so than usual."

"I was mugged."

"*What?*" His knee bangs against the bottom of the table and a drop of coffee splashes out of my cup.

"I. Was. Mugged."

He tries to respond, but the server's approached us, asking if we're finally ready to order.

"Just keep bringing coffee," I tell her, and George orders pancakes.

Once she leaves, George says, almost amusingly, "How the hell were you mugged?"

"In the parking lot. Someone pulled a knife on me."

"Are you all right?"

"I was stabbed, but only slightly."

"Only slightly?"

"It's just a flesh wound."

"Calm down there, Monty Python."

The server returns, refills my coffee and sets a new cup in front of George, fills that one up. She tells him his pancakes are on the way. We barely even acknowledge she exists.

I throw some cream and sugar into my coffee and stir, watching the waves go crazy. For a moment, I swear the cream takes the shape of an owl, then vanishes.

George clears his throat. "So, this guy *slightly* stabs you—"

I shake my head, grimacing at the taste of coffee overkill in my mouth. "The mugger was a woman, not a guy."

George pauses, waiting for the rest of a joke that was never born in the first place. "Seriously?"

"Yeah."

"Wow."

"Fuck you."

He sniggers, sipping his coffee. "Hey, man, I'm with you, that ain't funny at all."

"Fuck you. You weren't there. She had a knife."

"So she stabbed you—*slightly* stabbed you—and . . . what, robbed you, I guess? Took your wallet?"

I don't respond, just stare at him, and he stares back, trying to solve the puzzle. The server comes to the table with a plate of pancakes, and as she sets it down, George suddenly shouts, "Oh shit, the wallet!"

The Nightly Disease

The server screams, jumps back, dropping George's pancakes to the floor.

After George apologizes a thousand times and helps the server clean up the mess, he collapses back into the booth. "That asshole's wallet? She took it?"

I nod. My body's shaking from too much coffee. It's a tick I've grown accustomed to since starting at the hotel.

"Ha-ha-ha, oh my god, I can't believe it."

"Yeah."

"Forty-five fuckin' hundred dollars, man."

"I know."

"Jesus Christ."

"I think I'm going to kill myself."

"What did the police say?"

"I didn't call them."

"What? Why not?"

"Well, I'd just finished drinking with you. What if they could tell?"

"So what?"

"I'd get fired, for one thing."

"There's no law that says you can't drink on the job. It's just frowned upon."

I don't know enough about the law to challenge him on this point, so I move on. "Anyway, what does it matter? I didn't really have shit in my own wallet besides my license and a debit card to an empty bank account. It'll be a pain in the ass to get a new license, but whatever, I can handle that. But Hobbs's wallet? Shit. I can't talk about that to the police. I wouldn't just get fired, dude. They'd fucking arrest me."

George sighs, drinking his coffee. His face tells me it's finally sinking in what I came to terms with hours ago. There's not a damn thing I can do about any of this. I robbed somebody, and now somebody robbed me. The circle of life. "Well," he says, "this sucks."

And I nod, because that's all that's left to say about it.

This sucks.

#201

It dawns on me too late that no wallet means no debit card, which means no way to pay for my coffee. George spots me, and I tell him next time I'll pay. He laughs and tells me that's what I always say.

When I get home, it's a little past ten, and all I want to do is pass out. Stress has eaten me to nothing. But I can't yet, because I have to call my bank and cancel my debit card before my thief spends what little money I do have in my account. I give some thought to busting my iPad out from my bag and watching some porn, but fall asleep before I can seriously consider the idea.

The alarm clock on my bookshelf tells me it's 2:34 P.M. when my eyes open again. I'm still sitting down, my neck sore from leaning back against the headrest of the futon. My work clothes stick to my body, glued by sweat. I undress and peel off the bandage on my stomach. The cut is barely visible, save for the dried blood smeared around it. I hop in the shower and throw on a flannel and some jeans. The coffee pot brewing in the kitchen sounds like heaven. It's the only noise that can calm me down, that can numb thoughts of suicide and self-loathing. I pour a cup into an unwashed glass and lace it with sugar and cream. Most of the characters in books I read tend to drink their coffee black. It's supposed to signify someone is a badass. I tried it black once. It tasted fucking awful. I climb on top of the bar stool in my minuscule kitchen and eat on my shitty excuse of a dining table. It's really just half a brick of white concrete built into the side of the wall. But from here I have a decent view of my sliding back door, which I suppose doesn't come with every studio apartment in the world, so maybe I'm not as poor as I'm convinced I am. Of course, outside my backdoor, the only visible landscape is the wooden fence built around my tiny porch. It's a good fence, though. I'm proud of this fence. I may not have a license or forty-five hundred dollars or a job that's worth a damn, but at least I have a fence, so maybe life isn't too bad, after all.

A rectangular flat object falls from the sky and lands in my backyard, in the small patch of grass between my porch and fence. I set my coffee down and step outside. The porch is cold and wet against the soles of my feet. In the grass, amidst the dead insects and discarded cigarette butts, is a welcome mat. I straighten it out and read on the front: "FUCK OFF AND DIE". Probably the most welcoming welcome mat I've ever seen. It'd fallen from the balcony above my apartment.

I roll it up and go through my apartment and out the front door. An elderly woman stands across the patio, in front of her own apartment, arm raised and key inserted into the lock. She stares at me, body frozen except her face, which smiles and says, "Good morning."

"Good morning." I jog up the cagey steps to the second landing, hoping she doesn't try to continue the conversation.

The door is slightly ajar, so I knock lightly on the frame and shout, "Hello?" through the revealed crack. Thirty seconds pass and nobody answers, so I do it again. Another thirty seconds, still nothing. Fuck it. I drop the welcome mat in front of the door and go back downstairs. The woman is still standing across the patio from my apartment, holding the key in the lock.

She tells me good morning.

#202

Hobbs stands in front of the hotel smoking a cigarette when I pull up at five past eleven. He's not as loose and out-of-it as usual, but standing straight, skin actually a normal complexion. There's a look in his eyes like he has a purpose for once.

Those eyes arc directed straight at me as I hesitantly get out of my car, lock it, and head toward the entrance.

Looking at me like he knows what I did, but that's bullshit. There's no way in hell he knows.

"Good evening, Mr. Hobbs." I step around him, holding my breath.

As I enter the lobby, he calls out, "You got my money?"

But he doesn't follow me inside, so I pretend like I didn't hear him, I pretend like a trickle of piss didn't just spurt from my dick. If not for the color of my work pants being black, the color of my crotch would be a prime target for ridicule.

Yas waits behind the front desk, making a whole

show of checking her wristwatch as I come around. Who even wears wristwatches anymore?

"Sorry I'm a little late."

"Tell it to Javier." She walks out without another word and tosses the register keys behind her. They smack against the wall and drop to the floor.

I shout and tell her to drive safe, leaning over the front desk and watching her walk out, except I'm more worried about Hobbs standing by the trash can. What happens once he finishes his cigarette? I scan the front desk for anything that could potentially be used as a weapon. Maybe a stapler.

This is why the hotel needs a shotgun. This is the exact fucking reason.

The front doors slide open and I've run out of time. I grab the stapler without thinking, flicking the top open with my thumb.

"So did anyone find it or what?" Hobbs says.

"Find what?" I grab the stapler tighter, concealing it behind the front desk. One false move and I won't hesitate to take out one of his eyes or, at the very least, slightly graze his cheek.

"My wallet, man. I fucking lost it last tonight. Javier told me he'd have y'all looking for it."

"Oh." The piss in my trousers recede back into my dick. "I just walked in, haven't heard anything about it. Let me check."

I walk around the front desk, picking up random papers and acting like they hold some kind of importance. I pause and think. "Let me go check the lost and found."

I run to the back office, through the laundry room, and open up the head of housekeeping's office. The room is dark and cold and pleasant so I sit on her desk

Max Booth III

for a moment, waiting the appropriate amount of time someone would take to check for a lost wallet.

When I return to the lobby, Hobbs is half over the front desk, snooping through random documents.

"Hey, man, cut that out."

He jumps up, at first startled, then angry. "Did you find my fucking wallet?"

"Nah. I'll keep an eye out for it, though."

He rubs his eyes, grinding his teeth. "I need that wallet back."

"I'm sorry."

He punches the front desk and winces. "You don't even fucking understand, man. You don't know how much money was in it."

"I think I have some idea," I say, and immediately scream in my head. *Why did I just say that?*

Hobbs eyes me strangely. "You do, huh?"

I pause, clear my throat. "I imagine quite a bit, is all I'm saying. Since you're so worked up about it."

"Uh-huh."

"If I find it, I'll let you know."

Hobbs steps forward, sober for the first time since he's started staying at the hotel. "And if you don't find it, I won't be the only one who ends up with a switchblade up his asshole."

#203

He knows. No he doesn't. He does. He can't. He's onto me. Fuck him. Prove it. He doesn't need to. Courts don't issue switchblades up assholes. Dangerous criminals do. Psychopaths do.

There's only two ways he could find out I took the wallet. One, I crack and admit to it, which ain't gonna happen. Two, he bumps into the bitch who mugged me, which seems unlikely, unless Hobbs is in cahoots with the mugger and he's just screwing with me.

Otherwise, he doesn't know shit, and he isn't *going* to know shit. I'm not talking. Nobody else knows. Nobody except . . . shit.

I call the Other Goddamn Hotel. George answers on the eighth ring.

"Thanks for calling the—"

"Did you tell anybody?"

"Uh . . . ?"

"Did you tell anybody about the wallet?"

"No, man, you know I wouldn't. What the hell?"

"Hobbs is on my ass about it."

"Who"

"Hobbs. The—the fuckin' guy whose wallet I took."

"Oh. Oh shit."

"I think he may just be fishing for a confession. He might not know anything."

"Should we kill him?"

"Not yet. But keep the lye out and ready."

The elevator beeps, but not to signal somebody is coming down. It's the sound indicating someone's already down in the lobby, and they're about to board the elevator and go up to their room.

Who the fuck is in the lobby?

Shit shit shit.

By the time I climb over the front desk and get a look at the elevator station, the person is already inside and the doors are closed.

I want to laugh but I can't remember how.

The rest of the night is spent pacing from one wall of the back office to the other. I haven't even touched my book. Who the fuck can read in a time like this? The words would melt off the page and burn into my flesh like acid.

I'm too scared to nap, too freaked out to masturbate on the roof. My night is ruined. I walk outside and stare at the owl logo for TripAdvisor stuck to the front door and an hour passes. I print out guest receipts and slide them underneath doors. When I reach Hobbs's room, I stand outside it for a moment, afraid to disturb the frame. In the end, I can't do it and just toss the receipt in the trash can behind the second floor elevator.

I'm moving on hyperspeed as I prepare breakfast. It's not even 4:30 by the time I finish, a half hour before the cook is scheduled to show. I sit down in the dining section, alone, trying to calm down in the darkness. My heart's going to break out of my chest and a part of me can't figure out why that would be such a bad thing.-

I pour a cup of shitty coffee and sip it as I wait for the cook to show up. At ten 'til five, the phone rings. Not an outside call, either, but from a guest's room.

I don't register the importance of room 209 until Hobbs speaks.

"Hey, there, partner, I'm gonna need some new towels up to my room, pronto."

"Uh."

"Hello? Some towels? You think you can do that?"

"Yeah. Sure." I clear my throat, swallow dead lip skin I've managed to suck into my mouth. "I'll have them waiting for you at the front desk."

"Nah, I don't think so. I'm not getting dressed again. Just bring them up, all right?"

"Well—"

"Thanks, buddy. See you soon."

He hangs up and I sit in the dining area a few more minutes, sipping my coffee. It's awful, but it beats the alternative. It beats a switchblade up my asshole.

The phone rings again.

"How's those pillows coming along?"

"I thought you wanted towels."

"Yeah. You coming or what?"

I hang up. Fuck this. Fuck him. This doesn't feel right at all. I stare at the phone, expecting it to ring again. If it does, I don't intend on answering. Instead I call Javier and ask him if he can come in early so I can go home, I tell him I'm feeling like shit, some stomach bug, I've been vomiting all night.

"Actually, I'm just across the street at the Walmart. Since we need bananas and bread."

I quickly put together my audit pack and close my shift. I pack my bag and stand outside and wait for him to arrive. A line of guests wanting to check-out builds in the lobby but I don't care. They're not my problem. Eventually they'll lose their patience and leave their keys on the front desk. One might lack the intelligence to follow along and instead stand in the lobby until starvation takes him down. At least, that's the dream.

Once I make it home, I actually do puke. My stomach's all in knots. A mixture of stress, fear, and paranoia. I text Javier and ask him if he can get Mandy to cover me tonight, see if she's willing to work three nights in a row, since tonight's my last night of the week, anyway. When I first send the text, I wonder who he'll think I'm talking about: Mandy 1 or Mandy 2. Maybe it wouldn't be such a bad idea, propping up a corpse at the front desk to cover a shift now and again. She wouldn't be any less effective as I am most days. Javier's first response is a negative, so I send him a JPG of a man inserting an eel into his anus. Ten minutes later he calls me and tells me to take the night off and he'll see me Monday morning, after my return on Sunday night. I manage a weak "thanks" and collapse on my bed, shaking.

Hobbs fucking knows. He *knows*.

But maybe he doesn't.

Of course he does.

He heard my phone call. I *admitted* to it.

Oh, Isaac. You stupid garbage person.

#204

Three days to kill. Three days of worrying about Hobbs and what he's going to do with me. I call and cancel my debit card and request a new one in the mail. I masturbate a lot. I do not shower. I eat. I replay the brief conversation I shared with the bulimic girl the other night and realize I probably should have been more sensitive about the bulimia. Now I may never get a never chance to speak with her. What business was it of mine, anyway? What do I care if she throws up her food? That's her choice. People do tons of disgusting shit to their bodies. They insert golfball-sized plugs into their earlobes. They tattoo their genitalia and anuses. They subject their eyeballs to Tyler Perry movies. They stick their dicks into practically anything that they can fit them in. I once read an article about a guy who had gotten arrested for fucking one of those umbrella stand holes found on top of park benches. Apparently it's not that uncommon. So what the hell. Who cares if someone wants to puke up their breakfast? It doesn't make a person less beautiful. It just makes them more human. I think about the amount of time I masturbate in a given week. What's more shameful?

I frequent bulimia support forums I'd previously bookmarked to distract myself from thinking about Hobbs. No one's talking about "the hotel asshole" yet, and the more I think about it, the more I doubt she has access to the Internet. If she can't afford food or a second set of clothing, then she probably doesn't own a laptop. A cell phone, maybe. Even homeless people have cell phones. If she frequents these kinds of boards, I'm clearly not intelligent enough to crack the case.

The forum is still interesting, despite the lack of people complaining about me. A whole community of those suffering from bulimia, bonded together. The way they talk about the illness, none of them seem too proud of their actions. Like most "mental disorders"— their words—purging is out of their control. Sometimes posters start threads to document their progress as they attempt to get better. A cynical part of me suspects these threads serve as entertainment to the other posters, the ones encouraging the thread-starter's progress. Maybe they take bets on the side, predicting how long it'll take before he or she purges again. Like some kind of twisted countdown. Three, two, one—puke.

Other threads attempt to romanticize bulimia. They share war stories about past purges. People who've burst blood vessels in their eyeballs or have gotten toothbrushes stuck in their throats. Women who have accidentally dunked their breasts in the toilet bowl or have forgotten to tie their hair back before kneeling down.

Many complain of constipation. Constant

vomiting blocks you up. Your body grows dependent on rejecting food and forgets how to properly digest, so all the food just sits in your stomach looking at you stupidly, wondering, "Well, what the fuck do you expect to do now?" Laxatives are on every bulimic's budget. Maybe I should buy some for the girl who comes to my hotel. Some kind of peace offering. She walks into the hotel and I hand her over a small gift-wrapped box containing laxatives. She'd probably do much worse than punch me in the face this time.

If she *does* decide to show back up, I just won't mention the bulimia. It's none of my business. I don't even know this person. I'm only incredibly in love with her for some stupid goddamn reason.

The next day I sit on my porch and read about owls on my iPad. I had to take a rest from the bulimia forums. Too many unexpected photos kept popping up and seriously got me debating a conversion. I know this owl obsession is unhealthy, but I can't just forget about it. A girl was killed by one of these fucking things. That isn't in my head. Her death is as real as the thin line of blood streaming down my nostril. The more I read about them, the more innocent they appear. I'm not inputting the correct key words. These results are too safe. Something's hidden here, something buried beyond the bullshit facade of Google's page one.

I continue digging. If this were an actual shovel, my hands would be raw and blistered. Owls aren't exactly known for killing human beings. Sometimes they'll attack joggers, but never anything too serious. They're more likely to pick up a small dog in someone's backyard and chow down. But no people have been killed. Except for Mandy 2. Why her? What the fuck happened that night?

Birds typically get aggressive when they feel their young is in danger. It's possible Mandy 2 got her hands on a baby owl, tried to pet it, maybe dressed it up in tiny owl clothing, and the mother owl got offended. Took one look at her precious baby and went berserk. Broke Owl Code and murdered a human. Now all the owls in the world are freaking out because the truce is gone, human blood has been spilled. First an owl eats a woman's face, then a night auditor gets mugged. How many more seals need to be broken until the apocalypse gets in full swing?

I search "owls eating humans" online and come across a series of graphic anime illustrations depicting young boys receiving oral sex from anthropomorphic owls. I close out of the browse, but not quick enough for the NSA to now surely be on my trail. To throw them off track, I enter in one of my favorite porn URLs and click on a video that doesn't seem as disturbing as owl-on-human sex—which can sometimes prove to be quite the challenge. I go back inside the apartment before cranking up the volume.

If Hobbs doesn't get me, at least the government will have a chance.

#205

Sometimes my mother calls and asks how I'm spending my time in Texas and I just don't know what to say. You can't tell your mother you spend the majority of your days and nights either eating, sleeping, or masturbating. I could have done all that back home. You can't tell her you work at a job you hate with guests you wish were dead. You can't say you fantasize about murder more than Ed Gein. You can't tell her some redneck's planning to murder you because you stole his wallet, which you then lost after being mugged by some chick in a ski mask.

So what can you do? Me, I clear my throat and tell her I'm furthering my education, which is a bigger lie than the existence of a happy night auditor. I couldn't afford community college with my current wages, plus student aid denied my application thanks to my father earning too high of an income. But I don't want his help. Asking him for help proves I can't make it on my own. I don't want to need my parents. I don't want to be like my older brothers and still live at home in my thirties. I don't want to be useless. I'd tried explaining this to the student aid counselor who rejected my application. Like she gave a shit.

"I don't even live in the same state as my father. Why does he still have to be a factor in all of this?"

"You're only twenty-one," the lady said over the phone.

"So fucking what?"

"Please don't take that language with me. I am trying to help you."

"Is that what you call this?"

"If you want us to void out your parents' financial information, you have to provide a valid reason."

"I'm a legal adult and I live alone. What more of a valid reason do you people want?"

"What do you mean, 'you people'?"

"What?"

"I will not tolerate racism, sir."

"We're on the phone. I have no idea what color you are."

"Uh-huh."

"Well? What reason do you want?"

"Maybe if your parents abused you as a child or abandoned you, then we could reconsider."

"Wait. Are you seriously telling me the only way I'll receive any student aid is if my dad used to hit me?"

"It would certainly help, yes."

"Okay, fine, he used to beat the shit out of me. Guy broke my nose about twenty times over the years. Real cold-hearted bastard, that one."

"Sir, is that true?"

" . . . No."

So, yeah, I lie to my mother when she calls. But it's only to hide the truth that my aspirations for a college degree are credited to her and my father's lack of childhood abuse. She wouldn't be able to handle that kind of guilt.

On my second day off, my mother calls to tell me my older brother is having trouble with his wife and has moved back in with my parents for the indefinite future. This is not news. My brother moves back home every few months. It is a part of his cycle.

"You should make him live on the street," I tell her, lying in bed. The ceiling spins and distorts my vision.

"You don't have to be so nasty," she says, although I know a secret part of her agrees.

"Well, Mom, he doesn't have to be so pathetic and helpless, now does he?"

"Isaac, that's enough."

I stand up and walk into the kitchen, yawning. "I'm sorry. You just caught me when I was asleep."

"Are you still working at . . . that hotel?"

"Mom, you know I am."

"Such a shame. No boy as young as you should be spending his nights working. You need to get out and have fun. You shouldn't have to be worrying about bills right now."

I start brewing coffee as she lectures me. Her words quickly grind deep into my nerves and I lose my patience and pop open a beer instead. Halfway through the bottle, she abandons the concept of me randomly hopping on a plane to Indiana and asks what's new in my life. I make up some bullshit about a tough college test coming up that's stressing me out.

"What is the test about?"

"Owls."

"Owls?"

"Yeah."

"What kind of class is *that*?"

"Uh. Ornithology, I guess."

"Ornith-*what*?"

I finish off the beer. "Ornithology."

"What on Earth is that?"

"You know. The study of birds. Owls and all that."

"What made you want to take a class about birds?" She almost sounds disgusted.

"I don't know, Mom. What's wrong with birds? Jesus Christ."

"Nothing's wrong with birds. You just didn't tell me."

"Well, I am now, okay?"

"To be honest, I'm surprised you would be interested in owls *at all*. After what happened when you were a kid."

The coffee pot finishes brewing and begins beeping at me. The sound matches my sudden rapid heartbeat. "What are you talking about, Mom? What happened to me when I was a kid?"

She laughs. "Don't act like you don't know."

"I'm not acting."

"What, you're going to tell me that you don't remember what happened at that field trip you took in kindergarten?"

"That's what I'm telling you, yeah."

"I find that hard to believe."

"Humor me."

She pauses before answering, maybe regretting she'd even mentioned anything in the first place. "It's not even that big of a deal."

"Mom."

"You really don't remember going on a field trip

to the Lincoln Park Zoo? All you wanted to do was see the owls. You talked about those things for weeks before the trip."

"I don't remember *ever* talking about owls."

"Yeah, they were like your favorite things in the world for a while there. You had the owl lunchbox, the owl backpack . . . "

"What happened at the zoo, Mom?"

"You were attacked."

"I was *what*?"

"Attacked."

"By . . . by *owls*?"

"It was a very upsetting day for you."

"How was I attacked? This doesn't make any sense."

"I don't know exactly. It's not like I was there. But from what your teachers and the paramedics told me, you had wandered away from your chaperone and somehow managed to sneak into the owl habitat. No one noticed until you were screaming for help. The zoo workers found you covered with them."

"Are you fucking serious?"

"Isaac!"

"I'm sorry, Mom, but seriously, what the fucking fuck?"

"Isaac, watch your fucking language!"

"Why don't I remember this? Why don't I have any scars?" Sometime during the last five minutes I had drank a second beer. I open a third one without putting too much thought into it. The coffee can wait.

"You weren't really injured. I mean, they scratched you a little bit, but nothing too serious. They mostly just . . . I don't know, I guess perched on you."

"*Perched* on me?"

" . . . Yeah."

"But *why*?"

"Maybe they liked you. I don't know. But it really disturbed you. You had to take therapy for a while there."

"I was in therapy?" I finish off the third beer and reach inside the fridge for another, but there's none left.

"Only for two months or so. How can you not remember any of this?"

"I'm not sure I believe you. Are you positive this didn't happen to James?"

"No, Isaac, I know what happened to my own sons."

"Then *why* don't I remember any of this?"

"I don't know. I guess the therapy worked. The guy told us it was best not to talk about it—to make it feel like a dream you had, that none of it was real."

I walk into the bathroom, no longer listening to my mother. My nose throbs from where the bulimic girl punched me the other day. When I look into the mirror, I anticipate a swollen, black and blue nose. But it's not even my own nose in the mirror. It's been replaced by a small, pointy beak. And my face has flattened to an impossible smoothness, like a cartoon character who's been flattened by a steamroller.

An owl. I am an owl.

Hoot hoot hoot. Hoot hoot.

"Isaac, are you still there?"

The mirror ripples like it's water and, when it finally stills, my face has returned to normalcy. But I don't trust it. This mirror is a liar.

"Isaac? Hello?"

"I gotta go, Mom."

#206

Time doesn't always travel at a consistent speed. Our mentalities control the accelerators. The same way a pot of water only boils if you aren't looking at it. If there's something important and exciting coming up in the future, something you're actually looking forward to, then the time is just going to drag and drag. You look at the clock, go do something, and five hours later you look at the clock again and it turns out only three minutes have passed. But, say, something's coming up that you are absolutely dreading, something like a pissed-off hotel guest waiting to shove a switchblade up your asshole, well, then that time is going to pass like gravity swallowed up by a black hole.

And that's exactly what happened to my three-day weekend. Swallowed by a black hole. Erased by the shadow people.

I pull up to work at ten 'til and just sit in my car until 11:00 hits. I've done a mildly convincing job of telling myself everything is in the clear, that last week I had allowed paranoia to overcome logic. Hobbs had just been pissed that he'd lost his wallet. He didn't know I'd been the one to take it, and even if he *does* know, there's not shit he can do about it. The asshole switchblade threat had been all talk. A bunch of macho man bullshit used as audible lube to stroke his dick. I've been interacting with Hobbs for over a year now and he's never come across as anything less than a miserable drunken coward who likes to run his mouth. I'm not a good fighter or anything, I'm out of shape and I easily bruise, but I like to think I could put that fucker in his place if it comes down to it. I'm pretty sure he's some kind of shoe salesman. I'd throw down with a shoe salesman.

I'm not above kicking someone in the balls.

Before going inside, I stop by the trashcans and glance at the TripAdvisor owl logo on the front door.

"This is all your fault."

Hobbs is still at the hotel. It's the first thing I check when I make it behind the front desk. I ask Yas if he's been hanging out in the lobby or the dining area tonight, but she hasn't seen him all evening. I still can't decide if that's a good sign or a terrifying one. That guy's always down here, talking about what the queers are doing to the soil.

Maybe he's just gotten drunk enough to pass out. Or maybe Brenda's with him. The last few times he's stayed here, she's been mysteriously absent. Which is odd, since the reservation is always in her name, considering she's the associate and thus is the only one allowed the cheap rate. I still don't understand why we allow him to check-in without her presence.

The phone rings and my heart nearly stops cold.

Not Hobbs. Just George.

"Where the hell have you been, man? I've been

trying to call you all weekend. What happened to you on Thursday? What the fuck?"

"Good evening to you, too."

"Well?"

"I called in sick on Thursday. Couldn't handle it anymore. All the shit had gotten to me."

"You all right now?"

"What do you think?"

"Is that drunk asshole still at the hotel?"

"Yeah, plus . . . there's something else."

"What?"

I hesitate before speaking, feeling a migraine returning. "When I called you on Wednesday, I think maybe he heard me talking to you."

He responds with laughter.

"Oh, fuck you."

"You're screwed."

"Asshole."

I replace the phone into the receiver just as a tall man in a straw cowboy hat strolls into the lobby. The spurs of his boots clang against the floor. Typical Texas asshole.

He nods at me and tips his hat, says, "Howdy," and sits down on the lobby sofa. He pulls out a cell phone and begins fucking around with it, not caring whether I say anything back to him or not. I've quickly grown to loathe cell phones. They're too addicting. Every five minutes I reach into my pocket to take it out and play with it. They've replaced the heartbeat with biggest necessity. The thing that kills me the most is when guests come to check-in to their rooms and they can't even stop texting to look me in the eyes as they throw their information on the front desk. I'm not even human to these fucking pissants. I'm toxic garbage. I'm just another machine designed to jerk them off at their earliest convenience. I'm the self-checkout robot guzzling their cum as they aimlessly play *Farmville* or *Trivia Crack* or whatever other dumbass game is currently consuming the hive mind.

The cowboy doesn't seem familiar, which means he's probably going to want a room. That or he's waiting on a guest to come down. Or maybe he's staking the joint out long enough to determine there's nobody here but me, then he'll signal the rest of his cowboy gang in to murder me and clear out the cash register. Well, I got bad news for them: I'm already dead and there isn't even three hundred dollars waiting for them here.

I pick up random documents and pretend they hold some kind of significance, and maybe they do, I honestly don't know, I've never bothered to actually learn the duties of the audit shift. It's an easy enough job to fake—at least, until something goes horribly wrong.

When I look back up from the documents, the cowboy's standing in front of me, smiling his clean shaven face at me.

I jump back a little and he laughs. "Didn't mean to scare you there, buddy."

"It's all right. I'm easily startled. How can I help you?"

"My brother's staying here. I was hoping you could tell me what room he's in. I want to surprise him."

I force a frown. It's harder than it seems. Painful, almost. "Sorry, I wouldn't be able to tell you any guests' rooms. It's hotel policy."

"Even if he stays here all the time?" All this time,

he's still looking at his fucking cell phone, jacking off the touchscreen with his thumb.

"Um, well . . . who's your brother?"

"John Hobbs."

I choke for a moment but he doesn't seem to notice.

"Hobbs, you say?" A part of me's convinced I'm hallucinating. Hearing stupid crazy shit. Like I always seem to do on this fucking shift. But another part of me knows this is for real. Of course it is.

The cowboy nods. "Uh-huh. Stupid sumbitch's got somethin' that don't belong to him. I reckon I come to take it back."

"I'm sorry, but I can't tell you what room he's in. I can give him a call, though, tell him you're down here."

The cowboy ignores me, keeps messing around on his cell phone. "The damnedest thing, about the object that belongs to me. When I asked him about it the other day, he claims it was stolen. Says there's this fat little asshole who works overnight at the hotel he stays at, says he's the one who took my little somethin'."

The cowboy looks up, possessing the kind of smile villains in horror movies wear. "You wouldn't happen to know anything about that, would you?"

There is nothing left to say. Even if I wanted to talk, there's not enough oxygen traveling through my lungs to produce anything coherent. I turn around and bolt into the back office. The cowboy shouts for me to stop and scrambles over the front desk, but I'm already out of the back office and running through the laundry room.

Something heavy smacks against the back of my

head and for a brief moment the universe is a derailing rollercoaster, then my vision clears and I'm on my back, staring up at the cowboy and John Hobbs, who's holding an aluminum baseball bat.

Fucker must have snuck in from the back exit of the elevator, the same way all the housekeepers get into the laundry room with their cleaning carts.

He was waiting for me.

I desperately cling for any chance of escape, but they have me trapped. There's two of them and one of me. Hell, even one-on-one I'd still be fucked. I'm overweight and afraid of getting punched in the face. Not exactly the best qualities in a fighter. Nor a lover, for the matter. But I don't think these lunatics see me as a potential sex-partner.

At least, I hope not.

The cowboy no longer has his cell phone out. Instead all his attention's focused on me. Him and John both sneer like I'm an injured pig they've cornered that they're fixin' to take turns fucking.

"So my little brother here says you may have claimed his wallet for yourself," the cowboy says.

"What? No. No I don't."

Hobbs nods his head. "Uh-huh, uh-huh, the fuck you didn't. I heard you on the goddamn phone, ya stupid faggot. *I heard you.*"

"*No*, please, there's been some kinda misunderstanding." I hold up my hands to block the baseball bat from smashing into my stomach. Every finger at once jams as it connects.

I scream but I don't think it does any good. This laundry room is damn near soundproof. The guests across the hall and in the floor above us are undoubtedly still sleeping peacefully.

The Nightly Disease

"How you gonna continue bullshitting me, huh?" Hobbs says. "After I done heard you on the phone, talkin' to whoever the fuck."

Is there a way I can talk my way out of this? If there is, it's not the clearest solution. Nah, I'm screwed. He swings the bat again and I manage to turn in time to block the impact with my shoulder. It doesn't change the fact that it still hurts like hell.

"Please stop hitting me." At this point I'm practically sobbing.

The cowboy holds up his hand, calls Hobbs off. "Let's hear what the fat boy's got to say."

Maybe I can lie, make up some story about seeing someone else take the wallet. Except no, that won't work. He heard me talking to George. I fucking knew it. What did I even say on the phone that night? Did I spill it all, or just imply I knew more than what I'd been letting on? Fuck. Think, think. Why can't human beings be equipped with a rewind option?

Hobbs swings the bat into my stomach again and all the contents inside move around a bit.

"WHERE'S MY FUCKING WALLET?"

"I don't have it!"

"Bullshit." He hits me again and this time urine or blood or maybe both spurt out of my dick and wet my pants.

"I'm telling you the truth. I don't have your wallet."

He raises the bat and licks his lips. "Where. Is. The. Wallet?"

"I'd tell my brother what he wants to know," the cowboy says. "There ain't no controlling him when he's riding crank."

"Okay, okay, okay." I sit up and lean my back

against the wall, holding my throbbing hands up as a feeble method of protection. "I found your wallet, all right? You'd dropped it in the lobby last week when you checked-in."

"Well, where the fuck is it?" Hobbs says.

"I . . . uh . . . I don't know."

"What you mean—you don't know?" He raises the bat higher, ready to strike.

"Somebody stole it!"

Hobbs laughs. "No shit, we've already done come to that conclusion."

"I mean, somebody stole it from *me*."

Hobbs lowers the bat, eyebrow cocked, finally at a lost for words. The cowboy just laughs. "Who?"

"Somebody out in the parking lot, last week." Fuck it, might as well tell them the truth. Ain't no lies that would fare better. "They had a ski mask on and robbed me at knife-point. Took my wallet *and* your wallet. Even got my cell phone all wet and dirty."

"Fuck your cell phone," Hobbs says. "I'm'a get your face all wet and dirty."

"You're going to make-out with me . . . ?"

Hobbs raises the bat and the cowboy stops him, shaking his head and rubbing his temple. For a moment, the only sound in the laundry room is my own frantic heartbeat.

"Surely you counted how much money was in that wallet," the cowboy says.

"I may have looked."

"And I'm gonna hazard a guess that you don't have that kind of cash just laying around."

I shake my head.

"How fast is it gonna take you to come up with five thousand, plus interest—for, you know, all the shit you've put us through by not returning the wallet when you first found it?"

"Uh . . ."

"'Uh' ain't no answer." Hobbs swings the bat again. Something in my knee cracks and I'm too busy crying to pray that it's not broken.

"Well?" the cowboy says, seemingly unaffected by his brother's lunacy.

"How—how much is interest?"

"Let's call it double from what you stole from me."

"Double?"

He nods.

"Ten thousand dollars?" I gasp, still crying, clutching my knees.

"This ain't a fuckin' math class, bitch," Hobbs says.

"How long?" the cowboy says.

I barely make fourteen hundred a month. By the time I've paid rent and other various bills, I'm stealing hotel bagels to prevent starvation. Ten thousand is going to be impossible, but I can't tell him that, because he'll probably just kill me, or tell his asshole brother to do it with his little baseball bat.

"I don't know. A few weeks?"

The cowboy laughs. "How you reckon you're gonna pull that one off? Hotels pay more than I thought? Shit, maybe I'm in the wrong business."

"I'll figure it out. I promise. Please."

"Look, I'll make this simple." The cowboy pushes Hobbs's bat away. "You stole from me. If someone else in my field did this, I would not hesitate to end their life. But you're basically just a fucking pedestrian who didn't know any better. I can understand that. I truly can. I would have probably done the same thing if our positions were reversed. Problem is, though, I wouldn't have been stupid enough to talk about it on the phone in front of the person you robbed. So now we're in this situation, and I can't just let it go unanswered for. So if you repay me, plus the interest I mentioned, two weeks from now, then we ain't gonna have no problems. You don't pay me back? Well, I think you can probably figure out what happens, right?"

"Switchblade up my asshole?" I ask.

The cowboy steps back. "Um . . . "

Hobbs laughs. "I may have fucked with him earlier."

"Actually, that ain't the worst of ideas."

#207

Maybe I lose consciousness. Or maybe Hobbs and his brother just dissolve from existence, like dead movie characters fading out of picture during the narrative epilogue. Either way, one moment they're standing above me, then they're not. I blink hard and fast to make sure my vision isn't fucked up, then crawl through the laundry room, into the employee restroom. I climb up toward the toilet and vomit a good chunk of blood into the bowl. My stomach spasms and I give some thought to dunking my head into the bloody puke water and forcing it to stay until all the pain disappears. The smell convinces me to abandon the idea.

I wash my face and head back toward the front desk, but stop in the laundry room at the sight of a navy blue t-shirt tacked to the wall next to the washing machines.

The T-shirt says: "i'm really excited to be here"

Suddenly I can't stop laughing.

I kneel down in front of it and worship its majesty. I demand answers. Solutions to the mess I'm in. I consider abandoning the hotel and fleeing back home to Indiana. I could live with my parents and share a room with my thirtysomething-year-old brother. We could swap stories of failure and drink ourselves to death until beautiful, glorious alcohol poisoning kicks in. I could give-up. There's nothing wrong with giving up. There's nothing to fight for. There's nothing to win here except death. I could go home. I could finally sleep.

But I can't help wondering what would be more painful: a switchblade up the asshole or my mother smiling and telling me she knew I couldn't make it on my own.

I am not my brother. I am not my brother. I am not my brother.

I don't know what I am but I know what I'm not.

Hobbs pops up at the front desk at ten 'til seven, whistling and smiling like nothing had gone down last night, like everything was candy and ice cream.

"Howdy, Eye Sick," he says, and I just look at him, wincing the same way a beaten dog would at the reappearance of his abuser. "I'm gonna need you to go ahead and extend my stay."

"How long?" I whisper, groaning as I lift my hands up to type on the hotel computer.

"Hmm." He glances at the ceiling for a moment, contemplating. "Let's say, oh, two weeks from now."

Somehow I'm not surprised.

"Two weeks it is."

He keeps smiling, waiting for me to bring up the subject of payment, which I refuse to do. Fuck him. I won't give him the satisfaction.

"Don't you want to know my method of payment?" he finally asks.

The Nightly Disease

"No."

Hobbs laughs. "You're all right, Eye Sick. You're a-okay."

There is a bottle of coconut rum under my sink. When I get home, the first thing I do is open it and I don't stop drinking until everything becomes numb.

Part Three

Hotel Love

#300

Two **little kids,** maybe five or six years-old, talking by the pool as their parents gather supplies and I wait for them to leave:

Boy: "Well, that was a really good day for swimming, wasn't it, Alexis?"

Girl: "I guess."

Boy: "I really liked the hot tub because it was hot. But I also liked the swimming pool because it looks like a bean. What a really good day for swimming."

Girl: "Jeffrey, I'm tired, leave me alone. My body requires rest."

Then, when I return to the front desk, there's a group of drunks in the lobby slowly making their way to the elevator. One man is extremely pissed, and to prove it, he starts shouting. "No, goddammit, listen, in Mexican culture . . . "

Another man says, "Goddamn, I'm sick of your Mexican culture shit. Shut up!"

"No, you shut up and listen for once. In Mexican culture—in real, honest-to-God Mexican culture—the woman in the marriage does not get to talk back to the husband."

"Jesus Christ."

"Listen, in true Mexican culture, the man is allowed to smack his bitch if she gives him lip. It's true."

"You need to go to bed, man."

"Fuck you—"

The drunk walks into the wall, face-first. Embarrassed, he storms toward the elevator.

The other guy shouts, "In Mexican culture, are you supposed to walk into walls, too?"

I don't expect to see the bulimic girl again, not after telling me to go fuck myself, so when 2:00 A.M. hits and she's knocking on the front doors, I have to blink a few times to convince myself I'm not hallucinating. It wouldn't be the first time. Hallucinations are in a night auditor's job description.

I let her inside and she rushes to the front desk. Her eyes are raccoon-black and her skin is ghost-pale. "Where have you been?" she says.

"What?"

"I've come back here the last two nights," she holds up two ugly, scarred fingers, "to apologize to your stupid ass, and some other bitch was here instead."

"I'm off Friday and Saturday nights. That was Mandy, the part-time auditor."

"She threatened to call the cops on me."

"Why? What did you do?"

"Man, who cares? Fuck that lady."

"She can be irritating."

"Ya think?"

"Wait. I was here last night. You didn't come

here." Unless she tried to get in while Hobbs went to town on me with his baseball bat.

"Wait, what's today?"

I pause, struggling to remember. "I don't know. It's someday, any day. Mayday, mayday. Wait, what are you doing here?"

"I'm fuckin' dying, man."

"*What*?"

"I'm *dying*. I can't fucking take this much longer. I need your help, okay?"

I reach into my pocket for my cell phone. "I'll call an ambulance . . ."

"No!" She lunges at me and I step back, forgetting about the front desk between us. "Don't call the police. I don't need *their* help."

"Then . . . what do you need?"

For one insane moment I'm convinced she's going to look up at me and say, "I need your hard cock, Isaac." But of course she doesn't. That's crazy. Porn has rotted my brain.

Instead, she says, "Food. I need to binge so fucking bad."

"Oh."

My first instinct is to shame her, tell her to get her disgusting ass out of the hotel before I call the police. Normal people don't puke up what they eat. But I'm not an asshole—at least, I don't *want* to be an asshole. Besides, the whole reason I'd tried to confront her last week was to let her know it's cool if she comes to the hotel earlier than usual, when it's just me here. So what the hell is my problem then?

"Please," she says.

I head through the lobby and unlock the kitchen. When I turn around, she's shaking, teeth chattering, arms crossed over her chest. "Uh. What kind of food would you like?"

"I don't suppose there's any ice cream?"

"No . . . sorry."

"Okay. Can we cook up some waffles maybe?"

Preparing the waffle mix is a pain in the ass—especially for someone who prefers to do zero work. My hesitation shows.

"If it's not too much trouble," she adds, looking at me in a way that vibrates my heart.

"No problem."

As I pour the waffle mix into a large salad bowl and add water and butter, I ask her to go flip on the waffle irons so they can begin heating. I stir the mix with a wooden spoon, listening to her soft footsteps as she returns to the kitchen.

"So how long have you worked here?" Her voice sounds distracted. She doesn't care about me. Only gives a shit about the food. I'm just a necessary evil, like making awkward smalltalk with the delivery guy as you look for your wallet.

"I don't remember."

"You don't remember how long you've worked here?"

I shrug, staring at the bowl of waffle mix. "As far as I can recollect, I've been here since the moon first hatched. This is where I'm meant to be. Forever. When I die, my ashes will be buried in the garden out front."

"That's a little weird, man." She coughs. "Dude, what the hell happened to you? You look like someone beat the shit out of you."

"Well, there's your answer."

"Why?"

The Nightly Disease

"A guest was unhappy about his stay."

I pour the waffle mix into its proper container and drag it to the waffle irons out in the dining area. I unlock the cabinets below and bring out the plates, silverware, and syrup. The butter is already out. I guess she found it in the fridge as my back was turned. I wonder what else she snatched. She's giddy and anxious now as she utilizes both waffle irons, shaking like a drug addict waiting on her dealer to arrive.

"This is going to be so fucking good," she says. Even though it'll take a few minutes to cook, she can't seem to take her eyes off the irons. "Water. I need lots of water."

"Okay."

"Hurry."

I fill up a pitcher with cold sink water and she pries it out of my hands and begins chugging it before I have a chance to retrieve the cups. She shoves the empty container back at me a minute later and requests a refill. This time I bring her two pitchers.

The waffles are finished and she's already making two more while simultaneously applying butter to the finished ones on her plate. Impressive. She drowns them in syrup and breathes them in. I stand aside, feeling like a third wheel. This is a date between a woman and some waffles. There's no room for a night auditor here.

"So, what's your name?" I ask.

"My name?" She looks up, still chewing, remembering I'm still here.

"Yeah. What do I call you?"

"The bulimic freak. The fat cow. The gross slut. The Queen of STDs. Take your pick."

"Come on . . . "

"Look, if you want to talk, at least start heating up more waffles. And refill the water. Please."

After she's had her third helping, she belches and says, "Kia."

"What?"

"My name is Kia."

"Like the car?"

"Yeah. Like the car."

"Weird. Your parents just like the sound of it, or . . . ?"

Focusing on the waffles, she says, "It's where I was conceived."

"Oh."

"I guess they exhausted their imagination with my older brothers. Out I come, they couldn't have given less of a shit."

The silence that follows is painful and exhausting. I avoid it lingering by returning to the kitchen to refill her pitchers of water. When I come back out, she's heating up another round of waffles. I set the pitchers down and ask her if she wants to know my name, and she laughs and says, "I already know your name, Isaac."

I freeze, a thousand thoughts racing through my mind. Thinking I'm dreaming. Thinking there's a conspiracy afoot. Some secret government plot to murder me. The CIA can't allow this night auditor to continue breathing. I know too much. The fucking owls gave me away. First they took Mandy 2, now they're coming for me. Forget about the switchblade.

"How do you know my name?" I step forward, feeling aggressive, fucking violent. God, I'm tired.

She shakes her head, amused. "Maybe I'm a witch, or maybe I can read the name tag attached to your shirt."

The Nightly Disease

"Oh, yeah."

She leans forward, over her waffles. A thick line of syrup drips down her chin and it's the cutest fucking thing. "But it's still possible I could be a witch."

"At least I haven't been turned into a newt yet."

"What?"

"Uh, never mind."

Maybe on our first date we can watch *Monty Python and the Holy Grail* together. Wait, maybe this is our first date. We're talking, having a meal together—well, *she's* having a meal. I'm probably the only one who's thinking of this as a date, though. Who knows what this is to her. Nothing, maybe less than nothing.

The mobile house phone lights up on the table and begins beeping. Some guy wants to be connected to room 317. I connect him without responding, my mind far away from hotel duties.

Kia wipes her mouth with a napkin and chugs from the water pitcher. "You know, I've seen you."

"You've seen me?"

She points to the ceiling, smiling. "On the roof."

Oxygen leaves my lungs and I can no longer breathe. I spin around and head back into the kitchen, thinking I can't ever talk to this girl again. I'm going to have to call the police and have her escorted off the premises. I wash the bowl I used to stir the waffle mix in the sink and try not to think about how many times the girl in the other room has watched me masturbating. Maybe if I stay in here long enough, she'll be gone by the time I come out. But the question is whether or not I really want her gone, or if I want to watch her eat waffles until we both grow old and die together.

Max Booth III

I'm not given a choice. Once I finish washing the dishes and exit the kitchen, she's absent from the table. The plate and syrup and water pitcher are also missing, and for a moment I become convinced tonight has all been some kind of fever dream and Kia's entire existence has been this ongoing hallucination gradually fueling my schizophrenia.

Then I hear her vomiting in the lobby bathroom and my heart calms. The sound of her gagging serves as the equivalent of a baby's crib mobile. Peaceful. Soothing. Jesus, that's fucked up.

The hotel phone rings again. I answer it, half-hypnotized by the pleasant lullaby of puke. "This is the front desk. How can I help you?"

"Are your computers broken?" a woman asks.

"Uh . . . what?"

"Are your computers down? Are they broken? What's going on?"

"No, the computers here are working just fine, ma'am."

"Where's the other guy at?"

"*What* other guy?"

"The other front desk employee."

"Ma'am, I am the only person working this shift. There is no one else here."

The woman is silent for a moment, then sighs loudly. "Shit."

"What's going on?" I ask, rushing behind the front desk. The computers seem fine.

"I just received a phone call from the front desk. He told me your computers were down and he needed to reenter my credit card information."

Shit. The guy who called while I was talking to Kia. I hadn't asked him for the guest's name before connecting him over. "You didn't tell him your credit card number, did you?"

"Well, of course I did. You guys asked for it."

"No, ma'am. I'm the only one here, and I definitely did not ask for it."

"I just don't understand this. You guys *just called me.*"

"Nobody from the front desk called you."

"Then how did they get through?"

"I . . . I don't know. Maybe some kind of glitch in our system." I don't tell her the real reason, that I'm a shitty employee and an even shittier human being.

"This is unacceptable. Let me speak to your manager."

"Um."

"I said, let me speak to your manager."

"Um," I say again, because my brain's swarmed by the memos management posted last year when this same exact scam was hitting local hotels. The memo informed us all that if we didn't confirm the first and last name of a guest before transferring a caller over, we would receive an immediate termination, no exceptions.

Part of me wants to just hang up on this guest and start browsing the job listings online. Get away from the hotel, escape the cowboy's switchblade. But another part of me—the lazier part that just wants to continue sitting around every night jacking-off on the roof and watching horror movies on my iPad—wants to fix the situation before it becomes an even bigger issue. Before this lady drags Javier into the picture.

"Hello?" the woman says. "Are you there?" She sounds out of breath, like she's getting out of bed and putting clothes on. Shit, she's planning on coming down here. If I can convince her to stay in her room and calm her down over the phone, then I still might have a chance.

"I apologize, ma'am, I'm still here. I was just talking to my manager."

"No, let *me* talk to him."

"Of course, ma'am, of course. *However,* first we need you to hang up with us and call your bank, okay? It's crucial that you cancel your credit card before whoever you gave your information to uses it."

"Now, hold on a second—"

"Ma'am! They could be emptying your account right now, right this *very second.* Please, cancel your card, then call the front desk and you can speak to my manager."

"Oh, well, okay . . . "

"Thank you, and once again, ma'am, I do apologize."

As soon as she hangs up, I'm calling the Other Goddamn Hotel, desperately praying George isn't too drunk to answer the phone. It picks up after only two rings, which is always a bad sign.

"Thank you for calling the Other Goddamn Hotel. This is Chad. How may I help you?"

"Where the fuck is George?"

"Uh. George called off tonight. Who the *fuck* is *this*?"

I hang up. Well, there went my only plan. At this point I may as well sit back and wait for the executioner to drop his axe. Plop, down goes my head. Maybe poor children will use it as a soccer ball. Recycle the waste.

The gagging continues from the bathroom. But instead of a mentally ill girl emptying her stomach, I hear what possibly may be my last hope. Insert *Star Wars* reference. Insert a desperate night auditor left with no other options. Insert the word "fuck".

I grab the mobile and sprint across the lobby. I don't knock before opening the bathroom door, but the stall is locked, securing her privacy.

Between gagging, Kia says, "Occupado, you stupid bitch."

"It's Isaac. Open the door."

She laughs, and it's a painful, exhausted laugh. "What? Get the fuck out of here."

"No, seriously, I need your help. It's an emergency."

"Dude, fuck off."

I pound on the stall. "Please."

Silence on the other side, then a heavy sigh followed by the toilet flushing. The door unlocks and swings open and she's standing in front of me, hair pulled back in a ponytail, her face red and swollen, wet with vomit.

"What? Jesus Christ, what the fuck do you want?"

"I screwed up and connected a scammer to a random guest, and he stole her credit card information. Now she's pissed off at me."

"Okay?" She looks at the toilet, grimaces, then looks back at me, grimacing again, like I'm just as vile as whatever she just vomited. "What do you want me to do about it?"

"She's going to call back any second, and she's expecting to speak to my manager."

Her eyes widen, paranoid. "Shit, I thought you were the only one here."

"I am . . . but the guest doesn't know that."

When she doesn't catch on at first, I hold out the

mobile, and she backs away into the stall, shaking her head. "No, no, *hell* no. No way."

I step into the stall with her, holding the mobile between us like a fragile jewel. "It won't be that bad. I promise."

The smell of vomit hits me and I try to breathe out of my mouth. "She'll be pissed off, but all you have to do is apologize a lot and say you're gonna give me a stern talking to or something. Just say whatever it takes to calm her down."

"I'm sorry, Isaac, but I can't."

"After I gave you waffles? Come on, you can do this."

"No."

The mobile lights up in my hands. We both jump. She shakes her head harder and backpedals until she's against the wall.

"You can do this," I whisper, then answer the phone and shove it against her chest.

She grabs the phone, but leaves her eyes on me, annoyed. She presses the mobile against her ear and I notice just how bad the scars are on her fingers.

"Uh, yeah, hello?" Kia says, clearing her throat. "Yeah, uh, that's me, yes, uh-huh, right, right. Yeah, okay." She nods to the invisible guest. "Yeah, yeah, yeah . . . yeah. Yeah. Yes. Of course. Uh-huh. Yeah. Sure. Okay."

She hangs up the mobile and hands it back to me. When she doesn't say anything, I lean forward and say, "Well?"

She shrugs. "Well what, man?"

"Well what did she say? What's happening?"

She relaxes against the wall. "Ah, she's cool, don't worry about her."

"Really?"

"Yeah, man. She got her card taken care of. Obviously the same card she gave you guys for her room, so it probably won't work now. But I said she can stay here tonight for free, so, like, whatever, I guess."

"Shit, I can't comp her stay."

"Hey, you asked me to talk to the bitch, so I talked to the bitch. Don't be so ungrateful."

I tuck the mobile back into my pocket, brainstorming game plans that won't result with Javier asking a million questions. Fuck it. Maybe I'll just heavily discount the stay then put my MasterCard on file, eat the charge for my own stupidity.

Except my card was recently stolen, so what's the use in living.

"Thank you," I say. "You really did help."

"Uh, okay." She rolls her eyes and points to the door. "Now do you mind getting the fuck out of here?"

Back in the lobby a line of guests waits to either check-out or call me an asshole. As I listen to their abuse, Kia slips out of the bathroom and escapes the hotel, and I don't expect to ever see her again.

#301

But the next night, barely ten minutes after the 3-11 shift walks out the door, Kia's knocking on the front desk, shouting that she needs more towels because her husband's giant cock sprayed their entire room with cum. In the back office, I'm sitting at Javier's desk, thinking oh shit, not again. I rush to the laundry room, grab a stack of towels, and sprint back to the front desk, only to find Kia standing there, laughing her ass off.

I drop the towels on the front desk and wait for her to stop. "How did you even get in here?" I've already locked the doors, so maybe she slipped in when someone walked out.

"I transformed into a cloud of fog and drifted through the cracks."

"What are you, a vampire?"

"That would make things perfect, wouldn't it?" she says. "It's why I have to puke up my food, my body can't process it. But I just love the taste so much!"

I'm silent, suddenly terrified.

"So," she says, "are they gonna fire you or what?"

The Nightly Disease

"Looks like I'm home-free."

"Awesome." She holds out her tiny fist and I tap it with my own. "So I guess you owe me more waffles then."

I laugh and immediately feel guilty when she doesn't laugh with me. "Yeah, okay, no problem. But I can't until, like, two in the morning. I have too many reservations left to check-in, so I don't really want any of them seeing me making waffles and risk them mentioning it to the morning shift. Plus, what if they want some? There's only so many people I can make waffles for before waffling out. I'm only so strong."

She nods, thinking it over. "All right, then what should we do to kill time?"

"Uh. I don't know. There's a TV in the dining area."

"We could always go masturbate on the roof."

"Um."

She giggles, then slides over the front desk, nearly kicking me in the face as she sweeps her legs across. "Relax, I'm just fucking with you. Jerk-off wherever you please. It's a free country."

"What, do you live out in the woods or something? Where've you seen me? How many times? Do you . . . watch . . . all of it?"

"I live nowhere and everywhere, and I watch until you finish."

"Why?" I feel violated, yet hard at the same time. What a fucking creep I am. What fucking creeps we both are.

"I dunno. How often do you see someone doing that on a roof in the middle of the night? You kinda have to watch. Like a car crash. You know?"

"I'm not sure if I should feel insulted right now or not."

Kia shrugs and starts exploring the back office, picking up random objects and sitting them down without really inspecting them. Like she's performing on stage, like I'm her audience. "So, what do you do around here when you aren't pulling your meat?"

"I guess I read a lot."

"Who do you read? Like Bukowski or some shit?"

"You know Bukowski?"

"Are you a dirty old man, Isaac?"

I clear my throat, sweating in undesirable areas. "I like more genre stuff. Mostly horror."

She laughs. "You must regularly jack-off to *The Shining*."

"Only irregularly."

It warms me to see her smile. Warms me like the whiskey in George's flask. Maybe the world is not so miserable, but it probably is.

Just to remind me of my place in the universe, the front desk rings and some guy immediately calls me an imbecile for not properly installing the toilet in his room.

"It just won't flush!" he says.

One of the oldest complaints in the book, an issue typically solved by utilizing the miracle of the opposable thumb. "Sir, have you tried pushing all the way down on the flusher?"

"Of course I've tried that! How dare you insinuate I'm some kind of moron? I'll fucking sue your ass and take you for every last dime your pathetic minimum wage job offers."

"Sir, please go try again. Humor me, okay? Just press all the way down."

The guy sighs. "All right, whatever." Pause. In the background, I hear the toilet flushing. A few seconds later the line goes dead. Not so much as a single "thank you" or "fuck you".

"So," Kia says after I return to the back office, "do you often have to teach adults how to flush toilets?"

"About once a night." I yawn. Fear convinces me any moment now Hobbs and his brother will poke their heads down here and try to screw with me. Maybe they'll have a baseball bat again, and maybe they won't just take it out on me this time. But I can't push her away. I've dreamt of her being back here with me so many nights, I can't ruin it now. It's happening, it's actually happening, and if I do anything to fuck it up next time I jerk-off on the roof I'll follow my cum to the pavement. Splat, splat. "And what do you read?"

"Books written by dead people."

"Dead people who write books or people who used to write books but are now dead?"

"What do you think?"

"Well, ghouls penning novels *would* be pretty rad."

"Ha, you said 'rad'. One quarter in the asshole jar."

She holds out her hand and doesn't move or say anything until I steal a quarter from the cash register and drop it into her palm. Satisfied, she shoves the coin into her pants pocket.

"I wasn't aware your hand was the asshole jar."

"The more you know . . . "

I imagine a shooting star exploding out of her head. "Does that mean your hand smells like ass?"

"Only on Fridays."

"I think my uncle had that same medical condition."

Kia sniffs her hand for affect, then grimaces. "Shit, what's today?"

"Well, it's not Friday, otherwise I wouldn't be here."

"Oh." She lays her hand down in her lap. "It must be some other day."

"Yeah. One of those."

She catches me staring at her fingers and quickly hides them in her jacket pockets. "It's rude to stare."

"I know. Sorry."

She rolls her eyes. "Go ahead and ask."

"Ask what?"

"Saying 'ask what' when you damn well know 'what' is a good way to owe more money to the asshole jar, a.k.a. my ugly, fucked-up hand."

"Your hand isn't fucked-up. I think it's beautiful." The words sound like a lie, but they're not. There's something wrong with the wiring in my brain.

"And this isn't a Nicholas Sparks's novel, so stop trying to have sex in the rain. That's how a motherfucker catches pneumonia, man."

"All right, fine. What happened to your fingers? Is it . . . uh . . . from the bulimia?"

She nods, stuffing her hands deeper into her pockets. "When I first started purging, I would use my hands. First just two fingers, then I learned three or four is the way to go. Anyway, yeah, my teeth really did a number on them. These days, though, I just use a toothbrush."

"I've read that's highly dangerous," I say, not realizing my implication before it's too late to take it back.

"You've been reading about bulimia?" She raises her brow, maybe amused, maybe deeply offended.

"I read about a lot of things."

"Is that so?"

"Yeah, that's so."

"What else do you read about when you aren't stalking me?"

"Owls."

"*Owls?*"

"An owl killed one of the front desk girls a while back. They're dangerous creatures and they must be stopped."

She waits for a punch line that doesn't exist. "Owls?"

I nod. "I'm one of the few who's onto them. All the rest of you people have been fooled."

She laughs, more relaxed now, and rubs her scarred fingers through dirty hair. "Have I been fooled, too?"

"Evidently."

"The horror!"

"You laugh, but this shit is no joke. Do you know owls are a symbol of death?"

"Are they now?"

"Yeah, like, the Romans would freak out if they heard an owl hoot. Like an omen. Supposedly, an owl's hoot meant someone was about to die. If an owl hooted while perched on your house, you were supposed to kill it and nail the corpse to your front door."

"Shit—for how long? A night, a week, what?"

"I don't know. The article didn't specify."

"That'd begin to smell pretty fast."

"Well, given the choice of death or—"

"I'd probably take death." She pauses. "Wait. What about homeless people? Did they nail the owl corpses to, uh, I don't know, their assholes?"

"Quite possibly."

"The Romans were fucking hardcore, dude."

"Hell yeah."

Kia stops laughing. "Hold up. Did you say an owl *killed* someone who used to work here?"

"Yeah, but she wasn't killed at the hotel. The owl attacked her at home."

"What happened?"

"It ate her face off."

"You're fucking with me."

"Go Google it if you want."

"Holy shit. Owls suck."

"They're the worst."

She rubs her eyes, clearly exhausted. So am I. I debate asking if she wants to go nap with me in a vacant dirty room, but before I can find the courage to speak, she says, "So, how about those waffles?"

#302

I'm afraid to sleep because I don't know who will be standing over me when I wake up, watching. A guest might hop over the front desk and touch himself and drool over my unconscious body—or worse, my manager might decide to come in early and bust me doing something I'm not supposed to be doing. Then I'm out of a job and I'm sleeping on the streets, which honestly doesn't sound so bad most nights. But I can just imagine sleeping in an alley and waking up to some stranger pissing on me. At least at the hotel, the strangers are up front about pissing in your face. They do it while you're awake.

So tired my motor functions are out of sync, like a universe that's been split into a dozen tiny universes all attempting to work together, like different alternative realities just a second slower than the previous, like an online video game lagging due to shitty Internet service. I walk forward but end up leaning against a wall covered in dirty handprints and spattered condiments, resting my head against the cold surface, listening to the machines vibrate in my skull only I can hear. Somewhere Kia is asking me if she can eat something. I may have answered, but my voice is distant and muffled, like a drowning victim pleading for a fish's help. There is never enough sleep. I could sleep for a thousand years and none of it would matter because right now I must be awake, right now I must function. I am a robot disobeying its programming. At this rate, my creator will disarm me any moment, and goddamn it can't happen soon enough. And goddamn will it be great. And goddamn, I said, and goddamn. I try to drink cold coffee from two years ago and it spills down my chin because I forget the exact location of my mouth, and it's all right, yeah it's all right, because who needs coffee when you don't have a mouth, and who needs a mouth when you don't have a brain—at least, not a proper brain, more of a brain that someone accidentally installed while downloading pornography, like a virus that's eating up all the good things in me and replacing it all with a self-destruct sequence that'll be triggered in five, three, one.

Boom.

There's this sensation that overwhelms me when I'm in that nodding-off stage. Like my skin is an inch from bone, caught in stagnation, floating as its own entity. I try to scratch my skull and my scalp peels off like the skin of a rotten orange. My flesh is artificial and my guts are gravy. Nobody remembers the last few seconds before sleep snuffs them. When you wake up, there is no memory of your surrender. It is like time travel. One moment you're in bed, tossing and turning, and then five hours have passed within the blink of an eye. Or four hours. Or three. Or twenty minutes. How much sleep does a person even need?

The Nightly Disease

The moment before you become unconscious, something terrible happens that none of us remembers. I never remember it, either. I am not special. But I'm sure it exists. Something painful, agonizing. A great pain overwhelms our senses, and it is only after this orgasmic, awful moment that human beings are allowed sleep.

I try telling this theory to Kia and she laughs, tells me I'm a psychiatrist's wet dream, but don't worry about it too much, because so is everybody. She's following me around the meeting room as I clean up after an oil company that'd rented it out earlier today. Like true savages, they had left their mark behind with piles of trash and abandoned food. To Kia, this room is paradise. I wipe down tables sporting puddles of barbecue sauce and peel pickles off the wall while I tell Kia that sleep isn't a reward, it's a punishment.

"Time is all we get in this stupid life," I say, tossing a handful of sliced onions in the trash. "And sleep goes out of its way to take that from us. Think about it, each day consists of twenty-four hours. But do we actually get to experience all twenty-four?"

"You're spending a good chunk of your twenty-four hours cleaning up someone else's trash." Kia hovers over a Styrofoam container of half-eaten pasta and feasts.

"Yeah, and you're spending it eating someone else's trash."

She holds up her scarred finger and finishes chewing. "The difference here is, I'm content with my current actions. Can you say the same?"

"Contentment is a disease to which I am immune."

Kia laughs so hard she practically chokes on her

cup of water. "What-the-fuck-ever, dude." She moves along the room, picking through the abandoned food and filling up the Styrofoam container with whatever she deems suitable for a bulimic's diet.

Somewhere above the meeting room, a baby is crying. If I listen hard enough, there is always a baby crying at this hotel. The meeting room carpet needs to be vacuumed, but it's not happening at this time of night. The sound wouldn't drown out the baby's crying but it would annoy the neighboring rooms. Last time I tried to vacuum on my shift, a lunatic in the room next door attempted to bludgeon me with his television remote. The memory of his extraordinarily long, veiny dong dangling from out of his boxers still haunts me to this day. I'd been less afraid of the remote than I had been of the prospect of his penis detaching itself from his groin and attacking me like a rabid ferret. Never again.

"I wish someone would shut that fucking kid up. It's almost three in the morning."

Kia stops eating. "What kid?"

"You fucking know." The urge to slap the pasta from her hands is overwhelming. I bite my lip and resist tackling her and beating her face in, resist kneeling down and proposing marriage and devoting the rest of my life to her happiness.

"Man, how long have you been awake?"

"You can melt reality, you get tired enough. Deprive yourself of sleep for a few days and the universe starts to make sense."

She shakes her head, laughing again, digging her fork back in the day-old pasta. "You've finally cracked, Isaac. Congratulations."

"You don't hear a baby crying?"

The Nightly Disease

"Only you, darlin'. Only you." Then she pauses, staring at the pasta, and drops the container to the floor. "I think I gotta go."

"What?"

"I'm sorry. Uh, thanks for the grub." She's spinning and running out the door before I have a chance to give her shit for further staining the carpet, before I have a chance to beg her never to leave me again. Two hours pass before I realize she never stopped in the bathroom to purge.

#303

Every time I try to get Kia to open up to me, she shuts down. I've read that a relationship will never blossom without both partners sharing personal details about themselves. Obviously she isn't ready for this relationship to blossom. Obviously this is not a relationship. I am suffering from a delusion. She does not like me. She tolerates my presence in order to score free food. I'm nothing more than a waffle maker and a free toilet bowl to puke into. The only reason she comes here is because she's too poor too afford her own food, her own toilet. I am as replaceable as porcelain.

"Why are you looking at me like that?" she says one night, inhaling a plate of waffles. I'm standing by the waffle iron, heating up a new batch. A few minutes ago, Hobbs had stumbled through the lobby after smoking a cigarette by the front trash cans. He had winked and grabbed his junk before heading into the elevator. I'm still on edge, waiting for him to come back down and give me shit. He's been remarkably quiet these days, mostly keeping to himself, doing whatever the hell it is he does up in his room.

"Isaac, what the hell is wrong with you?"

"I'm not looking at you like anything."

She stops eating and pushes the plate away. "I'm sorry, but do I disgust you?"

"What?" My voice squeaks.

"I said, do I disgust you? Do you find me fucking repulsive?"

"No. Why would . . . why would you think that?"

"Because you're looking at me like I'm dogshit."

"I'm not even looking at you. I'm just . . . tired. I haven't been sleeping well." I debate telling her about Hobbs and the stolen wallet fiasco, but she wouldn't care, not really. She'd probably just laugh like George did. She only pretends to want to hear what I say because otherwise I might not give her waffles.

Kia shakes her head, sneering. "You have no idea what I've gone through. You have no fucking right to judge me."

"I'm not judging. I'm not doing anything."

"What do you know? You don't know shit, man. You've never suffered. You've never had a truly bad day in your whole fuckin' life."

I turn off the waffle iron and sit down across from her. "You can make your own damn food if that's how you want to speak to me."

"Whatever."

"I've been nothing but nice to you. I don't know why suddenly you think I'm some kind of asshole."

"I don't know." She leans her head back and sighs. "I'm sorry. I've been going through some shit. My brothers have been real dicks lately and they're just . . . you know. Just really pissing me off."

"I didn't know you had brothers."

She falls silent, then clears her throat. "Yeah, well, Isaac, there's a lot you don't know about me. So what?"

"So tell me."

"I'm not a writer. I don't tell stories."

"Anybody can tell a story."

"Not me."

I reach out to grab her hands but she yanks them off the table. "Look," I say, "I think at this point you have to understand that I'm not a stranger. We've become friends, haven't we? At least tell me that's true."

She slowly nods. "I suppose."

"Then what are you afraid of?"

She laughs, nervous. "I don't like talking about my life. Why must you know everything? Some things are better left in the dark. Like cockroaches."

"I understand what it's like to have a shitty past. Believe me, I totally understand. But, like, I know absolutely zero things about you. Don't you think that's a little weird?"

"Why don't you tell me about your shitty past then?"

"What? No. I asked you first."

She smiles and takes a huge bite out of her waffle. "And I asked you second."

"Uh."

Kia leans forward, pointing an accusing finger. "That's because you *don't* know shit, just like I said. If you did know, you'd understand that it's better to keep it to yourself. And if you *were* my friend, like you claim, then you would respect my privacy. I mean, come on, dude, for fuck's sake."

The Nightly Disease

Her face is so close I could kiss her if I wanted to. And I want to. But does she? Doubtful. A gust of sewage dust expels from her mouth and hits my face and I pull my head away, grimacing at her murderous breath.

"When I was twelve years-old, back when I was still in Indiana, we lived in various motels and hotels until I was almost sixteen." I gasp and grind my fingers into my thighs. Oxygen escapes. I've never told anybody that before.

She shrugs. "So you lived in some hotels. Shit, kid, you *work* at a hotel. What's the big deal?"

"Well, I didn't go to school from ages twelve to fifteen. Completely skipped high school. Never got that experience everyone else gets. I have a difficult time relating to the films of John Hughes."

"Man, not having to go to school." She shakes her head with faux sadness in her eyes. "What a terrible childhood."

"The state was under the impression that I was being home-schooled. But that was bullshit. No one taught me anything. I lost all my friends. All my belongings. One day everything just changed. We left our house, our town, and just . . . moved on. Isolated from the world like psychotic conspiracy theorists."

"Watch out, Mel Gibson."

"Seriously. I know it sounds like a fun way to grow up, traveling from motel to hotel to motel without having to worry about school . . . but you gotta realize how fucking disturbing and awkward it is to go through puberty while sleeping in the same room as your mom and dad. Every minute of every day. Zero privacy. Every friend you ever hung out with is gone. Every shop you have ever loitered at is miles and miles away. You are alone. All that's left is you and your thoughts to drive you crazy."

Kia stops smiling. She looks at me the same way I look at her when she's eating. "Why was this happening?"

I shrug. "To this day, I still don't know. One morning, our house lost electricity. This was common. We were always behind on bills. I went to school, then when I came home my mom had packed a bag of clothes and said we had to stay at a hotel for a few days. A few days stretched into a few years. I never saw the house again."

"Jesus fuck. What does your mom say now when you ask her?"

"She just . . . screams. Like I'm being an asshole for bringing up the past. I don't know. I'll never know."

"That's fucked up, dude."

"I know."

"What did you do to pass the time? That's like, what, three years? Shit."

"I read a lot. Also, like I said. I was going through puberty."

Kia laughs. "You were jerkin' it like crazy."

"Pretty much."

"In front of your parents?"

"Uh . . . no. There was a bathroom."

"You little perv." She chomps down on the rest of her waffle. Between mouthfuls, she says, "So I've always been curious. What's the difference between a motel and a hotel?"

"The first letters."

"Ass."

"This is my take on it. Hotels are the kind of places

you don't mind bringing your family to—you can expect good service, a nice breakfast. *Mo*tels, on the other hand, are where people take cheap dates for quick fucks. The walls are stained with nicotine and moans, the sheets are photographs of past orgasms and homicides and the floors are infested with bugs you never even knew existed."

"Hmm. And where are we now?" She motions around the dining area.

"Purgatory."

She nods approvingly. "And are you the nihilistic psychopomp guiding all these poor souls from check-in to check-out?"

Instead of answering, I get up and plop a new waffle on her plate. "Okay, I told you. Now you tell me something."

"Ugh. Okay, what do you want to know?"

"Are you homeless?"

"Next question."

"How long have you been bulimic?"

"I've been purging since the womb, son."

"Do you have any family?"

"I already told you I got some brothers."

"Parents?"

"Never knew 'em."

"Did your brothers raise you?"

She laughs, but it comes off as more depressed than amused. "If you could call it that."

"Did they abuse you?"

She's quiet for a moment.

I prod on. I don't know why. "How—"

She raises her hand, palm out. "I think that's enough questions."

"But—"

She shakes her head. "Nah, I actually think I gotta go. Thanks for the waffles." She rises and heads toward the hotel entrance.

I attempt to follow. "What about the bathroom?"

"Fuck it," she says, not turning back.

Then she's gone.

#304

In the beginning we stayed in dozens of different motels. At first we mostly lived in the hotel by the casino, since we had a lot of comped rooms due to my mother's uncontrollable gambling habits. But eventually those went away and we had to settle for anything with four walls and a door. We stayed in a lot of shit, but we stayed in some pretty nice places as well. After about a year and a half, we settled down in a Pretty Shitty Motel, as it had the cheapest rates with the least amount of cockroaches.

It certainly wasn't the worst motel. It had two beds, a TV with a hundred channels, a desk, a window, a closet, a bathroom. It even had a refrigerator, which comes to a surprise to me now, since the hotel I am presently working at is ranked like sixty-five out of the six hundred-something Goddamn Hotels in the world, and our standards don't even have fridges.

But it was a Pretty Shitty Motel, and the rates were extremely cheap, especially after we'd stayed there so long and worked up a discounted weekly price, so obviously the scumbags were expected to loiter about.

If you didn't lock your car before going inside, you could pretty much be guaranteed to lose some shit when you came back out. Across the street, at the Dirtiest Motel in the USA, you saw hookers and business men coming in and out hourly. The guests at the Pretty Shitty Motel weren't as bad, but we did encounter our fair share of crazies.

I rarely slept at night while living in the motel. I'd stay up until the sun came up and then just pass out. Funnily enough, I do the same thing now, only I get paid to stay up. It's pennies, but at least it's something. What I'm getting at is, I was awake when most were asleep, more alert when everyone else was out of it. So, when the night came that the Meth Freaks of Room 123 stayed at the Pretty Shitty Motel, I was the first one to hear anything out of the ordinary.

It was winter in Indiana, which is dramatically different than winter in Texas. Hence why it was so odd for the window below us to be wide open. Of course, *our* window was open a tad, but that was only because I was insane and needed to be frozen in order to be comfortable. It was obvious *theirs* was open since I could hear everything going on below us. Taking a break from the book I was reading, I approached the window and looked down, doing what every American does best: eavesdropping. It was two of them down there, talking real fast, "fuck" this and "fuck" that, "police" here and "pigs" there. Who knows what they were actually talking about. I doubted it even made much sense in their drug-addled minds, much less anyone else's.

The Nightly Disease

Just from the sound of their voices I could tell they were up to something. When a pillow went hurling out the window and into the snow, this only backed up my theory. Another pillow soon followed. I stood by the window and waited for something else to happen. If this was a movie or TV show, there would have probably been a gunshot, and then a body would have followed the pillows out the window, into the snow. The killer would stick his head out the window to make sure his friend really was dead, and I'd see his face, marking me as the only witness to the crime. Worst of all, he'd see me up there looking at him, and he'd know he would have to take care of me if he wanted any chance of escaping the law. So he'd run up the stairs to our room, kick down the door and shoot both of my parents who'd still be fast asleep. Only I would be nowhere in the room because I'd be long gone. I'd have tossed on my shoes, grabbed my books and jacket and gotten the hell out of there. He'd run back out of the room and back outside, trying to track me down. His mistake would be in thinking I had fled the motel completely, where in reality I had simply jumped down the laundry chute by the vending machine. The police would already be on their way because I was just so goddamn smart. I wouldn't have gotten my ass killed at all. If that had happened.

But of course, this wasn't a movie, and instead of a body falling out the window, I was met with unexpected silence as the two men below trailed off with their ramblings. Naturally it didn't take long for me to grow bored of waiting and return to my book. After a while, my brain began to fizzle out and I dozed off, only to wake up to an earthquake in the room below. The sun of a new morning temporarily blinded me as I rose and approached the window once more. My vision clearing, I saw that the two pillows were still outside in the snow. However, they were no longer alone, not by any stretch.

Along with the pillows, there was now a pile of sheets, a blanket, a comforter, a lamp, and a TV. There were coat hangers scattered everywhere, along with broken chunks of wood from a desk that'd been obliterated by God knew what. Same went for the nightstand and TV stand. A mattress was stuck halfway out the window. Standing around this chaos were a group of policemen, each of them rubbing their chins and staring at it all, equally perplexed.

My first thought was: *How did I sleep through this?*

My second thought was, understandably: *What in the fuck?*

Now I'm a little older and instead of living in a shitty motel, I work in a slightly less shitty hotel.

My first week on the night shift, I was with the front desk manager, who'd been training me for the position. He's since quit for a better opportunity, meaning a taxi hit him while crossing a street and now he gets a disability check once a month.

But a few years ago, he was still training me. It's almost three in the morning, and we decide to go outside and walk around the hotel a few times to wake ourselves back up. Along the way, we take out the trash, since it's overflowing and we're already out there, so why not. He expresses interest in the fact that I used to live in motels, and asks what was it like being on the other side. I tell him it's similar, meaning both the guest and the clerk can experience some

The Nightly Disease

pretty surreal, unique moments. Naturally, this brings me to share one of my favorite anecdotes. I tell him, one night there were two brothers that stayed in the room below us. We can hear them arguing, and then, I guess one of the brothers leaves, all pissed off, and goes out drinking. The other brother stays behind and decides to smoke up some meth. Does it right there in the motel room, gets high as hell. He then decides the motel room would look much better outside than inside, so proceeds to empty the room of its contents. Throws it all out in the snow, only stopping when the mattress gets stuck. He passes out soon afterward on the floor and wakes up in the morning to his brother coming home, drunk and yelling about what's happened. Soon the police are called and they haul both brothers away, the drunk one yelling to the meth freak that the devil is inside him and he hopes he rots in hell with the rest of the demons.

And my trainer, he asks how I know some of those details. How did I know he was on meth, or that they were brothers, or that he fell asleep on the floor like that? And the strangest thing happens—I freeze up. I have no idea how I know any of this. I don't think I've made it up. I remember it all clear as day—those other details, which I shouldn't know, they don't seem made-up either. They make *sense*, too. So what the hell? Maybe someone told me, I suggest. Like the person working the front desk at the time. She would have known what had happened. She'd have to. And why wouldn't she tell me? She liked me. Of course she told me.

And the guy training me, he just shrugs and says this all reminds him of these legendary thieves that sometimes hit the area. Their MO, he tells me, is they'll check into a hotel, paying with stolen credit cards and using fake IDs, and throughout the night they'll proceed to clean out the hotel room. The TV, the lamps, the paintings, even the fuckin' beds. They'll have a pickup truck out waiting at one of the side doors, and they'll bring it all down on luggage carts.

I ask him, why the hell would anyone even steal a lamp? What's the point? And he tells me dude, those things can go for a few hundred dollars. You'd be surprised.

He tells me he has a friend who works at a different hotel a few towns away. The thieves tried hitting them, only something must've spooked them because when the housekeeping went up to their room the following day, they found three of the luggage carts stacked with everything from the room's interior. Like they were about to take it all down, but something happened and they all bailed on the job. This was a couple months ago, and no one had reported any similar burglary since. So who the hell knew what happened to them. It was strange as hell.

Then he tells me, about a year and a half ago, they struck the old hotel he used to work at. He tells me how he came in at seven in the morning, started his shift, and got a phone call from housekeeping about three hours later. The maid, she tells him he's gonna want to come up to this room. He asks why, but the maid just says he won't believe her, that he'll need to come up and see for himself. So he gets his manager and they both walk up to the room. Only the room is empty. No TV, no lamps, no bed, no fuckin' anything. It's all gone. The room might as well be brand new.

I ask him how he reacted when they got up to the room and discovered it all missing.

The Nightly Disease

And he tells me he began to laugh, and his manager began to curse, and neither one of them could stop.

#305

I almost kill a deer in the parking lot. Something large and brown flashes in my periphery and I slam on the brakes so hard and close to the ground I swear to god I hear Fred Flintstone somewhere screaming, "Yabba dabba doo!" The deer realizes its dilemma and tries to turn around, but it's too late. It jerks to the side and slams its giant ass into the driver's door. A thud fills the car, then frantic footsteps against concrete as the animal flees into the woods behind the hotel. I sit behind the wheel, stopped in the middle of the parking lot, breathing heavy and trying to locate it in the darkness. Goddammit. Why couldn't it have been a guest?

I debate circling the hotel a little longer until someone stumbles out into the parking lot for a smoke before bed. Would management really get that upset if I ran over one lousy guest? Doesn't seem likely. At worst, I might receive a verbal warning. Running over a guest would absolutely be worth a verbal warning. Hell yeah.

The Nightly Disease

Maybe I'll get lucky and happen upon Hobbs. Get rid of him once and for all.

After a couple laps around the hotel, all I see are more goddamn deer, so I give up and park under the awning and head inside. As I'm punching in my code at the time clock, Yas starts telling me about all the tasks Javier wants me to accomplish tonight.

A guest's dog shit in the elevator, or maybe the guest shit in it, who knows, either way the carpet needs to be properly scrubbed.

The back office has become overpopulated with old audit packs and I need to transport them upstairs to a storage room.

A guest can't figure out how to flush his toilet and has requested that a front desk agent print out specific instructions concerning the toilet and slide them under his door and knock twice, not once, not thrice, but twice. Anything more or less will result in an official complaint to Goddamn Corporate.

A guest complained of a small bump located on the rug between her microwave and closet. It is the size of a ladybug, according to Yas, who has already gone up to inspect the obstruction. The guest claims she has a bad leg and cannot possibly be expected to step over it. Yas suggested she walk around it instead and the guest kicked her out of the room. She is waiting for me to come up and make everything better.

Or else.

Always or else.

Or fucking else what.

"Oh yeah," she says, "and there's a snake outside, too."

I turn from the front desk computer and slowly

blink a couple times. "Did you say there's a snake outside?"

She nods, natural and calm, like she's talking about the weather. "Yup. Saw it when I was putting a luggage cart back by the doors. It was in the flowers."

"Oh." Terror attempts to rip my heart open. "No big deal. I kill snakes all the time."

Yas squints. "Yeah, that seems like a lie."

Nervous laughter escapes my throat. "Your face seems like a lie."

"What?"

"I'll go check it out."

I walk into the foyer, one leg outside, one leg inside, and peer through the window, expecting either a garter snake or a suspicious tree branch. Nothing's out there.

"Do you see it?" Yas shouts from the front desk, and I tell her no, she's crazy, hallucinating.

"Come show me."

She starts walking to the entrance and I'm looking at her, wishing she'd walk faster, hurry up and get them over with so I can watch an episode of *Gilmore Girls*.

Then she stops dead in her tracks and screams and turns around and runs away. Runs through the lobby and down the hallway. A few seconds pass and the side-door opens and slams shut.

What the hell?

I debate chasing after her, but a deep, terrible realization sinks in and I freeze, because this scene is in every horror movie I've ever seen. The killer is closer than I suspected. It always is. The scene. The one where the audience shouts at the screen: "HE'S RIGHT BEHIND YOU, YOU IDIOT. RUN."

The Nightly Disease

I slowly look down and . . .

There's a rattlesnake on the ground between my legs.

Rising in a curl. Hissing.

Fuck fuck fuck FUUUUUUUUU—

I jump away just as it strikes at my leg, barely missing me. Or does it? Difficult to say. Later tonight I'll have to undress and properly examine my flesh for any red irritations. Where is Kia when I need her?

Successfully dodging the snake, I rush inside the hotel and grab a broom and try brushing it away from the entrance since guests are walking past and it keeps hissing at them.

"Hey!" some drunk piece of shit shouts. "There's a snake out here!"

"Yeah." I nod, because what else am I supposed to do? "There sure is."

"I'm going to complain to management about this!"

I wave at him from across the lobby. "Have a good night."

"Maybe we ought to discuss a refund on my room."

"Sleep tight." I point upstairs, annoyed he isn't taking the hint.

The drunk piece of shit crinkles his brow and shakes his fist at me like an old man in a cartoon. "Well, fuck you and your ugly snake!" He stomps away, toward the elevator, pouting.

Outside, a crowd of guests have surrounded the snake. Cell phone cameras whip out of pockets and flash like a horde of paparazzi. A great temptation to reach out and push them onto the snake attempts to overwhelm me. Let the snake feast. Offer it a meaty sacrifice. Sign the hotel over in the snake's name and let it rule the kingdom.

Before I can decide which guest deserves to be pushed first, the snake retreats behind the trash can next to the entrance. I tell everybody to fuck off and they slowly scatter back to their rooms. According to my phone, there's only one pest control place still open at 11PM and of course they don't deal with snakes. Pussies.

Animal control isn't open, either. Out of options, I call the non-emergency police dispatch. The woman on the line gets super shitty with me and informs me snakes are not a police matter. I ask for suggestions. She suggests I google the issue. So, I google the issue, and Google tells me to call the police.

I debate ignoring the issue and returning to the front desk. If this snake is fated to bite somebody tonight, who am I to get in the way of its destiny? Of course, it's thinking like this that will probably end with my own leg being the one attacked. Maybe when I leave in the morning, or take the trash out. The goddamn thing will be waiting for me, I just know it.

I call Javier and tell him we need to talk about a raise before I even consider fucking around with a rattlesnake. He tells me to call 911. I tell him I already tried the non-emergency number and he says he doesn't give a shit, call 911 directly. So I do. They tell me they can't help. I ask what the fuck am I supposed to do. The lady pauses, then sighs, and tells me to hold on, she's gonna talk to her supervisor. She puts me on hold. A minute passes. The hold music is Smash Mouth's "All Star". She gets back on the line.

"Okay, I just talked to my supervisor."

"And you're going to send somebody out?"

The Nightly Disease

"Only if you call us again. And it won't be to arrest a snake."

"What?"

"Stop bothering us."

"Are you fucking serious?"

"Sir, it's illegal to use a profanity while on the phone with nine-one-one."

"That . . . doesn't seem true."

"Care to test it, asshole?"

The dispatch lady hangs up.

I squeeze the phone in my fist and try to smash it to pieces. Nothing happens. My hand starts hurting after a while. I give up and slide it back in my pocket.

I peek around the trash can. The snake hasn't moved in several minutes. It's just hanging out in the shape of a ball, taking a nap.

I point at the snake like a stern teacher might to a disobedient student. "Hey. Hey, you. No loitering."

The snake does not respond.

"Are you listening to me, you stupid snake? I said *no loitering*. It's against the rules. What, do you want me to call the police? Because I will. I will call the police and they will take you away to snake jail. Is that what you want?"

The smell of tobacco infiltrates my senses and a familiar voice crackles.

"Who the hell you talkin' to, boy?"

I don't have to turn around to know who's behind me. I point at the trash can again. "There's a rattlesnake hiding on the other side."

Hobbs chuckles. "So what."

"So . . . so it's causing a disturbance, that's what."

He pats me on the back and steps next to me. "Ah, rattlers don't mean no harm. They're just as scared of you as you are of it." He leans over the trash can and peers down at the snake for a moment, then straightens his spine and nods. "Now that there's a baby rattler, Eye Sick. Just a little wittle baby. You afraid of a baby?"

"Yes."

"Good, because that sumbitch would tear you apart." He steps back and motions for me to do the same. "The thing with baby rattlers is, they haven't exactly learned how to control the amount of venom they release during a bite. An adult is smart enough to know how much is needed just to stun its victim, but a baby, a baby's dumb as shit, it'll give you everything it's got. It's so goddamn eager to shoot its load, you know? Stay away from that thing, Eye Sick. As much as you annoy the piss out of me, I still need you hanging around for just a while longer."

"I can't just leave it here. It's going to bite a guest."

Hobbs shrugs. "Who gives a shit?"

"If it bites a guest because I left it here, then I lose my job. Who's going to pay for your room then?"

He scratches his chin hair and thinks about it. "I'll be back."

He turns and enters the lobby. Five minutes later he returns with a pistol in his hand. He aims it behind the trash can and tells me to plug my ears, it's about to get loud.

"Wait!" I grab his shoulder. "You can't shoot that here."

He cocks his eyebrow, pistol still aimed at the snake. "Why the hell not?"

"Do you want somebody calling the cops?"

"I don't give a shit about no cops."

"There has to be another way."

The Nightly Disease

"This here is the way, Eye Sick." He refocuses his aim.

"What if the bullet . . . uh, I don't know, like ricochets against the concrete and hits you?" Of course, I secretly hope that's exactly what happens, but I don't know how I would explain his death to the police, especially when it's discovered I've been paying for his room this whole time. Plus, what if the bullet hits me instead?

This time he lowers the pistol. "Won't it just go through the ground? Into, like, the earth or some shit?"

"But what if it doesn't?"

Hobbs looks at the pistol in his hand and sighs. "All right, well shit. You got one of them trash grabber things?"

I run to the maintenance closet and retrieve a grabber and bring it back out front. There's no way in hell I'm touching the thing, so I make Hobbs take it. He notices my fear and laughs.

"Eye Sick, you crack me up sometimes, swear to god."

Standing as far away from the trash can as possible, Hobbs extends the grabber behind it and squeezes the trigger. I watch from a good distance, terrified he might think it's funny to fling the snake in my direction. His arm tenses as he lifts the grabber, and sure enough, he's got the handle wrapped inches below the reptile's head and it's going ape shit, violently lashing its body back and forth, nearly smacking into Hobbs's junk.

Hobbs seems more annoyed than afraid. He points at a tree across the parking lot with his free hand. "Go break off a branch. Something long and thick. Quick."

I hear his words but don't quite understand them. "Wh-what?"

"Goddammit, Eye Sick. I ain't gonna hold this ugly sumbitch all night. Move."

I head to the tree and snap off a branch and meet Hobbs in the grass next to the hotel. I wonder if the phone's ringing at the front desk, if anyone's looking out their windows watching this whole scene transpire.

Hobbs lays the snake down in the grass and keeps it trapped with the grabber still clenched below its head. He takes the tree branch from my shaking grasp and presses it against its head and pushes down and twists the branch back and forth until it's been successfully decapitated. He tosses the stick aside and picks up the head with one hand and carries the body with the grabber. The snake's body continues lashing out, trying to bite Hobbs despite its sudden lack of a head. He drops it in the flower bed in front of the building and gives me back the grabber.

"There. You fuckin' happy now?"

"What are you going to do with its head?"

He holds it up like it's a trophy. "Funny thing about rattlesnakes. Even when you cut their heads off, they still got some venom in their fangs. You get poked with it and you're in deep shit." He grins. "Maybe I ought to hold on to it awhile. You try to cross me, any stupid shit like that, and I stick it on your little pecker. What do you think about that?"

"Well." I clear my throat and step back, tightening my fist around the grabber. "I'm not too fond of that idea."

"Guess you better not piss me off, huh?"

I open my mouth to answer but something nearby

makes a strange animal noise and before any of us can react, some kind of flying beast swoops past us and grabs the rattlesnake's decapitated head from Hobbs's hand. We watch it fly away, speechless.

Eventually Hobbs says, "Was that a fucking owl?"

#306

A list of some of the things guests have forgotten in their rooms: cell phone chargers, cell phones, headphones, wallets, money clips, jewelry, hats, pants, shirts, jackets, bandannas, underwear, socks, shoes, unopened and opened bottles of liquor, unused and used condoms, blocks of cheese, unscratched lottery tickets, pills, weed, cocaine, meth, heroin, Twinkies, switchblades, butterfly knives, steak knives, cloves of garlic, silver bullets, crucifixes, bags of salt, bags of fat, bags of hair, and—perhaps the strangest item commonly left behind—handguns.

Out of everything, I've yet to grasp how a guest can forget they've brought a gun with them to the hotel. I try to imagine myself staying in a hotel room, a gun in my drawer. I've never owned a gun much less held one before, but surely it's not a typical possession. Someone checks into a hotel room with their gun, that gun is gonna be all they're thinking about. It's not something you just forget. Yet it happens, over and over. Maybe it's a Texas thing. Maybe it's a human thing.

The Nightly Disease

So when a platinum member calls a little after two in the morning and informs me he forgot a very personal item in his room, I'm thinking handgun, I'm thinking here's another rich conservative Texan who's too busy measuring his own dick to keep track of shiny metal toys with the power to steal life.

"Uh, yes," the platinum member says, "so the thing is, I'm already two hours' away from the hotel, and I simply don't have the time in my schedule to turn around and come get it. As it is, I'm probably already going to be late for my meeting in Dallas. But, as you know, I have a reservation every Tuesday at your location."

I've never heard of this guest in my life, but I don't tell him that.

"So I was thinking maybe I could just pick it back up next Tuesday when I return."

"I don't see why that would be a problem."

"Well, okay, so, there is a *slight* problem."

"Yes, sir?"

"The item—as I already said—well, it's personal. Very personal. Not your typical, uh, well, you know."

Yup. Dude left his handgun. "No problem, sir. Quite understandable. Happens all the time."

"It *does*?" The surprise in his expression is perfectly visible despite our two hours' distance apart.

"Sure, sure it does. What we can do is, I'll let housekeeping know, and in the morning they'll collect it and give it to my manager, who'll keep it locked up in her desk until you arrive next week."

"Well for fuck's sake, kid, don't let the *housekeepers* see it. That's why I'm calling *you*."

"I . . . I see?" I'm lying. I don't see at all.

"Do you know what *personal* means, son? It

means . . . well, it means it's personal. *Very* personal. Hell, I don't even want *you* to see it, but I don't see how I have any choice, given my current predicament."

"What would you like me to do, sir?"

The platinum member clears his throat, struggling with his word choice. "I would like you to please, please walk up to my room, collect the . . . the item, and store it somewhere safe that nobody—not even your manager—will see it. And when I return on Tuesday, I would like you to personally give it to me."

Maybe he doesn't have a permit for the handgun, doesn't want to risk the chance of being busted. Which means there's most likely a rather big tip in it for me. "Sure, sir. I can do that. Where did you leave the item?"

"It's . . . under the bed. Please make sure you use gloves or something. I don't recall washing it off after I last used it."

"Why would you . . . ?"

"You'll also want a decent sized trash bag to store it in. I'd recommend double-bagging it, if not triple-bagging."

"Uh."

"Thank you so much. You don't know how much your discretion and cooperation means to me."

The phone dies. I don't move for five minutes, maybe ten years. Eventually my brain sends a message to my feet to move. I program a keycard for his room, scavenge gloves and trash bags from the kitchen, and hesitantly head upstairs. Why would you clean a handgun? Maybe to wipe his prints off, which means he's done something illegal with it, which means I'm about to become an accessory to some kind of fucked-up crime. Hell, I'm already an accessory to whatever crazy shoe shit Hobbs is doing in his room, so what's another one to the list? At this point, I could start throwing the guests off the roof and it wouldn't make a damn difference.

The platinum member's room is a typical vacant dirty room. Used bath towels on the bathroom tiles. Empty bottles of Shiner overflowing from the small trash bin beneath the desk. Under the bed, he'd said, the item, the very personal item. I already have the gloves on, fearing leaving my fingerprints behind on even the doorknob. I stare at the mattress, unable to move forward, not wanting to see what's underneath and at the same time absolutely wanting to see, wanting nothing more in this world than to see what the platinum guest forgot. If it's a gun, maybe I could plug Hobbs with a few bullets and blame it on the platinum guest.

I step forward once, twice, then the alarm clock on the nightstand begins screaming. I return the scream with my own lungs and flee the room. I'm halfway down the hallway before reality comes snapping back into focus and stops me cold. The alarm clock is still audible even from where I'm standing. Another few minutes of leaving it roaring like that and the front desk phone will start bitching and moaning about being disturbed.

I unplug the alarm clock and silence its screams. Why did the platinum guest set a wake-up call at this time of night, knowing that he'd be out of the hotel at least two hours beforehand? Some kind of sleep-in insurance? An accident? Another hotel mystery that'll never be solved. Add it to the cold-case files.

With the alarm clock DOA, all attention's glued

back onto the bed—and, more importantly, what's hiding beneath it. A handgun, maybe. Or something much more sinister. Like what? Like a heart, a human heart. And the worst part is, I can hear it thumping, beating, somehow still pumping, still alive, still thirsty.

"Fuck you, Poe," I whisper to nobody, and lift the mattress.

No, not a handgun. And not a heart, either.

A black leash.

No, yes, kind of.

A black leash with a giant rubber cock attached to it.

A strap-on harness. I'm looking at a strap-on harness. And it's looking right back at me.

Well now.

After I've finished laughing, I realize I still have to grab the thing, and that helps kill the humor in the situation. Hand trembling, I reach forward like a petty thief scooping up roadkill as part of his community service agreement. I hold in my breath and push the harness into the trash bag. The dildo nearly whacks me in the face as it flops in with the rest of the contraption.

I double-knot the bag and carry it downstairs, arm carefully extended out far enough to avoid the bag from swinging and connecting with my leg. The front desk phone's ringing when I reach the lobby, probably somebody complaining about the alarm clock, or maybe Hobbs needs help stitching together a shoe, or hell, maybe it's my boss inquiring about the many semen-stained windshields out in the parking lot. Except it's none of those.

"Uh, hi, me again," the platinum guest says. "I . . . uh . . . called a few minutes ago?"

"Yes, sir?"

"Did you, uh . . . retrieve the personal item we discussed?"

"I have, yes."

"Okay, great. So, uh, I was thinking."

"Okay."

"I was thinking that maybe it would be best for you to just toss the item in the dumpster, if that's all right."

"Sure, I can do that."

"I was also thinking that maybe I won't be coming back next Tuesday after all, so if you could just cancel the reservation, I'd really appreciate it."

"No problem. Would you like me to reschedule it for a future Tuesday, or just leave it in the air?"

"Uh . . . I . . . uh, I don't see myself ever staying there again, to be honest. I'm sorry."

"It's all right, I understand."

"Don't judge me, son."

"I ain't a judge, sir."

"Just . . . please throw it away."

"I'll try."

Come 7:00, as I'm punching my numbers in at the time clock, Javier's holding up the trash bag, asking who left it on his desk. There's a piece of paper stapled to it that reads "FOR MANAGEMENT'S EYES ONLY".

"It was on your desk when I came in last night," I tell him.

Too impatient to unravel my knots, he rips the side open and pulls the harness out, hand wrapped around the dildo. He holds it for a moment, staring, not sure how to react. Meanwhile, Kevin's standing off to the side, laughing so hard it's a miracle he doesn't collapse.

I'm out of the hotel and jumping into my car as the first scream fills the lobby.

#307

Kia smells like shit and I've never been more
turned-on by an odor. I've spread out a blanket
on the roof and thrown a couple pillows on top.
A lantern sits off to the side, turned on to its
maximum brightness. We haven't spoken of our little
interview session since she stormed off. When she
eventually returned a few days later, we continued on
as if it had never taken place. But since that night,
she's somehow acted even more distant than she
already had been. Something new has been on her
mind, something she obviously wants to spill, but
something's still holding back, something's still
fighting.

She's been asking to see the roof for a few nights
now, and tonight's the first time I've clocked into my
shift with no scheduled reservations in I don't know
how long. She's come to the hotel every other night
for a while now. We talk for a few, then she binges and
purges and gets tired and leaves. Maybe she's using
me for the free food. Maybe she actually likes me. At
least she talks to me and listens to what I have to say.

The Nightly Disease

Up until her, all I've had was George. And there's nothing wrong with George—except for the things that are also wrong with myself—but Kia is different. George and I are too similar. We get together and just poison our livers and bitch about guests. Our conversations are toxic and always leave me in a foul mood. We feed off the teat of cynicism. Or the dick. Whichever sounds more cynical. But with Kia, my brain feels like it's finally being put to use. Like the other night, she started talking about my future at the hotel. "Don't you want to be promoted?" she'd asked, and I laughed.

"Not really."

"Well, why not?"

"I don't know. The hotel industry is just boring, I guess. Everything is so fucking boring. Nobody should ever become an adult. Our minds expire at age twelve."

And she laughed and said, "Cut out that stupid goth high school bullshit, man. Life is only as boring as you make it. If you don't like the hotel, then fuckin' quit. Don't talk about quitting. Actually do it. Figure out what excites you and gun toward it like a goddamn fighter jet."

"I'm not sure anything excites me."

"Dude, all you do is read books. Have you never heard of a professional reviewer? Or an editor? Shit, man, think about it."

I knew she had a point. Part of me wished she'd just shut up, though. Ignorance and bliss and all that. "What about you?" I asked. "What do you do that excites you?"

She'd frowned then, not expecting my attack. "It's far too late for me."

"Now who's being a goth high schooler?"

"There are things about me you don't know, Isaac."

"Well, look what happened last time I asked you about your past."

She'd sighed and said, "Listen, you just have to trust me on some things. I've fucked up too many times in life for a do-over. You, though, there's nothing keeping you here. Get out of here while you still can."

"But what's keeping *you* here?"

"Isaac . . . I'm not going to talk about that."

"The only thing keeping you from talking is yourself."

"That's not fair."

"No. I guess it's not. I'm sorry. You're right. I should leave this job. I should quit and not look back. But . . . I don't know, it's just too reliable I guess. It's routine. If I quit, then what awaits me? Who the hell knows. My future becomes unpredictable, and that terrifies me." Plus, I wanted to add, if I leave, some crazy cowboy will track me down and stick a switchblade up my asshole.

"Maybe terror isn't always bad for you," she'd said.

Then I looked into her eyes, knowing the next words out of my mouth would probably ruin our friendship. "The thought of leaving this hotel freaks me out more than ever, because that means leaving you, and I just can't handle that."

And she'd just stared at me for a moment, teary-eyed, then ran out of the hotel, fleeing to wherever she calls home.

Now here we are on the roof, two days later.

We haven't said much. She knocked on the front

doors, I let her in, she said "hi" and I repeated the same meaningless syllable. I asked if she wanted to see the roof and she nodded.

As I lie on the blanket and stare at the polluted, starless night above us, she says, "So, this is where the magic happens."

"Ha."

"What inspired you to do that up here? The first time, I mean."

"You don't want to hear about that."

"I wouldn't have asked if I didn't want to."

"Seriously?"

"Seriously."

"Well. Okay. Uh. I had gone up on the roof one night because I thought this guy was going to break into a car. I'd noticed him earlier, through the window in the lobby, walking around in the parking lot." I pause, closing my eyes. Why should I tell this girl something so personal when she won't even tell me where she lives? Because I'd tell her anything, of course. Because I am an idiot. "Anyway, I lost sight of him. Odds are he was probably just drunk and couldn't remember where he parked. So after a few minutes of trying to find him from each side of the hotel, I gave up and tried to leave. Except, sometime during my wanderings on the roof, I'd dropped the front desk keys. Which meant I couldn't unlock the door that leads from the roof to the stairway."

"So what," Kia says, "you decided fuck it, if you're gonna go out, you might as well go out jacking it?"

"I was just bored, to be honest. I searched all over this roof for the keys, but even with the light from my cell phone it was a lost cause. I gave up, figured I'd have to wait it out until daylight broke."

"Couldn't you call your boss?"

"Well, cell phones aren't allowed at work, so I was afraid he'd be an asshole and write me up. I was still pretty new then. Now, if I thought someone was going to break into a guest's car, I wouldn't even give a shit. Not my problem."

"What if someone broke into your car?"

"Then I'd probably kill myself."

"I admire your honesty. But back on topic. You're stuck on the roof. What leads to your hand squeezing your dick?"

"How else was I supposed to pass the time?"

"You raise a good point."

"The fucked-up part of this story, though, is that the keys ended up being in my pocket the whole time."

"Get the hell out of here."

"Seriously."

"How does that even happen?"

"I . . . I am not quite sure."

The laughter that follows travels through the night sky. If the guests can hear her, then they've been given one of the best gifts a pair of ears could ever dream of receiving.

This is the moment. This is when I'm supposed to roll over and kiss her. This is what I've been waiting for since she first walked into the hotel and vomited in the bathroom. This is it.

Then her laughing evolves into crying and she says, "I'm sorry, Isaac, I can't see you anymore."

And the night sky burns red with fire and the hotel begins shaking beneath us and the universe has cracked and I'm stranded at the fault lines, holding on by a single trembling pinky finger. Let it swallow

The Nightly Disease

us. Let it consume us and shit us out into beautiful nothingness. Let it create us and let it erase us. Let it be our own personal apocalypse.

"Why?" I ask, although a thousand plausible answers flash through my mind like a dying film projector. I'm too fat. I'm too young. I smell. I obsess over owls. I'm creepy. I'm clingy. I'm a pussy. I ask too many questions. All I do is read books. I drink and masturbate too much. My dick is too small. Wait, *has* she seen my dick? Of course she has. If she's watched me masturbate then she's seen my dick—or *lack* of a dick, at least.

"It's complicated," she finally says. "It has nothing to do with you personally, I promise."

"Then why?"

"It's just . . . I'm not in my right head these days. I can't trust myself. I need to get right."

"There's nothing wrong with you, Kia. You're perfect just the way you are."

She laughs through her tears. "What did I tell you about sucking Hallmark's cock? You gotta cradle the balls, too."

"I'm serious."

"Me too. We can't see each other anymore."

"Please—" I reach out and she slaps my hand away.

"Isaac, I have a child."

"What?"

"I'm a mother."

"That's okay. There's nothing shameful about that."

"No, man, it's not okay. It's not okay *at all*. I should be with my kid, not raiding hotels all night and purging. I'm too fucked-up in the head. This shit needs to change." I try to argue, but she shushes me. "I'm sorry, Isaac. I should have never came here."

She leans forward and kisses me. Her breath smells terrible. I grow instantly hard despite my tears.

Then she stands up. "Please, do yourself a favor and quit this fucking job before it kills you."

And she leaves.

Well, she tries to, at least. The exit won't open without my key. I let her back inside the building then lie down on the roof again, crying harder now that I'm alone.

Somewhere, an owl hoots.

Part Four

Eye Sick

#400

George pounds on the front doors and I've never been more relieved to see him in my life. It's been twelve years since Kia walked away from me and in that gap I've successfully ditched all remaining sanity out on the curb. Or maybe it's only been twelve seconds. Time means nothing.

When I let him inside, he takes one look at me and says, "Dude, you look like shit."

"Thanks, man, you too!" I clap him on the back and lead him through the lobby. "I'm so glad you stopped by. You're just in time for key packet jenga."

"Uh, what?"

"Hotel olympics! It's the next best thing since the automatic wake-up call."

In the back office, I show him the stack of key packets towering from the carpet to the height of my abdomen. It'd taken me two hours to get them to balance. I gesture to the stack and laugh. "Key packet jenga!"

Saying the word "key" is as painful as slamming the register against my scrotum. One syllable, one vowel away from breaking my heart all over again.

"Key packet jen—?"

"Shhh." I press a finger to his lips and he slaps my hand. "It's my turn to perform."

I approach the tower and kneel down, carefully inspecting every possible strategy. Once I determine the best packet to grab, I reach up and immediately knock down the tower. I collapse to my knees and throw a temper tantrum.

George grabs my shoulders and forces me into one of the desk chairs. "You gotta calm down, dude. You're acting crazy."

"That's what the owls want you to think."

"What?"

"I don't know. I'm too tired to know. Always so goddamn fucking tired."

"Wait. Have you been neglecting your naps? Not even joking. Night auditors are required by law to nap at least one hour per eight-hour shift. Otherwise they lose their shit, as you clearly have."

"I miss her, George. I really miss her."

"Miss *who*? The throw-up girl?"

"I think I love her."

"Oh Jesus fucking Christ. You gotta forget about her, man. Move on until some other succubus scuttles along and deep-throats your soul."

I feel like crying again, so I get up and move around. Harder for the tears to reach lift-off. "I don't know how to move on. All I do all night is stand at the front desk staring at the entrance, waiting for her to show back up. But she's not going to. She's gone."

"I'm sorry. Shit sucks. I know. But look on the bright side."

"What's that?"

"I brought whiskey."

The Nightly Disease

He busts out his flask and we continue the inaugural session of hotel olympics. After the complete disaster of key packet jenga, we move on to Russian Roulette, which involves seeing who can get the closest to the front entrance before triggering the motion sensors, then the plate toss, which is exactly how it sounds, then the great throw-a-pen-into-a-cup game, and finally we conclude with our main event: the luggage cart races. We bring two luggage carts to the fifth floor and begin at opposite ends of the hallway. We both take off at the same time, riding the luggage carts like skateboards and meeting in the center. We click the elevator buttons and wait for one of them to arrive. It's a fight for us both to squeeze inside, as we attempt to push each other out. Eventually we realize the door is never going to fucking close if we keep interrupting the sensors. It's a long ride from the fifth to the first floor. We spend the way down sweating and panting, because we're fat bastards who haven't exercised since grade school P.E. class. I'm the first out of the elevator once we hit the ground floor and I ride the luggage cart around the hallway and into the lobby, then stop in my tracks at the sight of a line of guests waiting at the front desk. How did they even get inside? I smile and wave and George smashes into me with his own luggage cart. We fly over the lobby furniture, laughing and cursing. The guests just stand there, staring at us like we're all a part of some bad dream. And we are. But the thing is, none of us are ever going to wake up again. But the thing is, that's perfectly okay.

#401

I'm spreading cream cheese on a bagel when something pounds against the front doors. It's loud enough to hear across the hotel, in the kitchen. Rapid pace, like someone furiously knocking on the glass. Maybe Kia's returned after realizing she loves me and wants to grow old together. She's come to rescue me from this wicked place and run away. No more Hobbs. No more sleep deprivation. No more bad coffee.

I set down a serving of cream cheese and jog across the lobby, instantly running out of breath. A guest stands outside, his back to the hotel, smacking the locked front door with his fist as he talks with some other guy. A dark expensive looking car is parked next to them with the engine running. I recognize the guest who's knocking as a platinum elite member named Art Yates. I've never seen the other guy in my life, but he looks pissed about something.

They're yelling when I walk outside, cursing and threatening each other.

"What's going on here?" I ask, trying to sound

authoritative and not even coming close. The fight is long out of me. Let these savages kill each other. None of it matters anymore.

"I'll tell you what's going on," Yates says, pointing at the other guy. "Your fucking luggage boy here is praying to get his ass whooped."

The other guy, resembling a skeleton with leprosy, laughs. "I doubt you've ever been in a fight your entire life, Pops."

"Um, he's not our luggage boy," I say.

Yates screws up his face. "What?" He looks at the stranger. "You don't work here?"

He shrugs, laughing. "Not exactly, man."

"Well, then fuck you kindly."

The stranger raises his hands, preventing Yates from entering his car. "But that don't mean I don't deserve no tip, right? I helped you with your bags and shit, right?"

"Yeah, and I already thanked you, now back away before I call the police."

"What's the matter with you, huh? You can't afford to tip people who help you, now? Spent all that rich white-boy money on this stupid-ass car?"

He kicks the bumper of the car and Yates gasps. "For your information, if I so chose, I could tip you quite handsomely right now, but I do not choose, and I will never choose. Gratuity is a fairy tale invented by welfare babies."

Both the stranger and myself just stand and stare at Yates for a moment, at a loss for words. Then the stranger says, "I'm gonna pretend I didn't just hear all that, and instead go ahead and take my tip." He bends down and unzips one of Yates's bags and searches through its contents.

Max Booth III

"Release my belongings, nigger," Yates says, and attempts to punch the stranger. He doesn't even come close to connecting.

I stand aside watching the fight unfold in slow motion, unable to act, frozen on the sidewalk. The stranger tackles Yates to the ground and strikes him repeatedly in the face. Something eventually rewires in my brain and mobility returns. I push the guy off Yates and tell him to fuck off, reaching for the mobile hotel phone in my pocket.

"What the shit is wrong with you?" the stranger says. "John said you were cool. Fuck."

I pause, holding the phone but not dialing. Yates cries on the sidewalk, holding his bloody face. "What are you talking about?" I ask. "John who?"

"You know who the fuck who. He set this up. Told me to help guests with their bags, collect tips. Shit, man. Don't you know nothing?"

"I have nothing to do with this."

"Bullshit you don't," he says, and kicks Yate as he attempts to stand up. "He told me you and him have a deal worked out."

I return the mobile phone to my pocket, too tired and stressed to concentrate. Yates remains on the ground, saying nigger this, nigger that. The stranger's kicks serves as a backup vocal to Yates's bigotry.

I scan the front of the hotel, then the lobby. Nobody's noticed the fight yet. We are still nonexistent. But it won't last. We could keep standing here and get noticed and surrender as everything goes to hell, or I could take action, actually do something for once.

This guy, this pedestrial scam artist, he obviously doesn't know much more than I do. Just another

The Nightly Disease

pawn owned by Hobbs and the cowboy, although I doubt Hobbs has much say-so on anything important.

It's all the cowboy.

"You're all gonna fuckin' fry," Yates says.

I rub my eyes, hoping it'll wake me up, but it doesn't, because this kind of sleep you don't wake up from. "Shit," I say, and nod toward the lobby. "Bring him inside, hurry up."

We each grab one of Yates's arms and drag him back in the hotel, then down the hallway toward Hobbs's room. Yates starts to scream, and this time I'm the one who speaks up. "The louder you are, the worst it's going to be," I say, not sure if the words coming out of my mouth actually belong to me. Sometimes walkie-talkies accidentally stumble upon the wrong channel. Signals cross.

We throw him in the elevator and ride to the second floor, then knock on room 209. Nobody answers, so I knock harder, louder.

"Be careful, man," the stranger says. "People can get fucking paranoid when they sew. Don't want him thinking we're the feds or some shit and get a few holes in our faces."

I cock my head, face screwed up. "Did you just say 'sew'?"

The door opens slightly and Hobbs sticks his head out, eyes wide and bloodshot. "What the fuck do you want?"

"Yo, John, we got ourselves a situation here," the stranger says.

Hobbs eyes Yates. "Who's he?"

"The situation," he says, and pushes Yates inside the room. There's a brief moment where I'm the only one standing out in the hallway, then I'm dragged inside, directly into the fire.

#402

"**I**f we're going to kill him, it can't be in here," Hobbs says. "You try getting bloodstains out of Nikes. It's fuckin' impossible."

Yates goes wide-eyed and squirms. Hobbs hits him until he quiets down. I remain standing by the now closed door, trying my best to understand what I'm seeing in the room. I had expected glass canisters and other lab equipment shit. Basically anything out of *Breaking Bad*. Instead, the room is littered with hundreds, maybe even thousands of sneakers.

"What do you want me to do then?" the stranger asks, whose name turns out to be Leo.

"Jesus Christ," I say, stepping forward. "You guys can't seriously kill him. Come on now."

Hobbs glances at Yates, then at a wall of sneakers, then back at Yates. He shakes his head. "He's seen far too much."

"I won't say anything, I swear, please," Yates says.

"He called me a nigger," Leo says.

Hobbs shrugs. "Well, you are one."

"Man, fuck the both of you."

194

The Nightly Disease

"I'm sorry, I'm so sorry, I didn't mean any of it."

"What are we going to do?" Leo asks.

"Just let him go. He won't tell," I say. "C'mon, you guys have scared the shit out of him. He's learned his lesson." What that lesson is, I'm not quite sure. Don't be a cheap racist?

Yates sobs. "Yes, I've learned my lesson. I promise. Oh god, please, *please*."

"Maybe you should call your brother," Leo says, and Hobbs looks offended.

"What, you sayin' I can't make decisions without his approval?"

"Nah, man, it ain't like that."

"Then what the fuck is it like?"

Leo shrugs. "I don't know, John. What do you want to do with him?"

John looks at his sewing machine on the desk and at Yates, then back at the sewing machine. He scratches his head and a cloud of dandruff and lice drifts out of his hair, floats to the ceiling and explodes.

Yates continues to beg for his life, but it doesn't seem to faze Hobbs.

"He's seen too much," he says, and Yates screams loud enough to wake up every guest in the hotel. Hobbs tries to kick him to shut him up, but this time Yates is ready. He rolls out of the way, grabs Hobbs's foot, and flings him backward. Hobbs cries out and collapses over the desk, knocking over hammers and other strange looking tools with sharp points.

Yates runs past me and flees the room. Leo chases after him, but he isn't smart enough to move around me and the narrowness of the foyer traps us both.

"Get the fuck out of the way, hotel asshole!"

"I'm trying!"

Max Booth III

Across the room, Hobbs desperately attempts to clean up the shattered sewing machine. "If that motherfucker gets away, I'm killing both of you. That's a goddamn promise."

It's enough motivation to get us to discontinue our reenactment of a *Three Stooges* episode. Out in the hallway, Yates is punching the down button on the elevator, screaming for somebody to help him. Nobody's left their rooms yet, but it's only a matter of time. People do not want to help others in danger, they either want to ignore the issue or film it on their cameras for the world to laugh at.

If we catch Yates, he's a dead man. If I let him get away, I'm the dead man. Unless I escape the hotel with him. We could head to the police station together and give a full statement. Except Hobbs could be gone by the time we get back. What if him and his cowboy brother know where I live? Any one of them could have easily followed me home one morning after work, scoped out my apartment. Or hell, who cares about where I live? They know where I *work*. They know there's no guards, no security cameras. No way in hell I'm an important enough figure of the human race to warrant twenty-four hour surveillance for the rest of my life. If I die, the only person it will affect is the asshole who has to cover my shift until a suitable replacement is recruited from the stack of job applications growing fungus inside Javier's desk.

But still. I can't kill him, and I can't let him die, even if that means further endangering my own life. Fuck. None of this shit would be happening right now if I hadn't gotten drunk with George. Whoever mugged me better be enjoying themselves. Of course they are. They're $4500 richer.

The Nightly Disease

Leo's already on top of Yates, punching him in the face, making him scream louder, the dumbass. I rush them and push Leo off. "C'mon, man, you can't *do this* here."

The door to room #210 opens and a woman sticks her face out. "What's going on out here? Do you need the police?"

I freeze. We're busted. Caught by a grouchy guest before I'm given the chance to go to the police myself, now I'm guilty, there's no getting around this. Except I'm the one with the tie, I'm the one with the nametag. I'm the guardian of this hotel. In this building, I am the law.

I hold up my hand, trying to look calming and reassuring as Leo drags Yates down the hallway. "It's okay, ma'am, only a drunk guest having trouble walking. We're just trying to get him to his room."

"He sounds like he's hurt." The woman peeks her head farther out of her room, trying to get a better look at them.

I jump in front of her, smiling. "Yeah, I think he fell, but seriously, we have the situation under control. I do apologize about the noise. I'll be sure to discount your stay for the inconvenience."

The mentioning of a discount is enough for the lady to forget all about the man on the verge of death in the hallway. She smiles weakly, then frowns. "It's the least you can do. Can't even sleep in this miserable place."

She slams the door.

The good thing about hotels, you can do practically whatever you want and the next day all the witnesses leave the state. Well, at the very least, the block.

Leo's dragging Yates through the side-door into the stairway and I have to sprint to catch up with them.

"Leave me alone," Yates begs. He swings his arms to fight Leo off, but Yates is weak and disoriented. His punches are like kitten massages against Leo's chest. "Please. I beg you."

Leo laughs. "Listen to the racist beg the nigger for his life. Ain't that just grand?"

"What are you going to do?" I ask, praying there's nobody else in the stairwell.

"I don't know," Leo says. "I've never killed anybody before."

"Neither have I, so maybe we shouldn't start now?"

Leo looks at me like I'm crazy. "Did you not hear what John said?"

"So what?"

He pauses, contemplating my answer. "He called me a nigger."

"Doesn't mean he should die."

"He doesn't believe in tips."

"I'll tip you!" Yates says. "I'll give you whatever you want, oh god, please, don't kill me."

Leo looks around, obviously out of his element. This guy's no killer, and I certainly am not one, either.

"Well," he says, "what are we supposed to do?"

He releases his grip on Yates, and Yates immediately pushes Leo down the stairs. Leo tumbles down the steps and smacks his head at the bottom of the landing. Yates laughs and extends his middle fingers. "Fuck you, nigger!"

Leo groans and gives Yates a death glare. Yates turns around and bolts up the steps toward the third floor.

The Nightly Disease

"Follow that motherfucker!" Leo screams, struggling to stand.

I run after Yates. He sees me coming and cries, continues running up the stairs instead of entering one of the hallways. Maybe he doesn't realize this hotel's only five stories, but he eventually reaches the door to the roof. He tries to open it, but it's locked, so he punches the metal and curses.

Gasping, I near in on him, thinking fuck, I gotta lose weight. "You idiot, I'm trying to help you."

"Help me?" Yates says. "You were going to *kill* me."

"Ugh. Shut up. Move." I pull out my cashier keys and unlock the door, push Yates out onto the roof and close the door behind us. It automatically locks once it's shut, trapping us in pitch blackness. Up here on the roof, there are no lights. I hold my hand out in front of my face and I see nothing. "Why the hell did you run *up* the stairs, anyway? You dumbass."

"Where else was I supposed to go?" Yates asks in the darkness. "You and that *nigger* were planning my death."

"If you had stopped and listened, I'd talked him out of the idea, then you went and pushed him. Jesus Christ. Stop using that word."

"What word?"

"You know what word."

"Nigger?"

"Ugh. I should've let him kill you. You're the worst fucking guest in the world."

"Wait until your manager hears about this in the morning. I'll have your job."

"I just saved your life, man."

Yates chuckles. "No, you failed at *ending* my life, you pathetic little man. Now you will face the consequences."

His face lights up about ten feet in front of me. His cell phone.

I ask him what he's doing and he tells me he's calling the police.

"You're going to tell them I helped you, right?" I ask. "That I wasn't the one who tried to hurt you."

Yates raises his eyebrow, amused. "Why would I lie?"

"It's not a lie."

"You are obviously in cahoots with those . . . those *thugs.*"

"It's not like that, man." I step toward him, but he doesn't move. It's too dark, he can't see shit. Maybe a foot or two in front of him thanks to the light of his cell phone.

He doesn't seem intimidated by me, isn't afraid to ridicule. He knows I won't do anything. I'm too much of a coward. I'm not a fighter. I'm not someone who breaks noses or blackens eyes. I'm just the night auditor. I'm nobody.

Yet I step forward again, and this time I'm close enough for him to see me.

A fist bangs on the roof door. Leo shouts for us to open it, that we're both dead, that we're so dead it's not even funny.

Yates gasps and drops his cell phone, and the screen shines up at us from the ground. The stupid motherfucker's checking his text messages.

"I thought you were calling the police."

"I was getting there, Jesus, that's private."

I bend down and pick up the cell phone. He'd been

in the process of composing a text to somebody named Lauren:

Me: "sorry 4 not calling all nite been meeting important clients luv u"

As I read his message, his cell receives a text from somebody else. Someone named Perfect Edge Paper Manufacturer.

Perfect Edge Paper Manufacturer: "already miss that big cock"

Three more messages arrive almost instantaneously:

Perfect Edge Paper Manufacturer: "have you left your hotel yet? :*"

Perfect Edge Paper Manufacturer: "I'm still close by, want 1 more quickie? ;)"

Perfect Edge Paper Manufacturer: "I'M SO WET!!!! ;) ;) :*"

Yates tries to swipe the phone out of my hands, but I'm quicker. I push him back and hold the phone up. His face evolves from angry, to desperate, to complete surrender.

"You don't understand," he says.

"I don't want to understand."

I think about smashing the phone, but it's our only source of light, so I just close out of the text screen and bring up the built-in flashlight app, illuminating the majority of the roof. The reality of being trapped up here with Yates sinks in as he stares at me, trembling, covered in his own blood.

What are we doing?

"Okay," I say. "I'm gonna call the police, but you're going to tell them I tried my best to help you and it's because of me that you even survived the night. Otherwise, I know your name. Thanks to the folio downstairs in the hotel computer, I even know your phone number and address. You fuck with me, and your wife gets a call about Miss Perfect Edge Paper Manufacturer. How's that sound?"

He nods, knowing I've got him, and I can barely hold myself together, because I've never sounded so cool in my life. I can't wait to tell George about this.

Yates holds out his hand for the phone, but before I can give it to him, something screeches from above us. Not just one thing, but many things.

"Ho-ho-hoo hoo hoo."

"What the fuck was that?" Yates asks, and I can't speak, because this isn't real.

"Ho-ho-hoo hoo hoo."

"Ho-ho-hoo hoo hoo."

"You-still-up? Me too."

Shaking, I raise the cell phone up and shine the flashlight on what I already know is flying above us.

Yates gasps. "Holy shit, are those—?"

"Yeah."

"There's so many."

"We gotta get out of here."

"What are they doing?"

I grab his shirt collar and drag him toward the roof door, toward the sound of Leo pounding against steel.

The Nightly Disease

"We can't," Yates says, "that nigger's still there."

For a moment, I forget about the creatures circling above us. Anger takes over and I slam both hands into his chest, pushing him back against an air vent. "Goddammit, man, stop *saying* that."

But he doesn't even seem to register I've pushed him. He's looking up, shaking, and pointing at the sky. "Something's wrong with them. This isn't right."

Then the owls swoop down upon us, maybe two dozen of them, maybe more. They don't touch me, don't even act like I exist. All their attention's targeted on Yates. I back away, feeling my pants grow warm and wet, and shine the flashlight forward. The owls dig their talons into Yates's flesh and peck at his face, then as if he possesses the weight of a feather, they carry him off the roof. All I can do is stand and watch as Yates flies away, screaming and kicking his legs. This can't be happening. This can't be fucking happening.

Maybe he breaks free of their grip. Maybe the owls simply tire of his company. Either way, Yates falls. It's not like in the movies. There's no slow motion special effect as his body drops through the sky, hard and fast. His scream is like a short-lived roar of thunder, barely hatched from his lungs before being silenced by the impact of the ground below.

I sprint across the roof, holding the flashlight out in front of me. I lean over the ledge, searching frantically for his body.

Then I see him, still in the parking lot. Maybe five feet from the actual hotel. There's something strange sticking out of his body and it takes me a moment to realize he's been impaled by a handicap sign.

When I look back up into the sky, the owls are gone.

#403

I run down the stairs with Leo close behind. He isn't chasing me now. Instead, we're racing. There's a corpse outside and we can't afford to let anybody discover it.

"So, what, he just jumped off the roof?" he asks between breaths.

"Basically." Nobody's going to believe a bunch of owls carried him into the sky and dropped him. Including me.

"You fuckin' pushed him, didn't you?"

I try to deny the accusation, but I'm too out of breath to answer, so he laughs and acts like my silence is enough of an answer. In actuality, my fatness has caught up and soaked all oxygen like a sponge. I'm supposed to be living a "sit around all night reading books" lifestyle, not a "run as fast as you can down five stories of stairs toward a corpse out in the parking lot" one.

"Go hide the body," he says. "I'm gonna stop and tell John what's going on. He'll know what to do."

He enters the second floor and I continue to the ground level, then sprint down the hallway. An invisible brick wall stops me dead at the sight of a man in the lobby. There's a pistol strapped to his hip and he's screwing around on his cell phone.

A cop.

Oh shit, he knows. He saw Yates fall from the hotel. But did he see the owls throw him?

Or did he see a hallucinating night auditor push him?

A woman sitting on the lobby furniture claps, laughing hysterically. "You've arrived, you've arrived! Hooray!"

I slowly step forward. "Uh, hi."

"We've come for the orgy," the woman says. "What room is the orgy?"

What the hell?

The cop glares at her. "I already told you to shut the fuck up. I don't like repeating myself."

"Okay, okay, sorry." She sinks back in the chair, looks at me and mouths the word "orgy", then squeezes her breast for emphasis.

The cop sighs and shakes his head, stuffing his cell in his pants pocket. "This lady needs a room for the night. Do you have any available?"

I consider lying and saying we're sold out, but the last thing I need right now is for the police to drive around the hotel and discover Yates. Unless I spill it all and tell him what happened, how a crank addict threw Yates off the roof and forced me to help dispose of the body. Except how do I know he'll believe me? I wouldn't have told the cops anything if he hadn't already been down in the lobby, which makes my whole story suspicious as hell. Shit. This is all screwed. I should have never filled out a job application for this place.

The cop snaps his fingers in front of my face. "Hey, do you have a room or not?"

"Yeah, I got a room."

I move past the cop and the drunk woman, punch in the office code, and join them again, only behind the front desk. The cop looks pissed enough to smash his fist into something and the woman looks drunk and horny enough to fuck lobby furniture. They both stand, leaning against the front desk, waiting.

"So, just the one bed, or . . . ?"

The cop rolls his eyes, like he's insulted for insinuating he'd ever be caught with this lady. "One bed, one night." He turns to the woman. "Give me your license and credit card."

"Fuck you, pig."

He sighs, doesn't say another word, just grabs her purse and dumps her shit out on the front desk.

"Hey!" she says, but the protest is weak.

The cop finds her license and credit card and tosses them at me. "The faster we get her to a room, the better."

I ignore her drunken ramblings and process her information into the system. I make a key packet and hand it back to the cop, along with the lady's cards. The cop pushes the purse and key packet into her chest and tells her to go straight up to her room and wait for her husband to arrive.

"I gotta go to the bathroom first," she says.

"There'll be a bathroom in your room," the cop says, rubbing his temple.

The lady—Tilda Smith, according to her license—looks at me, amazed. "Is that true?"

"Uh, yeah."

The Nightly Disease

"How futuristic." She pauses, staring at the front entrance. "I'm just gonna go smoke first."

"No," the cop says, "you're gonna go up to your room, or I'm going to arrest you."

"But I need a smoke."

"You had a chance to smoke, you chose not to take it. Now go up to your room and do as I said, or I will stop playing these games and just fucking arrest you. All right?"

"Fine, shit, all right."

"Seriously." The cop stares at her like she's a child hovering over a cookie jar. "I'm going to stay at this hotel until your husband gets here. If I see you try to leave, I *will* arrest you. There will be no more chances. I will take you to the station and let you sleep the night in a cell."

Tilda salutes. "Aye, aye." Before she leaves, she winks at me and says, "Give me a call when you find out more about that orgy."

"Okay."

After she's gone, the cop relaxes, rubs his darkened eyes. He's exhausted. Beaten to nothing. Another victim of the perpetual night shift. Another bag of meat shuffling sleep deprivation.

"I swear to God," he says, "that lady is gonna drive me insane."

I don't ask what her deal is, but he tells me anyway. Night auditors are psychiatrists. The lobby is a therapist's recliner, open to invitation.

"To be honest, I'm surprised she could even walk in here. She drank an entire fifth of vodka by herself. Shit, brother, if that was me, I'd be out. Just completely done for, you know?"

"Yeah."

Max Booth III

"It's kind of crazy, actually. She supposedly lives out in Austin, and every month I guess she attends these meetings, I don't know, some kind of bullshit women power kind of meeting. Well, tonight she goes to her meeting like everything's peachy, right? Except she don't come home. Her husband, poor guy, he's worried sick. No idea if she's gotten in a wreck or what. So he calls us, tells us the make and model of what she's driving, etcetera, and who happens to find her car parked on the side of the street in goddamn Omni, of all places? She's sitting behind the wheel, crying, sucking on a bottle like it's her husband's dick. Only maybe if it was his dick, she wouldn't be so screwed up in the head, I don't know."

His words are like acid raining from the sky, only I can't unleash my umbrella.

"I look at a receipt in her car, says she bought the vodka back in Austin, so she's been chugging this bastard for at least an hour, probably longer, driving the whole time. I mean, seriously. How she ain't dead, I don't know. I asked her what was out here in San Antone and she tells me some dumbass psycho bitch nonsense about owls. Says, 'The owls are coming.' I ask her where they at and she just laughs and tries to grab my dick. Crazy, right?"

I can't even nod. I just stare. The hotel disintegrates around us.

"So I take her cell, find her husband's number, give him a call. Dude's pissed. Rightfully so, too. I let him know I'll put her in a hotel until he can make the drive down. I figured she won't find no punishment better than what her man will enforce once he finds her. Because fuck. If that were my girl? Oh man. Oh *man*."

The Nightly Disease

The elevator dings and the doors open. Hobbs and Leo round the corner into the lobby, then freeze at the sight of the cop. The cop nods and backs away, gesturing at the front desk, telling them to go ahead and do their business, he won't get in the way.

I try to speak but end up choking on saliva. I clear my throat and give it another shot. "H-h-how can I help you gentlemen?"

Their mouths remain closed but their eyes scream: *what the fuck what the fuck what the fuck.*

"Was there anything you needed? Wake-up call, candy?"

Slowly catching on, Hobbs shakes his head. "We're just heading out. Thanks."

He grabs Leo's arm and drags him out of the hotel, telling him to shut his mouth and keep moving.

The cop watches them leave and snickers. "Probably off to rob a gas station. Bet you twenty bucks I get a call about those two sometime tonight." He pulls out his cell phone and says, "Hey, I don't suppose you're any good with technology, are you?"

"Uh. I don't know."

He leans over the front desk and pushes his cell phone at me until I take it. "Well, maybe you can help me. Last week I got a new cell phone, then threw my old one in the trash. Except I forgot I had all my crime scene photos still on it. Supposedly, there's like, I don't know, a cloud? And I can find the photos on my new phone. At least, that's what they tell me. I just . . . yeah. Where the hell do you find phone clouds, right?"

The cop looks up, like he's expecting to find the cloud hovering above him. I glance at the phone in my hands. My first thought is, damn, I need to get a new cell. It's easy to forget these kind of things when your life is under constant threat by a deranged shoe counterfeiter. I have no idea what I'm doing, but might as well pretend like I'm giving it a try. I access his photo library and I'm greeted with his most recent pic: a small, erect penis rubbing against a salt shaker. I close out of the photo library and hand it back to him.

"Sorry, I think they're lost forever."

The cop curses and returns the cell to his pocket. "I'm going to get so fired. Shit."

"That sucks."

"I actually enjoy the night shift, believe it or not," he says. "You work the day shift, they start paying attention when you park in the middle of nowhere and nap. Night shift, though? Nobody cares. It's a whole different universe, brother."

"Yeah. I know what you mean."

"Maybe they'll just write me up or something."

"It's possible."

The hotel's silent for a moment, then he sighs. "Well, I'm not waiting here all night. Her husband should be coming soon. Just let him know what room she's in when he arrives. Cool?"

"Sure."

As he walks toward the front door, reality slaps me in the face and I remember there's a corpse outside waiting to be discovered.

"Wait!" I shout, and he jumps, moving his hand to the pistol holstered at his side.

He spins around, not taking the pistol out, but keeping it close enough to draw at a moment's notice. "What?"

"Uh." Shit. Think. *Think.* "I was just going to say, don't drive around the side of the building." I point north. "Some idiot broke a bunch of beer bottles in the parking lot, I was on my way to clean it up when you guys came in. Wouldn't want to slash your tires or anything."

He doesn't respond at first, just studies me, letting me sweat it out. Then he smiles. "Thanks for the heads up, brother."

I watch his car make a U-turn and drive back out the front entrance of the parking lot. He pulls onto the access road and guns it toward the freeway.

Every ounce of me wants to collapse, but somehow I force myself outside, heart pounding.

#404

Yates is still impaled on the handicap parking sign. He lies with his back against the sidewalk, the pole sticking out of his stomach, like the metal's part of his body's architecture. Strips of gore hang from the parking sign, which is now bent and deformed from the impact. The sidewalk is stained with blood and the splat pattern reminds me of a dropped water balloon. Only full of red food coloring instead of water. His eyes are open but there's no life in 'em. Dude is dead.

Hobbs and Leo stand around him, scratching their balls.

"What are you doing?" I ask. "Why are you guys just standing there?"

Hobbs notices I've joined them, and flinches. "You're one hardcore motherfucker, Eye Sick."

"We were hiding until the cop left," Leo says. "What the hell did he want, anyway?"

"Nothing important. Just dropping off some guest."

Leo laughs. "Talk about timing. Goddamn, son."

The Nightly Disease

He looks at Yates again and gags, the humor lost just as quickly as it'd arrived.

I suck in oxygen. "I didn't push him."

Hobbs twitches. "Then how do you explain this?"

"I . . . I don't know."

"Uh-huh."

Leo steps forward, grabs the bloody pole, and attempts to yank it out of the concrete. It doesn't budge. "What are we supposed to do now?"

"Well, we can't just leave him here," Hobbs says. "Someone's bound to notice him eventually. Pigs will come back and question Eye Sick, and he'll crack. Rat us out. Then we'll have to bring out the switchblade, open up his sweet little cheeks."

I think about vomiting, but the thought of lowering my head next to Yates's blood is enough to make me swallow any hint of discharge building up in my throat.

Hobbs walks around the corpse, inspecting the damage. "The way I see it, we have two options. Since the pole ain't coming out of the ground without us making far too much noise than I'm comfortable with, we either gotta cut this poor bastard in half or—"

I groan. "Jesus."

"—or we lift the body, bring him up the way he came down."

"He's pretty fat, man," Leo says. "You think we can do that?"

Hobbs shrugs. "Unless you want to go find a hacksaw, I reckon this is our best bet."

"Shit." Leo kneels and stares at the corpse. "You sure you don't want to call your brother? He's gonna want to know about this."

"My brother ain't got shit to do with this."

"Okay. Just sayin' is all."

"C'mon, let's lift this fat bastard up."

We move forward then all three freeze as music bursts into the night. I recognize the song immediately, but refuse to believe it's real.

It's "Yakety Sax".

I follow the sound of the song and watch as a featureless white van zips through the parking lot. We witness it drive past us in awe, dumbfounded. It circles the hotel three times, blaring "Yakety Sax" through some kind of surround sound.

Then it drives away and the song fades out as the highway eats it up.

"What in the fuck is going on?" Leo asks.

"This hotel is a piece of shit," Hobbs says. "Let's get this over with before they come back."

He motions for us both to help and we surround the corpse. Even with the three of us combining our strength, his body is still nearly impossible to free from the pole. We groan and lift, but progress is slow. His wet innards scrape against the pole and make a repulsive grating noise. Blood spills from his back and soaks into our shoes.

The side door of the hotel opens and closes and we're frozen like deer in headlights. Deer who have recently murdered somebody and are trying their damnedest to dispose of the evidence.

"Is this the orgy?" Tilda Smith asks, planting her ass down on the bench and lighting a cigarette. I peek my head around the corpse in our arms and watch her smoke. She's looking at us, but not in a way that shows she's horrified. Her eyelashes flutter and she smiles and I realize she's more horny than anything.

Hobbs looks at me for advice. I mouth, "She's

drunk," and he seems to relax, as much as someone can relax while holding a corpse impaled with a handicap parking sign.

"Aren't you supposed to stay in your room, ma'am?" I ask.

Tilda laughs. "That pig is a joke. I follow the orders of a higher force. I obey only the owls."

"What?" Leo says. "What the fuck is she talking about?"

"What are you boys doing over there?" Tilda leans forward on the bench. Maybe it's too dark to make out Yates, or maybe she's simply too drunk. Or maybe she notices and doesn't care, maybe the owls already warned her that this would happen. "You start that orgy without me?"

I let go of Yates and step forward, thinking Hobbs and Leo have a good enough grip by themselves. Wrong. The corpse drops back down to the sidewalk. When I glance behind me, I notice there's now a long string of what only looks like melted lasagna cheese hanging from the pole. Leo vomits. Hobbs curses. Tilda doesn't seem fazed. None of this is real. I never showed up for tonight's shift. I'm still at my apartment, sleeping off a drunk. This is just some fucked-up dream, a punishment for not knowing my limit with rum.

"Is that fella okay?" Now Tilda shows concern. She tries to rise off the bench, but only falls back down, laughing and belching. I approach her and take her by the arm.

"C'mon, ma'am, let's get you back to your room."

"Back to the owl room."

"Sure."

"Hoot, hoot. Hoot, hoot."

Max Booth III

I hear her words but I can't ascertain if she's actually saying them. Reality itself is a hallucination. I lead her upstairs and settle her into bed. Somehow she's already trashed the room. She's drawn an owl on the wall with black nail polish. Her bank account will pay dearly for this action, and so will my psyche.

She falls asleep almost immediately and I stand above her, wondering if she's even real. I feel my own face and it's numb. This is not my body. Not my mind. I am an alien marathoning star projections. Rotting my brain on reruns of annihilated galaxies.

Back outside, Hobbs and Leo have gotten Yates off the pole. They throw the corpse in the dumpster across the parking lot. Leo crawls inside and shuffles trash bags around, thoroughly burying the dead hotel guest. Meanwhile, I inspect the pole. The sign is practically destroyed, folded up into a C. The pole itself is slightly bent, but it's also still dripping with intestines, stained with blood. Same goes for the surrounding sidewalk. There may no longer be a corpse here, but there's plenty evidence of *something* shady happening. It wouldn't take a lot of imagination to figure out what, either.

Hobbs and Leo return to the deformed pole and admire the owls' (my) handiwork. All of our clothes are soaked in sweat and blood. We're not even close to being home-free. It's absurd to assume we'll ever be.

I straighten my tie, which now resembles something found hanging in a slaughterhouse. I check my phone. Half an hour 'til Virginia strolls into the building. She's going to be pissed enough I haven't set up breakfast yet. "What now?"

Leo wipes sweat out of his eyes. "That dude's car is still out front, right? We can't just let it sit there.

The Nightly Disease

It'll get towed. When the police figure out he's missing, they'll know he never left the hotel."

Hobbs nods. His face looks like a Halloween mask. "My brother's friends with this mechanic asshole. He'll make the car disappear." He flinches and snaps his head to the sky, terrified. "Wait, shit. The fucking car keys. Are they still in his pocket?"

Leo kicks a rock into the grass. "I ain't going dumpster diving again."

I shake my head, nauseated. "The car was running when you guys started fighting. The keys are still in the ignition."

"Oh, yeah." Leo mouths a silent prayer.

"Smooth thinking, Eye Sick," Hobbs says, then turns to his partner. "You take his car, I'll get in my truck and you follow me. I just hope this asshole is at the shop right now."

"Why don't you call him?" Leo asks.

Hobbs pauses. "My brother has his phone number."

"Dude, I'm telling you, he's gonna get pissed we didn't tell him what happened."

Hobbs grabs Leo by his shirt and pulls him close, eyes wide, nostrils flaring. "And I done told *you*, I can fucking handle myself. You see my brother in that room, busting his ass all goddamn day and night cooking up Jordans? I don't think so. I'm the man here. I get things done. So go get in that asshole's car before I break your fucking skull."

As Leo walks around the hotel, he mumbles, "Fucking psycho."

Hobbs laughs. "Leo thinks I'm dumb and deaf. Well, Eye Sick, I ain't dumb, and I certainly ain't deaf."

"Okay."

He waves to the mess on the sidewalk, to the deformed handicap pole. "You need to clean this shit up while we're gone. And quickly."

"What? How?"

He shrugs. "It ain't my job to clean up blood."

"Well, it's not mine, either."

"Boy, it became your job as soon as you pushed that sorry sumbitch off the roof."

"I didn't—"

"Look, just get the shit cleaned, all right? Otherwise we're *all* going down. You want to be some fat prison bitch?"

"I'm just the night auditor."

Hobbs sneers and looks at me like I'm just some kid who can't handle the incredibly complex concept of potty training. He turns around and heads toward his pickup truck. After he's driven off, I check the time again. Fifteen minutes until Virginia arrives. I wonder if anybody's called the hotel in the past hour or so. Maybe the lobby's full of pissed off guests waiting to slice my throat. I miss Kia.

I rush to the wall and grab the hose, then spray it against the handicap pole. Strips of gore fly off like dandelion seeds in the wind. I redirect the hose's aim to the sidewalk. The puddle of blood spreads against the cement. Some of it flows into the grass. Most of it remains in the cement, drying into its hard surface. Fuck. I keep spraying but the blood is stubborn and refuses to accept the water's friendship. I drop the hose on the sidewalk with the water still running, then sprint back into the hotel, through the lobby. A guest's sitting on the sofa, waiting to check-out.

"There was no receipt under my door."

The Nightly Disease

"I'm terribly sorry, sir. I've been a bit distracted tonight," I say as I print him out a receipt, because it's not like he's going to be emailed one, anyway.

"Son, you look like hell."

I try to laugh but it comes out sounding like a mental patient orgasming. "Those raccoons are vicious."

After he leaves, I run to the kitchen and turn the coffee pot on so Virginia can't say I've done nothing all night and fill a bucket with soapy water, then take the bucket and a sponge outside, through the side door. Walking down the hallway, I tried to convince myself that the blood wasn't as bad as I was making it out. My imagination had lost control. There were maybe a few drops at most. But of course that wasn't true. One step outside the hotel and the reality of the situation is like a bullet to the gut. This is the kind of job Harvey Keitel's character in *Pulp Fiction* would be hired to do. What the hell do I know about cleaning up human remains?

Except I don't really have a choice. It doesn't matter if I know what I'm doing or not. The crime scene either goes away or I go away. I'm far too involved to claim that I'd simply been forced into helping. I'm all alone now, and I'm still not calling the cops. That makes me less of a victim and more of an accessory.

I kneel down and attack the bloody concrete with the sponge. I scrub hard and fast and I don't stop until my arms can no longer move. The bucket is now full of red water and the sidewalk is still as chaotic as it'd been before I introduced the sponge. I check my phone. Virginia has to be here already. People are going to start coming down for breakfast. They're going to have complaints to direct at me about who the hell knows what. There are always complaints. If I still exist, then someone will be pissed.

The hose did nothing and the same for the sponge and soap. How would a person in a movie hide this? They'd probably call one of their friends who just so happened to be skilled in this area. Except the only friend I have is George, and he doesn't know shit. I could call him anyway, see what he thinks. But there's not enough time to explain all the insanity that's unfolded tonight. There might never be enough time. I can't call the police. I can't call George. I can't call Hobbs's brother because a) I don't have his phone number and b) I don't even know his name. Hobbs should have contacted him immediately, Leo was right. Hobbs is a bag of rocks, but his brother on the other hand, he's at least semi-intelligent.

A white car honks at me as it passes and for a moment the world freezes because I just know it's a cop car and now everything is fucked I've been caught I lost my chance to confess now I'm going down with Hobbs and it's all because of the fucking owls—but then the car nears, and it's only the newspaper lady, waving as she moves on the Other Goddamn Hotel. Christ, if she's already made her drop here, then I'm really running out of time. Think, goddammit, *think*.

I can't. So I run. Inside the hotel, I sprint down the hallway. A guest calls for assistance but I ignore him and continue toward the maintenance office on the second floor. I don't know what I'm looking for, but I'm certain the answer to all my problems can be found in this room. This is where you come when you need to fix something. Well, I need to fix something.

In the corner of the office there's multiple cans of

white paint. Maintenance uses them to touch up the walls every once in a while. The rooms age and disintegrate, just as humans and every other unfortunate creation in the universe. I grab a flathead screwdriver and slide it in my front shirt pocket, then pick up two cans of paint and hurry back outside. This time I manage to avoid any customer interaction. I'm too afraid to check the time on my cell phone.

Outside, I lower the cans to the ground and bring out the screwdriver. I lean one can to the side and position the flathead underneath the can's lid, then pop it up, successfully breaking the seal. I continue working the screwdriver until the lid's at least halfway off, then I grab the can with both hands and fling the paint against the abstract puddle of blood staining the sidewalk. It lands like a tsunami crashing over an already obliterated city, splattering against my bloodstained shoes and slacks. In the back of my mind I'm obsessing over how I'm going to explain my horror movie appearance to my shift relief, but it's a minimal concern compared to everything else that's happened tonight. I empty the rest of the first can and do the same with the second one, watching the paint and primer spread over the blood. I save a little bit to pour down the handicap pole as well. It looks stupid as hell, but at least it doesn't resemble a crime scene now. I set out a few CAUTION: WET FLOOR signs around the perimeter. All I need right now is an oblivious guest walking through the wet paint and bringing their half-blood-half-paint footprints into the hotel.

The roaring engine of a garbage truck grumbles from a distance, nearing the hotel. I throw both empty cans of paint into the overflowing dumpster just as the truck rounds the building. I flee from the dumpster and maneuver around the puddle of white paint and collapse on the bench next to the door, trying to catch my breath and relax my heartbeat. I'm overwhelmed with a strange feeling that everything's going to be all right now. Things are working out, in their own fucked-up ways. The sidewalk will still be noticed, and I'll almost definitely be questioned by management, but at least they won't be asking why the parking lot looks like the film set of the latest Eli Roth production. Instead, they'll be more curious why I randomly dumped two perfectly good cans of paint on the sidewalk. Plus, what happened to the handicap sign? As long as they never ask "What happened to Mr. Yates?" I should be able to cope. But of course the question will come up. A person doesn't go missing without anyone eventually noticing.

The garbage truck grinds its loud, hungry teeth into the dumpster and heaves it up like a drunk chugging a beer, emptying the dumpster's contents into the truck's greedy stomach. As expected, stray trash bags and cardboard boxes spill out the sides of the truck and splatter in the parking lot. One hundred eighteen rooms in this hotel, perpetually producing garbage.

The truck lowers the dumpster to the ground, backs up, and continues its journey through the parking lot toward the next dumpster awaiting to be eaten. As it passes me on the bench, the corpse of Mr. Yates waves at me as it hangs over the edge of the truck, one foot caught in its mouth, the rest of his body bouncing off the siding. As the truck turns onto the main road, Yates's foot releases from the crusher and he drops, landing in the entrance of the parking lot. The truck continues down the road, as if everything's perfectly okay in the world and it hasn't just ruined my fucking life.

It takes a minute or two for me to find the strength to open my eyes. My face becomes stuck in this expression of pure terror, the kind of horrified look you get when you're going seventy miles per hour down a two hundred foot, ninety degree rollercoaster drop. Except instead of falling, I'm just standing next to the hotel, staring at the corpse of Mr. Yates laying out in the open for the whole world to witness. I'm convinced a thousand spectators are circling around the body, just out of eyesight. The police are already on their way. Hobbs and Leo aren't going to return. In fact, they never existed. I made them up to conceal the reality of my insanity. I hallucinate shoe counterfeiters and owls to numb my own murderous desires.

I haul ass to the front of the hotel, covered in blood and paint. I look less like a night auditor and more like a distant relative of Leatherface. My car is boxed in under the awning by the shuttle van and a random jeep. Some jackass is in the lobby bouncing up and down. Probably the jeep's driver. The anger on his face is like grease in a pan of fried bacon. My relief will be in soon. She can deal with the guy. I rush into the foyer of the hotel, grab a luggage cart, and pause. Someone's gonna notice a dead guy on a luggage cart. Hell, someone's probably already noticed a dead guy in the street. I ignore the jeep driver's protests as I rush past him and slide over the front desk. I collect a couple sheets from the laundry room and exit through the side door, avoiding the jeep driver as I retrieve the luggage cart again and I sprint around the hotel.

Yates still hasn't moved. I guess a part of me was hoping he wasn't actually dead, he'd just been knocked unconscious, and any second he'd stand up and walk it off.

But he's no longer alone. A car has parked next to his corpse and a lady's gotten out. She's standing above it, crying. I pick up my pace, my chest on fire. Gotta start exercising more. Fuck.

"Miss!" I shout.

She looks up from the corpse and stares at me. "He's dead! This man is dead!"

I shake my head, trying to act reassuring, when I realize my entire body is shaking, not just my head. "He's badly hurt, but he's not dead. He's gonna be okay."

"He isn't moving. I gotta call the police. He needs an ambulance, for Christ's sake. Just look at him."

"Ma'am, I am fully aware of how he looks. And I've already called. An ambulance should be here any moment."

She exhales, calming down. Then she steals another glance at the corpse and squeals. "What happened to him?"

"He got a little too drunk and fell off the curb."

"That's it?"

I nod. "Looks worse than it is, I promise."

"I'll stay here with you, make sure he's okay. God, I've never seen anything like this."

"No, no, I can't let you do that. The police instructed me to wheel his body into the hotel, so he'll be safe and sound inside."

"I thought you weren't supposed to move the body. Like, isn't there a risk of causing a spinal injury or something?"

The Nightly Disease

"Trust me, ma'am. Everything is taken care of. Please get back in your car and continue on with your day. Thank you for helping as much as you have."

She hesitates, looking at the body, then at her car, then the body again, then me. "You sure he isn't dead?"

I force a laugh. "It's gonna take a lot more than a lousy fall to kill old Mr. . . . . Johnson, here."

She exhales. "Well, all right. I just hope he's okay, is all."

"He'll be fine in no time. Have a good day, ma'am."

"You too."

After she drives away, I wrap Yates in three layers of bed sheets and drag his corpse onto the luggage cart. It feels like a million eyes are on me as I push the cart around the hotel. Every window is occupied by a guest, witnessing my descent into hell.

I'm five feet from my car when a man steps in front of me, his eyes glued on Yates's corpse.

"What is that, a dead body?" he asks.

"Uh."

He laughs and looks up at me. "I'm here to pick up my drunk crazy wife."

"What?"

"A cop dropped her off here last night, right? She got drunk and went on a little road trip."

"Oh, yeah. She's in her room."

"You mind telling me where that might be?"

I tell him.

"Thanks." Before he walks away, he glances once more at the corpse. "Your, uh, luggage is bleeding."

"It does that, sometimes."

Once my trunk is popped, I let out a loud, pained

groan as I lift Yates inside. I lock up my car and return the luggage cart to the foyer, then stumble into the now empty lobby. Behind the front desk, the on-hold function is still beeping on the phone. I don't remember putting anyone on hold, but a lot of shit's gone down in the past couple hours, so who knows what else I've forgotten. I take it off hold and apologize for the wait.

"It's all right, dear," the woman on the other end says.

"How may I help you?" I ask, staring at my hand. It's covered in blood and dirt and paint. I wonder if my face looks the same.

"I was just wondering if your hotel offered adult films to rent on pay-per-view."

"You waited on hold all this time just to ask that?"

"I'm very lonely."

"We don't. I'm sorry."

"Aww."

I hang up just as my relief comes in. Fortunately, it's Yas and not Javier.

"What the hell happened to you, Isaac?"

I drop the register keys on the front desk and shrug. "It's been a long night."

I leave the hotel without closing my shift. I'm not even sure if I ran the audit last night. Did I print out the receipts? Who cares. None of it matters. Nothing is important when there's a corpse in the trunk of your car. Everything is just TV static you can't mute fast enough.

I drive away from the hotel wondering how long it takes before a dead body begins to smell.

I turn on the radio and "Yakety Sax" blares out of the speakers.

#405

I desperately scan through the dozens of gangster movies I watched growing up. If Joe Pesci was here, he'd direct me to an already dug hole out in the desert. But shit, this is San Antonio. I'm not driving five hours out to the Chihuahuan Desert when the hole is yet to be dug. *Casino* made a smart point: who knew how many more hours I'd end up digging before the job was done? Besides, I'm not a killer. I did not throw Yates off the roof. I'll keep repeating it until it starts to sound like the truth. It might not sink in until I'm bouncing off the walls of a padded cell, tongue half-chewed off. Owls picked him up and dropped him from the clouds.

If the desert's out of the question, then what? I don't know a Mr. Wolf and I certainly don't own a wood chipper. How much *are* wood chippers, anyway? Christ, the mess that would make. I'd never get back my deposit. I could just leave Yates in the trunk and drive it into a lake, except then I'm out of a car, and besides, what's to stop the car from floating back up above the surface sometime in the future?

Cops take one look at the registration and I'm fucked. Unless I'm already in the car, blue and bloated. At least then I'm fucked on my own terms. If I'm dead, can I even comprehend the idea of being fucked? I guess if a necrophiliac happened to discover me . . . hey, thinking of things to do with a dead body! Yeah, no, that's wrong. I'm a piece of shit. How did this happen? How did a corpse end up in my trunk?

"Because you pushed him off the roof, you sadistic motherfucker," an owl says from the passenger seat. Somehow, I already know his name is Owlbert.

I scream and swerve the car, struggling to reclaim control of the steering wheel.

Next to him, another owl probably named Chowls says, "You better keep your eyes on the road, buddy, or you're gonna have a few more bodies to add to that trunk."

"And there was barely enough room to fit the one!" Owlbert laughs. "Imagine another dozen!"

"You guys aren't real. Owls can't talk."

"Then what the fuck is it do you think we're doing?" Owlbert asks.

"You're just figments of my imagination."

"Hey," Chowls says, "maybe you're *our* imagination, asshole."

I grip the steering wheel tighter. I don't know where I'm driving. If I stop, everything becomes real again.

"You know," Owlbert says, "you could always just chop that old fucker up and bake him into some scrumptious meat pies."

Chowls sighs fondly. "*Sweeney Todd* is my favorite musical. So bloody, so pretty."

"Oh, wait, wait," Owlbert says. "Shit, you work at

a hotel. *Barton Fink* it the fuck up! Cut off the guy's head and carry it around with you in a box. Embrace your inner Madman Mundt."

"*What's in the box?*" Chowls squeaks. "*What's in the box? Oh God, what's in the box?*"

"No, that's from *Seven,* dumbass."

"Well," Chowls says, "what about *Seven* then?"

"What about it?"

"How did the killer dispose of his victims?"

"He didn't, he left them out for the police to find. Then he turned himself in."

"Oh. How thoughtful."

"Which is precisely what Isaac is attempting *not* to do."

"I thought that movie was called *Sesevenen.*"

"What the fuck did you just say?"

I clear my throat. "What if I just melted them? Poured some hydrofluoric acid in a bathtub, like in *Breaking Bad.*"

Owlbert shakes his tiny head, disgusted. "Obviously you know that idea is a turd and a half, considering the acid ended up melting through the tub."

"Actually," Chowls says, "they tried that out on *Mythbusters* and it didn't eat through the tub. Turns out Vince Gilligan is a fraud."

"Well fuck me sideways," Owlbert says.

"Why don't we do what they did to Jimmy Hoffa?"

"No one knows what *they* did to Jimmy Hoffa."

"Exactly."

"How is it possible to be so fucking stupid?"

"I'm not hearing any brilliant ideas from *you,*" Chowls says.

"Maybe we could slice him up and—"

"We already suggested *Sweeney Todd*."

"—*and* tie the body parts to balloon strings, then, just . . . let the sky eat them, or something."

"Is that from *Up*?"

"Close, but not even. I'm thinking of this weird Polish flick called *How to Get Rid of Cellulite*."

"Ah."

I slam on the brakes and scream, "Will you two shut the fuck up? You're *owls*. You can't watch movies, so fucking *stop it*."

The passenger seat is empty. The car is silent. I look through the rearview mirror, anticipating a collision caused from stopping suddenly in the middle of the road, but I'm not even in the road. I'm parked in front of my apartment.

I sit behind the wheel, listening to the static of my own rotting brain. If I get up, then I have to take action. But if I keep sitting here, then I can continue to not exist. If I wasn't covered in blood, I might do just that, but my shirt's beginning to get sticky and who knows how long it's going to take to scrub this shit off.

I enter my apartment and take the most significant shower of my life.

I'm going to die.

I'm going to die.

I'm going to die.

This isn't going to end until I've killed myself.

In the shower I travel through time, back to the days of living in a Super Shitty Hotel. I spent a lot of time in the motel shower, the water hot as Satan's piss, digging my nails furiously into my flesh. I was plagued by the perpetual itch. I scratched and scratched, and of course it did no good. But it didn't matter. At the time, I couldn't stop.

The Nightly Disease

The Mayo Clinic describes obsessive-compulsive disorder as: *"an anxiety disorder characterized by unreasonable thoughts and fears (obsessions) that lead you to do repetitive behaviors (compulsions)."*

Like an addict surrounded by infinite crack, like a bulimic drowning in free waffles, I used to binge big time. The insides of my fingernails were raw and caked with tiny specks of blood. My stomach always on fire. I couldn't stop attacking it with my fingers. The bleeding only made the skin itch more.

Stop imagining blood gushing like a waterfall. These thoughts do nobody any good. This isn't a splatterpunk exploitational TV drama. The truth was, it wasn't much more blood than what you'd get after scratching a dozen mosquito bites. It was enough to send me into full on freak mode, though. Enough to block out all logic and make me go blind with panic—scratching deeper, scratching faster. Jesus Christ, how it itched. Now, standing in the shower of my own apartment, I scratch the scars on my stomach, wondering how much pressure it'd take to reopen them.

I was around fourteen when I first started suffering from obsessive compulsive disorder. I'd been living in motels for a little over a year by then. A room smaller than my old bedroom, housing two beds, one for me and one for my parents. The queen-sized mattress by the window was my only personal space. I looked out that window a lot, sat at the desk and read. Watched TV. My father went to work during the day. My mother stayed "home" every day, unemployed. Sometimes I went for walks, but didn't go too far, considering most of the hotels were right smack in the middle of some lost highway with nowhere to go.

Max Booth III

I remember counting the cracks on the ceiling while lying in bed. I remember listening to the sound the TV made as my mother clicked through each channel, searching for the next great stupid afternoon sitcom to drown our boredom with the laughter of dead people. I remember the rattling the vending machines would make after I'd found enough change in the hallway to buy a pack of Zingers. I remember the poetic sound of cum-soaked tissues softly splashing into toilet water. Everything has a rotation, everything is on its own schedule. My mind zoned in on it all. There was simply nowhere else for it to go.

I counted the seconds ticking by on the alarm clock between our two beds. I counted how many steps it would take to go from my bed to the bathroom, the steps from the door to the ice machine, to the elevator. How long it took the elevator to travel from one floor to the next.

The counting wasn't too bothersome, at first. But then, like most things, it got weird. Whenever I checked the time, I would have to look at the clock, blink, look at it, blink, look at it, blink, and look again before turning my head quickly away. It was either that, or sometimes I would have to look at the clock, turn away, and repeat the action three more times. Everything was always in threes. Sometimes I would have to look at the clock nine times, going three times three. It didn't make any goddamn sense to me but it still made me feel good.

No, "good" isn't the right word. "Complete" is more appropriate. If I didn't obey this strange obsessive command, my whole world would shatter. Everything would feel wrong. I would gain this sense of panic, this consuming dread that something was about to go to shit. I'd feel dirty and awful, and then the itching would kick in. It would be minor at first, and I wouldn't think anything of it and scratch—this, of course, only increased irritation and it didn't stop until I carried out my insane ritual of three. All willpower was out the door, as if a demon had possessed my fingers. They'd dig into my flesh and keep going at it until I put an end to it and gave in. Which I, of course, always did. Although that's what made it worse, what made the OCD continue. The constant fear of this silly superstition I'd somehow convinced myself of believing.

It wasn't just looking at clocks, either. When I closed doors, they had to be shut three times. When I ate food, I'd have to chew in quotients of three. I don't mean I had to chew only three times and then swallow—just that I couldn't swallow without having chewed it at least three or six or nine or twelve times.

I couldn't walk on the right side of anyone. If someone else and I were side-by-side, then I had to be on the left side, or else . . . well, I'm not sure, but I bet something horrible would have happened. And God forbid we were on a sidewalk. I didn't mind the cracks too much, but it was the big open space between the cracks—if I didn't take three steps within each space, then Hell would surely open right below my feet and devour me whole.

It even affected my speech. At certain, seemingly random moments, I would get this, I don't know, this *craving* I guess, to say things three times. Luckily, most of the time I would figure out ways to suppress this without coming off as too weird. Like if someone asked me a question, and I didn't hear them, I'd act all dramatic and over-the-top deaf by going, "What?

What? WHAT DID YOU SAY?" It didn't always make sense of course. Try answering what you want to drink by saying "Coke Zero-Zero-Zero, Coke Zero-Zero-Zero, Coke Zero-Zero-Zero" and you come off as a fucking coked up nutcase.

The Merriam-Webster Dictionary describes insanity as: *"a deranged state of the mind usually occurring as a specific disorder."*

Sometimes, when the TV was off, I would count the moans of my neighbors. In a motel room of silence, there are *always* moans. Sometimes, even, people moan in threes. What heaven these rare moments are, what pure fucking bliss.

Left in a room with nothing to do, you start grasping onto anything that'll accept you. And that's when you enter the bizarre. Sometimes isolation can be angelic, yes, but other times it can be absolute torture. Your mind becomes dependent on things that you've decided matter in the big scheme of things, despite how insignificant they are to reality. Of course they seem silly to everyone else—but to you, it's fucking life or death, man. There is an omniscient force that you create but it becomes so real that it controls you.

You have to do what it tells you to do or else you die.

At least, that was my mindset. Thankfully, as my period of living in motels ended, so did my OCD. It didn't go away *like that*, but over time it became a habit I dropped, thanks to new distractions in life, such as being wanted by the police for pretending to shoot all those mimes. But that wasn't my fault, anyway, I just wanted to see how far they would take their act.

The Nightly Disease

And boy, did I get my answer.

The Merriam-Webster Dictionary describes a pathological liar as: *"an individual who habitually tells lies so exaggerated or bizarre that they are suggestive of mental disorder."*

I still can't walk on the right side of somebody, though. I'd rather risk walking on the road and getting hit by a car than going through that kind of hell.

In my apartment, I scrub my flesh harder, thinking about the days I once lived and the days I now live. How much has changed? This isn't my blood washing down my body.

This isn't my blood.

This isn't my blood.

This isn't my blood.

I'm seeing talking owls and I'm smuggling corpses and I'm saying things in threes again and nothing is the way is should be, nothing is the way I want it to be, nothing is the way I need it to be.

Nothing is.

Nothing is.

Nothing is.

#406

"**T**hank you for calling the Goddamn Hotel—no, we don't have any fucking rooms, go kill yourself."

I stand behind the front desk wondering if I actually just said that on the phone or if I dreamed it. Am I awake? Is the hotel even real?

A man storms into the lobby and slams his credit card on the desk. "I need one room."

"I apologize, sir, but we're all booked up tonight."

He literally scoffs. "That cannot be possible."

"Well, I'm afraid it is. It happens quite a bit around this time of year."

"I want to speak to your manager."

"I am the night manager. We do not have any rooms." The truth is, we have plenty of rooms. But fuck this guy. In fact, fuck all human beings.

"Well, where can I go?"

"I'm honestly not sure. The entire town is all booked up tonight."

He slams both hands on the desk, making the impact echo throughout the lobby, and says, "What is a *town?*"

The Nightly Disease

He's practically snarling at me now and it takes all I have in me to resist laughter. "It's, uh, it's like a city," I tell him, "but smaller . . . "

"Ugh, bullshit!" he shouts. "I fucking hate Texas!" He runs out of the hotel and drives away.

Just as the doors begin closing, the cowboy calls down to the front desk and says, "We need to talk," then hangs up. It's the night after Yates's death and I still can't remove the now phantom sensation of blood sticking to my skin. I lock the register and drag myself upstairs, wondering why I'm obeying his orders, wondering why I don't run away, what I'm trying to prove.

Hobbs lets me in and plops down on the bed after maneuvering around his various sewing paraphernalia. The cowboy sits in the corner of the room, at the desk, still wearing the ridiculous straw Stetson. If anyone else was wearing it, I might laugh. But after all the shit that went down last night, the sight of his hat is enough to make my work shirt stick to my spine. Although he doesn't exactly seem pissed. More amused than anything. The smile on his face proves hard to distinguish. Somewhere between "I'm gonna kill this motherfucker" and "I wonder how this night auditor would react if I started juggling fruit".

He waves his hand at the bed, so I sit down next to Hobbs. The springs sink under our weight, sounding like a gunshot through my nerves.

"So," the cowboy says, "John here tells me y'all had quite the time last night."

I lick the roof of my mouth, scavenging for courage. "You could say that."

Hobbs laughs, but with less confidence than when his brother isn't around. "Should've seen him. He turned into a lunatic, threw the motherfucker off the hotel. Fuckin' split down the handicap sign. Reminded me of goddamn *Mortal Kombat*. Talk about a motherfuckin' fatal fatality, shit."

"And you put the body in the dumpster?" the cowboy asks. The question seems open to either of us, yet he's staring at me only. Like he knows something. Like he's caught on to my insanity.

"Yeah," I whisper, "that's right." Except that's not right at all, but who knows how he'd react if he found out the body is currently hanging out at my apartment. What kind of lunatic brings home a corpse? He'd have to kill me on the spot out of fear of me trying to blackmail him and his brother by threatening to show the body to the police.

"Well, I gotta admit," the cowboy says, "I didn't think you had it in you. You've definitely surprised me."

"Last night was bad, real bad," I say. "I can't keep doing stuff like this. I know I stole your brother's wallet and I'm real fucking sorry but I just can't do this anymore. Someone died last night. That's nuts. Don't you think we should just go our separate ways after something like that? Please. What's it going to take to leave me alone?"

The cowboy's smile vanishes. I guess he was hoping I'd kneel down and suck his dick after all those compliments. "Pay us back what you stole, times three, and we'll leave. Until then, you continue entertaining us, or else you'll end up in the dumpster, too."

"I can't afford that kind of money. As it is I'm paying for this room every night so my boss doesn't get suspicious."

"Not my problem, kid. Can't do the time, then don't do the crime. Or at least don't get caught. Right, John?"

Hobbs jerks awake, having nodded off. "Are we gonna kill him now?"

The cowboy laughs. "Not yet, John, not yet."

I rise from the bed. "Can you at least stop having your goons assaulting the guests?"

"What are you talking about?"

"Nothing," Hobbs says. "Ignore him. He's stupid."

The cowboy eyes me. "Did my brother leave something out about last night?"

"I don't know. What did he tell you?"

Hobbs grabs my wrist. "Kid, I will crack your fucking skull open."

"John, shut up," the cowboy says, then returns his full attention on me. "The way I heard it was, you somehow accidentally checked the now dead man into our room here, and he discovered our little counterfeit shoe operation. To take care of the situation, you dragged him up to the room and threw him off."

I laugh and my chest burns. "I didn't check the guy into anything. Some friend of yours named Leo tried to mug him in front of the hotel, then when he wouldn't cooperate, we dragged him up here to your room. John decided he should die. The guest fought back and escaped. I followed him up to the roof. He was scared. He fell off. I never pushed him. I didn't do anything."

Both Hobbs brothers are silent. John's the first one to speak.

"Look, Billy, I'm sorry, okay?"

The cowboy's eyes remain closed when he speaks.

"You brought your shithead friend to our place of operation? And you had him pulling petty shit outside?"

"You don't—"

"Do you have any idea how much shit we'd be in if the cops discovered our little shoe racket in here? Because if you did, you sure as hell wouldn't be socializing with scumbags like Leo."

"Billy, please."

The cowboy clears his throat. "Isaac, I'm going to have to ask you to leave us now. I need to speak to my little brother in private."

I don't need to be told twice. Halfway down the hallway, I can hear Hobbs screaming.

#407

After our talk, things begin spiraling even further into chaos. Maybe Hobbs and his brother feel like now that I've allegedly murdered a guest, they can pressure me into not only paying for their room, but also assisting them with their criminal activities. Before Yates died, they had only sewn shoes at the hotel, which I guess isn't a crime? Hell, I don't know. But now they've grown ballsier and have started selling the shoes at the hotel, too. Knockoff brands, counterfeit Nikes.

I learn the hard way they intend on using me as the go-between when a man covered in dust rings the buzzer outside the front doors. He doesn't look entirely trustworthy, but of course none of the guests at this hotel can really be trusted. He approaches the front desk, eyes full of expectation.

"Good evening, sir. Do you need a room?" I'm out of reservations, so I'm thinking either he's a walk-in or he's here to rob me. At this point, I'm welcoming a robbery.

"I'm here for the presidential suite," the man says, licking his sore-infested lips.

"Uh, I'm sorry, but we don't have a presidential suite. We do have suites, however. Our double queen suite has—"

"No." He raises his hand, cutting me off. He's wearing fingerless cotton gloves. "You're not getting me, man. I'm here for the *presidential suite*. You know what I'm talking about?"

"No . . ."

He grunts. "Goddammit, John told me that was the code word."

"The code word for what?"

He lays out both hands, perhaps holding an imaginary Halloween treat bag. "I'm looking for a new pair of Jordans, man. This *is* the new place, ain't it?"

I eventually come to terms with reality and send him up to room #209. Later on, after the man leaves wearing a new, remarkably clean pair of shoes, Hobbs comes down to the lobby reeking of booze and unwashed genitals. His left eye is black and swollen. "You done did a fine job tonight, Eye Sick. Not sure what my brother told you, but this will be the way things go from now on, ya hear? Customers come to you, you send them to me. But you gotta screen them, all right? If they look like a pig, you send them squealing the other direction."

"I don't want to be involved in this."

"Well, I reckon you should have considered that before snatching a wallet that didn't belong to you."

"How am I supposed to tell if someone's a cop?"

"You'll smell bacon."

"Funny."

"Funny, sure, but also true."

The Nightly Disease

"You know they can't come here on my nights off, right? We'll all get busted if you try pulling this with the girl who works Fridays and Saturdays."

He frowns. "Those are my two best nights to sell."

"I can't switch schedules. Those are the nights she works, and she's not gonna put up with any of this. She even gets a whiff of . . . whatever the hell it is you're doing, and she's calling the cops."

"I don't know how I feel about this, Eye Sick. I thought you were a team player."

"What if I never come up with the money I owe?" I ask, balling my fists. "Are you guys just gonna stay here and torture me forever?"

He appears to think about it for a moment, then nods. "Yeah, I reckon so."

"What if I get fired? What if I quit?"

"You're not gonna quit."

"I might."

"Then we'll probably fuckin' kill you."

"You guys don't even know where I live."

"Or maybe we've just never told you we know where you live." He spits tobacco on the lobby floor. "Like, we could be saving that twist for later down the road, when you try to flake out on us. We show up at your apartment unexpectedly and shove a switchblade up your asshole, something along them lines."

After he leaves I search for Air Jordans on Amazon. The prices range from $200 to $700. Why cook meth when you can sew shoes? I scroll through a list of third-party vendors. It's meant for people selling used products, stuff they no longer want, typically at a slightly cheaper price than what you'd pay for something brand new. Any one of these users could be the Hobbs brothers. Considering how many shoes are stored in room #209, it only makes sense that they'd be selling them online as well as in person. After all, how many degenerates are going to randomly stroll into a hotel hoping to score counterfeit shoes?

Well, at least one person, so far.

I lock up the front desk and escape to the roof and drink a pint of Shiner I'd bought at the gas station before clocking in. I lean against the ledge and drink and stare at the sorry sons of bitches passing by on the highway. This has become my new ritual. I barely even talk to George, although he calls about every other night, wanting to hang out. I'm too embarrassed to approach him. I can't tell him how bad things have gotten over here. He'd just call me a pussy and tell me to man-up or something. "If it were me," he'd say, "I'd beat the shit out of every last one of 'em." Although in reality George is my clone and can't fight to save his life. Hobbs and his brother would break out that baseball bat and kick his ass, and George would be in the same exact situation that I'm in now.

On the roof, I scan the Other Goddamn Hotel for a sighting of George on top of the building. Doubtful, since he almost never explores his own roof alone. He might be afraid of heights, but refuses to admit it, so whenever I want to come here he sucks it up and joins me. The last time we were up here together on my roof, it was Halloween night. We'd each purchased the biggest pumpkin we could find. George went first and pushed it off the ledge. I watched it drop like an anchor. One moment it's on the roof, the next it's exploding next to the swimming pool behind the hotel. The impact sounded like a gunshot and echoed across the parking lot. "Oh shit," George had said, laughing, "you think we woke anybody up?"

"They can sleep when they die!" I screamed, and threw my own pumpkin over the ledge. A second gunshot and everything felt beautiful in the world.

I want to relive that night. I want to go back in time before all the horrible things happened. I want to erase the errors.

The breeze up here is strong and cool and some other night when the weight of the universe isn't collapsing upon me, I might enjoy it. But tonight it's only irritating. I continue drowning my lungs in beer. When the bottle is empty I close my eyes and throw it as hard as I can and wait for the sound of glass shattering, but I hear nothing. No gunshot. Probably overshot it into the trees, or more likely, one of the fucking owls caught it and flew off with it.

I keep my eyes closed and lie down on the roof, shivering and biting my lip. The last time I lied down on the roof was with Kia, back during that brief moment when life felt somewhat meaningful, back before I was evicted from planet delusion. I can't even bring myself to masturbate on the roof anymore. She might be somewhere out there, still watching. Let her find someone new to watch. Let her hurt someone else.

Somewhere below me, another shoe customer might be buzzing the front doors, waiting for me to let him or her in so they can go up and get their fix. Hobbs will wander down to the lobby and discover my absence and get pissed. Maybe he'll bring out his switchblade, maybe he won't do anything. Maybe I don't care.

I fall asleep on the roof, embracing the simplicity of the void.

#408

At the next afternoon meeting, management serves overdone hamburgers and potato salad that tastes just as bad as it smells. I take a bite of each and throw the rest away, then return to my seat off in the corner where I'm least likely to be approached. I can't remember the last time I got a haircut or shaved or showered or changed my clothes. My eyelids tremble as I struggle to force them open. Behind the mask of my face a hive of insects participate in an orgy. A strange hum emits from my throat but I can't figure out why or how to stop it.

Javier takes one look at me and laughs, says, "Oh, Isaac, you're such a goof." I think about inviting him up to the roof and it's real hard to keep my mouth shut, especially since I keep drooling for some reason. Every time the answers to all of the universe's questions comes close to fruition, I nod off for a few seconds and disassemble my train of thought.

Javier's talking about guest survey cards and how housekeeping needs to shape up and soon a little league group will be staying at the hotel and none of it matters, none of it ever matters. The only important words the man has said at one of these meetings were passing on the news of Owl Girl's death, and I haven't forgiven him since. A theory begins to form about the afterlife. Our souls could travel into the nearest owl and possess its body, then we live forever in this feathery carcass. Do owls live forever? Has anyone ever seen a dead one?

Then Javier asks if anyone remembers seeing Mr. Yates checking out last week and the room's volume goes quiet as everybody one-by-one shakes their heads and mumbles "no". Javier's gaze turns to me and I repeat the same response as everyone else.

"Well," Javier says, "Mr. Yates stayed here last week, like he does once a month. However, he seems to be missing. A detective contacted me this morning and asked me to keep her in touch in case I find anything out from you. He was scheduled to check-out last week, but we have no records of him coming to the desk. He was supposed to catch a plane, too, but apparently never arrived. His car is missing from the parking lot, so odds are he left the hotel without an issue. Just, if you remember anything weird about Mr. Yates from last week, anything out of the ordinary, please let me know ASAP."

One of the housekeepers raises her hand. "Do you think he's dead?"

"I have no idea," Javier says. "But if I had to guess, yeah, probably."

I stand up. "Can we go?"

"Where are you off to in such a hurry?"

"I'm rotting. I need to recharge. Need to sleep."

Javier rolls his eyes. "All right, if your beauty sleep is so important to you, fine."

I'm out of the hotel before he can add another smartass comment. Back at the apartment, Yates is still in the closet where I left him. The odor triggers my gag reflexes as soon as I arrive. I light a dozen candles and hang more car fresheners and sit on my mattress and rock back and forth, desperately trying to think of a solution. I can't keep Yates here forever. The smell is eventually going to attract the attention of my neighbors. But what do I do with him?

In the corner of my apartment, Chowls whispers, "Meat pies, meat pies, meat pies . . . "

I close my eyes tighter and wake up at twenty 'til eleven. No time to shower, not that I was going to, anyway. I search my fridge for food. I haven't gone shopping in months. Who can afford food? I'll just eat tonight at the hotel. Pig out on some bagels. Consume an ocean of cereal. I check on Yates before leaving and vomit a little in my mouth. No time to brush my teeth, either.

The 3-11 shift gives me crap as soon as I walk into the hotel. "You're late. I'm sick of always waiting on you."

"So go kill yourself. It's the latest craze."

"You're a psycho. I should report you for harassment." She throws the front desk keys at me before leaving. They bounce off my chest and fall to the floor. I stare at them for a while, contemplating not retrieving them, just leaving them on the carpet, abandoned until the next shift finds them or some hopeless bum hops over the front desk counter and discovers them. But I'm not that far gone yet. I bend down to scoop them up and someone immediately buzzes the front doors. I shove the keys into my pocket and trigger the entrance to open.

The Nightly Disease

A man with bloodshot eyes stumbles forward. A black baseball cap is tilted to the side of his head and his nostrils look raw, like he's been suffering some major allergy attacks. "Hey, what's the rate tonight?"

"One-nineteen, plus tax."

"That's the best you can do?"

I debate giving him the room for free. The energy to haggle with a guest is nonexistent tonight. Instead I nod. "Yes, that's the best."

"How come?"

"Because that is the rate the gods have determined."

"What *gods*?"

"The owl gods."

This answer seems to make sense to him. "Okay, then I'd like to stay tonight on points."

"Sure, but you have to make the reservation online first."

"Why can't you just do it?"

"I don't have access to members' profiles. Only a member can make a points-stay online, while logged into their account."

"This is bullshit. I've stayed at countless Goddamn Hotels that let me pay with my points at the front desk."

"No, you haven't."

"Are you calling me a liar?"

"Yes."

He spits in my face and says, "Fuck you, buddy," and stomps out of the hotel. I rush for a towel and clean the spit off my cheek. It's not the first time someone has spit on me at this job and I doubt it'll be the last. Come to think about it, I've probably contacted a couple STDs from phlegm over my years here, so it's a good thing Kia never had sex with me before abandoning the hotel for good. I am simply not destined for love. At the end of my tunnel the only thing waiting for me is a fresh pile of shit.

I toast some bagels and attempt to eat an apple as I wait, but the apple is disgusting so I drop it in the trash bin. It's a Red Delicious, which is anything but delicious. Pink Ladies, now those I can get behind, and not just because they sound perverted. Unfortunately the hotel is too cheap to dish out on decent fruit—nevertheless decent security, otherwise I wouldn't even be involved in this miserable trainwreck with the Hobbs brothers.

I eat two bagels and use the leftover cream cheese to draw a crude owl on the kitchen wall. To someone else it will probably look like an abstract glob, but to me it clearly resembles the winged beast that goes "hoot" in the night. I think about Mandy 2 and feel sad at the realization that she only got to pet one of those deranged monsters as it was in the process of chewing her face off. And it was more likely a desperate grasp of self-defense than a soft gentle stroke of love. Sometimes I wonder if I'll eventually wake up to an owl planted on my own face and I think, of course I will. It's the only possible outcome to this stupid life that makes any sort of sense.

Guests continue to pour in. I give them keys and send them on their way. My eyes burn and vibrate like rails beneath a subway. This will not end. I am caught in a loop of infinity. 'Round and 'round I go, forever.

"Uh, yes, I would, um, like, um, the presidential suite, please," a woman tells me in the lobby. She's sitting on the sofa looking down at her feet, refusing to make eye contact. I send her to Hobbs's room without hesitation and return to the book I was reading. The less I focus on reality and the more I absorb myself in someone else's fiction, the more likely I am to survive each night. Whichever night it is. My brain can no longer keep track of such trivial details. Seconds and minutes and hours and days and nights and weeks and months and years and centuries, it's all illusions invented by man, cheap parlor tricks to make humanity feel better about the vast nothingness slowly devouring the universe.

A half hour later the woman comes down with Hobbs. She's wearing new, clean shoes that look more expensive than any piece of clothing I've ever purchased. I wonder how much it cost Hobbs to make them. He guides her out of the hotel then sits down on the lobby furniture, belching loudly. He leans back against the sofa and rubs his stomach. "My, my, Eye Sick, my, my. What did you think of that fine piece of ass that just walked out of here?"

"My mind has become separated from the rest of my body. I am a balloon detached from its string."

"That's a weird thing to say, Eye Sick." Hobbs licks his lips. "That little lady comes up to me and says she don't have no cash, but she'd be willing to pay up in other ways. Know what I mean? Now what do you think? Would you have taken her up on that kind of offer?"

"Probably not."

"Yeah, but you're a faggot, though, so of course you wouldn't." He cracks his neck and laughs. "Boy, I tell ya, that gal, now she could suck a mean cock, Jesus Lord Almighty."

"Whatever happened to Brenda?" I ask, knowing I'm about to hit a nerve but unable to stop myself.

Hobbs stops smiling. "Don't you ever fuckin' mention that name to me again. You know shit-all about me, so don't go pretendin' otherwise."

The phone rings. It's room #209. I pick up and say, "Yeah."

"Is my dumbass brother down there still?"

"He is."

"Tell him to get his ass up here right now. We got more orders to package and I have no idea what I'm doing. He's the one who passed Home Ec."

I hang up the phone and ask Hobbs if it's true. "Did you really pass Home Ec?"

He opens his mouth, confused but still attempting to spit out a retort, then gives up and sprints toward the stairwell.

#409

A white Toyota Corolla rolls in at a little past one in the morning and parks in front of the automatic doors. It takes a few minutes, but eventually an elderly man steps out of the car and approaches the front desk. His eyes seem to have a difficult time staying open, and when he speaks he sounds like he's a second away from nodding off.

He wants to know the rate for a room tonight, but the hotel's already sold out. He asks if I'm sure, and I nod, yeah, I'm sure. The man stands there for a few moments in deep contemplation, then asks if he can use the bathroom before he gets back on the road.

I am not a complete monster. Of course he can use the bathroom.

The man stays in the bathroom for a full hour before I start to seriously worry. The man either decided fuck it, he's old and he's gonna sleep wherever the hell he pleases, or he has died. After everything that happened with Yates, I am fucking finished with messing with the dead. I try to pretend the man simply no longer exists, until another hour passes and the man exits the bathroom, yawning. He nods and returns to his car, where he promptly falls asleep.

The man stays asleep until 5:00 A.M. I confront him as he stands outside, sniffling and nodding off against the hotel. I have to shout at him to get his attention. I tell the man I didn't mind him sleeping like that for a few hours, since every hotel in the area is sold out and he obviously couldn't have continued driving in the exhausted state he'd been in, but now it's time to get going.

"Could I stay another few hours?" the man asks, groggy.

"No. I'm sorry."

"Well, I need to at least take a shower first. Where can I do that?"

"I don't know."

"Don't you guys have some sort of guest shower for weary travelers?"

"Nah, only in the rooms. And the rooms are sold-out."

"Shit. Even truck stops have showers."

"This ain't a truck stop, man."

The man sighs. "Okay, well then how about this: I'm gonna need to leave my car here, just for a few hours. I gotta walk down the street and meet up with my sponsor."

"Your sponsor?"

"Yeah. My sponsor's expecting me. I'm already late."

"You can't leave your car here, no."

He sighs again and kicks some gravel. "Okay, fine. I understand. Could I at least use the restroom one last time? Sir, I believe I need to tinkle again."

The Nightly Disease

I can't bring it in me to decline a request with the word "tinkle" involved. As the man uses the restroom, I attend to some spilled trash by the dumpster. When I return inside the lobby, I find the man wandering down the hallway trying to open random guests' doors.

"Hey, man, what the fuck?" I ask him. It's a valid question.

The man spins around, holding his hands up. "Oh, I'm sorry, I'm sorry. I'm very tired, you see. Very tired."

He flees into the restroom before another word can be uttered. He leaves an assortment of random grocery bags on the floor by the sink and locks himself in the stall.

In the stall, he begins snorting.

Loudly.

Over and over, followed by a content sigh.

Ten minutes later, he comes out, sniffling, eyes wide, talking fast.

He asks if I want to hire him to write anything. Apparently he's a writer. Of course he's a fucking writer.

The man tells me that he could write me a resume or a novel or a poetry collection, anything I want, if I have the money.

"I have no money," I tell him.

Defeated, the man grabs his bags and leaves. I follow him outside and watch him get in his car. But instead of leaving, he just sits there. A few minutes pass. He gets out, tells me he lost his cell phone and asks if he can leave his name and address in case somebody finds it.

"Hurry up."

Max Booth III

The man opens the backdoor and digs through the seat. He pulls out a notebook, along with a stack of ancient *Penthouse* magazines. He places the notebook on the trunk, and steadies a pencil against an empty sheet.

Instead of writing anything, though, he asks me what kind of books I like to read.

No, I don't know why I'm still talking to this guy, but here I am, entertaining the insane.

"Crime."

"Crime?" The man turns toward me. "I *love* crime! Have you ever been in a crime?"

"Just the other day, I had to dispose of a dead body."

The man nods. "Wow, now that's something."

He writes down his name, then attempts to follow it up with his address, and repeatedly nods off.

After I wake him up, the man tells me he's written two or three novels, he can't remember anymore. He says it's a shame we hadn't met earlier in life, because we could have partnered up together and ruled the world.

"I agree," I say. "It's a real shame."

The man hands me the sheet of paper and leaves, just as mysteriously as he fucking appeared.

#410

"**S**o you're saying you don't remember seeing Mr. Yates leaving the hotel?" Detective Garcia asks. We're sitting down in the back office, sipping on bad hotel coffee. It's a little after six in the morning. No management yet, but I figured they wouldn't mind if I brought a cop behind the front desk for our discussion. Might be bad business to talk about a missing guest in the middle of the lobby. Although the guest isn't exactly missing. He's stinking up my apartment. The other day my landlord slapped a notice on my door that stated they were getting complaints from my neighbors. If I didn't do something soon, they'd let themselves in and personally investigate the foul odors. But Detective Garcia doesn't know anything about that. At least I hope not.

"That's right," I tell her. "I'm usually very busy in the mornings, handing out guest receipts, taking out the trash, preparing breakfast. It's very likely he just slipped out when I was preoccupied."

My voice sounds calm but my heart's going a mile

a second. I knew someone would eventually question me, but never thought it'd be so soon. The reality sinks in like an anchor. A man is dead and I am partially to blame. Maybe it's all my fault. Maybe there weren't any owls. But maybe there were. There probably were.

"Is Mr. Yates a frequent guest?" Her eyes look baggier than mine. Probably works the same shift as I do and is long overdue for a good nap. We could go to my apartment together and snuggle up on my mattress and sleep until the sun explodes, except she might get curious about what's in my closet. And if she doesn't notice, there's a good chance I'll end up falling in love with her, then she'll abandon me just when I'm starting to believe the feeling's mutual.

I'm too young to be this fucking bitter.

"He stays a week every month or so," I tell the detective. "Something to do with his job, I guess."

"Which is?"

"I forget, to be honest." Seems odd that she doesn't know, either, although she probably does and is just testing to see how much *I* know about him.

"If he stays here so much, then it's safe to assume you've had the occasional conversation with the man. Correct?"

"Not really. I work the graveyard shift, and he was pretty old, so he's usually in bed long before I clock-in."

She narrows her eyes on me and I think, did I say '*was* pretty old'?

"Have you ever seen him with anybody?" she asks.

I start to say 'no' but bite my tongue, remembering the text messages I discovered on his cell phone seconds before the owls tossed him off the roof. An

258

idea forms. "Just his wife," I say, my stomach uneasy with regret.

The detective pauses, clearly caught off-guard. "Mrs. Yates informed me she's never been in Texas, so I don't think that was his wife you've seen."

I force an expression that I hope shows confusion. "Oh . . . "

"Any idea who that might have been?"

"I don't know. They were pretty friendly. I assumed she was his wife."

Detective Garcia shifts her position on the desk chair. She steadies her grip on the pen she's using to take notes. She must be thinking, wow, this fat piece of shit might have something of importance to add, after all.

If only you knew . . .

"Can you describe what this woman looks like, Isaac?"

I struggle, emphasizing the wince my face makes as I attempt to recall some foggy memory. The truth is, Yates could have brought a different girl to the hotel every night, but it doesn't mean I actually noticed. If they're not calling for help, they don't exist. I try to be away from the front desk as much as humanly possible. Hell, the guy could have brought in a dozen clowns and took turns fucking them in the lobby—if they were quiet enough, I wouldn't have known. But still. She wants some kind of answer. I can't give her anything too specific, because if she does track down this girlfriend and she turns out to be a four-foot-three redhead, the detective may have some questions concerning my credibility.

I finally shrug. "Honestly, I don't remember. I think maybe she's blonde, kind of youngish?"

Basically, your common mistress. "It's been a while since I've seen her."

"So you didn't see her last week?"

"No, but that doesn't mean she wasn't here. I don't see a lot of people."

"Mmm hmm."

"Do you think maybe he ran off with this girlfriend? Abandoned his wife?" I'm planting a seed, but my lack of gardening experience is obvious.

She closes her notepad. "Everything's a possibility at this point. If you remember any more details, here's my card." She hands me her card. It's dull and beautiful.

"I'll do that, thank you." I slide the card in my front shirt pocket, thinking the next time she tries to contact me I'll be long gone. Gone from Texas, gone from the U.S. Hello, Mexico. Hello, slightly optimistic bullfighting career. Hello, bottomless bottle of tequila.

Detective Garcia stops at the office door and looks over her shoulder. "Oh, one more thing."

"Yes?"

"What happened to that handicap sign on the side of the hotel? Looks like it took some real damage."

I blink at her, unable to respond. Then my mouth opens and some alien parasite inside me commands my vocal cords to rub together and release a string of syllables. "Deer hit it."

"A deer?"

"Uh, yeah, ran right into it, it was pretty crazy."

"And it just walked away?"

"It was very tough."

"Huh." She turns to the door, then stops again, hand curled around the handle. "You know, it's funny. The other day, I asked your manager about the sign, and he told me a slightly different story."

The Nightly Disease

"Oh yeah?"

Javier, you utter piece of shit, you've ruined everything.

"Yeah, he said a drunk driver crashed into it. Didn't it happen during your shift?" She squints. "I could be misremembering his words."

She isn't misremembering anything and she knows it. I make a face that is universally recognized as "ohhh, oohhh yeah" and say, "No, no, that's true, but you see, what happened was this drunk driver almost hit a deer, but he swerved out of the deer's way and hit the pole."

"Oh. I see."

She's onto my bullshit, but she isn't calling me out on it—just standing there, waiting for me to dig my own grave. So I oblige and grip the shovel. "Sorry for the confusion. I'm just, you know, pretty tired. Sometimes this shift makes me go a little out of mind."

Her eyes say, "Out of your mind enough to murder a guest?" but her mouth says, "Sure, I can understand that. Happens to the best of us."

After she leaves, I'm a mess until the 7:00 A.M. shift arrives. I run out of the hotel, leaving the keys on the front desk. I'm in my car and gunning toward the Other Goddamn Hotel and notice George entering the access road in his crappy jeep. I lay my hand down on the horn and increase my speed. He gives me the finger without looking back, probably figuring I'm some guest he's pissed off for whatever reason. I continue honking until he pulls off into the IHOP parking lot along the highway.

"George!" I shout, running up to his jeep.

"Dude, what the fuck?" He opens the door and

steps out, expression reminding me of a bystander in a horror movie.

"We gotta talk, man."

"You look like hell. Are you back on crack?"

"What? I've never smoked crack."

"Spoken like a true crackhead."

"I'm not fucking around, George. I'm in deep shit."

"Okay, well." He pauses, sighs. "Are you going to tell me or do you want me to guess?"

A pair of elderly women pass us as they get into their car. The IHOP parking lot is packed with arrivals and departures. "No, not here. Somewhere private. Follow me to my apartment. We can talk there. No one will hear us besides the owls."

"Well, you certainly sound more insane than usual."

"Please."

His eyes bounce from his jeep to me, then his jeep and back to me again. He sags in surrender. "I have a burrito at my house that I've been thinking about all night, so this better be worth it."

"I'm sorry. I have food at my place."

"Yeah, but it won't be no burrito."

Ten minutes later, we're walking into my apartment and he's going through my fridge, ignoring what I'm trying to tell him. He eventually settles for a handful of stale Cheerios. "I was right," he says. "This isn't no burrito."

"You mean, 'this *is* no burrito.'"

"What?" he says through a mouthful of food.

"Double negatives, you know? Very unattractive."

"Inviting me over and insulting my grammar is *unattractive*. Asshole." Then he grimaces and spits out the cereal. "What the fuck is that *smell*?"

"Maybe you should sit down." I guide him to the

couch, but stay standing as he sits. I pace back and forth in front of him, aware of his confusion and annoyance.

"Dude, this reeks. Seriously. I'm gonna leave."

"You can't. Not yet."

"Then hurry the hell up. For fuck's sake, it smells like something died in here."

"Well . . ."

"Wait, *did* something die in here?" He scans my studio for a corpse. He doesn't look hard enough.

I lick the roof of my mouth, dry and doubtful. "No, something didn't die *here,* but . . ."

"But?"

"But some*one* did die at *the hotel*, and he is now in my closet."

It's like he wants to laugh but his face is broken. "Shut up, Isaac. You're currently too crazy to start making jokes."

I point to the closet. "Go ahead and check if you think I'm joking. What do you think that smell is?"

Hesitant, George rises and approaches the closet. He glances over his shoulder one last time, waiting for me to confirm what he wants to hear, that this is all some stupid joke, that he's still at work, asleep at the front desk.

He opens the closet and screams, then slams the door and attempts to flee from my apartment. I wedge myself between him and the front door, hands held up as a pathetic peace offering. Dude just saw a badly decomposed corpse in my closet. The concept of "peace" has clearly left the table.

"Please, let me explain."

"Who the fuck? What the fuck? How the fuck? What. The. Fuck. Fuck. *Fuck!*"

I push him and he backpedals until his ankles hit the couch and he sits down. His mouth keeps moving up and down but no words come out, just a series of unintelligible mumbles. He motions to the closet over and over like a toddler terrified of the monster underneath his bed.

"Just let me explain, okay? Please."

"Fuckin' explain *what?* Who the fuck *is* that? What did you do?"

"That's Mr. Yates, a former guest of my hotel."

"Holy shit, you actually killed a guest, holy shit, Isaac—Isaac, *holy shit.*"

"My neighbors are going to hear you. You gotta be quiet."

"Be *quiet?* Dude, I can't be *quiet.* You fucking killed somebody."

"I did not. I . . . just have the body."

"Then why do you have it? Who killed him?" He stands up, sits down, stands up, then sits down. If he leaves in this current state, he'll head straight to the police station and tell them about what he's seen in my closet. Detective Garcia herself will make it her duty to personally slap the cuffs around my wrists.

"Just—will you calm down? Let me explain what happened."

"You fucking calm down. I'm too hungry and sober to deal with this shit, man. I can't do this."

I sit down on the coffee table across from him, ready to tackle him to the floor should he attempt an escape. "Okay, so you remember I took that guy's wallet a while back, right?"

"Yeah, then you got mugged, and he came back asking about it."

"Well, the story didn't exactly end there."

The Nightly Disease

In the end, I don't tell him one hundred percent of the truth. Instead of owls throwing him off the roof, in this retelling of events, Yates just stumbles and trips off the edge. I try to save him, but I'm not fast enough, and he falls. Everything else, mostly, is what happened. I try to avoid discussing Chowls and Owlbert, because even I know that's fucking crazy. And besides, they're not relevant to Yates's story.

"I don't understand why this guy is still at your apartment. Why haven't you dumped him someplace?"

"Someplace like where . . . ? If I knew of some magical corpse disposing store, don't you think I would have tried it?"

"I don't know, but it shouldn't be as complicated as you're making it sound. You could bury him in the woods."

"But what about dogs?"

George raises his brow. "What *about* dogs?"

"They might dig him up."

"Then dig deeper."

"I don't own a shovel."

"Buy one."

"I don't have any money."

"Steal one."

"I'm not a criminal."

"There's a dead body in your closet, dude. You sure aren't *not* a criminal."

I bury my face in my hands and groan. "What am I gonna do about the detective? She knows something's off. She's gonna come here with a warrant or something."

George stands and opens the glass door to my

patio. "I doubt she'll need a warrant. The smell alone will grant her plenty of probable cause."

"Gee, thank you for that glimmer of hope."

"It's why you dragged me here, right? Wait, why *did* you drag me here? I was perfectly content living in ignorance. I could be eating a burrito right now."

"Because I don't know what to do. I'm going out of my mind and I can't hold it all in any longer. I needed to tell somebody with less morals than myself."

"I know you meant that as an insult, but I'll take it as a compliment."

"George. Please."

"Please what?" He spins around, face squinted. "What do you think I can do? Do you think I am experienced when it comes to shit like this? Maybe I have an uncle on the force? Something like that? Well, I don't. I would have mentioned that a long time ago. I would have convinced him to let us drive his squad car and pull over stoners."

I bite my lip and blurt out the idea that's been gnawing away at me all morning. "I want to rob our hotels."

George halts. His panic seems to evaporate like smoke into a vacuum. "Both of them?"

"Yeah."

"If you pay off that Hobbs fucker, you still have the cop to worry about. Plus, who says the shoe freak is even going to leave you alone?"

"The money isn't for Hobbs."

George sits back down on the couch. "You're gonna flee the country, aren't you?"

"I think so. Yeah."

"Mexico?"

"It's a start."

"They cut people's heads off in Mexico."

"They cut people's heads off here, too."

"True."

"Well?"

"We split it fifty-fifty?"

"That sounds fair."

"All right. Fuck it. We've talked about it enough over the years, might as well get it over with. When?"

"Tonight."

#411

A t 1:15 A.M. I lock up the front desk and walk over to the Other Goddamn Hotel. George waits in the lobby, no laptop out, no flask, not even his cell phone. He's shaky and bug-eyed, like he hasn't slept at all before coming in tonight, which would make two of us. Who could possibly sleep under these circumstances? Al Capone must've tossed and turned every night before a big heist. Or maybe he slept like a baby. He was a professional, after all. Robbing places was his thing. George and I, we're just a couple of fat deadbeats with no real social skills. If we walked into the casting call of a heist film, we'd be laughed out of the room before we even got a chance to speak.

"So are we gonna do this?" George asks. He's biting his lip, hands behind his back. He's never been this nervous around me before. This is a different George. A George with emotions.

"You sure you want to?"

"Of course I do. I've never wanted to do anything more in my life."

The Nightly Disease

"What if we get busted?"

"Prison can't be any worse than a hotel."

He raises a valid point. In prison, you don't have to worry about bills. You don't have to feed your gas tank. You don't have to worry about sleeping through alarms. You don't have to worry about masturbating at an inappropriate time, because any moment in prison is an appropriate time to masturbate. You don't have guests, but you do have fellow convicts, and yeah, they'll probably be assholes, but at least you can be an asshole back to them without fearing the loss of your job. What are they going to do in prison if you act out of line? Throw you in the hole? A small room with no other human interaction? Where do I sign up?

We sit down in the back office of his hotel, which is almost identical to the back office of my hotel, and share a bag of Cheetos as we discuss robbery methods.

"So, how are you thinking we do this?" George says.

"Well, right off the bat, we should empty the register, get that out of the way. Then we figure out how to crack the safe here in the back. Afterward, we go to my hotel and do the same thing."

George clears his throat, glancing at the safe in the corner of the back office. "Uh, I don't know about you, but I'm no expert safe cracker. I can barely crack open pistachios."

I stand up and kneel down at the safe. It's the same as the one at my hotel. At the top, there's a slot to slide in receipts of each shift's cash deposit. There are buttons next to the slot that shoots out small amounts of change whenever the front desk register runs out. At the bottom of the safe, there are two key slots. One of the front desk keys goes into one slot, and the other key belongs to the general manager. To open the safe, both keys must be inserted simultaneously.

"Maybe we could smash it with a sledgehammer," I say.

"Do you have a sledgehammer?"

"No."

"I think I have a regular hammer."

"That might work."

George goes through a series of random drawers until he pulls out a small hammer. He hands it to me, eyes glued on the safe, like he's expecting it to explode. I grip the hammer and search for a weak spot in the safe to smack. It looks pretty impenetrable. The hotel did not cheap-out when it came to protecting their precious money.

"What are you gonna do?" George asks.

"I guess I'm going to hit it."

"You think that's gonna work?"

"I don't know."

"Try."

"All right." I pull my arm back and *twack* the hammer against the safe, near the key locks. A tingling pain shoots down the handle of the hammer and into my hand and wrist. The same kind of vibration I used to feel when I was in Little League and I'd smack a ball just inches from the sweet spot. I hit it again with the same result.

"That doesn't seem to be working," George says.

"No shit."

"I guess we should have thought this out better."

I toss the hammer on the desk and sit back down,

pathetically out of breath from my brief stint of exercise. "I wish we had some TNT."

George rubs his chin. "Or some fat."

I spin in the chair toward him. "What?"

"Fat. Like, human fat. From liposuctions or whatever."

"Gross. Why?"

"We could turn it into napalm."

"Uh . . . how?"

He shrugs. "I don't know. Brad Pitt did it in *Fight Club*."

"Technically, Edward Norton did it. Brad Pitt was a figment of Norton's imagination."

"Whoever the fuck did it. It still worked."

"Maybe you're a figment of my imagination." Somehow this makes perfect sense. "Maybe you're my Brad Pitt."

"I'm more of a Robert Paulson," George says.

"We are all Robert Paulson."

"Sometimes I think we're wasting our lives watching all these movies, but then situations like tonight arise and, finally, they serve a purpose."

"Well, we don't have any fat, so this conversation is pointless."

We spin around for a while, staring at the ceiling. George coughs. "Where would we even blow it up?"

"I don't know." I hadn't thought about that. "I guess in the parking lot."

"We'd definitely wake up the guests."

"Fuck the guests."

George sniggers. "And cheat on throw-up girl?"

"You're an asshole."

The phone rings. George answers and hangs up. He retrieves the flask from his bag and takes a swig. I decline a turn when he offers it to me and instead return to the safe, wondering what would happen if I just started screaming at it. Would it suddenly pop open out of common courtesy?

George continues drinking. "Forget about it," he says between swigs. "Might as well get drunk and take a nap. This was a dumb idea."

I grab the flask from his hand and slam it on the desk, standing over him. "I don't have any other choice. I can't just take a nap and forget about my problems. You saw my fucking closet. The universe is collapsing and I don't have much longer before it's too late to escape. I need to do this *tonight*. Are you with me or not?"

George holds up his hands, leaning back in the chair. "Yeah, man, shit, okay, I'm with you. Now will you please back off? Your breath smells like ass."

I give him some space and kneel down by the safe. If I can't get this open, I'm not going to get very far before either the police or Hobbs's people find me. Money is fuel and I'm running on an empty tank.

I wrap my arms around it and try to pick it up. It budges slightly, and with another pull it slides a few inches forward.

"You're going to throw your back out doing that," George says.

"Do you think if we both tried picking it up, we could carry it somewhere?"

"Carry it where?"

"The roof."

" . . . And why exactly would we carry it there?"

"Maybe if we push it over the edge, it'll explode open when it hits the ground." Much how Yates exploded when he landed on the handicap pole outside my own hotel—except, instead of blood and guts coming out, we'll be greeted with white envelopes full of cash.

"That sounds a little bit too much like a *Looney Toons* episode. Aren't safes supposed to be, like, safe? You know, indestructible?"

"I seriously doubt people who run our hotels dished out on anything too top of the line. They won't even install cameras. Which is, coincidentally, why they're about to get their asses ripped off."

"Getting your ass ripped off sounds super painful."

"I imagine it is. Now go grab a luggage cart."

It takes some patience and a lot of energy, but we eventually drag the safe on top of the luggage cart. The large contraption settles in on the thin board of metal and the screws creak and tighten as the cart struggles to maintain the new weight.

"It's going to break the goddamn cart," George says.

"It might not."

"But it might."

"It might also rain flaccid penises from the sky. So what."

"It might rain hard penises, too."

I wipe sweat from my eyes and crack my neck. "Let's get this over with. We still have the safe at my hotel to bust open tonight."

"Heists are exhausting," George says. "I haven't worked this much since your mom came to visit that one time—"

"Shut up and push."

We get the cart to the elevator and ride up to the sixth floor. Despite being one floor taller, my hotel still has twenty more rooms than George's. We push it down the hallway, cursing under our breaths and snapping our heads around every few steps, afraid a guest is going to exit their room and catch us in the act. But so what if they do? This shit is nobody's business but ours. Well, ours and the hotel owners.

The flaw in our plan doesn't sink in until we're standing in front of the stairway leading up to the roof, luggage cart between us.

"I don't think we can carry it up that far," George says.

"We're gonna have to try."

"What if I pull my back? I'm not in the best shape, in case you haven't noticed. And neither are you."

"We don't have any other choice."

George looks at the safe, then the stairs. He sighs. "This is not going to end well."

"I think you're underestimating our strengths."

"I think you're vastly overestimating."

I flex, but he doesn't seem too impressed. Screw him. "Okay, on three, we lift."

"Ugh. All right."

We kneel down and position our hands around the safe. There's a brief moment of silence before we take action, like the last few seconds before a presidential assassination.

We lift and it's immediately clear this plan has a few flaws. I'd been anticipating one of those "mother lifts car over screaming child" superpower moments—instead, I am hit with the side-effects of never having worked out once in my life. Rather than carrying the safe up the flight of steps and onto the roof, I let out a long, wet fart and scream, "No, I can't!" and release my grip. The safe drops on George's foot, who squeals

The Nightly Disease

at a volume equivalent to a dying hyena. But the safe is not quite finished, as it then tips over and begins rolling down the stairs we'd just climbed. George and I watch it tumble down not just one flight, but two flights, then it's out of sight but still not stable. Frozen, we listen to it crash to the ground floor.

Tears flow down George's face as he sits on the landing and holds his foot.

I stand above him, watching him cry, then peeking over the banister and trying to locate the safe down on the bottom. It's nowhere in sight, but the stairway leading down has definitely taken a very visible pounding. "Well, that sucked."

"No fucking shit," George says.

Helping him balance, we slowly descend to the ground floor. The safe awaits at the end of the stairway, lock busted and door wide open. My plan has worked. I am a genius. Inside the safe are dozens of small white envelopes, and inside these envelopes are various amounts of cash. I pull out a trash bag from my pocket and fill it with envelopes, figuring I'll count it later today once I'm a safe distance from the crime scene.

George collapses on the steps, still groaning.

I hold up the bag. "Dude, relax. We did it. We actually did it."

"Yeah, and we also broke my foot in the process, you insensitive asshole."

"I'll buy you a new foot in Mexico."

"I know you're joking, but that sounds kind of cool."

If we leave the safe here, the police will undoubtedly wonder why the robbers went through all the trouble of bringing the safe to the top of the hotel and dropping it down the stairs instead of just taking the whole thing with them. However, even if we do move the safe, there's still plenty of damage done to the stairwell. But that's only cause for concern if the police decide to search the stairs, which they shouldn't have any reason to if George explains the imaginary thieves were never near that area. When the maintenance man discovers the vandalism tomorrow, he can blame a group of drunks who'd gotten lost on the way to their rooms. This explanation works because there are always drunks, every night, forever lost and accidentally breaking things.

I leave George on the steps holding his foot and retrieve the luggage cart from the top floor. Somehow I roll the safe back on the cart without any help and we wheel it to the back office. The lobby is empty. I don't know how we would explain ourselves to any guests who might witness us wheeling around a cracked open, empty safe. I don't know why we would have to explain ourselves. Guests are just that: guests. The only thing we truly owe them is a pillow pressed gently over their sleeping faces, and they're lucky to get that. I push the safe off the luggage carts so it lands back where we'd originally taken it from and tell George perhaps he can explain the robbers had come in wielding sledgehammers.

"Man, they're not gonna believe me," George says. "How am I going to explain my foot?"

"Why would they know about that?"

"I can't exactly hide it, Isaac." He winces as he adjusts in his seat. "In case you haven't noticed, it's fucking broken."

"Well, I guess you could say they hit you with the sledgehammer, too."

The Nightly Disease

"Who are *they*? How many? What did they look like?"

I shrug. "I don't know. You were the one who got robbed. You make it up."

"Yeah, but they're also gonna hit your hotel up, so don't you think we should figure these details out so our stories match?"

He has a point. I check the time and gasp at how late it's getting. Or early, depending on how you look at it. If we're going to rob my hotel too, then we gotta get moving.

"Okay." I visualize what I assume a group of sledgehammer-wielding hotel robbers would look like and see a couple of young black guys. Unhealthy black guys. Like maybe they're addicted to crack or heroin. Wait. No. That's extremely racist. But also, this is Texas. The police are already hoping the robbers are black. This way, when someone calls them out on being racist pieces of shit, they can use this incident as proof that they are right. But it is still troublesome my mind immediately went there. Perhaps I am also a racist piece of shit. But on the other hand, perhaps I am simply a genius. Maybe there isn't a difference. Maybe both the racist pieces of shit and the geniuses will all eventually be dust and none of it matters, none of it has ever mattered.

"Wait," George says. "Why even bother explaining ourselves to the police? Why don't we just go empty out your safe then get the fuck out of here?"

I laugh at the realization of what he's been saying. "Since when are you coming with me?"

He shrugs. "It's either that or I hang myself in the lobby."

I nod. "All right. Well. Before I thought we'd need

to talk to the police because you were staying here, but now that you're coming with me . . . we should probably still go along with the plan."

"Uh. Okay."

"I think we'd probably have a way easier chance of getting to Mexico without being wanted. It's bad enough Hobbs will be after me, but at the same time, I don't think I'm important enough for him to actually hunt me down. So this Mexico trip would really be more of a vacation than anything. I just don't intend on ever coming back to Texas, even when we do eventually leave Mexico. *If* we ever leave. It might be awesome."

"It's obviously going to be awesome."

"At this point, I'm pretty sure the shitter of a Taco Bell would be awesome compared to my current situation."

George frowns. "What about the guy you killed?"

"I'll figure something out." If it comes down to it, I'll take the poor dead bastard with us to Mexico. But I'm not telling George that. He would probably disagree. George gets queasy when it comes to these kind of things. "Also, I didn't kill him. We've already been through this."

"Doesn't change the fact that he's still dead and in your apartment. Cops find the body, I doubt they're gonna give you the benefit of the doubt." He readjusts his leg and groans. "Mexico better have some great feet, man, because this one is just bullshit."

"I'm sure if you Googled 'Mexican feet', you would be impressed. But in the meantime." I clap my hands together, like maybe I'm a high school football coach now or something. "We're running out of night."

George bites his lip. "I think the cops are gonna think my foot injury is suspicious."

The Nightly Disease

"Most foot injuries are suspicious. So what?"

"So . . . it just seems weird the robbers would just bash my foot. Like. I think if they're okay with breaking a guy's foot, then they're probably not going to hesitate to really rough you up."

I check the time again. Shit. "Dude, what are you saying?"

"I think if we want to make this realistic, if we want to come out of this looking like the victims, we're going to have to really sell it. We're going to have to beat the ever-living shit out of each other."

If I wasn't so tired, I'd try to think of an alternative option. But right now, his words make more sense than anything else in the universe. I laugh and I don't know if it's a laugh of amusement or sadness or madness or what. Sometimes a laugh does not need an agenda. Sometimes it can just be a laugh.

"You're serious, aren't you?"

George nods. "Sure. Why the hell not."

"So you want me to hit you?"

George stands up and moans at the weight he puts on his broken foot. "Once I've had some sleep, I will probably hate you. But that's in the future. This is the only way we do this without getting caught. You hit me. I hit you. We gotta *Detroit Rock City* this shit."

I clench my hands into fists and loosen them. This is silly. "Okay, man. Fuck it. You're right. Let's do this. Where do you want it?"

George shakes his head and closes his eyes. "Don't tell me. Just do it. Hurry before I change my mind."

"All right . . . I can't believe we're really—"

"Fucking *hit me*."

I hit him.

Hard.

Max Booth III

Blood flies from his mouth like coffee from a lidless mug in a cup holder. I start to apologize, then fall silent as he trips and tumbles. It unravels in slow-motion and I'm still not fast enough to save him. A loud crack fills the back office as his head connects with his assistant manager's desk and his neck snaps in a ninety degree angle. Then he's on the ground, completely still, and I'm standing above him with a heartbeat loud enough to shatter eardrums.

"Uh," I say, because it is the only thing to say. "Uh."

I nudge him with my foot. He does not move. I nudge him harder. He remains motionless.

"Uh."

I scream and flee the back office. I am no longer tired. Feet slap against the outside pavement as I haul ass back to my hotel. There's a junkie outside waiting for me to let him in. He tries to give me hell about making him wait so long, but I push past him and escape into the lobby bathroom. I dive into the stall and project a steady stream of vomit into the toilet bowl, and suddenly I miss Kia so much it seems impossible to continue living another second without her company, her warmth. Where did she go? Does she still watch the hotel from a distance, hoping to catch a glimpse of me on the roof? Or has she skipped town? Did the owls get to her? Did she ever even exist?

The junkie is still in the lobby when I exit the bathroom. Green goo drips from the corners of his eyeballs. "I need the presidential suite, please."

"Two-oh-nine."

"How do I get there?"

"Slice your throat and swim to it in your own pool of blood."

The Nightly Disease

I stumble around him and hide in the back office. Eventually the junkie discovers the elevator. My breathing matches the pace of an out-of-control street racer and everything inside me burns. Maybe he isn't dead. Maybe he's back at the Other Goddamn Hotel, struggling to get to a phone because his best friend abandoned him. Maybe there's still time to save him. But maybe that's all wishful thinking. Maybe I've killed my best friend over a few thousand dollars. Maybe I've . . .

Shit, the money.

I check the time. I'm no longer worried about my own breakfast lady, but now I'm racing against the Other Goddamn Hotel's breakfast lady, who will be arriving within the hour. If I leave the money, the scene will only confuse police. Why would the thieves just leave the cash there after killing the auditor? Unless he knew the auditor, and didn't mean to kill him . . . unless the other person was in fact the auditor next door, one of his only friends in the universe.

No. The money can't stay.

This time I drive to the Other Goddamn Hotel. I'm afraid if I run any more I'm going to have a heart attack, which actually might be the only real solution to my situation. Except I don't have the willpower or ability to drop dead at the tip of a hat, so instead I sneak into the Other Goddamn Hotel. It's still empty and George hasn't moved since I left him. That's because he is dead. That's because I have killed him. That's because I am a fucking moron and do not deserve to rot on this planet any longer. Or maybe I do. Maybe this is my punishment. Maybe immortality only comes to those who are true pieces of shit. And I'm not just any piece of shit. I am the faith-healer-leader-of-a-revival-cult-kool-aid-mixer piece of shit. I'm the Jesus Christ of pieces of shit. Not only did I convince another human being to commit a felony with me, but then I fucking killed him afterward because I don't know how to properly throw a punch.

I collect the trash bag of cash-filled envelopes, but I can't bring myself to leave George alone. He had been a good friend. Not a great friend, but a damn good one. He can't be dead. Twenty minutes ago he was alive. Twenty minutes ago, we were going to Mexico. We probably would have rented a Mexican prostitute together. Maybe we would have seen a donkey show or gotten into a fight with the cartel. Now we will do none of these things. Now he will decompose and I will sweat and panic until I'm also decomposing.

I can't abandon George. I can't leave his body here. I can't pretend this didn't happen.

This happened.

This happened because of my poor decisions.

I have to make things right. I have to react. I have to show courage.

I have to cover this up.

It takes fifteen minutes to roll his corpse on a luggage cart then push him outside and lift him into my trunk. His weight proves greater than the safe, but at least I'm well-practiced when it comes to disposing dead bodies. I wonder if I can include that on my resume if I'm ever in the market for a new job. Like "prison librarian". I return to the back office of George's hotel and wipe down various spots that I may have touched tonight. I don't know if this will actually throw the police off my trail, but that's what everybody always does in the movies, so I figure it's worth a shot.

Back at my hotel, the breakfast lady is standing outside, ready to bitch at me in Spanish for not being around to let her inside on time. I nod and apologize and pretend like I understand what she's saying, then help her set-up breakfast.

Meanwhile, George waits patiently in my trunk.

#412

Fifteen-hundred dollars. That's how much money was in the Other Goddamn Hotel's safe. I don't count it until I wake up in the afternoon. Once I got home and managed to sneak George's gargantuan lifeless body into my apartment, I was useless. I passed out for a solid six hours. I would have probably slept for the rest of my life if my cell phone hadn't woken me up. No, wait, not my cell phone. George's.

I fish the phone out of his pocket. The caller ID reads "DON'T ANSWER", which must mean it's his boss calling. I obey the caller ID and click the ignore button. His phone has been attacked with dozens of missed calls and text messages. All of the messages are from his manager, demanding to know his location and letting him know the police are looking for him. Of course they are. Not only is he missing, but the money inside the safe is also gone.

And it's not even two months' worth of rent. I don't know what I expected. Most guests don't pay cash anymore, and the safe is emptied at the end of every

The Nightly Disease

week, so what the fuck, I'm no Al Capone—hell, I'm not even Owlcapone. What I should have done was instead of freaking out and bringing George to my apartment, I should've gone directly back to my hotel and cleaned out whatever little was in our safe, then hightailed it directly to Mexico before anyone could figure out what happened. But now I have to return to work tonight. I have to continue like everything is normal. Until . . . until when? Until I regain the courage to rob my own hotel, then flee to a country that speaks a language I don't understand? What the fuck is wrong with me? What do I know about Mexico?

What I need is an actual plan. I can't go into this sleep-deprived and desperate. That's how George ended up dead. No more half-assed schemes that inevitably backfire. If I'm going to get myself out of this mess, I'm going to have to use my brain.

There are two key issues currently ruining my life: One, the corpses decomposing in my apartment, and two, the Hobbs brothers. Realistically, the first issue will solve the second issue. I just have to smuggle the bodies into their room. Except the only time John ever seems to leave his shoe lab is either for a smoke break or to give me shit about something. If he sleeps, it's when I'm off the clock. But, knowing what I know from the plethora of trashy crime books I've read, it's doubtful he ever sleeps. The meth works as a superpower, disabling the need to rest and turning him into a constant work machine. Only death will stop this force—death, or a riot squad acting off an anonymous tip about some dead bodies in the man's closet.

George's cell phone continues ringing as if its owner hasn't expired, as if he's just oversleeping and any second now he'll wake up and give it the love and

attention it believes it deserves. The caller ID still says
"DON'T ANSWER". I pace around my apartment,
holding the cell phone and listening to it ring while
exchanging glances with George. I can't just leave him
on the carpet. Not only will it ruin the material, but
I'll eventually trip over his body.

Yates is beyond thrilled to receive a new friend. It
gets lonely, hanging out in a closet all day. Sometimes
you need someone to talk to. Sometimes you need to
know you aren't the only person in the world, even if
you're both dead.

I try not to eavesdrop on their conversation. I
wash dishes that haven't been cleaned in weeks but
the hatred in the corpses' tones is loud enough to
drown out the sink water. I suppose I can't blame
them. I am not only their imprisoner, but also their
murderer. At least they have stuff in common.

I am not losing my mind. I am not losing my
mind. I am not losing my mind.

The phone goes off again, except this time the
ringtone is different. Weirder. Distorted. The caller
ID reads: "OWLBERT".

I answer.

"Uh, hello?"

"You stupid fuck. They can track the phone."

It hadn't even occurred to me. First thing the
police probably did was track down George's cell
phone signal. He is, after all, currently their best
suspect.

But there's a more pressing issue at hand. "How
did you dial my number? You . . . you don't have
thumbs."

Owlbert sighs and calls me a mean name, then the
phone goes dead. The phone that's going to lead a

The Nightly Disease

firing squad straight to my front door. This thing might as well be my executioner. The microwave above the sink sings my name. A sexy siren guiding me to my unavoidable crash. I feed it George's cell phone and click the POPCORN button. Radiation seduces and penetrates its new lover. The phone sizzles and pops and bursts into a tiny ball of flame, and the sound of its death carries a better rhythm than any rock song I've ever heard, and I can't stop headbanging to the beat. Because this is real. Destroying phones. Hiding evidence. Disposing corpses. I am no longer a person. I am a movie character. I am a John McClane. I am a James Bond. I am a superhero and the hotel gig was my origins story. Every great character hatches from someplace horrible. From someplace totally repugnant and evil. The hotel serves both as my birth and my death. It is my Uncle Ben and my Venom. I can't leave it behind for the same reason Batman can't leave Gotham. I am its protector and its destroyer. The only way to save it is to let it burn. I am the hotel's savior. I am the hotel's death sentence. I am the hotel's everything. I am the hotel. I am the hotel. I. Am. The. Hotel.

The doorbell rings.

The world collapses.

The rock song in my end ceases.

Somewhere, an owl is laughing.

"Isaac?" a voice shouts from outside. "This is Detective Garcia. Please open the door. I know you're home. I can hear you."

Hear me? I'm not making any—oh shit, wait, I'm the one laughing. I'm the goddamn owl. What's so funny, anyway?

What's so funny?

"One minute," I tell the detective. "I'm naked." Which isn't true, but it buys me some time to change out of my dirty work uniform and throw on something clean. I had thought the smell of death was coming from my uniform, but taking it off doesn't seem to help. The smell is coming from inside me. My soul is tainted with violence. Whatever the fuck a soul is. Whatever the fuck anything is.

The detective looks the same as the first time we met. I only open the door a crack and peek my head out. Does my face show any guilt? Do my eyes tell her all my little secrets?

"Can I help you?" I ask, and I realize I'm already acting suspicious, and I realize I am unable to act any other way.

Detective Garcia starts to smile, then frowns and strains her nose. "What in the world is that smell?"

"Uh." She tries to push her way inside, but I refuse to budge. "I don't know anything else about Mr. Yates, I'm sorry."

But she doesn't care about dead bodies. She nods to my apartment, grimacing. "What *is* that? Good lord, it's horrendous."

"I'm afraid I don't know what you're talking about." But of course I know. The stench of Yates and George's decaying corpses can be detected for miles. I'm more obvious than a child with cherry pie smeared across his face. I fake an expression of recognition. "Oh, yeah, my popcorn."

She raises her brow. "Popcorn?"

"Yeah. I just burned a bag of it in the microwave. Wasn't paying attention."

"I see."

She's a detective. Obviously she's able to

determine the difference between burnt popcorn and decayed corpses. It is her job, after all. Garcia nods. "Ugh. I do that all the time. Why don't you step outside so we can talk without having to choke ourselves to death?"

Of course, I'm not very good at my job, either.

I suck in my groaning gut—when was the last time I've eaten?—and slip through the crack in the door without risking to open it any wider and possibly reveal evidence of my unintentional wickedness.

The elderly lady across the pavement waves at us as she attempts to unlock her front door. "Good morning!"

The detective waves back. "Good morning, ma'am." She lowers her voice. "You think she realizes what time it is?"

I nod. "Yeah, it's morning."

She squints. "I need to ask you some questions about the gentleman who works the night shift at the hotel next to yours."

"George?"

"So you know him."

I scratch the back of my head, hair dripping sweat. This being-out-in-the-sun bullshit isn't meant for me. "Yeah, we gotta call each other every night to compare rates and occupancies. What . . . what's going on? Did something happen to him?"

Detective Garcia nods. "I'm afraid he's currently missing. Do you remember talking to him last night?"

Last night was a decade ago. Did I call him before heading over? Surely the police will check the phone records to confirm my story, either way. "You know, I don't recall if I did or not."

"You don't recall."

I shrug. What does she want from me? "Most nights tend to just blend together, it seems. Almost like my entire time employed at the hotel has been one long shift that'll never end."

"Sounds like you need to reconsider careers."

"Yeah, maybe."

"Before I joined the academy, I was an overnight cashier at Walmart, so I understand what you're feeling. Trust me when I tell you it doesn't get better."

"What?"

Her eyes seem to darken and her voice deepens. "Face it, Eye Sick. You're two steps away from tripping in your own grave. The universe is collapsing and you are the magnet guilty of annihilation."

"Uh."

Her eyes return to normal. The demonic tone in her voice disappears. "Did you notice anything strange last night?"

"Strange like how?"

"Strange like anything."

I try to clear my throat but my mouth is too dry. "No. Not really. It was just a regular night. I came in, I checked in guests, I did my paperwork, and I left."

"Do you think it's sort of strange that two people have gone missing from the same area within a month?"

"Uh, I suppose."

"Do you suspect these two disappearances are related?"

"Um." I rub sweat out of my eyes. The burn is torture. "Why are you asking me this? You're the detective. I . . . I don't know anything."

"Just brainstorming, I guess. Hearing myself think."

Across the walkway, my neighbor waves again and

tells us good morning. She's still fighting to unlock her door.

"Look," I tell the detective, blood boiling in this Satanic heat, "I don't know where George is. He didn't exactly tell me he was planning on robbing his hotel. Shit just happens. One day someone's here, the next day they're gone."

I realized halfway through talking how much I just fucked up, but it was too late to stop. The words spat out of my mouth beyond my control. But maybe she wasn't listening. Maybe her detective skills really are as poor as my customer service skills.

"I never mentioned anything about a robbery."

"Excuse me?" Now's the time to strategize: do I flee or attempt to smooth the situation over with my charm?

"You just said you don't know why Mr. George Wilk robbed his hotel. But I haven't said anything about a burglary."

"What? Uh. Yeah you did. It was one of the first things you mentioned when I answered the door."

"How do you know the hotel was robbed, Isaac?" The detective steps forward and I know if I try to flee now she would probably just shoot me in the back. Maybe that wouldn't be so bad. Maybe that's the solution I'm been searching for all this time."

"I, uh, I . . . "

Detective Garcia nods at the door. "Is he in there? Are you hiding him in your apartment?"

"What. No. What."

"Is he armed?" She draws a pistol from her hip holster. "Is he?"

"No."

She hesitates. "Did you guys partner up, or what's the story here? Is he forcing you to hide him?"

"No."

"Then what?"

"What."

I can't talk, can't think. It's too hot. It's too cold. Reality continues disintegrating as she slaps a pair of handcuffs around my right wrist and connects the opposite cuff to the stairwell. She approaches my apartment holding her gun like all the cops do in movies. Her approach is so authentic it doesn't seem real. And that's because nothing is real. Detective Garcia is a figment of my imagination just as Owlbert and Chowls are figments of my imagination. Everything is a figment of something else's imagination. It is the way the world works, and only when you begin doubting this universal truth does nothing make sense.

The detective shouts, "I know you're in there! I'm armed, so don't try anything funny. I'm coming in. Again, I am armed. I will shoot you. Keep your hands up." She kicks the door open and storms into my apartment, waving her pistol in every direction. From my handcuffed angle, I'm still given enough of a clear view of the apartment's interior. She frantically explores inside, yelling for George to surrender himself before an accident happens. Then she opens up the closet door and she's no longer yelling, no longer running around in search for the dead.

The detective is frozen in time. The contents of the closet have struck her dumb. I desperately try to pull free of the handcuffs, but only succeed in bruising my wrists. Fuck. This is bad.

Out of view, the sound of spurs rustling gives birth

into the wind, and before I can piece together why the melody is so familiar I am greeted with Hobbs's brother rounding the apartment building. He tips his cowboy hat at me as he passes and calmly enters my apartment. Despite the spurs, the detective doesn't even notice his presence. She's too distracted by the sight of two corpses in my closet. Too distracted by how dumb she had been to not have suspected me of being capable of absolute evil. Too distracted to realize she's no longer alone.

Helpless, I watch as the cowboy unsheathes a large hunting knife from his boot and slices the detective's throat. The pistol falls from her grasp as she collapses to her knees, hands jerking to her neck in a worthless cause to prevent the flow of blood. I want to scream but I don't know who I would be screaming for. I want to cry but I no longer remember how.

The cowboy wipes off the blade of his hunting knife with a towel and slides it back into his boot. He kneels at the detective's body, still draining of life, and searches through her pockets, then strolls out of the apartment and unlocks my handcuffs. He's smirking like this is all a game and he knows he's the world champion. Smiling like he's my buddy and he just did me a big favor.

I rub my wrist, now raw from my uneventful escape attempts, and glare at him. "What the fuck."

His expression is of genuine confusion. "What are you so pissed about?"

"Why did you kill her?"

"Why do you have two bodies in your apartment?"

"That's none of your business."

He doesn't know what Yates looks like, and he

isn't even aware of George's existence. These bodies could be totally unrelated to the hotel.

"I reckon one of 'em is the guest you tossed off the roof."

" . . . Yeah."

"And the other?"

I shuffle my feet. "It's kind of complicated."

"What was the cop doing here?"

"I don't know."

"Don't fuck with me, kid."

"She had questions about the missing night auditor from the hotel next to mine."

The cowboy pauses, then recognition hits. "That's the guy in the closet, I assume."

"Yeah."

"Well, it's a good thing I was nearby to save your ass. You're welcome."

"What were you doing here?"

He winks. "Keeping an eye out on my new friend."

How long had he been outside, watching me? Does he have so much free time in his day that he can just hang around apartment buildings on the off chance that he'll have to murder a cop? Is he the only one watching?

Does he know the owls?

Across the pavement, my neighbor tells us both good morning. One day she'll figure out that lock and release all the demons waiting to burst from the underworld.

The cowboy stares at her like he's considering getting out his hunting knife again. Then he nudges my arm. "C'mon. Let's go inside and discuss matters in private."

Inside the apartment, his cool-guy character

breaks and he slams me against the wall. His nails dig around my throat and I'm too startled to fight back. "There's things you aren't telling me, boy."

"What? No. I promise." The words come out as a series of gargled chokes.

His grip tightens. Oxygen abandons me. "Tell me why the cop was really here. What have you told her about me? Who else knows?" He pauses, glances over his shoulder at the opened closet, and bounces my skull against the wall. "And why do the contents of your apartment contain so much death?"

It takes him another twenty seconds or so to realize I can't answer him when my air supply is cut off. He releases his hands and steps back. "Answer me, boy."

I gag and spit and kneel over, still unable to properly breathe. The toes of his boot sink into my gut and I fall to the floor. A mouthful of vomit drips down my chin.

"You best not start telling me stories of wires attached to your chest, either. And that includes your little ballsack, too."

"I don't have a wire. Jesus Christ, please stop." I sit, holding my hands up in a plea for mercy. "I didn't tell the cops anything. You said so yourself. You were watching. You saw her handcuff me. She was in the process of arresting me when you arrived. Why would I be fucking around with a cop when there's dead bodies in my apartment? I want their attention even less than you do."

The cowboy seems to contemplate the facts. "Why did you kill the fat boy?"

"It was an accident. He's a friend."

"A friend."

"Yeah. And I killed him. It . . . we were just messing around. But it looks like I murdered him. I didn't know what else to do."

"And the other guy?" He nods to the closet. "That's the guest you and my little brother tossed off the roof, correct?"

"Yeah."

"Last time we met, you informed us you'd done taken care of that mess. I don't appreciate liars, boy. I don't appreciate them one bit."

"I'm fucking sorry, okay? You act like I'm one of you. Well, I'm not. I'm fucking not."

The cowboy laughs. "What're you sayin', then?"

"I'm saying I don't know what the fuck you expect from me. I'm just a night auditor. I can't . . . I can't fucking *do* this."

The cowboy laughs harder and it reminds me of when I was a kid and my older brother would tease me in front of my friends, only on this occasion we're instead surrounded by owls and dead bodies. And I'm pretty sure at least one of them exists only in my head.

"Boy, you're all cute and shit, I tell you what." He rubs his chin. "Okay, listen. Gettin' rid of bodies ain't no thing, really. Movies and shit, they put it in your mind that it's this impossible task, but really, all it takes is a shovel and a quality level of seclusion. Now, you got a shovel?"

"No."

'Well, I got one in my trunk you can borrow. You know the woods out on thirty-five? Behind those ghetto strip-malls."

"I think so."

"Well, here is what you do. You gather up this entourage of death you've done collected and you take them out in them woods. You dig yourself a great big hole. In fact, you dig yourself three great big holes. One for each body. Wait. I assume there's just the three, right? Have I missed anybody?" He looks around the apartment.

"Just the three."

"Okay, good. So you dig up three holes and you bury 'em deep, deep, deep into the earth. This ain't a funeral, so you best stretch beyond the standard six feet. You might wanna bring a stepstool or somethin' to get yourself out of the hole once you've dug it up, or you'll find yourself slapping off vultures come mornin'."

"I have to work tonight." Wait, do I? What day is it?

"Well, you best hurry up then, I reckon."

"What about the detective's car?"

"Huh?"

"She probably drove here. Don't cop cars have a GPS installed or something?" I'm sure I once saw that in a movie, so it must be true. "It'll be tracked once she doesn't show back up at the station, right?"

"Hmm. Good call." He scavenges through Detective Garcia's pockets and scoops out a set of keys, then examines the various tools connected to the chain. He pulls out his cell phone and dials a number. "Hey, yeah, it's me. Listen. Word is, if you bring yourself down to Universal City and take a stroll through an apartment complex called The Meadows, you'll happen upon a Crown Vic with the keys on the hood. I reckon it'll probably be black or dark grey. Yeah, Carl, that's right, like a cop's. Well, who gives a shit? You best move your ass, though. You have an hour and it's gone. But you ain't heard shit from me, and if you say you have, well, yeah, come on, I don't think I need to discuss consequences."

The cowboy returns the cell phone to his pocket. "The car is no longer an issue. Help me find which one is hers so I can drop the keys on the hood, then I'll lend you my shovel."

"This is really happening."

He nods. "Yes. This is really happening."

Part Five

The Last
Check–Out

#500

As it turns out, tonight's one of my off-nights at the hotel. Despite this, I still have no intention of wasting my time out in the woods. With the bodies gone, I would have no upper hand. I would be the Hobbses' slave. Fuck that and fuck them. These dead bodies belong to me.

I realize this train-of-thought is unhealthy to whatever sanity remains in my hard drive and is probably what most people tell themselves the day before a flock of white-coated doctors drag them into a padded van. But I am not like those people. My horrors are real. These bodies are not my fault. The Hobbs brothers are not my fault. The owls are not my fault. It's pretty clear what is to blame. The hotel. The hotel is behind all of this. At the root of this dumb conspiracy is a giant hotel sporting a throbbing erection and we're sucking it off and soon it's going to finally come all over our faces.

I allow the cowboy to help me drag the bodies into my trunk. Of course, only one fits, so we store George and Detective Garcia in the backseat. The idea is that the least decomposed of the group will be the most pleasant to see while passing by the car. It amazes me the amount of times I've transported corpses around my apartment without anyone saying something to me. Although, if I saw some dudes dragging a body outside, I sincerely doubt I would interrupt them. That shit's nobody's business.

After the cowboy leaves, I still drive away with the bodies and his shovel in my car. He might still be hanging around, watching to confirm I'm not ignoring his orders. But I don't drive to the woods. Hell, I don't even know how I would carry three individual corpses far enough to locate a spot isolated enough to dig holes. Most days I can barely carry the hotel coffee pots without struggling. I drive aimlessly down I-35 with no real destination in mind. I can't sit down somewhere and eat. My bank account is mostly bone-dry, plus there's the matter of two dead bodies chilling in my backseat. Someone's bound to take notice.

An hour passes and my car's on its last few trickles of gasoline and the radio has been overthrown by a strict commercial-only broadcast and my bladder's one bump away from bursting and the bodies in the backseat smell so fucking terrible that at this point I'm perpetually swallowing my own vomit and it's all fucked, every last second of my life is a virtual "KICK ME" sign, and I'm the one doing the majority of the kicking.

When I regain consciousness, I'm parked at the San Antonio Zoo and Aquarium. I don't know what I'm doing here. I can't afford to enter. I can't even afford to drive back home. I don't have time for zoos. I have to strategize. If this was a videogame, the final boss fight wouldn't take it easy on me. I'd already be torn to pieces.

The Nightly Disease

On the other hand, if this was a videogame, I could just press PAUSE.

So I press PAUSE.

On the floor of the passenger's seat, the bag of stolen cash deposits from the Other Goddamn Hotel calls my name. I take out a few envelopes and count out a hundred dollars. I don't remember bringing the bag back out to the car. I had taken it inside to count. Why did I return the money to the envelopes?

All of my memories are lost film reels. When I struggle and try to think back, volcanoes burst in my skull.

I pay the ticket holder at the zoo the eight dollars to enter. It's late in the evening and the lady at the front booth informs me they'll be closing in less than an hour. Perhaps I would like to save my money for tomorrow. I tell her perhaps I wouldn't. Inside, the zoo is absent of all other human beings besides myself and the few stray employees still unfortunate enough to be on the clock. They all stare at me the same way I stare at my guests. They hate me and I haven't even said anything to them. My presence alone goes against everything they stand for. I am the enemy.

The various animals in cages stare at me, confused, wondering what I'm still doing here. I could set them all free, I realize. I could be a hero in the animal kingdom. But I don't. These animals are not part of my story. They would only become distractions. What if a tiger ran out onto the highway and got plowed by a semi-truck? It's bad enough I have George's death on my conscience. I couldn't handle a tiger, too.

I don't stop to inspect the other animals. I ignore

them and continue to my destination. There's only one reason I would come to a zoo.

The barn owl stares at me from inside its cage, claws curled around a wooden perch. Its head remains cocked as it takes me in. Our eyes become one. I try to ask it what the meaning of life is and it refuses to answer. Mandy 2 would be proud. I finally made it. This trip is for her. Everything is for her. All she wanted to do was pet an owl. In the end, the owl had petted her.

Next to the cage stands a standard information sign about the inhabited animal:

COMMON BARN OWL
Tyto alba
Range: The length of a scream.
Habitat: Behind you. Watching. Waiting.
Size: Equivalent to a shadow stretching infinitely across sizzling cement.
Diet: Hotel night auditors.
Fun fact: Death is inevitable.

I blink hard and long but the words don't change. Hallucinations don't mean a damn thing when reality's never entered the equation. I ask the owl what I'm supposed to do. How do I climb out of this hole I've dug myself? Save me, goddamn, just please *save me*.

The owl doesn't respond. Maybe because it finds amusement in teasing me, or—more likely—it's an owl and understandably doesn't understand English.

"You fuck," I whisper, and the owl flinches. "I know you can hear me, you crafty piece of shit. This is all one big game to you, isn't it? *Isn't it?*"

The Nightly Disease

"Hoot," the owl says.

A woman next to me clears her throat. "Uh, sir, you can't curse at the animals. It's against regulations."

"Is it?"

She points at a sign that reads "PLEASE DO NOT INSULT THE ANIMALS".

"Oh. I'm sorry."

"I'm gonna have to ask you to leave, sir."

"Okay."

We stand in silence for three very awkward minutes before she finally throws her hands up in the air. "Well?"

"Well what?"

"I said I'm gonna have to ask you to leave."

"But you haven't asked yet."

"Get the fuck out of here, dude."

On the way out, I notice another sign next to an empty cage. Well, mostly empty. The only object inside is a mirror propped up on a stand, so whoever's in front of the cage can look at their own reflection.

The sign is very similar to the owl's.

HOTEL NIGHT AUDITOR
Hospitality dicksnot
Range: Just low enough to be perpetually stomped on by the human race.
Habitat: A bottomless ocean of his own tears and cum.
Size: Chris Farley.
Diet: Will literally eat anything that incorporates grease.
Fun fact: Nothing is real.

Max Booth III

I try to kick the sign down but miss and tumble to the ground. A crowd of zoo employees surround me like vultures and laugh. "Are you all right?" they ask. "Were you trying to destroy our sign?" they ask. "Do you even hoot, bro?" they ask.

Then, in unison, they begin chanting: "Where are the owls? Where are the owls? Where are the owls?"

The owl cage is opened and the prisoner has escaped. Did I free it? Did it free itself? Was I the one in the cage?

Am I free?

"Where are the owls? Where are the owls? Where are the owls?"

I push past the zoo employees and flee the property. Hundreds of footsteps seem to echo behind me as they give chase, but when I glance over my shoulder there's not a single soul present. I turn back around and the lady from the ticket booth is in front of me, telling me the zoo's been closed for over a century and there's no way in hell I'm getting a refund over some bullshit bird attack that occurred when I was on an elementary school field trip.

Her face melts as she talks and drips down her cleavage. What bird attack? What field trip? This isn't a zoo. This is hell. I've died and gone to hell and there is no escape, there is no escape.

I have escaped.

In the parking lot, an owl waits on top of my car. It is not Owlbert or Chowls but the owl from the zoo. The one everyone accused me of stealing.

Did I steal it?

"You aren't real," I whisper, and unlock the car.

"Yes I am," it says.

The Nightly Disease

"Oh." There's really no arguing this kind of hard evidence. "Okay, get in, I guess."

I open the door and let the owl fly into the passenger seat. Did George switch seats with Detective Garcia? Fuck. Someone is messing with me. Maybe the cowboy has been following me. Maybe he's watching right this very second.

"Right. Okay. What's your name?" I ask the owl, and begin driving.

"Steve."

"Steve?"

"Yeah. You got a problem with 'Steve'?"

"No, uh, it's just not what I expected."

"And what is *that* supposed to mean?" The owl emits a loud hoot.

"Nothing, nothing. Just other owls I know, their names are ridiculous."

"Well, my name is Steve. I am quite proud of it."

"It's a good name."

"Thank you, Isaac."

"I never told you mine."

"Sure you did, Isaac," Steve says. "Sure you did."

"What do you want with me?"

"Hey, man, you're the one who busted me out. What do *you* want with *me?*"

"I want everything to go back to normal."

"What's normal?"

"I don't know."

"Has there ever been a 'normal'?"

"No."

"Then what do you want?"

"I want to leave."

"Then you should leave."

"I can't."

"Why not?"

"I don't know."

We drive into the night. I don't want to go back to the apartment. Cops might be there, waiting for my arrival. I walk up to my front door and I get swarmed by a hail of bullets. Cop-killers don't get brought into the station without a few obliterated organs. Even if I wasn't the one who slit Detective Garcia's throat, they won't know any better. My apartment, her blood. My backseat, her corpse.

I stop at a truck stop and use the stolen hotel money to refill my gas tank. I park in the shadows of the parking lot and head toward the promised restaurant inside. Steve follows.

"I don't think you're allowed in here."

"It's okay," he says, "I'm friends with the owner's nephew."

"Oh, cool."

The server looks at me strangely and I can't tell if it's because of me or my dinner companion. She leads us to a booth without a word and hands me a menu.

"What do you want?" I ask Steve, who's sitting across from me.

"A mouse would be superb."

"I don't think they have mice here."

"At least not on the menu."

I order a coffee and a cheeseburger. The way my stomach growls, it might have been days since the last time I've eaten. The best diet in the world is accidentally stumbling into a series of murders. Forget about Atkins and South Beach. Just go kill a couple motherfuckers and deal with the ensuing fallout.

The truck stop coffee reminds me that not all

coffee is terrible. The hotel has ruined me in more ways than one. I tell Steve he should try some of it. It's really good.

"I don't drink coffee," he says, "but thanks."

"What kind of owl doesn't drink coffee?"

"I'm pretty sure coffee would give me a heart attack."

I laugh. Steve's got jokes. "Owls don't have hearts."

"Well, fuck you too," he says.

"I'm sorry. I didn't mean to offend you."

Steve steps forward on the table. "Where do you want to go?"

"What do you mean?" Mayo drips down my chin and I shamelessly lick it off.

"You said you wanted to leave. Leave where?"

"Oh. Uh. I don't know. Anywhere but here sounds good. The plan has been Mexico, since that's what everybody does in movies. But I don't speak Spanish, and I'm afraid of the cartel confusing me for someone else and decapitating me due to an awful misunderstanding."

"That might be racist," Steve says.

I nod. It certainly might.

"Then if not Mexico, where?"

"I don't know. Maybe London."

"London?"

"Yeah. There's this hotel there called the Langham Hotel. Mark Twain and Oscar Wilde stayed there before. It's supposed to be crazy haunted."

Steve laughs. "Do you believe in ghosts, Isaac?"

"Well, you're here."

"I'm not a ghost."

"You're something, all right."

"Why would you leave a hotel to go to another hotel?"

I shrug, hating this spotlight treatment. But it is a good question. "Hotels are all I know."

"That's the saddest thing I've ever heard."

"If Shakespeare wrote my biography, they'd be teaching that shit in high schools right now."

"The Great Hotel Tragedy."

"Exactly."

"Or maybe the Great *Whooo-tell* Tragedy." Steve chuckles a little too loudly.

"Ugh."

"Get it?" he says. "*Whooo-tell. Whooo.* Because I'm an owl."

"Yeah, I . . . I get it, man."

I finish the cheeseburger and drain the coffee mug. I feel like I could sit here for the rest of time, drinking coffee refills until my flesh deteriorates and my bones turn to ash. The scene would make a great painting, at least. Not so much a great way to live, though.

"Okay," Steve says, "so the plan is to go to London and get a job at this Langham Hotel."

"I don't know. It's a possibility."

"How are you going to get to London? Do you have any money?"

"A little. Just what I got from George's hotel. I'll need more. A lot more."

"And how are you going to do that?"

"I guess I could bust open the safe at my own hotel. Empty it and get the hell out of Texas before anyone notices I'm gone."

Steve steps closer and whispers, "What are you going to do about the bodies in your car?"

The Nightly Disease

No response. I don't have the answers to everything—hell, anything.

"Well, you can't just leave them where they currently reside. That's a wee bit suspicious, don't you think?"

"I suppose."

"Make them the cowboy's problem."

"How?"

"You're asking questions you already know the answers to."

"I'm taking advice from a hallucination."

Steve spits on the table. "Hey, fuck you. Your *dick's* a hallucination, pal."

I grip the empty coffee mug and whip it across the table. Steve's eyes widen and he squeals, but the mug passes through him as it would a ghost and shatters against the wall next to us. Shards of glass bounce off my face but I don't mind. The other patrons of the restaurant stare at me, gasping and whispering amongst themselves, and I don't mind that so much either.

"That was a real asshole move," Steve says, and vanishes. Clap on, clap off. Clap on, clap off.

The server tells me if I don't lift myself out of the booth and put one leg in front of the other until my body has exited the truck stop's premises, she will dial a set of three digits into a telephone and request the assistance of the authorities. I consider the bodies in my car. I consider the things left to be done. I consider the existence of humanity.

I stand up. I walk. I smile at the restaurant patrons as I pass but they do not smile back. No one is smiling except for me and I can't even be sure I am really smiling because I think maybe one of those shards of glass from the shattered coffee mug has cut open my cheek and now this mask of a face has become inside-out. But maybe that's also a hallucination.

I drive. I do not know where. I kill time like I kill my friends. Like I kill hotel guests. I kill time like I kill myself.

A person can only drive as far as their bank account will allow. The corpses in the backseat tell me if I stop, I'll die. If I even slightly ease my foot off the pedal, I'm fucked. Don't bother looking in the rearview because I'll only freak out at the sight of a thousand black-and-whites trailing behind me, sirens blaring. Except I do look, and the road is dark and empty. Detective Garcia's lifeless eyes stare at me in the mirror, casting blame for her death.

"This isn't my fault," I tell her. "I didn't kill you."

"You didn't save me, either."

The detective tries to laugh, but ends up coughing out something wet and cold against the back of my neck. "If you'd just come clean in the beginning, I would still be alive. George would still be alive."

A fist bangs against the passenger seat's head rest and a voice shouts, "Yeah, asshole!"

"I am innocent here," I tell the dead bodies in my car. "I am a victim just as much you all are."

"Who's the one still breathing?"

I focus on the road, which blossoms into a parking lot. In the center of the parking lot, a five-story tall building sits in hibernation. Soon the building will awake and devour the universe. The hotel. I'm not scheduled to work tonight yet I'm still here, because where else is a night auditor supposed to go? This building is my only destiny. Night auditors die in their hotels, like soldiers on a battlefield, like Chucky Cheese janitors at the bottom of a ball pit. Spin a night auditor around for five minutes and every direction they take will lead them back to the front desk. Metal to the magnet. Bumblebee to the pollen. Toilet paper to the asshole.

I cut off the engine at the edge of the parking lot, next to the dumpster. The corpses have stopped talking. We sit in silence, waiting for a solution that's never coming. Plane crash survivors jumping up and down on an island undetected by radars.

The smell of the corpses hit me hard and I have to run from the car, blindly into the woods, and find a comfortable place to discharge the cheeseburger and coffee I'd guzzled down at the truck stop. Afterward, I stand up and continue walking into the woods. I don't want to go back to the car. I can't deal with the corpses any longer. They expect results and I'm only going to disappoint them. If I keep walking into the woods, maybe I'll stumble across the edge of the universe, and maybe I'll leap off.

Instead, I walk into a wall. My nose cracks and I stumble back, one step, two steps, three, then fall on my ass. The woods are the definition of darkness but I can still make out the shape of a small house. Barely even a house. More like a shed. An abandoned shed in the woods behind the hotel. It exists. Kevin had told me about it many times, said he'd spotted it while cleaning the trash that'd blown out of the dumpster. I thought he'd been bullshitting me.

The edge of the universe is a shed in the woods.
Salvation.
I scramble toward it, knowing whatever's waiting inside this place will save my life, will make

everything better again. I push open the door, expecting a treasure chest in the center of the room, and instead find a small baby lying on a blanket, the inside of the shed illuminated by a pair of lanterns.

Regret is instantaneous. A burst dam flooding a town.

I turn around with plans to flee and stop at what—*who*—is in front of me, and stumble into the shed until I'm backpedaling against a wall, and Kia steps inside and closes the door.

#501

"**I**saac, what are you doing here?"

"Me? What the fuck are *you* doing here?" I point at the baby on the floor. "Is this yours?"

She's eyeing me like I'm some lunatic, like finding a baby on the floor of an abandoned shed in the woods is a perfectly normal thing for a person to do. Her stare says to lighten up, to chill the fuck out. Her stare is saying the impossible.

Kia scoops up the baby and hugs it against her chest. "Of course she's mine. This is Saturn."

"Saturn?"

"Yeah, Saturn."

"She was conceived in a Saturn, wasn't she?"

"As a matter of fact—"

I hold up my hand, not wanting to hear the rest of her answer. "What are you doing here? I thought you left."

"Dude, I never said I was moving away or any kind of shit like that. I just said I couldn't keep hanging out with you."

"But . . ."

"I don't know who you think you are, but c'mon, you aren't my dad, man. You don't have me by some kind of twisted, fucked-up leash."

"All this time, you've been behind the hotel."

"Well, most of the time, sure. This is my home."

"This place is abandoned."

"It was abandoned up until the time we claimed it."

"We?"

"Yeah, me and my brothers."

"Right, your brothers. And where are they again?"

"I don't know, man. They don't show their faces here that often. Hell, you probably have a better idea than I do. Why are you bothering me with this dumb shit?"

"I'm sorry." I step forward, intending to caress her cheek as a better apology, then think better of it and step back, step forward, step back, step back, step back. "What do you mean, 'I'd have a better idea'?"

She rocks the baby in her arms. "What are you talking about?"

"What are *you* talking about?"

"What?"

"You said I'd have a better idea about where your brothers are than you do. Why would you say that?"

But she doesn't need to answer me, because it's so fucking obvious I could kill myself.

"They're not," I say, but they are, of course they are.

I want to keep stepping back but I've run out of floor space. If I was a stronger person I'd just step through the wall, through the trees, finally find that edge of the universe once and for all, say hello to whatever's at the bottom.

The Nightly Disease

Kia's cool girl, I-don't-care-about-your-emotions attitude drops at the sight of my expression. "Oh, shit, Isaac, they told me they told you, said you knew everything."

"I . . . I . . . "

"Shit, I'm sorry, I thought . . . "

Anger drives me forward, hands balling into fists. Don't strike a woman holding a baby. Don't strike a woman holding a baby. "They're your fucking *brothers*. Those two pieces of shit? Goddammit, are you serious?"

"You can't pick your family."

"This whole time, you guys were . . . were . . . what?" I want to hit something. I want to hit everything. "Explain this to me, please, help it make some sort of sense, otherwise I'm going to explode, and you'll have to clean up my blood and guts off your stupid baby."

"Hey, fuck you, man, don't talk about Saturn that way."

"Fuck Saturn," I say. "That's a terrible name for a baby."

"So is 'Eye Sick', you asshole." And because I'm concentrated on the baby in her arms, I don't notice her leg until it's between my legs, and my testicles are on fire and I'm falling to the floor.

Hands cupping my junk, I groan and roll around on the floor, anything to make the pain go away. "You bitch," I shout, "what have you done to me?"

"Well, if I'm wrong and there actually is a god, then I just prohibited you from ever reproducing, but we'll have to play that one by ear," Kia says, shushing Saturn, who's in the early stages of a crying fit. "They told me you killed a guy, you know. Said you threw him off the roof, that you were crazy."

"And you believed them?" I try to laugh but only end up gasping, half-convinced she split my scrotum.

"So it's not true."

"Not exactly."

"Did you a kill a guest?"

"I don't know. Maybe."

"What happened to you?"

"You left me."

"Oh, fuck off, don't you dare make me responsible for your own shitty decisions. In case you forgot, I'm the one who tried to convince you to quit that stupid fucking job."

"I would have run away with you."

"You don't even know me, Isaac."

"I could have learned."

"You have learned *what?*"

"You. Everything there's to know about you."

"That, right there, man."

"What?"

"That's psycho, stalker talk."

"No it's not."

"That's, like, what someone says before they fuckin' skin ya and wear ya as a suit."

"It doesn't matter now. Everything is ruined. Everything is so fucked."

"Look, Isaac, I'm sorry about what's happened. I really am. When my brothers told me to get close to you, learn about the hotel, you were just some dickhead behind a desk. I was doing what I thought was best for Saturn. There's not a lot of ways to make money when you're a homeless bulimic single girl with a baby. You gotta do what you gotta do to survive."

"There are other ways to survive."

The Nightly Disease

"You don't know the kind of life I've had."

"You're right. And at this point, I don't even give a shit."

"That's the spirit." She pauses, shushing the baby, then looks up at me again. "Listen, I never meant to actually stab you, okay? I only meant to scare you. I didn't think it'd actually break the skin."

"What are you talking about? You've never stabbed—oh . . . oh, motherfucker." I punch the floor and my knuckles crack. "You were the one who mugged me? Are you fucking serious? What the fuck?"

"Well, yeah . . . who else did you think it was?"

"Fuck."

"I'm sorry."

"Are you?"

"Kind of, yeah."

"You stabbed me."

"It was an accident."

"I can't believe this." I breathe in deeply and slowly exhale. "Wait, so those assholes have had the wallet all this time?"

"I guess, yeah."

"I'm going to kill them. I'm going to fucking kill them."

The baby begins crying harder.

"You're upsetting Saturn."

"I don't give a shit. I have a right to be upset right now. Your stupid baby needs to see how evil her mother is."

"I am not evil."

"You're practically Satan at this point."

"Man, fuck you. I could have stabbed you a whole lot deeper than what I did."

I don't respond, just continue trying to prevent a panic attack. Somehow the shed shrinks even smaller than what it already is. I cross my arms over my chest and sit on the floor and rock back and forth. I scan the rest of the shed and notice the walls are lined with shoeboxes and bags of black sunglasses.

"What's going on with all this?"

"What?" Kia says, disgust in her voice as she rubs her baby's back.

"The sunglasses. I know about the shoes, but what's with the sunglasses?"

"Oh." Kia sighs. "You know those Ray-Ban sunglasses spam things that litter Facebook?"

"Uh, I guess."

"Well, you can thank my brothers for those."

"This doesn't surprise me."

"Listen, Isaac . . . "

"What?"

"I'm sorry for all of this. I really thought you knew about it. Billy, he said they told you. I thought about coming back to visit for old times' sake, but figured you never wanted to see me again."

"Well, he lied."

"Plus he said you had killed someone, that you'd gone crazy."

"So what?"

"So . . . I don't know. I have a baby."

"You keep saying that."

"Well, man, I do, okay? And you know what? This baby is the most important thing in the world to me."

"More important than purging?"

She spits in my face. "Fuck you."

I let the spit trickle down my cheek, then stand up and calmly walk out of the shed. I stop at the door and turn around. "You know, I had it all planned out in my head. None of this was supposed to happen this way. You and I were going to fall in love. We were going to rescue each other."

And Kia laughs and says, "Not everybody needs rescuing, Isaac."

#502

Eventually the sun rises. I park in front of a house on the opposite side of town and wait for Mandy 1 to pull into her driveway. She's just finished night one of her two-night work week at the hotel. She will not be clocking in tonight for her second shift, not if I have anything to say about it. Once she is inside her house I get out of my car, holding Detective Garcia's pistol. What am I doing. I know what I'm doing. These are the things I have to do. These are the things that must be done. I point the pistol and pull the trigger. I've never fired a gun before yet my aim is somehow perfect. The gas tank gives birth to a bullet hole. I flinch, expecting a massive explosion. Nothing happens. I shoot it again. Still nothing. Bells ring in my ears and I can't hear, I can't breathe. Bells ring in my ears and it is the only sound that has ever truly existed. But where is the fire. Where is the mayhem. Where is the apocalypse. Where are the owls. I dive back into my car and drive faster than I've ever driven in my life. Did she see me? Maybe my plan will still work despite the lack of an explosion. Maybe she will be so frightened, she will flee the state. Or maybe she recognized my car and I'm driving into an ambush. Maybe, maybe, maybe.

There are many flaws to my plan. Mandy 1 might not call off from work. Perhaps strangers attempt to explode her car on a daily basis and she's simply gotten used to this way of life. Or maybe she'll find refuge at the hotel. It might be the only place she feels safe now.

I punch the steering wheel and when it honks it sounds like an owl shouting an obscenity. I yell the same obscenity back at the steering wheel. I will not be spoken to in such a manner.

Somewhere between driving and crying uncontrollably, I fall asleep. When I wake up, I'm still driving, only I'm no longer on the road. Trees surround me yet somehow I have not crashed. I scream and press harder on the gas. This is the way I'm supposed to go. If there's one thing left in this world I can trust, it's the choices of the unconscious mind. The unconscious mind has no hidden agenda. It simply reacts. There is no thought process or outline. The unconscious mind is no one's bitch.

"Where the fuck are you going?" George screams from the backseat.

"Pull over!" Detective Garcia joins in. "You're under arrest, Eye Sick! Just give it up!"

I shake my head, eyes on the dark nothingness ahead. "The dead don't talk, so shut the fuck up."

"Dude, you can't talk to me that way," George says. "You killed me, asshole. The least you can do is show some respect."

"Dead or not," Garcia says, "I'm cuffing your ass and bringing you downtown."

"That doesn't make any sense," I say, finally giving in to this insane conversation. "Why would you take me downtown? Wouldn't you take me to the local police department that you work at?"

Garcia doesn't respond. Clearly I've won this argument.

I plunge deeper into oblivion. Texas farmland surrounds me and I can't quite shake a *Chainsaw Massacre* vibe. If my car suddenly breaks down, there is little doubt in my mind that someone won't come along and offer to give me a lift back to their trailer where they've prepared a feast with "night auditor" as the main course. But I don't break down. At least, my car doesn't. I've long broken down, and there isn't a spare in the world big enough to put me back together.

#503

Saturday night and I stroll in the hotel like I own the place, and really, once you consider everything I've been through in this building, I might as well. At this point, I've done plenty to mark my territory. Not quite eleven yet. Yas stands at the front desk, on her cell phone. When she sees me, her expression brightens, which is immediately peculiar considering how clear she's made her indifference toward me in the past.

"Isaac," she says, "I didn't know anyone had gotten a hold of you."

"Mandy can't come in tonight, right?"

She nods. "Yeah. Some crazy people tried to shoot her? I'm not exactly sure. But she refuses to come in, says she's hiding at a friend's house for a couple weeks until the police arrest somebody. It's super weird."

"It's a weird world."

"So Javier isn't coming to do audit tonight?"

I pause. "Did he say he was?"

"Well, nobody could contact you, so yeah, he said he would just do it."

"Could you give him a call and tell him I made it in, after all? I'm okay with working tonight. It's no problem."

"Sure." She stares at me longer than a person should stare at someone. "Uh, you know you're bleeding, right?"

"Yeah. I know." I touch my forehead and inspect my finger. She wasn't kidding. "I'll go clean up. Call Javier."

I don't know why I'm bleeding, but that's okay. Sometimes people bleed. Sometimes people bleed a lot. Sometimes I am a person, but only sometimes.

I wet paper towels and wipe my face. I must be presentable. I must give the impression that I am someone who doesn't currently have three corpses in his car. What if a guest sees them and calls the police and ruins everything? It won't happen. It can't. Nobody sees someone in a car and thinks, "Oh, hey, that person is probably dead." Someone sees two people in the backseat of a car in the middle of the night and they assume they are lovers. They assume someone's getting jerked-off. Only a lunatic like me would automatically think they're oozing maggots.

"Has the little league group showed up yet?" I ask Yas once I return to the front desk.

"No, but they called me about twenty minutes ago, said they'd be here around midnight or so."

"And they're paying cash, right?"

"Yeah, I think so." She laughs. "You're in for a hell of a night. Good luck."

She tosses me the keys and walks out of the hotel despite the fact that there's still a good half hour until eleven. It doesn't matter. Gives me more time to carry out my plans. I clock in and sit down in the back office, psyching myself up for what awaits. I go over my to-do list:

1. Check-in little league teams.
2. Steal their room payments.
3. Frame the Hobbs brothers for three separate murders.
4. Do my audit.
5. Get breakfast ready.
6. Close my shift.

Should be easy enough. I've had rougher nights at the hotel. If I survived the night Yates died, I can survive anything.

And, as if rising to the challenge, the front desk phone rings. I answer it and a lady says, "Yes, I need some help."

"What can I do for you?"

I know I watch too much porn because every time I ask someone this question, the dirtiest responses come to mind. Yet they never use any of the ones I imagine. I know I watch too much porn because life is a constant disappointment.

"I'm a guest at your hotel, but I'm trapped down the street."

"I see."

"I'm at this bar, and I called for a cab over an hour ago, but they still haven't shown up."

"Okay."

"What are you going to do about this?"

"Uh. Well. Nothing?"

"Nothing?"

"Correct."

"I don't think so, mister. I am a guest at your hotel. I paid for a room and I expect to sleep in that room."

"Have you called the cab company back and asked what's going on?"

The lady pauses. "Okay, so here's the thing. When I first talked to them, they told me they'd have a driver out in no less than twenty minutes. Then forty minutes pass and still nobody has shown up, so I called them and raised hell. They tried telling me some bullshit about how they been trying to call me for the last half hour, but I ain't pickin' up. Well of course I ain't pickin' up, my cell was at the bottom of my damn purse. How the hell was I supposed to know they was calling?"

"By the sound of the ringer?"

"Not if it was all the way at the bottom of my purse I wouldn't! Don't you know how big my purse is?"

"Well . . . no. I don't."

"Believe me right here and now when I tell you it's big. Real big. Now how am I supposed to hear my phone ringing if it's all the way at the bottom? Why didn't those stupid assholes think to tell me they might be calling me again? If I had known something might unexpectedly come up, I would have had my phone out ready for them, but they didn't tell me that. They didn't tell me anything of the sort."

"Those bastards."

"So now I'm still at this bar, waiting to be picked up, and I am just so sick of this shit. I need someone from the hotel to come get me."

"I'm sorry, ma'am, but I'm the only employee at night, and I can't leave the building."

"That is unacceptable."

"It's really not."

"Let me speak to your manager."

"Once again, I am the only person here." I hang

up the phone. Someone's at the front desk, pounding on the marble. I come around from the back office and find a lobby full of men and women wearing various baseball fandom T-shirts and sweatpants and trying their absolute best to look tough. They are sort of succeeding. Running amok through the crowd of coaches and parents are a thousand tiny ten-year-old boys flying on an apparent sugar-high. The woman trapped at the bar down the street had done such a grand job of screeching into my ear that I did not hear the little league group enter the hotel.

A short man with a long grey beard stands at the front desk. He smiles and reveals a set of black teeth. "We're a bit late, but we finally made it. We should have fifteen rooms reserved. We're the—"

"—little league group, yeah, I figured."

I pull up the reservations, hoping that housekeeping hadn't fucked up and we actually have the rooms available. For once, it looks like they did their jobs. I calculate the cost for all fifteen rooms throughout the weekend and tell him how much he owes me: $3,118.80. He doesn't even seem to blink at the amount. He hands me over thirty-two one hundred dollar bills and says to keep the change and for a moment I almost feel bad about pocketing the entire sum, but only for a moment.

The coaches and parents in the lobby laugh and shout, drunk and ready to party. The leader of the group takes all the room keys and distributes them, then asks me where the swimming pool is located.

"Outside, but it closed at ten. It's locked up now."

He stares, unfazed. "I just gave you an eighty dollar tip."

"The fence is short. If you hop it, I doubt I'll notice."

The leader grins. "You want to join us? We got moonshine and weed."

"Maybe later. My, uh, work is not yet done."

The leader holds out his hand and indicates for me to slap it. "I fuckin' love that book, man."

"What."

"You think because I coach a little league team, I don't read? Man, me and Ligotti once snorted lines of cocaine off a stripper's titties together."

"That . . . that isn't true."

He winks, then spins around and punches a random kid in the arm. "You motherfuckers ready to party?"

The lobby erupts with celebration. I flee to the back office as they finish entering the hotel. Their drunkenness increases in volume and I realize now why management reserved the entire first floor for this group. At least there shouldn't be too many complaints. It's my last night at the hotel, anyway. Fuck it. After tonight, I'm done. Either I'll be free of all charges and the Hobbs brothers will be behind bars, or I'll be the one with cuffs around his wrists. Either way, it's better than one more fucking shift in this pool of quicksand. After tonight, I will sleep better than any man has ever slept. I will be free.

Something made of glass shatters in the lobby and I run from the back office to investigate. A nude man stands above a broken beer bottle. He apologizes and quickly cleans it up with his bare hands. Once the glass has been disposed of in a trashcan, he returns to the puddle of beer and proceeds to lick it off the floor. Elsewhere, a woman screams, "You stretched his cock all to pieces, ya damn floozy!" Down the hallway, a group of children have created a human pyramid. The kid on top attempts to eat the tiled ceiling.

Little league coaches are insane, and the players' parents are even worse. They aren't of this world. I've learned this on more than one occasion.

Any other night and this group might be stressing me out. Any other night and I might be contemplating suicide. But it's not any other night. It's tonight. Everything is zen. There are three dead bodies out in my car and everything is going to be okay.

But first, I have to convince Hobbs to momentarily abandon his room. But why would a sketchy shoe counterfeiter abandon his sweatshop? Why would an owl leave its nest? To hunt. To feed. Maybe if I offer to pay, he'll make a trip to McDonald's. I call the room but nobody answers. Might be too invested in his needle and thread. Might be dead. This is a monster who sleeps probably less than I do. How long can you go without sleep before dying? How long can you work until combusting?

All questions I've been trying to answer for some time now.

The phone rings. My hopes rise then fall once the caller ID reveals a room other than Hobbs's. "Front desk. How can I help you?"

"Hi, uh, yes, there seems to be multiple men and women down in the jacuzzi. They're naked and . . . appear to be performing various sexual acts on each other."

I groan. Suddenly these little league coaches don't seem so harmless. I got a lot of shit to do tonight and they're just going to get in my way. But why is this my problem? Why can't these coaches and parents screw wherever they please? I've already decided tonight is my last night, which means I don't need to worry about potentially being fired. These concerns no longer belong to me, so why do I automatically own the responsibility? I am a machine with one simple set of coding, a customer service robot programmed to obtain satisfaction from all.

"I'm sorry, sir," I tell the guest. "Thank you for informing me of this unfortunate situation. I'll go take care of the situation right away."

"No! No, God no. Please don't."

"Excuse me?"

"There's no reason to stop a good thing, bro. I'm up in my room watching through my window. I just thought you might want to come up and watch with me. It's pretty hot."

"I . . . no. I'm gonna have to pass."

"Ah, dang, you're really missing out."

Three muscular women covered in tattoos wait patiently in the lobby for me to get off the phone. The logo for the Houston Astros cover their arms in large, bulging tattoos. One of them holds a giant industrial-sized can of refried beans. The possibilities of what they intend on doing with this can are terrifying, but that doesn't mean I don't desperately wish to find out.

"Can I help you ladies with anything?" I ask.

One of them says, "We was hoping you had some kinda big container for us to eat these beans in."

"We have many containers, yes." I lead them into the kitchen. They follow close behind, giggling. It occurs to me that this might be a trap, that they might be storing something other than beans in this cartoonishly large can. Something much more deadly. But once they use the can opener we have in the kitchen to cut open the lid, all suspicions of a conspiracy diminish. Unless they plan on force-feeding me a mythological god's portion of the musical fruit and having me fart myself to death, which I suppose is possible. At this point in my life I can't rule out any ridiculous ways to die. Look at George. Look at Mr. Yates.

Look at me.

Everything is ridiculous. The concept of existence alone is funny enough to make a clown piss its pants. Why should death be any better?

The women cook the refried beans in the bowl and take turns taking bites from a large metal spoon I give them. When I attempt to return to the front desk, they circle me like a pack of teenaged bullies on bicycles. Except they're passing around a hilariously large bowl of refried beans, so they aren't exactly the most menacing bunch.

"Excuse me, ladies," I say and attempt another escape, but they block me from passing.

One of them sniffs, then smiles. "Goddamn, boy, you smell goooood."

"Mmmm," another says, leaning forward and smelling me.

"Uh, what."

"You smell amazing."

"Seriously, what kind of cologne is that?"

"Mmm."

I can't remember the last time I've showered. I have never worn any type of body spray in my life. What they smell is death. I have been driving around for hours with three corpses in my car. They are in love with the scent of death. Fuck.

I break free of the trio of bean-guzzlers by claiming the phone's ringing.

Max Booth III

"We don't hear nothin', honey," one of them says, grabbing my crotch hard enough to squeeze tears from my eyes. Once I'm behind the front desk, I grab the phone and pretend I'm having a heated conversation with a guest in another room about the hypothetical cleanliness of their bed sheets. The three little league chaperones linger in the lobby for a moment, eavesdropping, until something down the hallway snags their attention, and they run off toward their next adventure. On the way down the hallway, one of them kicks the pyramid of children and they all go collapsing to the floor. The kid who was on top remains hanging from the ceiling, jaws hinged to a tile.

Every ounce of me wishes to just hide up on the roof until my shift's complete. But this isn't a normal shift. This is my last shift, and my actions tonight will determine the outcome of the rest of my life. Well, they'll at least keep me out of prison. Maybe.

This shift is a ticking time clock. The longer I wait, the less of a chance I have of pulling everything off successfully. As it is, the odds here aren't that great. It's a challenge not to pick up the phone and call the Other Goddamn Hotel. George would listen to me bitch about my problems. He'd agree with me that the world was created with the sole purpose of destroying me. But I can't talk to George because George is dead. My only friend is rotting in my backseat. I can't even tell him about Kia, that he'd been right, I should have never trusted her. She hadn't loved me. Yet still, despite this new knowledge, despite these revelations, I feel no less about her than I did the first morning she snuck into the lobby and puked in our restroom. She could saw my penis off and feed it to the owls and I would still owe her my heart.

The Nightly Disease

If George was still alive, this is the point where he'd laugh and tell me how pathetic I am, and I'd agree with him, but that still wouldn't change anything.

A man in the lobby is shouting the word "penis".

A woman shushes him. "You can't say penis in a hotel lobby."

"Why the fuck not? PENIS! PENIS! PENIS!"

"Stop it!"

"I can't believe nobody is at the fucking desk."

"You probably scared him off, penis this, penis that."

"Oh, suck my penis."

A few minutes pass, and just when I think the coast is clear, another gaggle of voices erupt in the lobby.

"Baby, please don't do this. You're gonna hurt my feelings and my feelings are like a million dollars right now, don't spend it all at once, honey."

Two little league coaches, drunk as hell. I peek around the corner of the back office. The man speaking is the nerdiest white guy I've ever seen.

"I'm a muthafuckin' kamikaze comin' down upon my destination, ya bitch ass nigga ho."

Just as they leave, another set of little league chaperones take their place.

"Martha, that isn't an elevator!"

"I'm taking the goddamn stairs!"

"Martha, that is a bathroom."

"Fuck you, no it ain't."

"Fine."

Silence, then:

"Hahahahahaha, you guys, you guys, Martha just ran into the wall, oh God, hahahaha, Martha just ran into the wall, I think she's bleeding, hahaha, fuck you, Martha, fuck you!"

I don't move, don't even breathe, until I'm sure whoever's at the front desk has given up and returned to whatever hole they crawled out of. I poke my head out from behind the back office wall to confirm the lobby is empty. It only lasts for a moment, as another group of little league monsters sprint down the hallway, shouting something about an overdose. It doesn't sound that serious. From the laundry room, I fetch bed sheets and a bungee cord, then cautiously exit the hotel and wheel a luggage cart to my car. Down the parking lot, a couple little league coaches have set a trashcan on fire and are using the flames to roast marshmallows and light their joints. A small boy rests on all fours nearby, howling at the moon. They don't seem to notice me. Or, if they do, they don't care. These people play by their own rules. If this was a normal night and I called the cops, would there be a shootout? Or maybe the dispatcher would tell me I was on my own, that cops and little league coaches, they got themselves an agreement, and hotels are off limits.

I open the backseat door and spread one of the bed sheets over the bottom of the luggage cart. I don't think the human body bleeds much once it's no longer living, but I'm a night auditor, not a doctor, so who am I to start taking chances? George's body drops like an anchor, nearly rolling off and smacking against the concrete if not for my shins acting as a temporary blockade. Next, I drag out Detective Garcia with her slit throat now dry and empty, then pull Yates out of the trunk, the stupid bastard who started it all by getting himself thrown off the roof. The bodies are stiff, which works to my advantage when trying to stack them on top of each other. Detective Garcia and Yates lie side by side on top of George's immense bloated fat. I wrap the extension cord underneath the luggage cart and bring both ends around the stack of corpses, clipping them together where the rigid hips of Detective Garcia and Yates connect, then cover them with the rest of the bed sheets, tucking the ends under George's arms. To an outsider, it will look like I am either transporting three corpses or a massive amount of oblong-shaped luggage. I do not need to keep them disguised for any extensive amount of time, just long enough to smuggle them into Hobbs's room.

I don't even make it back into the hotel before getting interrupted.

A young guy, maybe my age, cuts me off in front of the entrance, wearing a backpack and a red baseball cap turned backward. Just stands there with a big goofy smile across his face, the kinda smile that screams, "I'm about to rob you."

"Can I help you?" I ask, both hands wrapped around the luggage cart's handle.

"You work here, bro?" the kid asks, the words somehow leaking from his untampered grin.

"My attire would suggest it's likely."

"Okay, great. Well, I have a reservation for eight rooms."

"I just checked my system and I didn't have a single reservation left."

"Hmm. Weird. You'll need to check again. Search for the name: Dean. James Dean."

And I just look at him, thinking how easy it would be to add him to my collection of corpses. "I don't have the time for this."

"No, I'm serious." The kid holds his arms out, blocking me from walking around him. "All eight rooms should already be paid for under your PornHub account."

I release the luggage cart momentarily and push the kid out of my way, then continue pushing it into the hotel. He follows me through the lobby like a gnat on the back of my neck.

"Okay," he says, "I apologize for that. Sometimes it makes people laugh."

"What do you want?"

"Funny you should ask, actually." Again, he's standing in front of me, preventing me from continuing forward, but now he's reaching into the front of his pants and I'm convinced he's either about to pull out a dick or a pistol. I'm oddly indifferent to either outcome.

Except it's neither a dick nor a pistol, but a yellow sheet of paper I immediately recognize as the scent sampler card of a traveling bootleg cologne hustler. I've encountered these types many times over the years, usually lingering behind fast food restaurants or inside shopping malls, and not once have any of them exceeded beyond a stereotypical douchebag persona. The kid in front of me now shows no promise of exception.

"Tell me," he says, "what kind of cologne do you usually buy?"

"Oh, fuck right off."

"Excuse me?"

"I don't have time for this. *Nobody* has time for this. But I *especially* don't have time for this. Leave. Now."

"Now, c'mon bro, you're gonna wanna hear me out."

The Nightly Disease

"I seriously doubt it."

"Listen, bro, all right, just listen. I'm here to change your life, all right, bro? Change your *life*. You ain't never smelled so good 'til you met me. Now I got a variety of scents here, tell me what you usually prefer, and I'll hook you up. Trust me, bro."

"Dead skunk."

"What?"

"The only scent I prefer comes from rubbing the rotting carcasses of skunks against my naked body. So unless you have a dead skunk stored away in that backpack of yours, please fuck off. I'm very busy."

The kid's smile only trembles for a moment, then regains stability. "You're one of those weird ones, huh?"

I want to look at him and wink and tell him he has no idea, but I'm not a movie character so I just tell him to fuck off again and continue pushing the luggage cart through the lobby. The kid remains persistent and I remain impatient and the corpses remain remains. The only reason the kid doesn't notice the smell probably has to do with him constantly surrounding himself in the awful bootleg colognes he sells for a living. I don't delude myself into thinking he always strikes out with potential customers. It would not surprise me to hear these cologne salesmen make more than the pitiful amount the hotel has decided it's fair to pay me. At the mall, he probably hits gold. But I can't understand why he'd think it's a good idea to take his pitch to a hotel lobby at one, two in the morning. His desperation is evident even with that shit-eating grin plastered over it. He needs money. He needs help. He needs a savior.

I am no one's savior.

"You have five seconds to get the fuck out of here or I'm calling the cops," I tell him, and he's giving me a Judas look.

"You can't even smell a *few* of them? At least give me that, bro."

I sigh. Every ounce of my body aches with exhaustion. I glare at the cologne hustler like he's responsible for everything that's happened to me, then lean down and pull the bedsheet up, revealing Detective Garcia's haunted face staring straight up at us, a deep gash in her neck.

"Does it look like I give a shit about hygiene at the moment?" I ask the kid, but he's already backing up, muttering something unintelligible, then he's gone, out of my life, maybe running to the police station, maybe fleeing the state, it doesn't matter, he's just some asshole pushing bootleg cologne to irritated strangers, nobody's gonna give a shit what he says.

And if someone believes him, so what.

It's hard to care. It's so hard to care about anything.

I flip the sheet back over Detective Garcia's face and push the luggage cart into the elevator. None of this feels like I'm breaking the law. It's just more work, mechanical and draining. It doesn't matter how you spend your nine-to-five or your eleven-to-seven or whatever the fuck because it doesn't change the fact that you're still trapped, still confined, no room to breathe, no room to operate your thoughts without the fear of failure. Handling corpses is no goddamn different than anything else this hotel's required of me. But even after all this, I don't see an Employee of the Month plaque in my future.

One of the little league coaches joins me on the

elevator ride, presses the third floor button. His face is covered in white powder and he doesn't show any indication of giving a damn who notices. He asks how I'm doing and I tell him okay, I'm doing okay, and just as I exit the elevator on the second floor, I swear to God he hoots like an owl at me, but before I can turn around the doors have already closed and he's gone.

I stash the luggage cart of corpses in the laundry room down the hallway, then pound my fist against Hobbs's door. I don't slow down until a neighboring guest pokes his head out and tells me to shut the hell up. I apologize and he tells me to apologize to the whore he's about to bang and I say, "Sorry, whore," and he tells me he'll have my job and I tell him all right, then come take it, motherfucker. But he doesn't respond, just stares at me like I've lost my mind and closes the door, and I have never felt more like a gangster in my entire life. I am attracting unwanted attention and I don't care—even though I should, I don't, I can't, I've cared so long I've gone and overdrawn my giving-a-fuck account.

Either Hobbs isn't in the room or he's passed out in there, drunk or dead. I don't know much but I do know nobody's ever gotten many answers out in some hallway. I insert my master key into the lock and open the door. Darkness greets my presence.

"Hey," I whisper. "Hey, you in here?"

No response.

No one's here.

I don't flip on the light switch on the likelihood that Hobbs is outside smoking a cigarette. If he happened to glance at his window, he'd know someone was up here snooping around, and the plan would be ruined. Instead, I sneak back down the hallway and retrieve the luggage cart, then smuggle it into Hobbs's room under the cover of shadows. A straining series of grunts and "Jesus Christ"s later, the three corpses are secured inside Hobbs's closet. It's not the most conspicuous corpse storage, and it's not supposed to be. The bodies only need to remain undetected until the police arrive.

The gears in the elevator squeal on the way down. The sound reminds me of owls mating. Maybe a few of 'em sneaked in through the roof and got themselves trapped in the elevator shaft. Good. Hopefully they starve in there and rot for eternity. The smell will haunt the guests for weeks, months. I'll be long gone. A new state, a new country, a new world, anywhere but here.

Hobbs is sitting in the lobby when I reach the ground floor. He nods at me, grinning his tobacco-stained teeth and gripping the neck of a plastic Pepsi bottle. "Eye Sick! Thought we saw your car out front. What the hell you doin' here, man? Ain't tonight your night off?"

Before I can respond, a woman enters the hotel, eyes narrowed at me, jaw grinding. "Oh wow," she says, pointing an accusing finger at me, "you mean to tell me somebody actually works at this goddamn hotel?"

"That's an accurate statement, yes."

"Don't you get smart with me, dickhead! Do you have any idea how long I've been waiting at that bar for someone from *your* stupid hotel to come pick me up? Huh? Do you?"

It takes a moment for her identity to click. The woman who'd called earlier, in the beginning of my shift. The one stranded down the street. I'd assumed she had been abducted or murdered by this point.

The Nightly Disease

"As I told you, ma'am, it's just me here, so nobody could have picked you up."

"Sounds like a bunch of bullshit excuses to me. I hope you realize I am expecting a full refund for my stay tonight."

"That isn't going to happen."

"Excuse me?"

"You're not getting a free room, lady. You're lucky I don't kick you out right here and now. So just stop. Just . . . stop. Go to sleep. Piss off."

All the fight drains from her system at once. "Okay. I'm sorry." She lowers her head and boards the elevator.

Hobbs starts clapping. "Christ almighty, Eye Sick, that was fuckin' poetry."

I don't share his enthusiasm. Once upon a time I had dreamed of speaking to the guests in such a matter. Now, it feels underwhelming. Too many complications in life have dulled my sense of pleasure. I fear I won't even gain satisfaction when I turn in my resignation tomorrow.

The bathroom door down the hallway opens and the cowboy steps out, straightening his straw Stetson. He belches before saying, "Isaac! You really are here. How wonderful."

When I look at the cowboy, all I see is him strolling into my apartment and slicing Detective Garcia's throat as casual as someone might act brewing that first pot of coffee in the morning. This man is not a man but a monster. A devil in human flesh. A wolf in sheep's clothing.

He pats me on the shoulder and I stiffen, fearing the possibility of a blade hidden within his grasp. His sister's already stabbed me in the back plenty—surely it runs in the family.

"What's going on?" I ask, because clearly something is.

"Well," the cowboy says, "we were just driving by, heading out of town once and for all, when we saw your eyesore of a car parked out here, so we thought we'd stop and give you a proper goodbye. After everything we've been through, hell, I reckon we owe you at least that."

I listen to his words but I can't hear them, can't understand them. "What are you talking about?"

Now Hobbs is standing next to his brother, showing off his brown teeth. "We're packin' it up, Eye Sick. Movin' on. Our time here's done expired."

"You're . . . you're checking out?"

"Already done, my friend," the cowboy says. "Checked out this afternoon. We were on our way out of town tonight when we saw your car. Thought, hell, Isaac doesn't work tonight. He's made it abundantly clear he don't work on no *Saturdays.*"

"The . . . the other lady called off." I clear my throat, sweat trickling down my spine. "Did you say you *already* checked out?"

The cowboy nods. "Yeah, well, I figured we had outstayed our welcome here."

"What with my brother killing himself a cop and all," Hobbs says, and the cowboy elbows him in the gut. He doubles over and grunts. "Shit, Billy, that hurt."

"Good." He looks back at me, serious. "Listen, kid, I know we've been hard on you and all, and I'm sorry for that. Life's been stressful as all hell lately. Our Amazon account has been swamped with orders, which is great, just a lot of work needed to be done. Now, our stay here did not go over as ideally as I'd liked, but I think we all had a heck of a time, don't you think?"

"I, uh, I guess?"

The cowboy smiles and rustles my hair like I'm some grade-schooler saying goodbye to his father. "Excellent. Also, about the money you stole from us. I want you to forget about it. Shit happens." He laughs. "Hell, put me in your place and I'd've probably pulled the same shit. Except, of course, I wouldn't have allowed myself to go get mugged."

I push his hand away from me and tighten my fists. "You mean, you wouldn't have made your sister mug you. Wouldn't have made your sister hold up a knife to your throat and threaten to murder you."

Both brothers stare at me, silent. Fuck them. I step forward and they step back.

"You wouldn't have made your own goddamn sister trick you into falling in love with her. You wouldn't have made her break your heart. You're far too much of a tough sonofabitch to ever let anything like that happen, right? *Right?*"

The cowboy coughs out a nervous laugh. "Isaac, now, hold on, you don't know what you're talking about."

Hobbs matches my step forward and shoves me back. "Yeah, *Eye Sick,* why don't you watch your fuckin' mouth, huh?"

I return the shove. He's not expecting the retaliation and stumbles harder than I intended. The cowboy wedges his way between his, holding up his arms as a offer of peace. "I don't know what Key's told you, but I advise you to calm down and allow us to explain."

"Explain what?" The anger building up is hot

enough to boil. "Explain how everything that's happened to me has been *your* fault? Explain that you set me up to steal the wallet, that you forced your sister—the mother of your niece—to attack me in the parking lot? What if I had defended myself? What if I had killed her? Did you ever even think of that, you stupid shit? Did you ever stop and consider how much danger you were putting her in?"

Hobbs explodes with laughter. The cowboy lowers his head, shaking it slowly and rubbing his temple like he's sporting a headache. "Isaac . . . "

Hobbs cuts him off. "Eye Sick, you dumb motherfucker."

"Shut up, John," the cowboy says, then to me, "Look, you can think what you want. The truth is, you're right, we all fucked you over. But I never once forced my sister into anything. That whole mugging scheme, you think that was my idea? That was reckless, careless, completely stupid. By now, I would hope you know me better than that. But that doesn't change the fact that I'm still partly responsible, and for that, I do apologize, and so does John."

Hobbs shakes his head, waving his index finger back and forth. "Hell nah, I ain't sorry for shit. If Eye Sick here was such a good goddamn Samaritan, he would've never snatched my wallet in the first place. The way I see it, he got everything he fuckin' deserved, and you know what? I think he may have gotten off lightly. It's his own damn fault blood was shed here. I sure as hell didn't throw no sumbitch off the roof. That was all you, Eye Sick. Think about it, boy. You're the real asshole here. You're the one owing *us* apologies, not the other way around. Nuh-uh."

The fight in me deflates. The urge to bash their

faces in with my fists subsides. The black hole of the hotel swallows my energy. I debate retrieving Detective Garcia's gun from behind the front desk and putting a hole in each of them, then maybe turning it on myself. Just get it over with already. Finish it once and for all.

Except I still have a plan. They may be leaving, but before I left on Friday morning I made sure to extend their stay until next week. Which means they're still technically in the system. Which means the bodies up in room 209, they belong to the Hobbs brothers.

I got you, you fuckers. I got you.

A drunk little league coach stumbles into the lobby, dripping with water from the pool. "We need some towels," he says, drooling. "We need, like, a million towels. Also, I think one of us had an accident in the jacuzzi. It was me. I shit in the jacuzzi. I'm sorry. Towels?"

And the urge to inflict violence on every last soul in this building returns. The urge to drench the floors and walls with gasoline and light a thousand matches. The urge to fetch the dead cop's gun and make everything beautiful.

It doesn't matter that I'm in the middle of a dramatic conclusion to a terrifying situation. A guest needs towels. A guest in need of needing needs, needs to need like he needs to bleed.

Needs.

I will never not be a slave to hospitality. I will never leave here. Outside this hotel there is nothing. I cannot leave my home. I cannot leave my mother's womb. Instead of telling this guest to roll around in the grass to dry off, I know I will get him a stack of towels, because it is not just my job but my only real reason to exist. I was not conceived, I was coded. I don't get to decide whether I live or die. Night auditors are not given the ability to make their own decisions. We just do. We service. We are handymen of comfort. Mechanics of sleep. These thoughts aren't new. They've been engraved in the land since the big bang.

I glance at the Hobbs brothers, no longer feeling the intensity we'd been sharing a few moments ago, and lower my head in defeat.

"Okay," I tell the little league coach, "I'll get you some towels."

"*All* the towels."

"Okay. I'll get you all the towels."

Before I head toward the laundry room, the cowboy grabs my shoulder and whispers, "I really am sorry, Isaac. I want you to know that. And when the lady gave me our bill this afternoon, I saw how much you've paid just to let us stay here, and I can't tell you how much that means to me. All the shit we did to you, you still pulled through for us. If we're ever in the area again, I'll buy you a beer or something. Deal?"

I mouth the word "Receipt?" without actually saying it. The little league coach's own voice interrupts my confusion. "Hey, wait a second, I know you, don't I?" He points at Hobbs. "You look familiar as hell. Where do I know you from?"

Hobbs shrugs. "I get around, man. I don't know."

The little league coach squints, then laughs. "Oh shit. I know who you fuckin' are."

"All right." Hobbs laughs with him. "Care to enlighten me, brotha?"

The little league coach whips a cell phone out of

his shorts pocket and dials a number. Somehow it isn't destroyed from soaking in the water.

Behind me, the cowboy whispers, "John . . . I think we should go . . . "

And behind the cowboy, the automatic doors slide open and Kia Hobbs runs inside, face bright with excitement. She doesn't acknowledge her brothers, but looks straight at me, and gestures outside. "Isaac, dude, you aren't gonna fuckin' believe it."

"What?"

"The hotel is swarmed, man. Fuckin' swarmed."

"Swarmed with what?" Hobbs asks.

And when she answers, she's still looking at me, no one else:

"*Owls.*"

On the cell phone, the little league coach says, "You won't fuckin' believe who I just ran into in the lobby. You remember those assholes who ripped us off on those cleats? Yeah, the ones that fell apart during our first game. Yup, in the lobby. Right now. Looking at them as I speak. Uh-huh. You got it."

The little league coach slides the cell phone back in his pocket and stares at us, glowing. "Oh, you motherfuckers are in for it now. Think you can steal from a children's baseball team? Ha, oh shit. You're about to get fucked the fuck up, amigo."

"Shit," the cowboy and his brother say in unison.

"Owls," their sister says. "Everywhere."

And the sound I've been hearing, the heartbeat rising in volume, the sheer panic consuming me, it's real, it's more real than anything anybody's ever heard in the history of noise. That sound, it's the sound of a million owls swarming the hotel. Pissed off. Hungry. Ready.

Max Booth III

The elevator dings.

Then, three things happen.

One: the woman who'd gotten stranded at the bar earlier runs out of the elevator, screaming something about dead bodies in her closet.

Two: the cowboy pulls a pistol out from the back of his jeans and shoots the little league coach in the stomach.

Three: every window in the hotel explodes, and owls swarm the lobby.

#504

"**A**re those fucking owls?" Hobbs screams. The four of us leap to the floor and begin fighting off the birds from landing on us.

"I told you!" Kia says, barely loud enough to travel over the sound of the owls' wings flapping in the lobby. "Didn't I tell you?"

The little league coach remains standing by the front desk, legs shaking, hand holding his bleeding stomach. The gunshot and the sudden owl attack have sent him over the edge. Tears leak down his face. His mouth opens but I can't hear what he says. Then a dozen or so owls cover his body and feast. His screams match the owls' squeals of delight.

And I'm on the floor listening to it all, heart pounding, everybody understandably freaking out, realizing if I don't move right this second then I'm done, I'm dead, I'm owl-food. There's no use trying to understand the situation when I'm at risk of being erased from it.

Grinding my teeth, I rise into the cloud of owls. I reach down and find Kia's hand and pull her up with me. I don't care what she's done, she's still the love of my life. Owls bounce off my head as I drag her through the lobby, leaving her dirtbag brothers to fend for themselves.

The cowboy starts shooting and I don't know if he's aiming at me or the owls.

Down the hallway, a group of little league coaches rush toward us, armed and extremely pissed off. The owls attempt to attack them and they slap them away. One of the coaches—the one who had checked in—points a machine gun at me and shouts, "WHERE ARE THEY?" and I point behind me, back toward the lobby. I grip Kia's hand harder and pull her along as we take a sharp corner in front of the elevator, running to the end of the side-hallway. At this point, three potential routes present themselves. We either go outside through the backdoor and battle who the hell knows how many owls flying freely in the night, hide in the exercise room which contains a large picture window that's surely been shattered and infiltrated at this point, or flee into the Muzak room.

The little league coaches run past us, toward the sound of the cowboy shooting off his pistol.

I push Kia into the Muzak room and just as I'm closing the door behind us, a hand pokes through the opening. One of her brothers, presumably. I swat the hand away but it doesn't surrender, continues trying to squeeze the rest of the body attached to it inside. The gap widens enough for the perpetrator to stick his head through.

Not Hobbs and not his asshole brother, and not one of the little league coaches, either.

The fucking cologne salesman.

The Nightly Disease

"C'mon bro, open the door, I'm gonna die out here."

If not for Kia, I would've just locked the door and left him out in the hallway to fulfill his destiny of digesting in various owls' tiny stomachs.

I grab his shirt and drag him inside, then close the door. The lock clicks into place. The Muzak room is nearly soundproof and the owls' hooting and hollering decrease to mere muffles. We are immediately violated with an intense humidity. The Muzak room is not designed as a room to linger in, but to enter, adjust the Muzak volume, and exit. It is also where our Internet modem resides, as well as the first-floor breaker boxes.

Only seconds pass and we're drenched in sweat, panting, unable to comprehend what had just happened in the lobby. There are no answers. We can dig all night and the only substance we'll hit is dirt. So the hotel has been attacked by owls. Okay. So what. These things happen. Sometimes other things happen, but right now this is the thing that is happening.

It doesn't have to make sense.

I pound my skull against the door until my brain loosens.

It doesn't have to make sense.

Kia's crying and so am I.

It doesn't have to make sense.

"Were those . . . were those owls?" the cologne salesman asks, and I strike him in his fucking face.

It is the second time I've punched someone, but the first time I've punched someone and not killed them as a result.

"Ow," the cologne salesman says, rubbing his cheek. "Ow."

"What are you even still doing here?"

"Calm down, bro. I was just waiting for you to come back down, thought maybe you might want to buy a few bottles of my sweet-smelling goodness to keep me from blabbing to anybody about that dead chick you showed me."

Kia clears her throat, wipes tears from her face. "What dead chick?"

"Oh, just the cop your brother murdered at my apartment."

"John killed a cop?"

"No, the one with the dumb cowboy hat."

"Daaamn." She actually seems impressed. "Wait, why'd you show this guy?" She sticks her thumb at the kid.

"He was trying to sell me cologne."

"Ah." She pauses, considering it. "Where's she at now?"

"The dead cop?"

"Who else?"

"She's in your brother's room. Well, what used to be your brother's room. Now some other lady's staying there."

"I see. And what was the dead cop doing in what had once been my brother's room?"

"It wasn't just the dead cop. There was also my best friend, whom I killed, and a guest, whom the owls killed."

"Okay. So. What were *three* dead bodies doing in what had once been my brother's room?"

"I was trying to frame him."

"For what?"

"Murder?"

"Why would you do that?"

The Nightly Disease

"Do you really have to ask?"

"Well, he's my brother."

"Exactly."

"STOP!" the cologne salesman shouts, and we both look at him like he's some goddamn dog scratching at the backdoor needing to take a piss. "Shouldn't we be more worried about the . . . the . . . the fucking *owls* outside this door? What is even going on?"

"It seems pretty straightforward, dude," Kia says. "Some owls are trying to kill us. It's not that complicated."

"It's a little complicated," the cologne salesman says.

Kia shrugs, turns back to me. "I can't believe you were trying to set up my brother."

"Why do you suddenly give a shit? You're the one who said he forced you to mug me, to manipulate me into being intimate. Fuck him, right? Unless you were bullshitting me about that, too, of course."

"What are you talking about, Isaac?"

"I'm talking about maybe you hadn't been so honest with me last night. Which wouldn't exactly be out of character for you, right? I mean, it's sort of your whole schtick."

The expression on her face isn't apologetic. It's more guilty. The kind of face someone makes when caught in the act, but more irritated someone had the gull to confront them than they are for doing something wrong.

"Isaac, this is not the time to be discussing this."

"What are you even doing here? Shouldn't you be back in your shed, watching your baby?"

Kia's expression evolves from irritation to horror. "Oh shit, Saturn."

"What, you forget to change her diaper before abandoning her in the woods?"

"No, you fucking asshole. She's in the backseat of Billy's truck."

This hits me harder than anything else. "You were skipping town with them? You were . . . you were leaving me?" After everything we'd gone through, I'd hoped we still had some sort of chance, however small. But it'd been bullshit. If they hadn't noticed my car tonight, I would have never laid eyes on her again. She wasn't even going to say goodbye.

Hobbs hadn't been messing with me. Kia orchestrated everything. This whole time her brothers have merely been the marionettes, and her the puppeteer. She'd been responsible for it all. Yates, Garcia—hell, even George. If she hadn't walked into my life, things wouldn't be great, but they wouldn't be as horrible. I would still have a friend to talk to on nights when I get lonely.

At this point, it wouldn't even matter if I killed her. It'd just be adding another corpse to the closet. Is four really that different than three?

"You asshole," Kia says, "I mean Saturn's in the truck, outside the hotel, where the goddamn owls are going nuts. If they broke the lobby windows . . . "

And all murderous thoughts vanish, replaced with concern for the baby trapped in the midst of an orgy.

Fuck.

"We have to go back out there," Kia says. "Those fucking things are gonna eat my baby."

"Is this a dildo?" the cologne salesman says.

Our heads slowly turn to the side, remembering the kid exists. He's standing next to the Muzak station, holding a strap-on. A dildo hangs from it, staring at us menacingly.

"This hotel is fucking weird, man," Kia says.

The platinum guest's forgotten personal item. I hadn't seen it since Javier opened up the trash bag I left on his desk. Why didn't they throw it away?

"I got an idea," I say, and pry the dildo from the harness.

"I uh, I don't think this is the time, Isaac. Haven't you been listening to a word I'm saying? Unlock the door. Let me through."

"Just . . . just wait." I nod at the cologne salesman. "Give me a bottle of that shit you're peddling in your backpack."

The kid brightens up and unzips his bag. "I knew you'd come around."

I loosen my necktie and pull it off, then wrap it around the head of the rubber cock in my hands. I grab the first bottle of cheap bootleg cologne the kid takes out of the bag and pour the liquid on the tie.

"Hey!" the kid says. "That bottle costs fifty dollars."

"Wise to give up on that dream early."

"What the fuck are you doing?" Kia asks.

I hold out my free hand to her. "Give me your lighter."

"Why?"

"Just do it."

It takes a few seconds, but the flame eventually takes to the tie and they hit it off like two lovers in a dumpster. I hold the dildo up by its base and it wobbles left and right. The flame stays. Silicone melts down and burns my hand but I don't give it any attention. Let the pain fuel me forward.

"Okay." I open the door. "Let's go save a baby."

#505

If anything, the owls have increased in numbers during our brief intermission in the Muzak room. The parliament grows stronger! The parliament rises! The parliament annihilates all who resist! There's no use in attempting to further converse our plans. The dildo torch will only stay flamed for so many more seconds, and then we might as well hang signs over our necks that read "OPEN BUFFET". I rush forward through the hallway now filled from floor to ceiling with frantic, screeching owls flying in every direction. Like bats emerging from their cave. This is a new world and they intend on exploring every square inch.

The lobby is a bloodbath, a near-perfect reenactment of *Kill Bill*'s Crazy 88 scene.

The floor is covered in corpses. Little league coaches and parents torn open and devoured. Guts and gore sprinkled through the lobby like last-minute Christmas decorations. Owls dip and dive into the carcasses, snagging bits and pieces to munch on as they continue their aimless flight through this strange and majestic building of dreams.

The Nightly Disease

I can barely hear the fire alarm over the sound of their flying.

I wave the wobbly dildo torch at any owl ballsy enough to swoop down on us. The flame sends them back, tells them who's boss here. But we all know the score. Once that flame dies, there's gonna be a drastic change in management.

The floor is too slick with blood to run through. We move with caution toward the shattered entrance. Little league coaches aren't the only corpses littering the land. I step over the lady who'd taken over Hobbs's room. Her eyeballs are missing and her stomach is opened up like a trap door with a broken hinge.

It doesn't have to make sense.

Walk.

Walk.

Walk.

The cowboy sits on a lobby chair. We find his straw Stetson five feet behind him, next to the entrance. His head is still inside it.

If Kia notices, she doesn't show it. Her determination's narrowed in on the pickup truck parked outside. Once we make it into the foyer, she sprints outside. The truck's windows are miraculously still intact. Saturn looks up at us, smiling. She's having the time of her life. Kia doesn't open the door, just waves at the baby through the glass. The baby waves back.

The sky is black. I'm sure there's a moon somewhere, but it's covered by a sheet of owls circling the hotel. They're attracted to the building like it's a magnet pulling them in. Every window on the front-side of the hotel is shattered. Guests scream and claw the window frames as owls drag them out feet-first. They carry the guests high up into the cloud of owls above the building and release them. The guests rain down and splatter against the parking lot. Bodies explode like meat balloons. The awning above the pickup truck shields us from falling guests. The owls empty the hotel, claiming it for their own.

The dildo torch has melted down to the base. Pain hits like a bee sting. I drop the ashy sex toy to the ground and stomp on it.

"Please tell me you're gonna pay for that bottle, bro," the cologne salesman says. "My boss will have my ass."

I pull out the wad of cash I stole from the little league coach and hand him two hundred dollar bills. "Get as far away as you can. Don't give this to your boss. Just go. The owls have your scent now."

The cologne salesman grabs the money and sprints through the parking lot, barely dodging the rain of screaming guests.

"What do we do now?" I ask.

"I don't know," Kia says, leaning her face against the window and smiling at her baby.

"Are you still leaving?"

"Yeah."

"Can I come with?"

"Oh, Isaac."

"Yes?"

"No. You can't come with."

"Oh."

The keys dangle from the ignition. Before she leaves, she pats me on the shoulder and offers a faint smile. Then she gets in the pickup truck and drives away. The owls don't follow. They don't want her. And she doesn't want the one who does want her.

Somewhere, a fire engine screams into the night.

Defeated, I walk back into the hotel.

Arms wide, head up.

Offering myself to the owls.

Some of them land on my shoulders, perched.

But they don't bite.

They don't view me as an enemy. They don't view me as food.

The owls are here to protect me.

What would Mandy 2 say if she could see me now?

I step over dead bodies and punch in the code to enter the front desk door. Hobbs sits on the carpet, hiding in the shadows. Must have leaped over the counter during the battle. He holds a chunk of his own guts, breathing hard and fast.

His dirty, bloodstained eyes widen at the sight of me.

"Eye . . . Sick . . . what the . . . fuck . . . is . . . going . . . on?"

I shrug. There's no answer here. If there is, I certainly don't know it. I reach into the front desk drawer and pull out Detective Garcia's pistol, then aim it at Hobbs. I consider pulling the trigger. I consider a lot of things. I can't. I lower the pistol and Hobbs mouths his thanks, then coughs out something thick and wet.

The front desk phone rings.

I raise the pistol and shoot it and it explodes and it is the most beautiful thing.

I drop the pistol in Hobbs's lap and he stares at it, confused.

I want to say a clever goodbye line, something like,

"Here's your final receipt," but my mouth won't listen to my brain, so I walk out of the hotel and get in my car without saying anything.

Flames consume the hotel.

Fire engine sirens blare from around the corner.

The owls fly above me as I drive down the highway. Some of them are on fire, but that doesn't seem to slow them down. In the passenger seat, Chowls and Owlbert applaud. I don't know how they applaud. They just do.

"That was one hell of an ending," Owlbert says.

"Yeah," Chowls says. "Extremely satisfying."

"Kind of an deus ex machina, though."

"Hmm. Yeah. A little bit of a deus ex machina."

I pull over in the emergency lane and open the passenger door and push them both out.

"Hey!" Owlbert screeches.

"Fuck you too, asshole!" Chowls screams as I drive away, leaving them on the side of the road.

They don't follow.

Eventually, the owls above me also grow bored and venture off to stalk some other basketcase.

And once again I am blissfully alone.

#506

I**drive until** I run out of gas then I fill up the tank and drive until it's empty again. Maybe days pass. But the sun never rises, not once, so I can't be sure. I drive until my eyes crack like glass. I don't know where I'm going and it doesn't matter. I am driving away from the hotel and goddammit that's enough.

When my eyes start bleeding, I swerve off the highway and pull into a parking lot of a building with a sign that reads: ANOTHER GODDAMN HOTEL. The sign makes my stomach hurt, but maybe my stomach has always hurt.

The lobby is empty. I stand at the front desk, half-asleep, and shout for assistance. Nobody comes. I pound my fist against the counter. "Hello? Hello!"

No response.

Fucking lousy hotel dickhead. Probably somewhere watching Netflix instead of doing his job. Probably jerking-off on the roof, adding cum-stains to my car's windshield.

I sit down in the lobby chair and fall asleep. When

I wake up, some lady's standing above me, snapping her fingers.

"Hello?" she says, irritated. "Wake up, goddamn you."

"What do you want?"

"I've been driving all night and I'm exhausted."

"What?"

"Don't you work here?"

I look down at what I'm wearing. I'm still in my hotel uniform, minus the necktie, which is back at the Goddamn Hotel, melted into a burnt dildo. My clothes are covered in blood.

"I don't work anywhere," I tell her. "I've resigned."

"Well, I need a room."

She stands there with her arms crossed, staring at me like I'm the asshole here.

I stare back like she's the asshole instead.

It's a regular asshole-staring contest.

She wins.

I throw my hands up and stand. I don't know the code to get behind the front desk, so I just crawl over the counter. A man in a suit and tie's hiding on the carpet, out of sight from the lady in the lobby. Tears well in his eyes. He shakes his head slowly and mouths the word, "Please."

I stare at him then at the lady then back at him then the lady again.

The front desk phone begins ringing and I answer it before I know what I'm doing.

Except of course I know what I'm doing.

Of course I do.

"Thank you for calling Another Goddamn Hotel. This is Isaac. How may I help you?"

How was The Goddamn Hotel?

Thank you for choosing The Goddamn Hotel for your recent stay. We'd be grateful if you would leave a brief review about your experience with us, and we hope to see you again real soon. Thank you.

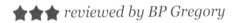

★★★ *reviewed by BP Gregory*

NOT A GREAT NIGHT'S SLEEP BUT BOY, THOSE OWLS

I gotta say, I'd some misgivings when we checked in and the concierge, or bell boy, or whatever they call them these days looked like he'd spent the night upside down in a dumpster. Kept staring all goggle-eyed past us like there was something behind, in a way that really gave us the creeps. Be sure to lock your door!

Linen acceptably clean. Complimentary owls got an extra star = amazing service. Would stay again.

Half a star removed for the amount of (bird crap?) on my windscreen next morning. Ought to put an awning in to protect guest cars.

★★★ *reviewed by Jay Wilburn*

Not the worst.

I don't normally write reviews as everyone has a bad night. Fires, flaming dildos, a mix up on a reservation. We are part of the Goddamn Hotel Rewards Program though and we were a few points away from GD-HR diamond level, but our points were canceled because we technically did not stay all the nights due to the fire. A drunk little league coach knocked on our door at 3 am and tried to talk us into a threesome. There was an owl which attacked and ruined the handle of my hard shell expandable rolling bag. We also did not get our complimentary bottled waters upon check-in. I'm giving this stay 3 stars due to the fact it was not actually our worst hotel experience. I wish the best to The Goddamn Hotel family as they rebuild and clear out the owls. God Bless The Goddamn Hotel.

★ *reviewed by Dave Goudsward*

Worst Hotel in Texas!

Normally, I only stay at [Brand Name Redacted], but I was tired, it was late and it was on the way. That was my first mistake. Based on all the owls flying around the parking lot, I'm assuming the building had a rodent problem. There was a loud party of drunks in the pool, and frankly, they looked old enough to know better. The creepy guy behind the desk kept glancing around like he was expecting the cops to come rushing in and destroy his meth lab. I asked him when the free continental breakfast started in the morning and his eyes got really wide and he muttered something about the road to eternal damnation being paved with waffles. I asked for a ground floor room. He twitched and said all he had was a third-floor room overlooking the pool. I mentioned the drunks and the noise at the pool. He walked in the back room and came out with a toaster and an extension cord, telling me he could quiet them down, but I wasn't allowed to complain about cold bagels in the breakfast buffet. I assumed he was kidding. I noticed bullet holes in the door leading to the back office and decided maybe I could drive another 50-60- miles and find a [Brand Name Redacted]. The clerk just looked at me as I told him I decided not to stay, and smiled this creepy little sad grin that still haunts my nightmares. I later heard they had a fire. Hopefully, that took care of the rats and the owls. But watch out for that night clerk—I think he's nuts.

⭐ *reviewed by Adrian Shotbolt*

Some twisted bird sanctuary.

The Goddamn Hotel wasn't much of a hotel at all. In fact, it was more like some twisted bird sanctuary, and a place where I came face-to-face with something truly horrific. It was late on Friday night and I simply wanted somewhere to get my head down and possibly masturbate. I should've known I checked into the wrong hotel when the rude night auditor refused me a complimentary biscuit on the grounds that there was no such thing . . .

It was far too late and I was far too tired to look for

somewhere else to stay, so up I went to my room. Imagine my surprise when upon entering the room I came across a large black dildo tucked into the bedding, the top of the dildo resting on the pillow as if sleeping. As somebody that travels the length and width of this country regularly, I've seen some weird shit in hotels. However, nothing could've prepared me for the small lump situated at the bottom of the bed. I approached with caution and peeled back the covers carefully. The last thing I expected to see was an owl . . . not just any owl, but an owl that had clearly been sodomised with the large black instrument that now lay dormant at the top of the bed. Suffice to say, I left rather quickly, but not before emptying the contents of my stomach onto the bed and the poor ravaged bird. No, I do not recommend The Goddamn Hotel.

 reviewed by Lawrence Ashley Wilson-Smythe

The worst Goddamn Hotel I've ever stayed in. EVER.

After a long flight from England (where good manners and great customer service were invented), I asked the young lady at reception for a cup of Earl Grey. she sneered and offered me COFFEE!

I declined her offer and headed for my room, narrowly avoiding a vagrant who stumbled into the foyer, unwashed, unshaven and bleeding from a cut on his head!

In my room, I had just closed my eyes when I heard a commotion from the pool. I then heard firecrackers from the foyer and then someone pulled the fire alarm! American teenagers! I tried to call reception to lodge an official complaint, but there was no answer. This would never happen in Kensington.

I tried to keep a stiff upper lip about it all. I made a note of my complaints and put my sleep mask on.

I was then rudely awoken by a loud banging. When I opened my door, I was confronted by an enormous brute of a man, claiming to be a fireman. He said that the hotel was on fire . . . *and overrun by owls.* Preposterous! I protested but he simply called me a dumb limey(!) and threw me over his shoulder, causing me to strike my head on the frame of the door.

I awoke in the hospital where I was informed all of my possessions (including my passport) had been stolen, the hotel was now a crime scene and covered in bird faeces and I would need to find somewhere else to stay. They are blaming a former employee called "Isaac". I shall be writing a strongly-worded letter of complaint to the owners of the hotel once I am settled in my new home at the trailer park, in between my shifts at McDonalds and trying to convince the authorities that I am a citizen of Her Majesty's British Empire.

★★ *reviewed by Brian Asman*

ENTOURAGE MARATHON!?!

Easily the second-worst hotel I've ever stayed in. I've

stayed in other Goddamn Hotels before, and thought I knew what to expect. I mean, it's a Goddamn Hotel, not the Four Seasons, right? The customer service was surly, and the gentleman who checked me in had a severe case of B.O. While the rooms were equipped with HBO, the network was apparently having an *Entourage* marathon so that sucked. My multiple requests for fresh towels went unfulfilled, and I was forced to drip-dry in the bathroom after possibly exposing myself to a staph infection in the filthy shower. I tried to use the pool, but a bunch of Little League coaches were having an orgy in the hot tub, and everyone was so out of shape I had a really hard time masturbating. By the time the hotel caught on fire, I was happy to be on my way. Also, what's up with all the owls? That kind of came out of nowhere.

The continental breakfast was serviceable but uninspired. Two stars.

---

 reviewed by anonymous

UR GOING TO GET IT

I HAD TO EXPLAIN TO MY G-DAMN DAUGHTER WHY A STRANGER WAS HOLDING SOMETHING THAT LOOKED LIKE MOMMY'S BACK MASSAGER AND WHY SOME ASSHOLE WAS CALLING IT A "DILDO" NOW SHE WONT STOP SAYING THAT WORD MY FRACKING SON SLIPPED ON THE GUTS OF A COWBOY AND AN OWL SHIT on ME.

I AM NOT TO BE TRIFLED WITH. I WILL RUIN YOU. I ONCE HAD A POST ON EEDDIT GET

UPVOYED 27 TIMES. I HAVE 253 FOLLOWERS ON
TWEETER AND THEY WILL*ALL*HEARBOUT HIS
AND UR GOING TO GET IT!!!!1!!

About the Author

Max Booth III is the co-founder and Editor-in-Chief of Perpetual Motion Machine and the Managing Editor of *Dark Moon Digest*. He co-hosts the podcast *Castle Rock Radio* with his partner, Lori Michelle, and writes online for LitReactor and *Gamut*. Born in Northern Indiana, he now lives in a small town outside San Antonio, TX where he works as a hotel night auditor.

Follow him on Twitter @GiveMeYourTeeth.

If you enjoyed
The Nightly Disease
don't pass up on these other titles from Perpetual Motion Machine . . .

INVASION OF THE WEIRDOS
BY ANDREW HILBERT

ISBN: 978-1-943720-20-0
Page count: 242
$16.95

After getting kicked out of his anarchist art collective for defending McDonald's, Ephraim develops an idea to create a robot/vending machine with the ability to hug children. He is no roboticist, but through dumb luck manages to hook up with a genius—a like-minded individual who also happens to be the last living Neanderthal. Meanwhile, a former personal assassin for a former president is fired from the CIA for sexual misconduct with a couple of blow-up dolls. He becomes determined to return to the government's good graces by infiltrating Ephraim's anarchist art collective in the hopes that they are actually terrorists. What follows is a bizarre, psychedelic journey that could only take place in the heart of Austin, Texas

DESTROYING THE TANGIBLE ILLUSION OF REALITY: OR, SEARCHING FOR ANDY KAUFMAN

BY T. FOX DUNHAM

ISBN: 978-0-9860594-2-1
Page count: 430
$14.95

In this surreal road novel, Anthony searches for the father he's never met: Andy Kaufman, the legendary song-and-dance man from the '70s. There's a few problems here, of course. Andy Kaufman died in 1984, and thanks to a recent cancer diagnosis, Anthony doesn't have much longer to live, either. However, new evidence has come to light that questions whether or not Kaufman is actually dead. Could he be in hiding, after all these years? Anthony is determined to discover the truth before his own clock runs out. During his travels, he will encounter shameless medicine men, grifters, Walmart shoppers, the ghosts of Elvis and Warhol, and the Devil himself.

THE GREEN KANGAROOS
BY JESSICA MCHUGH

ISBN: 978-0-9860594-6-9
Page count: 184
$12.95

Perry Samson loves drugs. He'll take what he can get, but raw atlys is his passion. Shot hard and fast into his testicles, atlys helps him forget that he lives in an abandoned Baltimore school, that his roommate exchanges lumps of flesh for drugs at the Kum Den Smokehouse, and that every day is a moldering motley of whores, cuntcutters, and disease. Unfortunately, atlys never helps Perry forget that, even though his older brother died from an atlys overdose, he will never stop being the tortured middle child. Set in 2099, *The Green Kangaroos* explores the disgusting world of Perry's addiction to atlys and the Samson family's addiction to his sobriety.

The Perpetual Motion Machine Catalog

Baby Powder and Other Terrifying Substances |
John C. Foster | Story Collection

Bleed | Various Authors | Anthology

Crabtown, USA:Essays & Observations |
Rafael Alvarez | Essays

Cruel | Eli Wilde | Novel

Dead Men | John Foster | Novel

*Destroying the Tangible Issue of Reality; or, Searching
for Andy Kaufmann* | T. Fox Dunham | Novel

Four Days | Eli Wilde & 'Anna DeVine | Novel

Gods on the Lam | Christopher David Rosales | Novel

Gory Hole | Craig Wallwork | Story Collection
(Full-Color Illustrations)

The Green Kangaroos | Jessica McHugh | Novel

Invasion of the Weirdos | Andrew Hilbert | Novel

Last Dance in Phoenix | Kurt Reichenbaugh | Novel

Like Jagged Teeth| Betty Rocksteady | Novella

Patreon:
www.patreon.com/PMMPublishing

Website:
www.PerpetualPublishing.com

Facebook:
www.facebook.com/PerpetualPublishing

Twitter:
@PMMPublishing

Instagram:
www.instagram.com/PMMPublishing

Newsletter:
www.PMMPNews.com

Email Us:
Contact@PerpetualPublishing.com